Riven

Titles by J. L. Jackola

Unbound Prophecy Series:
Ascension
Descent
Surfacing
Submerged

Riven

Unbound Prophecy

Book Five

J. L. Jackola

Tivshe Publishing

This is a work of fiction. Names, characters, places, events and incidents are either the products of the author's imagination or used in a fictitious manner. Any resemblance to actual persons, living or deceased, or actual events is purely coincidental.

Library of Congress Control Number 2021917315

Paperback ISBN 978-1-954175-11-2

Distributed by Tivshe Publishing
Printed in the United States of America

Cover design by Dark Queen Designs
Map design by D. B. Litteral and Alexis Jackola

Visit www.tivshepublishing.com

To those who believed in me:
the mentors, the teachers, my friends, and my family.

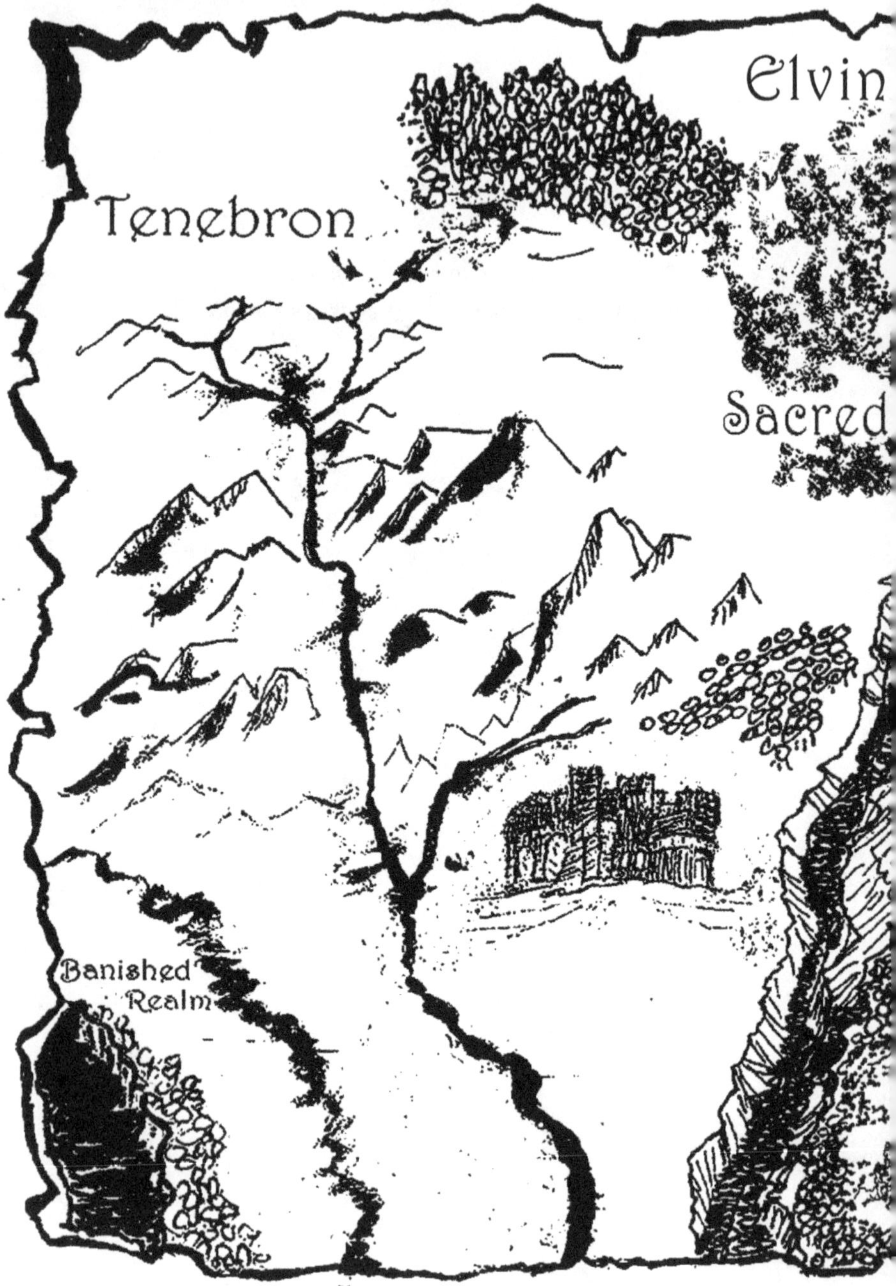
Elvin
Tenebron
Sacred
Banished
Realm

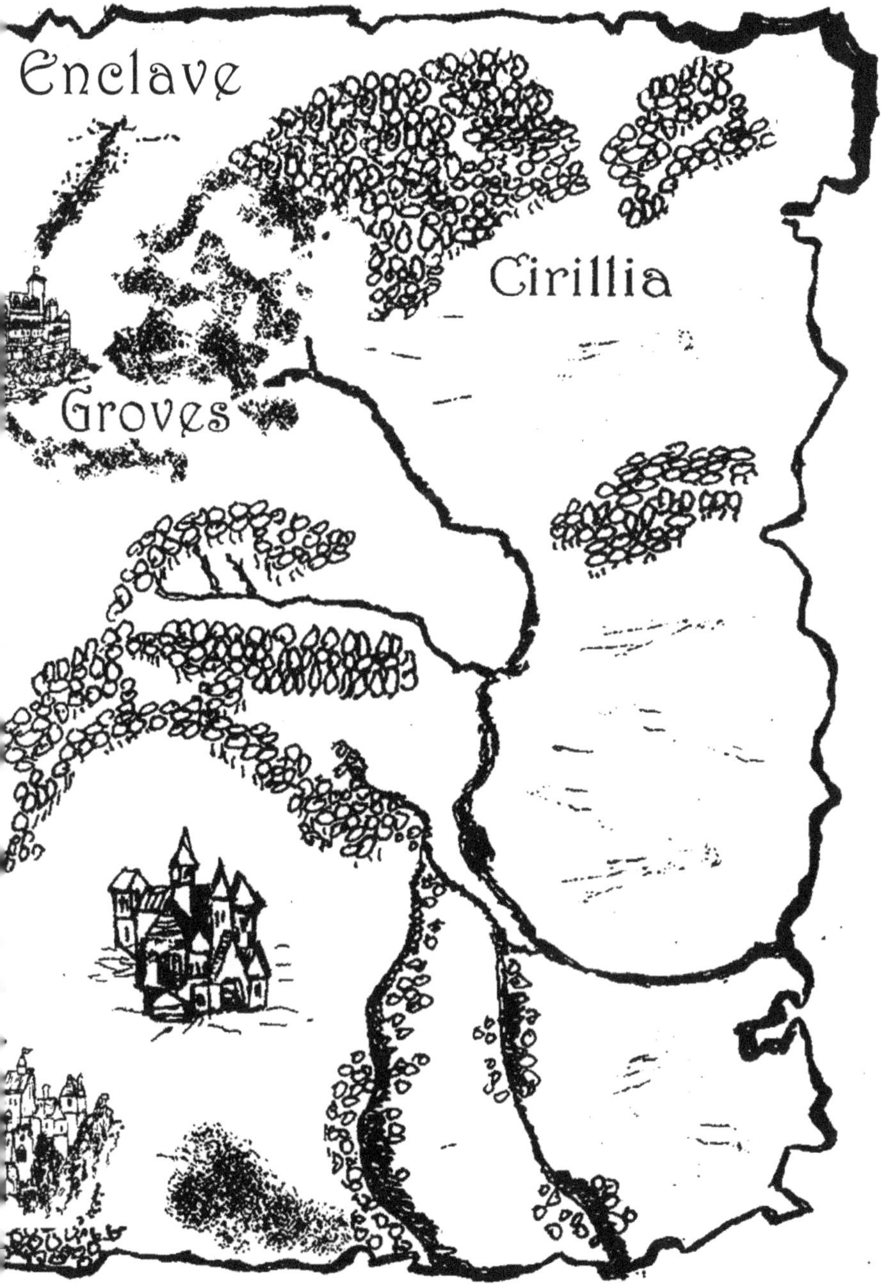
Enclave
Cirillia
Groves

Prologue

Violissa looked out across the land. From her vantage point, she could see atop the forests that comprised the Sacred Groves and beyond. To the west, she could see the mountains of northern Tenebron; to the east, the sprawling meadows of Cirillia. Night had yet to settle, the moons not quite ready for slumber, dawn just a hint beyond the horizon lending a dusting of pink to her view. Another restless night met by a pre-dawn awakening. She rubbed her eyes, a yawn rising from within her.

Looking to Tenebron, she wondered at the snow-covered terrain, winter's hold deep in its veins, the view from their northern home never ceasing to amaze her. She and Sinow had established their home in the meeting groves after her return just as they had planned. There, they had remained for centuries until the call of her heritage became too strong. Sinow had suggested they move to her birthplace, the castle where her parents had lived, her mother having passed and her father having returned to the Fates with her, saying he'd been blessed enough to have more time and was ready to sleep. It was decided Violissa and Sinow would split their time between the castles, and with that decision, the call of her Elvin blood had settled.

Standing there, she wondered if her mother had ever stood on this same balcony. Had she glanced upon the land as Violissa now did? Viewed the world her daughter would one day rule? She would not have seen Tenebron the way Violissa could. The castle had been moved to the west as to center it between Cirillia and Tenebron with the Elvin land still lying behind it. The view upon Cirillia would have been the same for Aradisa, however. Violissa smiled thinking of her mother standing where her own feet stood. She missed her parents, she'd been lucky to have time with them, time with her mother unlike any other ruler before her. They'd been gone for thousands of years, but she could still picture them, still feel their presence. As if sensing her thoughts, a gentle breeze drifted through her hair, lingering on her cheek.

"Hello, Mother," she whispered. She liked to think the spirits of both her parents were flowing through the world, but she knew better. The Elvin believed their spirits returned to the natural world, feeding the plants, encouraging the air, nurturing the animals. Immortals like her father, however, had different paths. Their spirits made up the stars above. Those who had proven their worth were selected by the Fates to join them or some, who preferred to stay closer to home simply chose to let their spirits drift among the living, continuing to watch over them as they always had. Violissa imagined that her father had chosen that form, the closest he could be to Aradisa.

Thinking of them brought on a melancholy she didn't want this day, but it settled upon her despite her attempts to avoid it, and her mind drifted to all those she'd lost through her lifetime. Generation after generation of her people had been born and died, countless cousins from her Elvin line, her uncle having passed at the same time as her mother. Born together and taken together. And then there was Paige, Violissa's most painful loss. She missed Paige every day as she knew Daneele did. He had taken Maggie's death hard but still had Paige to ease the pain. With Paige's death, there was nothing left to protect his heart, she having bore no children. It had been hard, but as the centuries passed, the pain eased though the memories remained. Thousands of years later, they would sit and reminisce, missing the small things that made Paige and Maggie special to them both. How she wished Paige were here now.

Violissa sensed Sinow before she felt his hand gently wrap around her stomach. She leaned into him as he brushed her hair back and kissed her neck.

"You're up earlier than usual. Trouble sleeping?" he asked.

"Mmm, something like that. You, too, are certainly up early this morn," she rebutted.

"If my wife awakens, I awaken," he replied softly.

She sighed, knowing there was more to his words than just the sweetness of them. The burden they'd both carried since that day long ago when they'd agreed to bury a past that should have been discussed; the fear that had lodged in his heart, taxing a heavy toll on him, on both of them.

He dropped his head into the curve of her shoulder, sensing where her thoughts had gone. Then raising his head, he asked, "And how is our son today?"

She smiled, moving her hand over his, feeling the swell of her stomach below it.

"Unusually quiet," she answered.

"The calm before the storm?" he asked as she felt the tension in his muscles.

"Perhaps. He'll be here any day now," she said softly, knowing it sent mixed emotions through him. She had no doubt he was happy about it, that he would love their son every bit as much as he loved her, that this was a wonderful thing for him. She also knew their son's birth was the start of a clock that neither could stop; the end of their lives, the end of their existence as they knew it. His ascension would come, too soon for them both, and so too would their requirement to return themselves to the Fates. It was expected, it was necessary. No two rulers could live in power at one time, Violissa's father had been the only example of any exception to this norm, but his full power had never returned, only his innate powers remaining upon his re-emergence to the physical world. No, there was no alternative. When their son ascended the throne, the first king to rule both realms on his own, she and Sinow would take their place among the stars with the rest of their ancestors.

"Are you worrying for me?" he asked. "I thought that was my job."

She laughed. "I thought you needed a bit of help."

He moved so that she was facing him, and she lost herself in those deep brown eyes, the cusp of black lying in wait just below. He fingered her wandering curl, once golden but now deep ebony, her son's Dark power evident in ways they hadn't expected. Only a few strands had turned, but it was evidence of his strength. He was powerful, more so than he should have been this early on, but he was different than any before him. He was a child of three powers, and no one knew of what he would be capable. For now, she could only sense his Dark power. It would spread through her as he moved, if he sensed she was uncomfortable or stressed, and whenever he felt his father near just as he had now. It should have scared her, but it didn't. Instead, the warmth of it was welcomed, familiar even. It reminded her of the feeling Sinow's power gave her, and she accepted it, her Elvin side accentuated by it. With his conception, her eyes had deepened, the green as bold as the forests she loved. They'd remained that way through her pregnancy. Her Elvin gifts seeming to call every piece of nature so that the keep was covered in vines constantly, the forest floors flourishing with thick life, the meadows outside the keep wild with flowers and flittering creatures.

"I do enough worrying for both of us," Sinow said, bringing Violissa in closer and kissing her. She gave herself over to his kiss, the feel of his lips against hers, the beat of his heart against her chest, the warmth, the security that was him. Then she felt a flurry of movement and gasped, pulling from his embrace.

"I'm not sure what he thought about that," she said, holding her stomach. The babe moved a bit more then went still again as he'd been the last few hours. "He's calm again."

Sinow got a look of pride in his eyes, one he'd been carrying since they'd discovered she was pregnant. It was as if he couldn't believe she was capable of carrying their son, awed by the miracle of it. "He'll be here soon, Vi. Our son."

"Our son," she said. She looked out at the horizon, the glow of the rising sun deepening just enough to reflect on the full moons above. *Moons that should have lowered*, she thought. The pinkish hue deepened and spread upward, the sky becoming a rich shade of red, blood red.

"Sinow," she said quietly, afraid to speak too loudly.

She heard him inhale sharply. "Vi?"

He reached his hand and pulled his fingers through her hair, lifting it to show her the ebony that was making its way through the rest of her locks. Pain crashed through her like a descending wave as Dark power rose from her son.

"It's time. He's coming" was her only answer as nature took hold, and her son began to force his way into their world.

One

Ren sat on the forest floor, eyes closed, listening to the world around him, letting it quiet his mind. This was where he came to escape, to be himself without the constraints that bound him in everyday life. The hush of the forest calmed him, and he opened himself to the life within—the rustle of the trees above, the patter of the animals all around, the stir of the breeze, the hum of the insects below. It filled him, renewing him. Opening his eyes, he moved his hand out to the fainna that stirred before him. It landed gently, eyeing him as if it knew his thoughts, knew what drove him to take refuge here this day.

"I know," Ren said. "I need to go back. I need to listen..." He stopped, the conversation with his father replaying in his head.

Conversation wasn't quite the right word. It had been a fight, the first he had ever had with his father. He'd seen his father angry before but never at him. It didn't feel good being on the wrong side of his temper.

Ren rubbed his face. “What am I going to do?” he asked the fainna, not expecting an answer.

It drifted closer to him and placed its paws on his cheeks. A knowing look crossed its features, and for a moment, Ren felt it understood him. Then, the moment was gone, and it fluttered off, leaving him to his own thoughts.

He sighed. *What am I going to do?*

His father was stubborn, and Ren even more so. Neither would bend, so Ren was left with a dilemma.

“Mother,” he said aloud. “Maybe she can help.”

His mother was the only one who could calm his father. Perhaps she could convince him. But would she? His decision impacted her as well. Would she side with his father? He had only one way of knowing. Rising, he brushed the forest from his pants then looked around once more, inhaling the rich forest smell one last time before he shifted.

Landing outside the keep, he spotted his parents and stepped behind a nearby tree to watch them in an attempt to ascertain his father’s mood. They were standing in his mother’s garden, her favorite place. Were they talking about him? He watched as his mother laughed, her head tilting back, golden locks shining in the sunlight. His father smiled, something he rarely did now, his eyes never straying from hers, filled with the adoration he held for her. His father pulled her into his arms and kissed her. Even after all this time, they loved each other beyond anything else. When Ren had been younger, he’d been embarrassed when they acted this way, but as he aged, he realized this was who they were. They shared a love that ran deeper, a love that was unique. The passion they had for each other was special and something he didn’t fully understand, but he knew it came from the Fates and something else, a history that bound them. Loss and pain, grief and fear that forever marked them but had also deepened their love for one another.

Drostiren, his father called him in enaigne, interrupting his thoughts.

He'd been hoping to wait and catch his mother alone, but he knew better; that was something that rarely happened. He moved from behind the tree and walked toward them. Running his hand through his hair, he waited for his father to say something more to determine if he was still angry. He was the only one who used Ren's full name, never reverting to the nickname his mother had given him, arguing that he should be proud of his full name, one derived from the names of both his grandfathers. His mother had insisted on using the nickname much to his father's frustration. One thing he knew about his parents was that his mother often frustrated his father with the things she did. It was the nature of their opposing powers he assumed.

"Ren," his mother said, her smile for him lighting up her face and Ren's heart.

She kissed his cheek.

"Mother, Father," he said, avoiding his father's eyes. "Have you thought any more about our discussion, Father?" he braved. The air thickened with a flare of his father's power, and Ren knew the answer. He met his father's eyes, coal black, no sign of brown to be seen.

"There is nothing to think about and no more to discuss."

His mother said nothing, merely remained quiet. She knew better than to pick a fight when his father was like this. She acquiesced, as she often did, something that infuriated Ren, but he would never tell her so. He knew it was a result of something deeper from their past. Something from which they'd never quite been able to move beyond, that had settled into their relationship long before he'd been born.

A look passed between them, and he could tell they were talking to each other. Then, his father shifted. There would be no talking to him, and he doubted his father would allow the subject to be broached again.

"You know you have a way of getting under your father's skin, Ren," his mother said, her emerald eyes shining at him, her smile full of love.

"I hear I inherited that trait from my mother," he replied.

She laughed. "Aye, you likely did. Walk with me, Ren."

She took his arm, and they walked back toward the castle.

"I'm surprised Father left without you," he said under his breath.

"That will be enough, Ren. Don't turn this into something about me. This is about you."

He huffed but remained silent. She stopped and turned to him.

"Turning away from your ascension, Ren? Did you really think your father would be happy about that?"

"I thought we could talk—"

"About what? You turning down your birthright? What did you expect him to say?"

She was scolding him, the Elvin in her slipping out, her tone harsher than normal.

"I don't know," he said, looking away from her and running his hand through his hair.

She lifted his face, bringing his eyes back to meet hers. "Ren, you can't turn your back on your destiny. I of all people know that. Your father and I fought with everything we had to be together and make your destiny possible."

"I'm not ready, Mother."

"Nor was I, nor was your father. Taking the throne is a big responsibility. Receiving your Fate-given gifts is traumatizing. But we all go through it, just as you will."

"But the two of you are the best to rule—"

"And we have ruled for nearly six thousand years, Ren. It is time for us to step down."

He lowered his eyes again.

"You still have fifty years left until your ascension. You'll be ready."

"No, it won't change anything. I won't take the throne, Mother."

He glanced back to meet her sad eyes, knowing he wouldn't convince her, then shifted to be by himself again.

Violissa stood in the wake of Ren's shift and sighed. He had inherited her stubbornness as well as Sinow's. Now she was stuck between the two of them. She knew she couldn't get either to change his mind. She lifted her eyes to the Fates, wondering if this was their doing or if it were her own. They had been silent for thousands of years. No more tests, no more punishments, just an uneasy feeling she and Sinow still carried. One which told them both to not accept complacency, never suspect that they had obtained their happy ending. Now, they were close to confirmation that they had. Almost to the time they would return themselves to the Fates and let their son assume the throne.

She looked over at the castle, knowing Sinow was watching. Ren had left her alone, and he would know, feeling their son's shift. She needed to go to Sinow before he came to her, his ever-vigilant guard over her present even after all this time.

She found Sinow in his study still staring out the window that looked out upon her garden. She laid her head on his shoulder, feeling the tension in him. It worried her. He'd been this way long before today. With every year that Ren grew closer to his ascension, Sinow's tension had grown. She knew it had nothing to do with the conversation she'd just had with their son and everything to do with what his ascension meant to the two of them; the finality of it, the end of them.

Caressing her hand along his back, she started to speak.

"Don't, Vi," he said first.

"Sinow," she said, "you need to talk about this with him."

He turned, and she saw the ire within, his coal black eyes revealing it.

"I won't discuss it any further. He will take the throne, Violissa. There has never been an ascending prince who has not."

Behind his eyes, she could see the pain discussing their son's ascension held for him, the underlying, unspoken piece of it that tormented him so. She brought her hand up and moved it down his cheek. He leaned into it, closing his eyes to her touch, a touch which to this day could still calm the Dark in him. When he opened them again, the slight of soft brown lie below. Her breath caught, and her heart skipped as if it were the first time she'd seen him.

He smiled. "You're trying to soften me."

"Is it working?"

He sighed then brought her hand down. "What would you have me do, Vi? What he is asking goes against everything we are."

"Talk to him. Father to son. Not king to prince. He's scared. Taking the throne is a big step. You know that. He'll be on his own—"

"Don't," he said, not wanting the reminder of it.

She leaned her head into his chest. "He's scared, Sinow, just as we were."

"He's not scared of the throne, Vi."

She pulled her head back and searched his eyes, questioning him.

"At least not completely. He's afraid of the power, the Darkness that comes with it."

"But he knows all three powers and knows his balance will keep him from experiencing what you did."

"Vi, he doesn't know that side of himself well enough to be reassured. He has embraced the Light, he spends his days wandering the forests, lost in his nature call, but he fears the Dark blood that runs through him. He lives in the Light, Vi."

"And that's a bad thing?" she asked, a little irritated.

"Yes, for a Dark king, it's a very bad place to be."

"But he is not a Dark king, Sinow. He is so much more."

"I understand that, but there are three sides to him. All three need to be present in order to rule this world, and he only allows for two. How will he punish? How will he protect? How will he lead a Council of Darkbearers if he cannot even rule that side of him?"

She chewed her lip, not sure what to say.

"Until he embraces the side of him that comes from my blood, he will remain afraid, and we both know what that fear can do to a Dark king," he said softly.

He moved his fingers through her stray curl. Leaning up, she kissed him, losing herself in him, letting everything else fall to the side. As always happened, just as it had when they were young, there was no returning. The need they had for one another overtaking everything else, the emotions of the day feeding into that need.

They made love, and she lost herself in his touch, his desire, needing him as much now as she had the first time they'd made love. It had been that way through the centuries never changing for her. Since Ren had been born, she'd noticed it had changed for Sinow. Every touch becoming more like it was the last one. The closer they had come to Ren's ascension, the more intense it had become. Now, he took her as if he would never be allowed to touch her again, never able to kiss her, as if it were their last time. It saddened her, not only because she knew the day was drawing near but because he was so consumed by it. That fear of losing her, always a burden, had now come to fruition. She understood what that did to him, to his Dark side, and after all this time with him, she still had yet to find a way to alleviate it.

Ren never returned to the castle that day. Sinow suspected he was either brooding in the Elvin enclave or trying to escape reality in the forests somewhere, his nature side always calling him. Sinow avoided any mention of their conversation through the rest of the day, at dinner and beyond. In his eyes, it was finished, but Violissa knew her son, he was too much like her, and so she knew the conversation was not over. As she and Sinow lay in bed that night, she thought about everything Ren's ascension meant to them.

"Sinow," she started, snuggling into his chest further. His arm pulled her in closer, and he kissed her head.

"Hmmm."

"What do you suppose would happen if Ren refuses the throne?" She knew she was pushing him, feeling his chest muscles tighten, hearing the frustrated inhale.

"Did you purposely wait until I was in this relaxed, weakened state to pin me down on this, Vi? Let me remind you that you are the cause of this state. I should have remembered your Elvin side might manipulate me into this conversation."

She laughed, then bringing herself up to look at him, replied, "I believe it was you who initiated it this time."

He ran a hand through his hair. "Aye, that I did." Then he looked at her, searching her eyes. "I don't know. The world would be rulerless. What does that do to the people? Does it cause chaos? Do we end up with a world with no laws, no higher order? Or a world like the human realm?"

"The Councils would still be in power. Could they rule as they did before my ascension?"

"The Councils are tired, Vi. I'm surprised none of them has stepped down before now, especially Cyric and Kanine, but I've a feeling they wanted to see our son ascend to the throne first." He sighed. "I'm sure most of them will step down, return themselves to the Fates when we..." He paused as if saying the words might bring it on sooner. "When we do so. It makes sense for him to start his reign with a few of the younger Council, Keary, Daneele possibly, but the others will make way for new Council to lead beside him."

She chewed her lip.

"No matter which way I look at it, there is no good that comes from his decision. He must assume the throne for proper order to remain, Vi, there is no other choice."

She laid back and looked at the ceiling. "He doesn't want it, Sinow."

He sat up and ran his hands over his face then rose from the bed, the full light of the moons illuminating him as he walked across the room. She watched him pick up his pants, the muscles in his back taut with tension.

"Warn me next time, Vi so I'm prepared for being jumped. I'm going for a walk. I was happy to go to sleep, but now ..."

She rose and walked over to him, his eyes following the movement of her body, as if they were both young lovers. She loved the fact that he never seemed to grow tired of her even after all these millennia. Of course, nor had she grown tired of him, still enjoying the feel of every muscle, the way his body moved, the strength of it.

She leaned into him, feeling the need for her grow in him again, as it always did.

"If he's afraid, then you must help him. Show him how to embrace his Dark side. Teach him not to fear it."

"I've tried, Violissa. When he was younger, he was eager to learn. There was such power there. You know that. Now, he hides from it. I can teach him all I want, but it doesn't mean he'll listen. He needs to embrace it on his own. If he's reliant on me, what happens when we're gone?" The harsh tone of his voice changed, softening with those final words.

She ran her hands along his chest, her eyes dropping to follow them. "What if...what if we're not gone?"

"What do you mean?"

"Well, what if we were to step down but not return to the Fates?"

She peeked her eyes back up at him. The sly grin on his face revealed his thoughts on her question.

"Well, well. Look who wants to challenge the Fates again. It looks like you and Drostiren have that in common."

"Who's to say it challenges the Fates, Sinow?"

"Vi, every king has returned to the Fates. Well, except my grandfather, and the Fates forced his power from him then took him."

"Well, he was an exception to the former kings, Sinow."

He searched her eyes. There was a heaviness to his eyes that showed he wasn't going along with her. Rubbing her arms, he said, "Vi, as much as I would love to step down and spend the rest of time with you, it's not meant to happen that way."

"Who says? We're an exception to every rule, Sinow. Why can't this be an exception? Even if they take our powers, we could still live, hide away in the Elvin enclave living a quiet life together until we felt it was time to give ourselves over."

She could tell he was thinking it through. He smiled and pushed her curl back. "That would be nice, but," he ran his hands down her arms, "it's not something we can count on. I just don't see that being a likely scenario."

"So, we accept our fate and pray the Fates show us kindness to allow us into their fold?"

"Something like that. Although with our track record of challenging them and as often as I know we've both cursed them, I'm guessing the Fates won't be inviting us to become one of them."

She knew he could see the sadness in her eyes. She'd been trying to tiptoe around the subject all this time, hoping to avoid forcing him to deal with the reality of their situation, and here she'd gone and upset herself by pushing it this evening.

"We'll be all right, Vi. Even if we end up stars in the night sky, I'll find my way to you. Not even immortal death will separate us."

"We'll combine to make the brightest star in the night sky?"

"Can stars make love?"

She laughed. "I suppose we'll find out."

She ran her hands up his chest and leaned into him. "For now, let's squeeze as much of that in as we can."

Giving her another sly grin, he replied, "You are quite insatiable for an eight-thousand-year-old woman."

He kissed her, and she lost herself again, putting their conversation aside just as he always did. Leaving it for another day until the day they could avoid it no longer.

Clouds of gray shrouded the full moon that shone above the lake, its water stirring slightly as it darkened to a shade of deep ebony. A mist rolled in over the park, shrouding the nightmare tree as its naked limbs began to quiver. The ground trembled below, dirt shifting as a crack formed, running jaggedly behind the tree, across the back of the park, and into the tree line. The trembling grew, the crack expanding with a force that cascaded across the town, buildings shaking at their foundation with the intensity, the sound of it splitting through the quiet of the night, followed by an eerie silence. The ground lay still again. From within the newly formed crevice, a thick black fog slithered its way into the world. One final quake shook the land, and the fog dissipated to reveal a figure.

Tynan breathed in the smell of freedom, rolling his neck and fully stretching for the first time since his imprisonment. He looked toward the lake and now understood what had been calling him all these millennia. Raising his hand over the water, he summoned the book, calling it home to its master. It hovered before him, its pages flipping to reveal its now unlocked secrets, spells that before had been hidden. He laughed, a sound that echoed shrilly in the silence that surrounded him. Revenge would be his, and this time there would be no mistakes. First, he needed to get home. Closing his eyes, he tuned out the strange wailing that was now filling the silence, instead concentrating on the Dark power that encased him, reaching out beyond, seeking what he knew was still there. Then, sensing it, he reached his hand out and felt for the strand, thin and fading yet still present as if awaiting his return. Opening his eyes, he summoned his power to meet the strand and opened the portal the Fates had saved for him. The path was still unbound, the game still on, and Tynan would be the crucial piece in the final move.

Two

Sinow stood on the edge of the ravine that divided Tenebron from Cirillia. The air was crisp, the cool season nearly upon them, having already settled on the mountainous northern region. All of Tenebron would soon be blanketed with snow, another season closer to the day he would be forced to give up everything, and he wasn't ready. Since the day he had gotten her back, he had held on tight to Violissa, kept her close, that fear of losing her ever present. It had never faded, even as time healed her wounds and dimmed her memories. A thousand years had seemed like a hundred, and every millennium that passed went too quickly.

When Drostiren had been born, they both knew the clock had begun ticking. It was bittersweet. He loved his son, had been surprised and proud as he'd grown and come into a mix of powers from all three lines. But his birth and his upcoming ascension meant Sinow would lose Violissa. There had never been a king who'd had so much to lose. Perhaps this was why the mothers of each king were mortals. Returning to the Fates was made easier if the woman you loved had died millennia before. Sure, there were some like his grandfather who had clung to the power, but love was greater. Sinow would give it all up for more time with her.

He sighed, dragging his hands through his hair. It didn't help any to dwell on it. He needed to get back to her. Over the years, he had managed to give her the private time she needed but always within his rules, always with both of them remaining on castle grounds, and only for as long as he could tolerate the anxiety of being away from her his constant companion. Reaching out his senses, he found her then shifted within a short distance of her. She was on the lawn with Drostiren, working with him on a Light spell. The sun shone down upon her golden locks and sparkled in her eyes. Her smile filled the surrounding area, and as always, he felt the wind knocked from his lungs. It didn't matter how long they'd been together, each time he saw her, every time he touched her, was like the first time.

Drawing his eyes from her, he watched their son. His Light powers were incredible, his Dark abilities as well, both equal, but Drostiren favored the Light. With his black hair and defined features, he resembled Sinow, even his height and build had come to match his father's. There was no real sign of Violissa in him save for his mannerisms and his personality, which were clearly gleaned from her. When he'd been young, his eyes had matched hers, the emerald presence a reminder of his Elvin heritage. As his Light powers grew, however, the green had faded, replaced by the vibrant blue of his Light forefathers. An equal balance of Light and Dark ever apparent in his appearance.

Sinow watched as Violissa called her powers forth, something he'd come to relish. The light tingle to the air, the soft feel of it that reached out and caressed him, calming him. Both her Elvin and Light sides had that calming effect, but the cool arcane of the Light enhanced the experience.

"Now draw yours, Ren," she coached him. Violissa insisted on calling him Ren, a term of endearment she'd given him as an infant, but Sinow had never taken to it, insisting that his full name be used to invoke the fear a Dark king needed. But he wasn't a Dark king, was he? He was much more, something new that none of them truly understood and none knew how to teach. Violissa was the only one who remotely understood, but Elvin and Light were compatible most of the time. Dark and Light, however, were like having a lit fuse inside you at all times. At least Sinow imagined it that way.

"Good. Now strike me with all you have," Violissa encouraged.

Drostiren looked at her with doubt in his eyes. Sinow had to laugh. The idea of his wife teaching their son fighting techniques with Light magic was humorous although he had to admit she could hold her own in a fight. Sinow had insisted she and her Council be taught to fight early on as a precaution, an attempt to allay his fears that was unsuccessful. The Councils sparred regularly now, and Violissa still trained with Sinow. They'd had many a fight in the sparring field, so he knew how capable she was.

"I really shouldn't, Mother," Drostiren said.

"Ha, don't patronize me, Ren. I could kick your ass in a heartbeat." She shifted her feet to a fighting stance.

Sinow chuckled. If Drostiren ever used his full power, she would be no match for him.

"I believe he doesn't want to hurt you, Vi," Sinow said, walking over to them.

She dropped her stance but not her power.

"Is that a challenge?" she asked, raising her eyebrow.

"If I were challenging you, you'd already be on the ground."

She huffed, but he winked, allowing a bit of playfulness in before addressing his son.

"Drostiren."

"Father. I should go," he replied, stirring Sinow's irritation. Running away just as Violissa had done when they were younger. The two were so alike and so enamored in self-doubt. Violissa had shed the doubt after the incident with Tynan. Something in her had been lost, building her self-assurance, her confidence. One of the few good things that had come from the nightmare.

"No, stay. You already have command of your mother's gifts. It is mine you need to hone."

Drostiren moved his feet uncomfortably.

"It's not necessary, Father."

"Yes, I believe it is. But this," he looked around the space, "this is not the place. Come," he commanded then shifted to the sparring fields, giving Drostiren no choice. He and Violissa followed within moments. Sinow had had no doubt Violissa would join; she knew he would want her nearby.

"Now, you've refused to spar with me for too long. Have you been working with the Council?"

Drostiren shrugged, reminding Sinow of a gloomy teenager. His irritation increased, and he called his power, feeling the Darkness and welcoming it.

"Draw your power, Drostiren. Put the Light aside and welcome the Dark."

Drostiren closed his eyes, and Sinow felt the air change, felt the Darkness increase. When his eyes opened, they matched Sinow's. He felt Violissa's power react to the increase in Dark power, then sensed her calm it.

"Now, hit me. Don't hesitate, don't think. Let the Darkness guide you."

Drostiren threw a bolt of power at him, which Sinow easily deflected. He retaliated and hit Drostiren who flew back a few yards before stopping himself.

"You've got more in you than that. Now show me what you've got."

Another strike came, a little harder than the last.

"Good, now remember what I taught you."

Another round then Sinow struck back, trying harder to encourage him. The blows were exchanging at a faster pace, each getting stronger.

"Release yourself to the Dark. Let it in."

They battled back and forth until Sinow, tired of Drostiren holding back, slammed him with a bolt of magic that sent him flying into the trees behind. He shifted, grabbing him from the ground.

"Stop holding back."

Drostiren's eyes grew blacker, and the ground rumbled, the air thickening. A hint of green filled his eyes, the sky turning pitch black. He roared, and Sinow was sent flying to the other end of the field, the force pushing him through miles of trees before he could stop himself. He stood, dusting himself off, and then shifted back.

"I'm not you," Drostiren yelled, his eyes a kaleidoscope of blue, green, and black hues. "I will never be you. That's why I can't ascend. Don't you see? I can't do it. The power is too much."

"Ren," Violissa started.

"No, Mother," he said sadly. "I'm not the ruler you both are. The world is better with you."

He shifted, leaving them both staring at the space where he had been. The air was filled with his power and something else. Fear. Sinow could feel it, heavy on his senses.

Violissa put a hand on his arm. "What are we going to do?"

He ran his hand through his hair. "I don't know. Did you feel the strength he has? Fates, Vi. He sent me flying without any movement. He has no idea how strong he is, and he's afraid of it."

"His powers are volatile, Sinow. That's why I was trying to get him to focus them earlier."

"Aye, the ascension is nearing. It will only grow worse."

The air changed, and something about it caught Sinow's attention. Reaching his senses out, below the tension in the air, the fear, below the residual of Drostiren's power, he detected a subtle something that felt familiar.

"Sinow?"

He walked toward the tree line where Drostiren had been, trying with everything he had to place it but to no avail.

"What's wrong?"

He tried focusing again, but the sensation was gone, lost in the residual of Drostiren's magic.

"Nothing, I suppose. I thought I sensed something, but I must have been wrong."

He stared into the woods, his Dark instinct telling him it was more than nothing.

Tynan shifted. He'd seen enough, he'd heard enough. He had exactly what he needed, and it was time to make his move. He landed, sure to keep himself cloaked. He'd remained cloaked since he'd returned from the other realm and would stay that way until the moment was right. Sinow was too sensitive to his power and would know the moment he dropped it.

So, they'd had a son. A strong one from the looks of it. The boy was a mix of all three powers, the first of his kind, which should have made him indestructible except for the fact that he didn't understand his power. He feared it, and that made him vulnerable.

Tynan paced the small spot where he'd hidden since his escape, the further most corner from Sinow's power, running his plan through his head one last time; every detail, every spell needed to be just right. He pulled the book from where he'd hidden it, knowing he would need it with him, for he would not be returning. Then he sat and ran through it all, the words from the spell flowing through his head. It was a beauty, one of the spells locked from him all those centuries he'd had the book. Violissa had foolishly unlocked it, and now she would pay for her fatal mistake. Thinking of her brought no desire but one to hurt her, all remnants of the man who had weakened in her presence gone now. In his place a Dark king. This was his end game; he would have the revenge he'd obsessed about for thousands of years locked away by his brother. Now the wrongs would be righted, and nothing would stop him.

He'd been locked in the past, an auditory witness to the last mortal life of Violissa and Sinow, Violet and Simon as he'd heard them referred. But he'd known his brother's voice, known the melodic sound of Violissa's, whether they knew who they were or not. Over and over, the same time played, a snapshot in their life but an important one, one in which they woke from the spell under which they'd been frozen, one in which they'd discovered each other and found their way home. Cursed to experience the same play of events repeatedly, Tynan learned and gleaned what he needed to concoct the perfect plan, and the book gave him the key to making it happen—time. A spell to manipulate it, travel the bounds of it within limits he'd discovered. He could travel a certain field in time that revolved around the events that had defined his relationship with Sinow and Violissa, starting with the day she and Sinow had met in this human life he'd been cursed to hear repeatedly.

At first, he'd been angry, the thought of going back to Sinow's birth and killing him had been tempting. Apparently, the Fates had anticipated that scenario and had instead bound him to these events. He had initially thought of killing them both in their human form, but he couldn't find a way back to that realm until now, the strand having disappeared from his grasp after last using it. Now that he'd seen the son, he knew he had found the way. But did he want to go back and kill them right away or have some fun with them first? After being locked away for millennia, he was ready to have some fun.

Three

Violissa lay spooned in Sinow's protective arms. Neither had discussed the events from earlier that day. Ren had not returned, which was not unusual. He came and went as he pleased regularly now. Still, Violissa wondered if he had stayed away purposely again. She cleared her mind, not wanting to lie awake all night worrying. Sinow's steady sleeping breaths provided a rhythm that lulled her to sleep and before long, she drifted off.

A light streamed in from the window, stirring her from sleep. She rose from the bed following the light's path out and through the balcony into the dew-tipped grass. She glanced back, seeing the balcony now high above her. Had she walked straight out? Looking down she found that a thin green gown now draped her previously naked body.

"A dream," she whispered to no one.

A shimmer pulled her attention back to the stream of light,

which she began following. Woods seemed to grow from nowhere, now surrounding her on all sides, still she walked, eventually coming to a small glade, a babbling stream running soundlessly through it.

"Daughter," a gentle voice spoke. Glancing back up she met the eyes of the Mother Fate, Orlaina. She should have dropped to her knees in respect but instead she stood frozen. The Fate's appearance caused fear to run through her, for it could only mean one thing.

"No," she said, backing away. "No, you can't do this." She brought her hand to her chest. "We righted our wrongs. You've left us in peace for six thousand years."

"We have, but the path is still to be followed, my child. The prophecy still unbound."

"No, we healed all the wounds—"

"You have yet to finish the path."

"What are they planning to do to us this time?"

The Fate smiled a sad smile. "This part of the path is not yours to follow."

"Sinow?" she asked, not understanding.

"No. The son must now walk for the parents and redirect the path to its conclusion. Only then will the prophecy be completed."

"Ren? Our son? You're going to punish him for my mistakes?"

"No, but this is his part of the journey." She paused. "And you must let him follow it no matter the fear in your heart. You must not let Sinow stand in the way, no matter the hatred in his. Both of you will fear, but you must trust."

"Hatred?" It was an unusual word for the sentence. He didn't hate their son, he loved him. Why would she have used that particular word? Violissa thought back to earlier in the day. Sinow had sensed something but couldn't determine its source. She inhaled sharply, her hand flying to her mouth.

"Tynan," she stated, the shake in her voice revealing her fear.

The Fate shimmered slightly. "You must have faith, both of you. Do not let Sinow stand in the way, no matter what happens. You both must let the boy go. This is his path and his alone." She began to fade.

"No! You can't! They can't do this!"

"Trust. Have faith," she said as she faded completely.

"No!" Violissa screamed, but there was no one left to hear her.

Waking, she shot up in bed and inhaled as if she hadn't breathed the entire time.

"Vi? What's wrong?" Sinow asked, sitting up next to her.

She looked at him, knowing her eyes reflected the fear his held and whispered, "Tynan."

Ren sat in the bed of long grass watching how the light from the moons illuminated the strands, keeping them from the shadows of night. He had gone to the Elvin enclave and spent the rest of the day with his cousins and their family. They were so far removed from his line in the family that there really wasn't a name to give their relation to him at this point, his mother's first cousin gone many generations now. It was on Elvin land that he truly felt at peace. That side of him quieting the two warring sides of him, the Light which he embraced fully and the Dark which he tried to keep submerged regardless of how it always seemed to claw its way up from the recesses of his soul.

Now, in the early pre-dawn hours, he sat in the only other place that gave him peace, the Sacred Groves. As a child he would find his way here, to the spot his mother had frozen in time when she'd returned to their world. No trees grew on the barren field, only grass and wildflowers. The souls of the dead which she had released, long departed. His mother's magic still lingered in the air here, further calming his restless spirit.

Behind him there was a slight stir in the air. He rose and turned, trying to determine its source. He could see nothing, but his senses tingled.

"Well, well. It would seem you have your father's annoyingly keen abilities," a voice said, movement revealing a man across from him. The air filled with a corrupt Darkness that fell foul on his skin. The man looked so similar to his father Ren knew it could be none other than Tynan.

"Hello, nephew," Tynan said, walking forward. Ren could hear the madness in Tynan's voice and see it in his eyes.

"That's close enough," he said, putting his hand out.

"Do you know who I am?"

"Yes, you are my uncle, although that's not a term we use in reference to you."

"Does your father still talk about me? Is there still fear in his eyes when he speaks my name?"

"He never speaks your name. In fact, no one talks about you, it is forbidden."

Tynan appeared a bit irritated by that fact, but he continued to talk.

"How long has it been, Drostiren? That is your name, am I right?"

"It's been almost six thousand years since my father defeated you."

Tynan laughed, a maniacal sound. "Is that what he told you? He defeated me? It would appear you've been told wrong, for here I am."

"What do you want, Tynan?"

"I want what's mine. I want revenge."

"You won't hurt my parents again," he said, not knowing quite where it had come from but feeling the need to protect his parents.

"And you're going to stop me? Your powers are unsteady, you've no control of your Dark power. How close are you to ascension, boy?"

Ren felt his Dark power stir, and his eyes began to darken, but before he could react, Tynan hit him with a force of magic. He was thrown across the field and through a patch of trees, each one stinging as his body knocked them over. Finally stopping, he picked himself up, too stunned to block Tynan's second attack. How was Tynan so powerful? Had his father been holding back during his training all this time? Pulling himself together, he managed to block Tynan's next attack.

His father's words played in his head, coaching him through the next moves. He heard his father say to embrace his Dark power, to release his hold on it. Closing his eyes, he did just that, feeling it course through him. He was about to release it when Tynan disappeared. He went to follow his shift, but Tynan shifted behind him and Ren felt his skin rip open.

"That's exactly what I needed," he heard as he tore himself away. He caught sight of a vial with what looked to be a small amount of blood in it before Tynan shifted.

Feeling the tear in his skin heal, he readied himself to follow but was stopped when his father, followed by his mother, shifted in front of him.

His father looked around frantically while his mother ran up to him.

"Are you all right? Did he hurt you?" she asked.

He pushed her hands away.

"He was here. I'm going after him," his father said, his eyes the deepest black Ren had ever seen them.

"No!" his mother yelled. "We are not to interfere. I told you that."

"They expect me to stand by and allow Tynan to surface, leaving my family vulnerable, leaving you vulnerable to him."

"He's not here for me, Sinow."

"He's here for me, isn't he?" Ren said.

They both looked at him.

"How did you know he was here? Did you feel him?" he asked.

His father sighed. "Your mother had a dream."

He knew about his mother's dreams, the ones his parents had shared with him. They tended to involve the Fates and almost always signaled that something was going to happen. As far as he knew, she hadn't had one since Tynan had taken her, a time they never spoke of, a time he'd had to pull teeth to find out about. Keary had been the only one willing to fill him in.

He swallowed. "You dreamed about him?"

"A Fate visited me, she warned me of his return."

"What happened, Ren?" his father asked with a worried tone.

"He attacked me. I fought back," Ren dropped his eyes, "not very well." He looked back up at his father. "You were right. All this time, you've been telling me to train, to use my Dark powers to fight, and I didn't listen."

His father came up to him and wrapped his arm around his neck.

"You did fine. You called your powers, I felt them. We'll work on strengthening them. Understand?"

"Yes, Father."

"Ren, why is there a rip in your shirt and blood on your back?" his mother asked.

His father let go of him and turned him around.

"You let him get close enough to harm you?"

"He shifted, and when I readied to follow, he surprised me by shifting behind me. He cut me with something before I could stop him."

His mother backed away, scanning him.

"Mother, I'm fine, there's no poison, no curse. He took some of my blood."

"What?" his father's eyes grew blacker. Ren could see the anger spilling from him. "Why would he take your blood?"

"I don't know why. I was about to chase after him when you arrived."

"Fates, Sinow, he's found the book."

"You can't know that, Violissa. He could be using it to create new creatures."

She shook her head, "No. He would never mix Dark blood with mortal blood."

"And you know this for certain?"

"Yes." She didn't elaborate, but Ren could tell his father's mind was filling in the pieces.

His father looked away for a moment; Ren could feel the thickness of his power on the air.

"If he found the book," he stopped and met her eyes, "then he's accessed the locked spells. Something in there requires King's blood, and Drostiren is next in line for the throne."

"The spells that had been locked to him, I unlocked them that day," his mother said. "Do you remember any of them, Sinow?"

"No, and not all of the book's spells made it to me. Remember, there were some left, the magic you used to open the portal."

Ren was fascinated. He'd never heard his parents talk about that time in their lives.

"Something he found needs Ren's blood."

"But why?" his father asked.

"Ren, what were you doing when he took it?"

"I had called my Dark powers."

"All three powers present with your Dark magic in full use. He waited for you to call your Dark powers, something you never do," his father said.

"He needed all three present when he drew the blood," his mother finished.

"But they weren't all equally present," Ren argued. "My Dark power was active—"

"And your other powers were still present," his mother said.

"I'm going after him, Vi. I can sense him out there now, he's no longer cloaked. I don't want to wait to find out what he's planning."

His mother stepped up to his father and placed a hand on

his chest. Ren could feel the calming spell she was using.

"Don't, Violissa. I'm going after him."

"You can't. She said we need to let whatever Tynan is planning happen."

"No matter what he does to our son?"

Ren wanted to say he was right here as they talked about him but bit his tongue.

"No matter what. I have challenged the Fates before and learned my lesson. We wait for Tynan's next move. This is Ren's journey, not ours this time."

His father sighed, and Ren could see the fight in his eyes, the battle of the Dark king to flush out an enemy, the father to protect his family, and the husband to trust his wife.

"You trust her?" his father asked.

"She's never steered us wrong before," his mother responded.

His father nodded in acceptance.

"Drostiren, first thing in the morning you train with me. Understood?"

"Yes, Father."

"Go home, get a few hours rest. I'm putting the Council on notice. I may not be able to stop him from whatever he's planning, but I will ensure our people are protected while he's out there."

The next morning, his father was waiting for Ren in the sparring ground. Ren hadn't slept; instead, he'd replayed the incident with Tynan in his head over and over then followed it by analyzing the conversation his parents had had. Something was going to happen, and the Fates wanted them to sit back and watch it play out regardless. It had to infuriate his father. Ren knew how his father disliked having things out of his control. That was why he'd gotten so angry when Ren had told him he didn't want to ascend the throne.

His mother sat to the side, ready to watch. He had figured she wouldn't be far, his father always keeping her within reach. Now with Tynan back, there was no chance he would leave her side, leave her vulnerable.

"Are you ready?" his father asked.

"Yes."

"Good, this time don't fight it, bring the Darkness forth."

Ren closed his eyes and listened for the Dark magic, hearing it deep within where he kept it buried. This time, like the previous night, he opened himself to it, letting it course through him, pushing the Light back, letting it claim its hold on him. He heard the rumble of the sky and the ground, felt the air grow heavy then opened his eyes to the blackness that now filled the space around them.

Four

Sinow watched as the world around them darkened. Drostiren was calling his full Dark power and inadvertently waking his Elvin side. It made sense; he'd found the two sides complemented each other more than anyone had ever realized. The ground shook beneath his feet, and the air grew thick with Dark magic. Sinow's own powers flared to meet his son's.

Drostiren opened his eyes; they were black as an endless night, all trace of blue gone from them.

He replaces one power with the other, Violissa said to him in enaigne. *That's why he fears the Dark so. He loses his Light when he embraces the Dark.*

He needs balance, he replied.

Yes.

"What now, Father?" Drostiren asked.

"Hit me. Take yourself back to the fight with Tynan and hit me as if you were fighting him once again."

They sparred for a long while, Drostiren finally allowing himself to stay in his Dark space. As Sinow fought with him, he evaluated him. It had been years since his son had sparred with him, and it felt good. Drostiren's powers were formidable, but he had a hard time controlling them, particularly his Dark powers. The pre-ascension didn't help, his strikes were sporadic, ebbing and flowing with the flickering of his power.

They spent the day together, breaking at times to rest and talk. Violissa conjured food and drinks midday, and they sat as a family, removed from the confines of their castle and of their titles. It had been a long time since they had been relaxed like this. As Drostiren had aged, he had distanced himself from Sinow, his way of distancing himself from the power he didn't understand. Tynan's return had forced Drostiren to embrace that side of himself and forced Sinow to view his son in a different light. Violissa had been right; Drostiren was not a Dark king, nor would he ever be. He was something new, something none of them truly understood, each of them identifying with pieces of him rather than the whole.

Sinow saw that now and regretted the distance it had placed between them.

"That's enough for today," he said, shifting to Drostiren who remained on the ground from the last hit and holding a hand out to help pull him up.

Drostiren stood, dusting himself off and laughing, something Sinow hadn't seen since he'd become what could only be described as a brooding teenager. The closer the ascension grew, the worse it had become. Sinow vaguely remembered going through a similar phase, but he had been cocky and overly confident as a result of the growing Darkness in him, not withdrawn and contemplative.

"When did it grow dark?" he asked.

"A while ago," Violissa said, coming over to them, her smile lighting the space that was dimly lit with spheres of magic she must have created when they'd been sparring.

"Are my two sweaty men ready to go home now?"

She reached up and kissed him, then pulled back with a wave of her hand saying, "I think a shower might be in order."

Only if I have company, he said in enaigne.

Hmmm, let's see. You ousted me to sit on the sidelines all day, never thinking I might want to join and now you want me to help you clean up?

"Are you two done?" Drostiren interrupted.

Violissa laughed. "Sorry, Ren. I was scolding your father and will continue when we get home."

Sinow chuckled and kissed her on the cheek. "Yes, you will after that shower," he whispered.

Turning back to Drostiren, he asked, "How do you feel?"

"Better, as long as I can keep it under control, I'm good."

The comment stirred Sinow's memories of his battle for control after the ascension.

"It's only going to worsen after the ascension. You can't keep it contained or controlled."

"No, he can't, can he?" Violissa said, understanding immediately.

"But if I don't, it's like this battle inside me. Constantly."

"I know, and it will always be that way until you give up that control," he said.

"What? That would be worse."

"No," Violissa said. "You have three powers in you, Ren. Each wants to own you, but it can't. They must work in harmony. You call each power separately when you use them, blocking the others off. I did that each time until one day I let them both flow through me. They worked together, weaving to make a power that was greater than they had been on their own."

"The day with the Torathar," Sinow stated, not realizing she had never done so before that day.

She smiled and nodded.

"The more you restrain your Dark power, the more it fights back," he said. "You have to allow all three the space to run through you, especially your Dark power."

"And how do I do that?" Drostiren asked.

Violissa chewed her lip then said, "I don't remember. I was so young then."

Drostiren looked to Sinow who shook his head. "Your mother had to help me. I only remember letting go for once, but I only had Dark magic in me."

"If I had the ability to ask my younger self, I would tell you, Ren. But you'll have to figure it out on your own."

"No way to go back to the past, trust me," Sinow said. He would have in a heartbeat if it meant keeping Violissa from the nightmare with Tynan.

Violissa took his hand; he was certain she could read his thoughts. "Let's go see if the Councils left any supper scraps behind for us," she said. "I thought giving them their own castles would alleviate that issue, but that didn't work out quite the way I had anticipated."

"Told you so," he joked, but his smile faded as he felt the change in the air, the stir from a shift he recognized all too well. The ground rippled below him as he threw a shield up around Violissa and Drostiren. Pushing Violissa behind him instinctively, he turned to face Tynan.

"Brother," Tynan said with a sneer.

"Tynan," he returned, stepping forward. "How did you escape?"

"It would seem you are more of a fool than I expected, Sinow. And you, Violissa. Tsk, tsk, I thought you were smarter than this." He waved his hand, and the book appeared before him.

Violissa moved from behind Sinow. "The book," she said in a hushed tone.

Tynan waved his hand, and the book faded from their view. "My, my Violissa, how you have bloomed with age. Have you missed me?"

Sinow's power flared. "Enough, Tynan," he said calling it forth.

"Sinow," Violissa said, her hand reaching for his, her other gripping his shoulder. "Remember."

"It would seem you've lost this time, brother. The Fates can't save you. Nothing can. There's something I came for, and I imagine you're going to attempt to stop me."

Sinow looked over at Violissa, tears were welling behind her eyes, but she was putting on a brave face.

"You're here for me," Drostiren said, taking a step forward.

Tynan's lips curved into a manic smile. "Why yes, I am. Are you prepared to fight your father's battle?"

"No, my father can fight his own as I can fight mine. But I will go with you. I know that's my course."

Sinow looked back at Violissa who dropped her head on his shoulder.

Let him go, Sinow. We must trust the Fates, she said in enaigne.

Drostiren looked back at them. "I love you both," he said then walked over to Tynan.

Sinow gripped Violissa's hand tighter, every part of him wanting to stop Drostiren, the power flaring around him begging for release, wanting only to attack Tynan and save his son.

"Once again you're a fool, Sinow, you always have been," Tynan said as he reached into the air behind him, summoning a portal.

He took a vial with a red mixture out and threw it into the portal where it shattered—the red, Drostiren's blood, spreading through the black space.

"This was almost too easy. First, I'll take the son who should have been mine." He grabbed Drostiren who, knowing his fate, remained obedient.

"No," Sinow said, stepping forward. "Vi, I need to—"

No, we can't, she replied, her voice quaking even in his head.

"Then I take the rest. All of it will be mine this time and even your blasted Fates can't stop me."

Drostiren looked back at them one last time before Tynan

dragged him through the portal.

Sinow freed himself from Violissa's grip and ran toward the portal.

"No!" he screamed as it disappeared. He looked over at Violissa who had followed him, her face layered with tears, her heart broken just as was his. She fell into his arms, all the courage gone from her. He held her tight and prayed to the Fates that they would watch over his son, that they would keep him safe rather than fail him as they had Violissa.

He buried his face in her hair and tried to fight the onslaught of pain in his chest by surrounding it with Darkness, pushing himself to a place he'd never wanted to return.

Five

Ren felt himself falling once he was pulled into the portal. He didn't know why he'd so calmly gone with Tynan, but he had known that was what he needed to do. The Fate had visited his mother, and from the way she'd held his father back, he knew the Fates needed him to go with his uncle. This was his journey, not theirs.

A tainted feel of corrupt Dark magic engulfed him, and he found it hard to breathe, the wind knocked from him. Tynan gripped his arm tightly. Wherever it was Tynan was going, he wanted Drostiren there with him. He felt a pressure against him then a forceful pull away from Tynan, who gripped him harder. The pull increased, and Tynan continued forward, arms flailing to reach for Drostiren who was suddenly ripped from his grip, the portal spitting him out moments later. He rolled hard onto a solid surface, bones breaking then healing with the impact. He stood, trying to get his bearings, a bit shaky from the trip. A loud noise invaded the silence, a blare of something he'd never heard cutting into the night, accompanied by bright lights he saw from his periphery.

Something slammed into him, and he was sent flying again. This time, catching himself in time to land on his feet, crouching down, ready to attack.

"Oh my god! Are you all right?" a woman's voice called as she ran toward him with another female. Her voice was so familiar.

"Paige, call 911."

Paige? He looked at the girl, her blue eyes shining, auburn hair surrounding a pretty face.

"Is he ok?" A male's voice shouted from where the object had stopped. What was it? He remembered hearing about something similar from Keary. Car? He thought that must be it, but then he was drawn back to the woman.

"He's standing," she said, approaching him. "Thank god. You're standing."

"Mother?" he asked, taking in the golden curls and emerald eyes that he'd known his entire life.

"Oh, honey. You must have hit your head hard," she replied, laughing.

"I don't see any wounds. I hit him dead-on. He appeared out of nowhere," the man said, but Ren continued to stare.

"Maybe he has a concussion?" she asked moving the hair aside on his forehead, looking for wounds.

"Either that or he got hit by the spell every man falls under when they see you, Violet."

Violet? Why had she called his mother Violet?

"Hush, Paige. Did you call 911 yet?"

From the side of the strange building next to them, he saw a figure run out.

"What in the hell is going on out here?"

He turned to the voice whose owner stopped dead in his tracks when he saw Ren. Keary. Did he recognize him? Why didn't his mother? Why were they all dressed so oddly? And how had a car gotten into their world?

A second figure came out, and Ren's heart raced as he pieced it all together.

"Everything all right out here?" his father said, then catching his mother's eyes added a breathless, "Vi."

They both appeared lost in each other as she returned his greeting with a smile and a "Simon."

"Fates," Ren muttered.

"Fates?" he heard Paige whisper to Keary.

"He just appeared out of nowhere. I didn't mean to hit him. One minute the road was clear, then boom, he was there," the man said.

"He looks fine to me. Why don't you pull your car to the curb and go in to the bar to sit down. Have Chelsea give you something to calm your nerves," Keary directed.

"I think he hit his head, Keary. We should have him looked at," his mother said. Violet. That's what she was known as here. But how was here even happening? "He called me his mother."

"Did he now? Simon, take Violet and Paige in. Let me take care of this," Keary responded, eyeing Ren suspiciously.

"I can stay and help," Paige said.

"Get him some ice for his head, Paige," Keary instructed.

"Come on, ladies, you've been entrusted to my care."

His mother smiled at him then disappeared into his father's eyes again. The two walked away with Paige following behind, curiously glancing back a few times. Keary watched until everyone was inside then, grabbing Ren, slammed him into the side of the building.

"Who the hell are you?" Keary said through gritted teeth.

"My father always says you have a tendency toward human words. It's Fates, Keary, not hell. Since I'm assuming you can sense my power, you must realize I could kill you right now for even touching me."

"I don't care. You are an unknown threat to my king and

queen, feel free to kill me, but I'll die fighting for them."

Typical Keary fashion, Ren thought.

"Good, now let me go and—"

Keary pushed him against the wall again. "Tell me who you are."

"I brought the ice," Paige said, running toward them. She was clearly eager not to be left out. Full of spirit just as his mother had said she was.

"Really, Paige? Do you think this is the safest place for you right now? He could kill you."

"If he were going to kill us, Keary, he'd have done it by now. Besides even as dark as it is out here, I can see that he has blue eyes. No Dark powers there."

Keary studied him for a moment then loosened his grip. "You have Dark power, I can feel it."

"Yes. I do. Now let go of me, and I'll tell you what I can. But first tell me, are they safe to leave alone?"

"You know?" Paige asked.

"Shit," Keary mumbled then grabbed Ren's face, tilting it to the left then the right. "They're safe. Now tell me why it matters to you?"

"I think you already know. My life depends upon it."

Keary let go of him and took a step back.

"My name is Drostiren, I am named for my grandfathers Drostan and Viliren." Keary took another step back, never breaking his eye contact. "I am Prince of the new world and Guardian of the Elvin domain. My father is Sinow Dark King of Tenebron, my mother Violissa Light Queen of Cirillia and Overqueen of the Elvin." Paige gasped. "Upon my ascension, I will be king of all three realms."

"No," Keary muttered. "It can't be."

"You know it to be true. You can see it. I am told I look—"

"Just like your father," Keary finished. "But Sinow told me of his vision, his son had green eyes."

"Aye, they were green, but as my Light powers grew, my

eyes became the color of my Light kin. My mother will be the only Light ruler who will ever bear the mark of the Elvin."

"No, this can't be..."

The door of the bar opened, and a woman hollered out, "Keary, are you planning to help me tend tonight or are you copping out on me?"

"Go back in, Chelsea. I need a few minutes."

Instead of listening, she walked over to them, her ebony hair straight and dark against her pale skin, brown eyes appraising the situation then Drostiren. She crossed her arms, which had several small inkings on them, something Ren found unusual.

"Why does he look just like Simon? I mean, Keary, you and Simon look alike, but this guy is the spitting image..." She paused, dropping her arms. "Wait, is this more magic stuff?"

Keary ran his hands over his face and gave Paige a dirty look. "You really need to keep your mouth shut."

"This is Chelsea?" Drostiren couldn't help but ask.

"How do you—" Keary started.

"You've shared a few stories."

"You talk about me?" she asked Keary. "That's so sweet."

"Not me, some other version of me."

"My head is starting to hurt," Paige said. "Can you just explain what you're doing here?" she asked Ren.

"Tynan brought me here."

"What?" they both asked at the same time.

"I don't think he meant for me to come out of the portal without him. I think the Fates pulled me here. My mother said they were involved."

"Wait, Violissa knew Tynan would bring you here?"

"Not quite, only that Tynan was going to take me."

"And Sinow allowed that?"

"Yes. It's a long story, but neither of them questions the Fates anymore."

"Ok, this is clearly going to be a long conversation, which I can't have right now. We need to hide you."

"Can we take him inside?"

"Drostiren, can you make a light sphere?"

"My mother calls me Ren and yes."

He made a sphere, and Paige gasped. "So that's what they look like with magic," she said.

"Wow," Chelsea said. "They were bright in the dark, but now they're amazing. Those eyes could make any girl—"

"Chelsea, don't corrupt him. This is my future king, have some respect. Now, go in and get us one of Chad's hoodies he's always leaving around."

"You take all the fun out of things, Keary," she retorted then ran back to the building.

"What's a hoodie?" Ren asked.

"What are we going to do, Keary? It's obvious he doesn't fit in," Paige said, ignoring Ren's question. "And he looks too much like Sinow."

"I don't know, but for now, we need to get back inside. Let's just be thankful it was so dark out here tonight."

Chelsea came running back out with a strange shirt in her hand. She handed it to Ren who wasn't quite sure how it functioned.

"It's a cape with sleeves," Keary explained, sensing his confusion.

"Here," Paige said, taking it and helping him into it.

She smelled good, like the red berries they had at home. When she stepped back, he could see a bit of her father in her. It was strange standing in front of someone he'd only heard of in stories, someone who had been dead for thousands of years.

"Now what? Everyone in town knows each other, Keary. They'll take notice to a random stranger."

"He's my cousin," Chelsea said.

"Seriously?" Keary asked.

"My cousin on my dad's side."

"Chelse, you've been here since you were a kid, no one's going to buy that."

"No one ever met my father or anyone on his side of the family for that matter," she stated, putting her hands on her hips. "He left us when I was young, that's why my mother moved here. Remember, I've got daddy issues."

"Ok, that may explain his sudden appearance. I guess. You come up with the rest of the story and figure out why he needs the hoodie on."

"He's got over sensitive eyes," Paige said. "I saw it on a show once. Photophobia I think it was called. That's why he was in the street and didn't move from the car. He has special glasses, but they dropped and got damaged."

"Fates, Paige, you sound like a mad woman. Where do you come up with these things?" Keary asked.

"It might just work," Chelsea said. She took his arm. "Come on, cuz, you and I are going to spend some time at the bar tonight."

"Keep him on the end away from everyone. Paige, you stick with him. When the bar closes, Ren, I want to know everything," Keary said.

Seated as far from his parents as possible, Ren couldn't take his eyes from them. But they weren't really his parents, not yet. They were Violet and Simon here, two people who had no idea who they were. Still, it seemed strange to be here watching them like some nightmare he couldn't escape. He went to run his hands through his hair but hit the thick hood instead. Frustrated, he dropped his hand and took a sip of what they called ale here.

"Same grimace Keary gets every time he drinks it," Chelsea said, walking by.

"How can you see his face, Chelse?" Paige asked, coming over to sit down next to him. She'd been tied up with his parents, and Ren had been stuck getting introduced by Chelsea to people he didn't care to know for what seemed forever.

"Tired of talking to people?" Paige asked. "I hear from Keary that it's not the normal thing for a Dark king."

"I suppose it's good I'm not your normal Dark king," he replied. "I'm used to it. You don't have my mother for a mother if you're not dragged from village to village from the moment you take your first step, much to my father's frustration might I add."

She laughed then looked over at them. "What's it like?"

"Strange. They're so relaxed, so free from the constraints of the crown, of their power, of...well just free. My father is laughing, it's not something I see him do often."

"Are they not happy? Not still in love?"

He heard the concern in her voice. "Of course, they are. There are no two people more in love than my parents. They can barely keep their hands to themselves. But I suppose they've had their share of challenges, and it has taken its toll on them in ways I can't say."

She studied him, then looked as if she were going to question him but was thankfully interrupted.

"Paige, I need your help," a man, said coming up behind her. "I can't get Violet to step away from Simon long enough to come sing."

"Sing?" Ren couldn't help asking, confused.

"Yes, it's Irish night. She sings every time we have it," Paige explained. "Keary has it once a month and shuts the bar down for locals only."

"But she never sings," Ren mumbled, "only on special occasions," he said, his memory of the stories coming back to him. He remembered distinctly that his mother never sang as a human.

"You've heard my sister sing?" the man asked.

"Sister?" Ren tried to keep from falling back on his stool.

"Ren, this is Cody, Violet's brother."

"Brother? But she doesn't have a brother."

"Is that what she's telling people these days? Always trying to trade me in. Well, Paige, if you can convince her to leave lover boy for a few minutes, the band and I can get started."

He slapped a hand on Ren's arm, "Good to meet you, Ren. No brother, that's a good one."

He walked away as Ren continued to stare at him.

"Well, that went well," Chelsea said, wiping down the bar and replacing his barely touched drink.

"Are you all right?" Paige asked.

"She doesn't have a brother."

"Could she have left that out?"

He shook his head, "No. I know this story by heart. It was a favorite of mine growing up. There is no sibling, there never is for either of them. They're royalty."

"But Tynan—"

"Was the Fates' doing," he replied before he realized he shouldn't have.

"What?" Paige asked.

"Never mind. There's something wrong, things are different. She doesn't sing in public either."

"She sings all the time. That's why I'm so surprised Simon hasn't heard her yet. Tonight will be the first." She seemed too excited, her eyes bright.

"No, she doesn't—"

He was interrupted again as Cody spoke, his voice carrying across the bar. He was speaking into something that was throwing his voice out. In his hands, he had a sort of fiddle. Ren remembered his mother telling him about the different instruments in this world. What had she called this one? Something similar to her name. Viol...he couldn't catch it so let the thought go.

"Simon, I'm stealing my sister," Cody said jovially.

She looked up at Cody and laughed.

"Paige, help me out here," Cody pleaded.

"Ah, ok. Ok," she yelled playfully. "I'll be back, duty calls," she told Ren, then leapt off the stool and skipped up to the front of the bar. Ren couldn't get over the fact that she had been sitting with him, that she was here, alive. But then neither could he believe he was here in the first place.

He watched as she hopped next to Cody, an endless bundle of energy, her auburn hair spilling over her shoulders as she tried to tame it by flicking her head to the side.

Cody started playing, and the rest of the group joined him but what Ren heard was nothing like music they had at home. The instruments different, made from materials he'd never seen, emitting sounds unlike any he'd heard. Paige began to sing, and Ren was drawn to her voice. It was pretty, and he knew if she were home and his mother in full power its beauty would be enhanced. He absently wondered what her first thoughts had been the moment that had happened. *The moment it would happen*, he corrected himself, remembering he was in her past.

His attention was pulled away as Keary patted the bar then helped his mother up to stand on it. His father looked puzzled, as puzzled as Ren currently was. Then his mother's voice filled the room, not quite the same, the power in it missing, the alluring quality still present, however. She delicately walked down the bar as she sang her verse then stopped to stand in the middle, continuing until Cody's part started.

Ren looked at his father. Paige had said it was his first time hearing her sing, and his expression was worth all of this. He was awestruck, the look in his eyes full of wonder and love as if there was no other woman in the world but his mother. He'd seen his father look at his mother that way every day of his life, but there was something innocent and pure about this, without the tainted past that haunted them.

"If you didn't want to marry her before, Simon, I guarantee you want to now," Cody joked as the music played. Everyone in the room laughed as did his father.

She began to sing again, her voice enthralling, wrapping itself through the room, capturing everyone in its spell. But there was something else there that shouldn't have been there: magic. Not the kind normally present but something subtle, innate.

Keary gestured to his father to pick up his mug, mouthing, "Trust me," and pointing to his mother whose voice was strengthening, crescendoing as it reached the peak of the song. Ren felt the ground tremble lightly, the bar shake, his ale sloshing. Someone ran to a set of glass doors and threw them open as she hit her last note, as if not doing so risked them shattering with the force of her voice.

Magic. Her voice held magic. She had innate powers. That couldn't be, though. Neither of his parents had their innate powers at this time. They wouldn't return until they kissed. This couldn't be right. What had Tynan done? What had the Fates done?

Six

Keary waited impatiently for everyone to leave the bar. He'd been jittery all night, running things through his head, trying his best to figure out how and why his future king was sitting at the bar watching the parents who would one day create him. His head was beginning to hurt. Having convinced Cody to chaperone Simon and Violet, Keary finally bid them goodnight, insisting he needed Paige's help with something. Slowly, he turned and faced the predicament before him.

Ren dropped his hood. Fates, his eyes were bright. Keary had never seen a Light king. Violissa's Council had eyes that had once shone strangely brighter than any normal persons, but Ren's were like two vibrant cerulean stars, revealing the power below.

"There's no way we're going to hide that," Paige said.

"Is that normal?" Chelsea asked.

"Just clean up, Chelsea," he told her, irritated that she was part of this at all. Paige and her big mouth.

Keary walked to the bar, pouring himself a shot as Ren removed the hoodie.

"These things are suffocating. How do you wear them?" Ren asked, revealing the standard garb of a Darkbearer below.

"Black?" Keary asked gesturing to his shirt. "With those eyes I would have guessed you'd be wearing lighter colors."

Keary watched as Ren's eyes darkened to match Sinow's. "Good Fates, so it's true."

His eyes lightened again, and he heard Chelsea exhale a shaky breath.

"I prefer my father's colors, but I favor my mother's power." He looked down at his hands and muttered, "Or at least that's what my father says."

There was something underneath that statement that Keary wished he could question, but it didn't seem pertinent to their situation.

"All right, tell me everything. How is it we get from where I was this morning to the unsettling sight of you in my bar tonight?"

"Never one to mince words, Keary," Ren said. He then proceeded to tell an abbreviated version of the past events, most centering on how Tynan had brought him here, none giving Keary any idea of the history behind it all.

"Wait, wait, you've left too much out. How did Sinow punish Tynan? How did he access a portal here? Why did Tynan take you and not Violissa?"

He noticed the cringe on Ren's face at the last question.

"I can't give too much away. It could change my past."

"It looks like Tynan has already done that," Paige said.

Keary rubbed his face in frustration.

"Do you know how Tynan escaped his punishment?"

"No, there wasn't enough time for questions."

"Any idea why he brought you here?"

"I don't think he meant to. I think I was supposed to go

wherever he ended up. I think the Fates intervened and redirected me here for some reason."

"Why is it always the Fates?" Keary muttered.

"There's more. I think they've changed things. The history isn't right."

"What do you mean?" Paige asked.

"Well, the brother for one. My mother never had a brother, not in any life, especially not this one."

"I always wondered about Cody," Keary said. "Why have a sibling when rulers don't normally have them. Why have the extra attachment to this world?"

"Is he an attachment to this world?" Ren asked. "Have you looked at him? He looks just like a Lightbearer. Even his eyes are brighter, like Paige's."

Keary noticed Paige blush.

Ren ran his hands through his hair just as Sinow always did. "Maybe Paige is right. Maybe Tynan has already changed my history."

"Because of that one thing?" Keary asked.

"No, it's more than that. What happened tonight never happened. My mother barely sang as a human."

"She sings all the time," Paige said. "Although I have to say, this is the first time she's sung since she and Simon, I mean Sinow, met. I think she was afraid of her power showing."

"She only sang twice when they were human, and she told me she barely sang before they met. Trust me, I was raised on this story. And powers. She never had powers here. Their innate powers were locked until they revealed their love for one another, and the Fate-given ones when they returned home. My mother's didn't even return until..." he dropped off as if realizing he'd said too much.

"Your mother's powers have been present since she was young," Paige said. "The town has always protected her and kept her secret."

Ren's power flared, Keary could feel it as his eyes turned a deep black.

"Paige, Chelsea, look down now."

Chelsea whimpered in fear, but Paige, her eyes cast downward, didn't seem bothered.

"She never had power nor did he. Something's off," he spoke as if he didn't notice he'd shifted to his Dark powers.

"Ren, when is your ascension?"

Ren met Keary's eyes, the black fading to a deep brown. "Soon, fifty years or so. Why?"

"Your powers are unstable." *And you can't control your Dark powers*, he wanted to add but decided to keep that from the girls. In that moment, Ren looked just as Sinow had before his ascension. He had struggled with the unsteady flow of Dark magic. Keary wondered why Ren was having the effects so early when Sinow hadn't shown any until right before his ascension.

"Calm yourself before you hurt one of them."

Ren closed his eyes, and Keary felt the room lighten. When he opened them again, they were a brilliant emerald that flickered with blue until the Light power in him took control. Keary was stunned watching it unfold before his eyes.

"You hold all three powers in you," he stated.

"Yes, a child of three races. It makes life interesting," Ren answered.

Keary sat, his legs unable to stand with the reality of what he'd just witnessed. This was their reason. This was why they were fighting to bring the prophecy to fruition. The future of their world stood before him, and the profoundness was almost too much for him.

"Maybe it's the Fates who are changing things," he said quietly. "Maybe it's all changing to protect you. That's why they sent you here."

"I don't understand," Ren said.

"You are the future of our world. Whatever Tynan is doing will influence the outcome that produces you. You're here—"

"No," Paige interrupted, "he's here to protect them. They

don't have the power to fight Tynan, even with what they have now. But he does."

"My father has power, too?"

"Yes, a small innate amount like Violissa but nothing that could stand up against Tynan. Maybe Paige is right. Whatever Tynan is planning, he'll do it when they're vulnerable. The Fates dropped you here so you could be a step ahead."

"Then we need to keep them safe until the festival."

"Festival?" Keary asked, not sure to what he was referring.

"The summer festival. The one that's held every year? She sings each year?"

Keary looked at Paige who shrugged. Neither of them had any idea about it.

"There's no festival?" Ren asked.

"No, there never has been. Besides, it's not summer. It's fall."

Ren looked defeated. "The night of the festival is the night they wake up. Everything's been changed."

"Whatever Tynan did by bringing you back, it must have disturbed the flow of time. The Fates are trying to intervene as much as they can it appears. We just need to sit back and let it unfold," Keary said.

"Not my favorite thing to do."

"Nor was it ever your father's," Keary said, laughing.

"There's something I don't understand," Paige said.

"You seriously understand any of this, Paige?" Chelsea chimed in.

Paige gave her a look, and she went back to cleaning up.

"If Tynan freed himself from whatever punishment he'd been given, why not simply fight your father?"

"My parents are too strong now. The union unleashed their full power. Tynan already lost to my father once, he won't risk that again. He's going to hit them when they're weak."

"Ok, I can see that but why involve you?"

Ren was quiet for a minute, but Keary knew what he was

thinking as his eyes grew dark again. He met Keary's eyes. Both understood the true reason, the way a Dark king would think.

"Revenge," he stated simply. "Payback for imprisoning him for six thousand years."

His eyes shifted to a rich green then back to blue.

Even though Keary had seen the shift to Dark power, he was still stunned to see the sudden transition in his eyes again. He rubbed his hand over his face, feeling overwhelmed by it all.

"I think that's enough for tonight," he said, not wanting to hear anymore, let alone think on it anymore.

"What are we going to do now?" Paige asked. "We need a place for him to stay."

"Aye, we do." Keary thought about it. With the shifting instability of his powers, it was too risky to have him stay with Chelsea...or Paige for that matter. This was going to be tricky.

"You'll have to stay with me, but under the radar. Can you calm those powers any?"

Ren closed his eyes, and Keary could see him relax. When he opened them again, they were a calm blue, still vibrant but more like Paige's. Something that would be less noticeable.

"That's better, how did you do that?"

"My father taught me. Mostly for my Dark powers. He spends a lot of time in the villages now and had to adapt."

"Sinow spends time in the villages?"

Keary noticed that slight tension again in Ren before he answered. "He and my mother are inseparable," he stated. Keary could tell there was more to it than that but knew Ren wouldn't divulge.

"We should go," he said to Keary, changing the subject.

"Yes, you should," Chelsea spoke up. "Paige and I can finish up here. Go get him settled. I'll take her home."

"Yeah, go. We've got this. Ren needs some time to adjust to this world. Remember those days?" Paige said, smiling.

"Too well," Keary replied. "Come on, let's go show you the advances this world holds."

"If the ale and the smell of the air are any indication, I think I'm good."

Keary laughed. "I think you've been tutored by me."

Ren shook his head and laughed. "Much to my father's chagrin."

They walked back to Keary's place, thankfully avoiding a run in with Simon. Keary thought it best to keep them apart; they looked too much alike for the similarities to go unnoticed.

After a brief tour of the apartment and an explanation of some of the modern amenities, Keary left Ren on the couch to get some sleep. Lying in bed, he stared at the ceiling, his mind sifting through it all, trying to make some sense of it. He doubted he'd sleep, it was something that had eluded him since Simon had come to town, initiating that tenuous dance they'd been in for the past month. Now he knew sleep wouldn't return until a resolution was at hand.

He couldn't wrap his head around the fact that Sinow's son was sleeping on his couch, the next king in line. It was impossible, yet he was here, and with his appearance was the knowledge that they'd been through this act before. Only now things were changed, a future that was fixed, one that had already played out, was now changing. Every move they made from this point could send it unraveling more.

How had Tynan found the power to do such a thing? He was powerful when Keary had still been in their world, casting spells that no king should have known. It always surprised him how Tynan had such abilities. Ren didn't appear surprised by it, however, and Keary had a nagging suspicion he knew, that they'd discovered from whence his powers had come. What had happened after they'd returned home? Something big enough to put fear in Sinow's heart. Keary had no doubt that was behind Ren's subtle comments and looks when questioned about his parents. What had happened? What had Tynan done? There were too many questions, unanswered questions, and Keary didn't like to be kept in the dark. He would find out more, needed to, or he would be no help to his king. Closing his eyes, he tried to push the thoughts away and braced himself for another long sleepless night.

Seven

Ren was gone, and a gut-wrenching ache filled Violissa's heart. They had taken her son, her only child, the only person she loved to the depths she loved Sinow. They stood together staring at the place he'd been, neither wanting to move, afraid doing so would make it real. The Councils all stood to the side, waiting on their king and queen, no one knowing what to do next.

Violissa looked up at Sinow, finally pulling her eyes away. His face was stoic, that of a Dark king showing no emotion, but she knew him, knew the subtle shifts of color in his eyes, the tightness of his arm around her, the tension in his body. Knew enough to see that he was hurting as she was. He looked down at her, eyes a prism of browns, each shade fighting to overcome the other, the heart of the man at odds with the will of the Dark king. His eyes searched hers as if they might offer an answer, but there was none to be found. Looking away, he loosened his hold on her and walked to the place where the portal had been. Her heart broke a little more as she watched him search for strands they both knew were not there. Strands of power to call the portal forth, a portal that had eluded them since the day he had punished Tynan, the day they had left it all behind.

The air around her stirred with a warmth that was unusual for the time of year. Then it filled with a sudden chill, the warm air remaining oddly present. The two wrapped themselves in a strand of juxtaposing temperatures. Violissa looked around to see if anyone else noticed, but they all remained fixed on Sinow. Time seemed to slow, and the air thickened, a spectrum of colors filled the world around her in streaks—some moving slow, some quick, some frozen. She brought her hand up to touch a strand, slowly, tenuously.

"Time," she whispered and felt Sinow's eyes turn to her. As if he understood what she meant, he turned back to where the portal had been, holding his hand up to feel for a different pattern of magic. She felt lightheaded, the colors still surrounding her, the flow of time only she could see, the land responding to it under her feet, creaking, humming. Keary came up to her, placing a hand on her back, and she sensed Daneele move closer.

"Are you all right, Violissa?" Keary asked, but she barely heard him, the river of time before her bursting into a kaleidoscope of colors as the multiple paths of their lives formed, each changing with every step further in their timeline Tynan dragged her son. Each changing the life she'd had, the possibilities now endless.

"The past is unraveling. He has disrupted the flow of time." As she said the words, the weight of thc air came crashing down upon her, and everything went black.

Pacing as he watched Violissa's steady breaths, Sinow's mind ran through the events of the day. A dark mist filled the space around him, his powers still drawn to keep his pain at bay. It was the only way he could move forward. Daneele had left some time ago, but Sinow didn't remember when.

Time, she had said before she'd tumbled back into Keary's arms. He had disrupted the flow of time. What had she meant?

He drew his eyes from her and looked out beyond their balcony. The reddish glow from the setting sun reflected on the clouds above, lending the sky a magical effect. Perhaps it was magic, residue from the portal that had stolen Drostiren. For a brief moment, the clouds stopped their eastward drift and stood frozen, a blanket of ruby cascading down upon them. He blinked, and they began moving once again. Had he imagined it, or did it have something to do with what she'd said?

Time.

He thought about the vial of Drostiren's blood Tynan had thrown into the portal. Pure Dark power laced with Light and nature. But why and what purpose had it served? His mind wandered again to Violissa's words.

Disrupted the flow of time.

"That was the reason for the vial," he muttered. Time. A connection. A spell he didn't know. "The book," he said aloud. "He's found a spell in the book."

"It had yet to serve its purpose," he heard Violissa say from behind.

He swiveled to see her emerald eyes watching him. Sitting on the side of the bed, he took her hand. "What happened, Vi?"

"Time is no longer constant. I can feel the pull on the land, in the air, see it in colors like ribbons unraveling." Her eyes had a distant look as they slipped to stare beyond him, seeing only something she could see.

"He's used a spell in the book to change time?"

"I don't know. Whatever he's done it is affecting the flow of time."

“The flow of time. He’s corrupted the portal to take him back. Only the book could have given him a spell like that.”

“That would explain what’s happening.” She bit her lip. “But why take Ren? And why take his blood?”

The Dark king in him knew exactly why Tynan would have taken their son. The more pain inflicted, the more rewarding the punishment. If he had distorted time, then he was going back to change things in his favor—to kill Violissa and as a result, Ren. Sinow’s heart raced. The ultimate punishment, the ultimate way to bring a weaker, younger Sinow to his knees. He met Violissa’s eyes as she too made the connection.

Before she could dwell on it, he said, “The vial must have offered a connection to wherever Tynan wanted to take them.”

“A connection to you?”

“Yes, it’s strong enough for a father to call his son. The connection within our blood binds us.” He didn’t explain any further, thinking it better she didn’t know the details, remembering the pain it had brought the first time his father had called him that way.

“Where did he take him?” she whispered.

“I think the question is when, Vi. When would we be most vulnerable?”

“The human realm, during our mortal lives. Fates, Sinow, he can kill us both easily.”

Her eyes teared, and he could sense her fear as it rolled in waves from her.

Brushing her curl back, he said, “Shhh. Vi, you said the Fates wanted this. That we were to let Drostiren go. We must maintain faith that they have their reasons. We need to trust them.”

“I thought we were done,” she said softly.

“No, you forgot just as I did and became complacent, too comfortable. The Fates like to test us when we let our guard down.”

“But you never let your guard down,” she replied, looking up at him. He knew exactly to what she was referring.

"Not with you. But I never raised it with Drostiren. I didn't think I had reason to."

He sighed and looked beyond her, avoiding her eyes. Eyes that always had a way of reading him, of seeing more than others could.

"He's not strong enough to fight Tynan. He's unsure of his Dark power, unstable from the pre-ascension. He..."

She brought his eyes back.

"You need to trust him."

"He doesn't trust his own powers, Vi."

"And I remember a time when you failed to trust yours. He's more complex, his Light constantly fighting the Dark, but once he accepts that they both belong, he will be amazing."

"That's not enough to stop Tynan."

"Maybe not now but perhaps that's not why the Fates took him. Perhaps stopping Tynan is not his purpose."

He looked at her, she had that knowledge in her eyes that came with seeing things beyond what others could. Call it instinct or second sight, whatever it was, he trusted it.

"I suppose we are being forced to sit back and watch," he said.

"Yes, I suppose we are." Her eyes had a far-off look.

"Vi, what happens if Tynan manages to change the past?"

Her focus returned to him. "He already has changed it, Sinow. The ribbons of time are altering. If he continues, our life will unravel, our existence will fade as who we are today may no longer be."

Her words brought a ripple of fear, the threat of losing her present once again. Shaking it off, he brought her against him and held her tight knowing all around him the ribbons she had spoken of swirled unbound, teetering precipitously on something he could not control.

Eight

The fear in the girl's eyes urged Tynan's actions. He preferred watching their eyes when he took them. The fear, the horror, the pain that filled their innocent eyes increased his desire, urging his movement on, bringing him closer to climax. And this girl's eyes held terror. Grabbing her breasts, he felt the end nearing and, in that instant, released his permission, pouring his Darkness out upon her. As the life left her eyes, he climaxed, the power of taking her life too erotic to contain his ecstasy. Grunting, he pushed himself from the dead girl's body, kneading her breasts again, feeling the urge return. He rolled his neck and walked to the other side of the room, leaving her there for the servants to dispose of.

"Who's ready to play this time," he said, grabbing another of his toys by her long ebony hair. He rubbed his body against hers. "Maybe I'll let you live again, you're especially fun to play with."

He began dragging her away when he sensed something new. A rise in Dark power. Dropping the girl, he reached out to find the source which he found close to his castle. It was strong but didn't carry the same aura as Sinow. Yet, there was something familiar about it. Curious, he shifted to confront it, disregarding his still naked state.

A thick fog covered the ground, Tynan could feel it layer his legs when he landed on the castle grounds. A lone figure cloaked in black awaited him.

"Who are you?" Tynan asked, his power drawn.

"Drop your power and put some clothes on," the figure said walking toward him.

Angered, Tynan did nothing, standing his ground. There was something familiar about the voice, about the feel of the man's power.

"You are on my land, in my kingdom. I suggest you identify yourself before—"

"Before what?" the figure asked, dropping his hood.

Tynan took a step back, startled by what he saw.

"Impossible," he said, returning to his senses but still staring at the wild, unkempt version of himself, madness screaming from his eyes.

"Not impossible. I am your future a few thousand years from now. Although I must admit I don't know exactly how many. Enough for our brother and his whore to bear a son."

"They live? How is that possible?"

"Put some clothes on, and I'll tell you the story then I'll tell you how I plan to destroy them once and for all."

He shifted, leaving Tynan alone to question his sanity.

After donning clothes, Tynan found his future self in the dining room, tearing into a hunk of meat he must have scrounged from the kitchens, leftovers from Tynan's earlier meal. He listened as his future self told his story, heard every misstep and every victory.

"I take Violissa?" he said, licking his lips instinctively,

feeling the rise in him and finding the thought of her in his bed tantalizing.

"Don't get distracted."

"Was she enjoyable?" he asked, curious as to why his future self wouldn't give him more details about the events involving her.

"Too enjoyable. She's a distraction and one we don't need. Now focus as I tell you how she becomes your downfall."

When the story came to an end, Tynan leaned back and stared at himself.

"Now we take our final revenge. We lost once, but we won't lose again."

"You lost," he said, leaning forward. "You lost, but I won't."

"You idiot, you are me. You will follow the same steps, make the same mistakes, and have the same outcome unless you do as I say."

"And what do you propose I do?"

"Bring down the barrier. Focus your forces on the western corner closest to the ocean's edge. The barrier is weaker there, and the people are all corralled close to that spot. This will secure the realms are completely yours."

"But Sinow and Violissa?"

"You will leave them to me. They are exactly where they need to be. They're vulnerable and I intend to take advantage of that vulnerability."

He stood and stretched.

"What if you don't succeed?" Tynan asked.

"I will. Now do you still have that castle in the Lost Realm?"

"Yes, why?"

"Once I've killed Violissa and Sinow, my timeline will end while your new one will begin. I haven't had a woman in eons, and I'd like to satisfy myself before my existence ends. Your head servant will be a good start, then maybe I'll work my way through a few more before I continue my journey. You know what to do, now make sure it's done right this time."

Tynan went to protest, but his future self had shifted. His anger at the final comment spilled over, the book on the table reacting to the Dark power that now surrounded it. He opened it again, staring at the new spells his future self had released for him. Violissa had been foolish enough to release them in the future giving his future self control of them and the power to easily unlock them from the version Tynan now riffled through. He would follow the plan and trust that his future self would follow his. Absently, he wondered why he would have asked about his head servant in the Lost Realm, Chara. There were plenty of younger, prettier servants and slaves to choose from. He let it go, holding his hand over the book, drawing the power from a spell that would strip away immortality and power from any immortal, king, or Council. He'd used the brother to this spell already, but this one was stronger. The Council were weak, but as he had just learned, there were greater powers involved in this story, and Tynan was not about to take a chance that those powers would stop him this time.

"Enter," Tynan commanded in answer to the rap on the door. It had been hours since he'd left his younger self, but he had yet to leave this time. There were things that needed his attention first, punishments that needed to be given, traitors to which to attend. He remained in the chair as he heard the door open, staring at the mangled body before him. Taking Chara had left him with a temporary satisfaction but killing her had fulfilled it. He watched as the blood pooled on the floor below, dripping steadily down the hand that draped limply from the edge of the bed.

"You called, Sire," the guard said. Tynan pulled his eyes away in time to catch the slight reaction to the body: the step back, the subtle shake of his hands. With the flick of a finger,

Tynan bid the guard's helmet to disappear, the face below reflecting the horror to the scene before him, his reaction too slow to hide it from Tynan.

The second guard stepped in behind the first. "Sire, you wanted to see me?" he said, the last word catching in his throat at the scene. They were used to his messes, all of his guards were. This, however, had been Tynan's most loyal servant, and the punishment was one reserved for those who broke his trust—torture, the kind that fed the mad king in him.

Tynan rose, ripping the helmet of the second guard off with his magic. He felt their pulses increase, their heartbeats strain.

"Do you know what I do to traitors?" he asked, rising to stand across from them.

"You punish them, my liege," the second one answered. What was his name? Tynan tried to reach it but couldn't, it was too far removed from his memory. He moved closer to the first guard, Donal. That name he remembered.

"Cirillian. Why did I trust you? Why didn't I listen to my gut?"

"Sire?"

"You will betray me, both of you will. She would have," he said, looking over at the dead woman, remembering the three of them, kneeling, heads bent. He had already punished the other guard, the one he had trusted to lead them all. Four of them he'd seen that night, catching only a quick glimpse during his fight with Sinow, but it had been enough.

"Traitors are punished," he said, revoking his permission from the second guard who screamed in pain before Tynan pushed him through the room and out the window that he would one day have removed to cage Violissa. He heard the body hit the ground, the sound of the shattering bones fueling his madness.

"Pity, he had potential before I placed him with you."

Tynan could see Donal trying to work it out, knowing he couldn't because none of it had happened yet.

"I couldn't take my revenge the first time around," Tynan said, the boards to the door behind Donal separating, then hanging suspended in the air in large slivers behind him. "But revenge is mine regardless of whether you've betrayed me yet or not. It matters not, you would betray me again, and I don't give second chances."

The slivers pierced the guard clear through his body in multiple places, a silent scream escaping, his eyes wide in surprise. Tynan made sure to keep his body upright so he could witness the pain in the man's eyes. Stepping closer, he said, "No damage to the heart or the brain. You'll die but you'll live long enough."

He grabbed him and shifted, Donal stumbling when they landed, the weight of the boards and the pain too much for his body. He fell to his knees, choking on blood.

"Rise and shine!" Tynan screamed, throwing bright light spheres out against the dark of the slave encampment.

"Donal! No!" Darragh, his brother, screamed.

Tynan froze him mid-movement then pulled his body closer with his power.

"Your brother is a traitor and has been punished with death, a slow death. Yours shall be faster."

"No," Donal gurgled.

Tynan turned to Donal. "Were you ever loyal to me? Was there ever a day when I was your king or was your loyalty always to Violissa? Always to that whore of a Light queen?"

"Always to my queen," Donal spat in defiance, blood splattering from his mouth.

"Even when she is lost to you? Even when I am the only one left standing?" he screamed.

"Always," his brother answered for him.

Tynan roared, picking a large stone up with his power and sending it straight at him. The brother collapsed, dead as it crushed his skull. Stones rose from the pits around them, hovering in the air.

"Traitors will be punished, and all of you will betray me. None can be trusted!" he screamed as the stones pummeled the men, slaves, and guards alike until none stood. With a final roar, he sent flames across the bodies. He knew his younger self would be irritated with the loss of his slaves, but there was no use for them; they were a distraction and a waste of resources. They were also a risk. He saw that now; too many living mortals kept in conditions like this where he couldn't watch them were an opening for conspiracy against his younger self.

He stepped through the charred remains, feeling for the portal once again, knowing the Fates would grant him access. What was it Violissa had said so long ago? That they were all pawns in the Fates' game? Well, someone wanted him in the game still; the portal had dropped him here after ripping the boy from him. He didn't mind—he rather enjoyed where this was headed, especially since it was turning in his favor. He would play his part, and he would play it to perfection. The portal appeared as he expected it to, reacting to his reach for the lingering trace of Dark magic that kept him attached to it, the feel of the boy's blood tracing through it still. Having no doubt as to its end destination, he stepped through, never once looking back at the trail of devastation he had left in his wake.

Nine

Ren woke, the morning sun streaming into the room, causing him to blink as he adjusted to its brightness. It took a moment to gather his surroundings and remember where he was. As reality came crashing back, he sat up, cupping his face in his hands. He wasn't home. It hadn't been a dream. He was truly here.

"Morning, sleepy head," Keary said, walking over and placing a mug of black liquid in front of him. "Drink up. If your sleep was anything like mine, you'll need it."

Ren picked up the cup, feeling the heat below his fingers. "What is it?"

"This, my friend, is the only beverage made by humans that I truly appreciate. This is—"

"Coffee," Ren finished for him.

"How did you guess?"

"It's all you complain about. Cursing the Fates for not giving us the ability to replicate coffee."

Keary's face fell. "I can't make it when we get our powers back?"

Ren laughed. "I suppose that piece of information is not event changing so no, you can't. You said it always turns out like muddy water. There's no match to this stuff."

Ren tasted the coffee; it was bitter and acrid on his tongue. His reaction made Keary laugh.

"It'll grow on you. Now, you look about my size. There's a set of clean clothes in the bathroom. Go wash up, and we'll talk more."

They never had time for that talk.

When Ren emerged from the bathroom, Keary was talking with Simon. It still seemed odd to call his father Simon, but he wasn't really his father yet and doing so made it easier on his confused mind.

Simon stopped talking and walked toward Ren, studying him. That's when Ren remembered he had nothing covering his head or his eyes. Keary leapt across the room and pushed something on his head and his face.

"Gotta keep those eyes covered," he said.

"That's amazing," Simon said. "They're so bright. Does the sensitivity make them that way?"

"Yes."

"No."

He and Keary answered at the same time.

Simon looked suspiciously at both of them. "Well, if you two aren't confusing. It's too early for this. Are you coming for breakfast or not, Keary?"

"Sure."

"Good. Ren, join us. I'm sure Violet will enjoy talking with you."

Ren exchanged a look with Keary, unsure if that was a wise idea, but Simon was on his way out the door. Keary shrugged.

"You're here for a reason, you might as well stay close to

them. As close as you can," he muttered to Ren.

They met Paige and Violet at a place Simon called a diner. His mother had told him how humans ate, but it was an entirely different thing to witness it. A gathering but one in which they gathered in small groups, their food served to them. Over the course of the meal, many people stopped by their table, and Ren got a glimpse of his mother in Violet. His father had once said the Fates could never hide her true self, no matter how much they tried; the attributes that made her special always came through.

They sat talking, Ren mostly listening to the casual chatter that took place, taking it all in, as he'd done the night before. There were questions directed at him, but Keary and Paige fielded most of them, garnering suspicious looks from both Simon and Violet. Ren was relieved when Violet stood and said, "Well, I hate to cut this short, but I'm due at the shop soon."

"I should probably check a few emails and do a little work as well," Simon said, standing up and pulling her in.

"Can you two take it somewhere else?" Keary joked.

Simon kissed her, disregarding his comment then stopping to say, "I do believe you still owe me some figures on the bar, Keary. Maybe I'll be heading over there instead."

Keary groaned. "I hate numbers, Simon."

"That's what makes it more fun," he replied.

"You two argue about your numbers. I need to go before I'm late."

"But you own the shop, Vi," Simon said, nuzzling her neck before Paige tossed a roll at them.

Simon laughed then, kissing Violet once more, said, "Ok, I yield."

"I think you'll survive the few hours until you see her again," Paige said.

It was odd to see them all acting so casual, normal people living their ordinary lives, Paige and Keary playing their parts to perfection.

Violet left, Simon's eyes following her out the door until Keary stood and landed a hand on Simon's back.

"All right, let's go. If you're going to make me look at figures, I'd like to get this torture over as soon as possible."

"Ahem." Paige made a sound to draw his attention back to them.

"Ah, Ren. Paige, why don't you show Ren around town?" Keary said. "I'm sure there are some historical sites he'd like to see."

"Historical sites?" Simon asked.

"Nothing you'd find exciting, Simon," he said as the two of them walked out, leaving Ren alone with Paige, a woman he'd only ever known from history. A living ghost.

"So," she said, turning to him, "looks like it's just you and me." She appeared confident, but he could sense her hesitation, the slight quiver in her voice.

"I scare you?" he asked.

"I'm not certain how to feel about you," she answered honestly.

"I suppose that's fair."

She stood, and he followed suit, accompanying her out of the diner and down the street.

"So, should I address you as your highness when others aren't around?"

"I prefer my liege," he answered quickly.

Her face dropped, and she looked taken aback.

"I'm joking," he said, holding up his hands. "My father gets that title and prefers it. You can just call me Ren."

She continued to look at him with trepidation.

"I'm sorry. Keary says I inherited my father's inability to deliver a joke. I suppose I failed at it again."

"No, no. It wasn't bad," she said. "Just unexpected."

He ran his hand through his hair, pushing his hood back before he realized he was doing it.

"Wow, you really are their son, aren't you?"

"Did I give you reason to doubt me?" he asked.

She smiled, and he noticed it was a pretty smile, lighting up her eyes.

"You have your father's eyes," he said before he could stop himself.

"So I've been told."

"Although they don't carry the magic that illuminates his." Yet they were brighter than a mortal Cirillian's would have been, clearly marking her as Daneele's daughter.

"Really?" she asked. "I've never seen a Lightbearer with power. Do they really glow brighter? Like yours?"

He had forgotten where he was on the timeline. Power had not been restored to the Councils, and it had been nearly a century since one had held any magical abilities.

"Almost. All Lightbearers have eyes that reflect the Light within them. Their king's eyes always run brighter, his power being greater. Or so I've been told."

They reached a house, bigger than any mortal in their world could perceive to live in. He was beginning to see that humans liked their things a lot larger than he had imagined.

"Where are we?"

"Your mother's house."

He looked back at her, surprised.

"I thought you might like to see it, a look into her life as a mortal."

He looked back at the house, taking in every detail from the peak of the roof to the swing on the front, to the rows of flowers that lined the walkway. Slowly, he walked until he reached the door, hesitating, unsure of whether he should fill in the missing pieces of a story he'd heard hundreds of times.

"Go on," Paige prompted behind him.

Ren turned the knob and entered. As he walked through the home, taking in the subtle reminders of his mother, Paige stayed quietly behind him. The lilac scent that he'd known since he was a babe lingered gently in the air. He climbed the stairs after wandering the first floor only to stop at the top, unsure where to go, not feeling he should invade Paige's privacy and choose the wrong door.

"To your right," she said.

He continued on, and, opening the door to his mother's room, took it all in. There were pieces of his mother throughout the room. Pieces of her that bled through the façade of Violet she was unknowingly forced to wear. He didn't move, simply stood looking at it, letting it fill the part of his mind that had always been fascinated with the mortal lives of his parents, never fully comprehending what it had meant until now.

Paige let him have his silence, saying nothing in respect.

Finally, he walked over and looked out the window where a cushioned seat lie, its cover worn from use. He ran his hand along it.

"It's as if the part of her the curse has locked away is screaming to be heard," he said softly.

"You can see that just by walking in here?"

"Yes, there are pieces of my mother's spirit throughout this room."

"I always wondered," Paige said. "Having never met her as my queen, I only had stories from which to judge."

She walked over and stood beside him.

"What's it like?" she asked.

"Hmm?"

"What's it like seeing them this way? Neither knowing each other, neither knowing you."

"Both oblivious to the story they are stuck in? Blind to the significance of their next moves?"

She laughed. "Something like that."

"Strange. I feel as if I'm stuck in some nightmare from which I cannot awake."

"I feel that way each day."

"Ah, but you know your purpose. You know why you are here and what you must do."

"And you don't?" Paige asked.

"No."

"But it's easy to see," she said.

He raised an eyebrow at her, awaiting the answer he couldn't determine himself.

"You're here to protect them, to keep them safe from Tynan."

He thought about what she'd said. It was something he'd already considered but discounted. "No, I don't think that's it, Paige. That's too easy, and the Fates do not work in ways that are easy to read. If that were the case, why not drop me with Tynan so I can do just that? Why separate me from him?"

"But you've got the power—"

"No, Paige. I don't. I'm pre-ascension. My powers are unstable, like Keary said. Even if they weren't, I will not have the ability to defeat him until I'm granted my full powers. My father barely defeated him..." He stopped, not wanting to give any more away.

She must have sensed his reticence, saying, "Well then, I guess we'll have to wait and see why the Fates brought you here. Let's go downstairs. I could use some water."

"Since you're stuck with me, do you mind if I ask you some questions?" he asked her.

"Not at all," she answered with a smile, her eyes shining.

They spent the rest of the day talking. He had so many questions, having only heard about her second hand. She told him about her life in the Banished Realm, about her mother, and shared stories about her father and the Councils that opened his eyes to an entirely different side of the men whom he'd only known with magic. Finally, Violet came home, followed by a visit from Keary and Simon soon after.

As the evening progressed, he fell into a comfortable

existence with them all, at times forgetting Violet and Simon were earlier versions of his parents.

Later that evening, as he lay on Keary's couch attempting to sleep, he thought of the one place he hadn't seen on his walk through the town with Paige: the park. He didn't quite know why, but he needed to see it. Needed to see the lake where his parents had opened the portal. Did this place have anything to do with Tynan's escape? It didn't make sense that it would, but the thought was there. He wished he knew where his father had imprisoned Tynan, but that part of the story was hidden along with most of that sequence of events. The only thing he knew for certain was that his prison was somewhere here. Inspired to view the lake, he dressed and snuck out of the apartment. He wasn't certain where to go, so he let his instinct guide him. Like his mother, his instinct as well as his tie to nature was strong.

Eventually, he came to the park, but there was no lake. He scanned the area, sending his senses out. What was he missing? He sensed something that didn't belong in this world, something Dark, filled with magic. Following that feeling, he discovered the other side of the park, divided by a grouping of trees, and came upon the source of his confusion. Before him lay the lake, black and corrupt, a strange yellow ribbon with black writing around it. Ignoring the ribbon, he walked toward the thing that disturbed him more than the water. A tree, its limbs warped and misshapen, devoid of any leaves. Its bark smooth and onyx colored. It was foreboding, ominous, frightening to anyone other than him, and it was filled with emotion that rolled across him in waves: pain, anger, desperation, longing. All of it hitting him with a force as he dared place his hand against it. He didn't need to ask to whom the emotions belonged. He knew immediately. He also knew of the tree.

Years pestering Keary had worn him down enough to get some details, one of which was how his mother had remained in the Light after her descent into her Elvin powers. Keary had said he had asked the same thing and been told she had left her pain behind in a tree. At the time, it had made no sense, but now, seeing it before him he understood. Unable to sustain the weight of her emotions, she had poured them all out, the tree growing from them, encapsulating them. He now understood the extent of all his mother had endured. Hearing it not in words but in emotion.

He stepped back, reeling from the intensity. *Why was it here?* he wondered. The tree shouldn't have appeared this soon, it hadn't been created yet.

"Quite intimidating, isn't it?" He heard Violet's voice behind him. He looked over to see her walking up to stand next to him. What was she doing out here so late? And by herself? Concern flared through him. With Tynan on the loose somewhere, her being out here alone was dangerous. Or was he simply being overprotective, stepping in for his father?

"Wow, you don't even flinch when someone comes up behind you in the middle of the night? Just like Simon."

"Does Simon know you're out here by yourself?" he dared ask.

"Simon holds my heart, but he is not my keeper."

He wanted to respond and tell her just how wrong she was, but he bit his tongue.

"I come out here sometimes. It's weird, I know, but this place calls me."

"That's a pretty disturbing thing to call you."

"Perhaps to some. It's called the nightmare tree."

Curious, he asked, "How long has it been here?"

"For as long as anyone can remember." She walked over the yellow binding just as Ren had and drew closer to the lake. Something stirred in him, and he grabbed her arm, pulling her back.

She turned and looked questioningly at him, and he dropped his hand.

"The water doesn't look right," he said. Then imagining his father's reaction to anyone touching her like that, he added, "I apologize."

She gave him a small smile. "That's sweet, but I wasn't planning to swim in it."

"Has the water always been like that?" he asked, changing the subject.

"It's always been murky, and nothing seems to grow over here, but that greasy color started a short while ago. Then, there was this quake that ran through town then an explosive sound. No one could figure out where it came from until the next morning when we saw the lake. It had turned completely black, and this fissure appeared."

She turned a light on what he now knew was a cell phone and pointed to a large divide that ran the water's edge to behind the tree and beyond. The moon broke from behind the clouds at that moment, giving it the illusion of a mouth belonging to a monstrous beast.

"Tynan," he muttered, walking to the edge of where the fissure almost touched the lake.

"Who?" Violet asked.

He ignored her, instead squatting down at the ledge. This was where his father had imprisoned Tynan and where Tynan had escaped. But how? He brushed his hand along the broken ground. He felt the remnants of his father's spell. It was weak, barely discernable. Had it broken down? Was that how Tynan had escaped, his cage no longer holding him, the magic no longer binding him? He remembered hearing that the god of this world disliked magic. Perhaps something here had broken it down.

"Ren?" he heard Violet say, but his attention was focused elsewhere. There was something else he sensed, something Dark. He stood and turned to the water.

"Vi?" he heard Simon's voice. "What are you doing out here?"

"Hey," she said sweetly, "I don't know, I just felt like I needed to come here."

"Not sleepwalking again, I hope?" he asked.

That caught Ren's attention. "You sleepwalk here? To this spot?"

"Ren? What are you doing here?"

Ren sensed the flare of concern mixed with jealousy.

"He was here when I arrived, standing as if it called to him as well."

"Do you sleepwalk to this spot?" Ren asked again.

"Yes. I mean, I have in the past. It's been a while."

"No, Vi. Remember the night of the quake? I found you on your way here. You were on the other side of the park disoriented."

Ren's heart raced. She'd been so close to Tynan. If she'd been here, he would have killed her, and that would have been it. He looked back at the water. Was this place still a danger to either of them? He bent down and ran his fingers through it. Darkness reached for him; he felt the residue of something foreign, smothering, powerful, something searching for Dark power. The book. This was where his mother had left the book. He didn't know how he knew, but he did. He reached out to sense any presence of it, but it was gone. Tynan had it again, that was how he'd bent time. His mother had unlocked the darkest spells, and they had lain there waiting for Tynan to take them. The history of the book was the only part of the story he'd been told in its entirety.

"It calls to you, something about the water," Simon said.

"It does the same for you, doesn't it?" Ren asked, rising. "She shouldn't be here. You need to keep her away. It's the Dark that calls you just as it may call him back."

"Who?" Simon asked.

He'd said too much. "Evil" was all he could think to say.

"But this calls me as well, Ren. I could never stop coming here," she said, moving closer to the tree.

He studied her for a moment. "Have you ever touched it?"

"No, it's so pure and untouched I never have."

"Place your hand on it," he said on impulse.

She looked at him as if to question him, then slowly moved her hand until it was touching the smooth bark.

"Now sing," he said, feeling Simon's eyes on him. Ren never took his eyes from her. Without questioning, she sang. It was a slow song, melancholy with its cadence, suiting to the tree's purpose as a vessel of pain and anger. Within moments of the first note, the tree reacted just as he had expected. Buds sprouted from its limbs, blooming to vibrant red, flowing, their color in stark contrast to the black limbs. The sky above them opened, the clouds dissipating, leaving the moon's iridescence to illuminate the macabre beauty of the scene.

Ren's eyes, drawn to the moon's reflection in the lake, watched as the black consistency retreated far below the surface water. He'd never realized his mother's innate powers were so strong, but he should have. Elvin power was not bound to one's core as Light and Dark powers were. It ran freely through their blood and was challenging to temper.

She stopped singing, and the world was still.

"You knew that would happen," Simon said. It wasn't a question but a statement. A fact.

"Yes," he returned, knowing there was no way to hide it and not certain if there was a reason. Violet was staring at her hands.

"I've never—"

"No, you wouldn't have," he finished for her, squatting next to the water again, watching the deep ebony climb back into the clear pool, the magic below stronger than Violet's innate abilities. As he brushed his fingers through the water, the Dark climbed to him, his own Dark powers beckoning it. He wondered at the power the book held that it would leave such residual magic long after it was gone.

"It has something to do with our connection, doesn't it?" Violet asked.

"Yes," he answered, validating their suspicions. They knew,

knew there was something more to them, knew their meeting was not chance.

"Star crossed lovers," Simon muttered. Ren turned in time to see him run his hands through his hair. He wanted to scream at them to wake up, to remember who they were, to get their story moving so he could find out where Tynan was lurking.

"You know the missing pieces," Violet said, looking into his eyes.

"Yes."

Without saying anything further, he looked at Simon. The situation was dire, they would awaken soon, and Tynan was bound to be a threat, waiting in the shadows to kill his mother or even his father before they could confess their love for one another and step through the portal.

"You need to stay away from this place, both of you, and you need to keep her away. It's dangerous, even if the tree is tied to her. There is Darkness here that will pull her away. You feel it. You've powers that urge it forth. Keep her away, keep her safe."

He walked past them, both too stunned to reply to him. He could see Simon trying to sort it out, to make sense of Ren's words, always needing to ground himself in reality, to find an explanation. He could sense them looking at each other, questioning. Then he heard footfalls, small and light.

"Ren," Violet called. He stopped and turned back to her. She was standing across from him, her emerald eyes still carrying a touch of Elvin magic. It hurt him to not be able to talk to her, to call her mother, to have her hold him as she had when he was young. As Simon walked up behind her, he realized how much he missed his parents.

Violet stepped closer to him and, reaching up, lowered his hood. His eyes not bound behind glasses elicited a slight gasp from her, but she remained where she was.

"Just like Paige's eyes," Simon said, moving next to her.

"Only brighter," she added.

"There's nothing wrong with your eyes, is there?" he asked.

Ren looked down and ran his hand through his hair.

"Just like you, Simon," she whispered. Then she took her hands and held his face, tipping it back so that his eyes met hers.

"Who are we to you, Ren?"

She was always so intuitive, on a level deeper than any before her.

"Everything," he answered honestly. Then he took her hands and lowered them, reminiscing in the warmth they held, before turning to walk away from them, knowing he'd be unable to hold himself together if he stayed longer.

Ten

Violet stood, unable to move, taking comfort in the closeness of Simon's body to hers, knowing he would catch her if she tumbled with the weight of what she was thinking.

Could it be? But how?

"Vi? Where is your head taking you?" Simon asked, knowing her too well after even this short time.

"He looks just like you, Simon," she whispered.

"It's a coincidence," he answered. She could hear him trying to convince himself.

"Is it? He moves like you, runs his hands through his hair—"

"Stop it, Violet. You're trying to make something more out of this than there is."

She turned to him. "Am I? And what of the tree and the water? How do you explain that?"

He looked down at her hands and sighed. "The same way I explain this," he said and walked back closer to the lake. Violet watched as he put his hand out toward the water. The color had returned to a dark ebony. As a cobra summoned by its charmer, the water rose and curled, slithering toward his hand. Violet inhaled sharply; he had magic just as she did. He clenched his fist, and the water fell to the ground in a sudden splash.

"I can't explain it, Vi. No more than I explain how things seem to happen when I'm angry, especially in reaction to injustices. Or that I can do certain things." He turned back to her. "Ren was right, something in the water beckons me. It draws me to it just as the tree does to you. I don't know who he is, Violet, or why he's suddenly here, but we both decided we would relax and see where all of this takes us."

He took her hand, then with his other hand brushed her loose curl back from her cheek.

"Let's go home," he said, kissing her. She let the feeling wash over her, losing herself in him and pushing aside the mystery of their place in their world, their place together.

They went back to his apartment, and as they always did, ignored their desire for one another as they lay in bed, remaining chaste on instinct, both too reluctant to push the boundary now that they'd established it. She lay on his chest, staring at the wall, playing the prior events through her head on repeat. No matter how she looked at it, she kept coming back to a truth that was too hard to grasp.

"Violet," Simon said, kissing her head.

She peeked up at him, her hair falling across her eyes and blocking her view. He pushed it back, smiling.

"You should get some sleep."

"I should, as should you, but..."

He raised his eyebrow, and she sighed wondering if she was simply being ridiculous.

"Aren't you the one who told me not to over analyze this, to just go with it all and let it happen?"

She laughed. "I do believe that was me."

"Then why aren't you doing that?"

"Because what my instinct tells me is impossible," she said, the words coming out in a whisper.

He shifted so he could meet her eyes, brow furrowed in that serious look he often had. He searched her eyes. "What does your instinct tell you, Vi?"

She bit her lip momentarily, "That he's someone very important to us. That he's—"

"What?"

"He's ours."

His face grew serious, but he didn't laugh. "And how would that be possible?"

"I don't know and that's what I'm grappling with...but, Simon, he looks just like you. Even his mannerisms are like yours."

"Yet he looks nothing like you, Vi, so how would you explain that?"

She took his hand and placed it on her heart. "With this. The same thing that tells me you are the one I've waited for forever. The same thing that tells me we're more than what we seem, that there's more to our story."

"You know in your heart that that man is our son?" He shook his head. "Even saying that out loud sounds crazy. You know that."

She rolled over and stared at the ceiling.

"Knowing I loved you when you were only a dream was crazy. Kissing you in the park that day was crazy. I'm pretty familiar with crazy, Simon," she said, laughing.

"Mmm, and I love that crazy part of you. If you say there's a connection, then I believe you. I don't know that I'd go as far as what you said, but it does feel like there's a familiarity about him. Something in the back of my mind telling me to see something I can't see."

She turned back to him. "You feel that, too?"

"Yes."

She took a deep breath, letting the scent of him strengthen

her. "Then we go with it, he's something to us. He knew that tree would react to me, he knew you could command the water—"

"Not the water, Violet, whatever is in the water."

A shiver ran through her, and he pulled her in close, kissing her hand.

"Let's stop talking about this and get some rest. It will be morning soon, and we both need some sleep."

"You're right. There's no use overthinking it. Whatever this is, we'll know when the time is right, I suppose."

"Maybe," he replied, pulling her in closer.

She snuggled against him and let the feel of his strength below his shirt calm her. A wave of need crested within her, but she bit it back. As much as she wanted to explore the defined muscles that lay beneath the shirt, she knew it wasn't the right time.

He groaned in frustration. "Whatever you were just thinking, you need to stop, Vi, or I'll have to move into the other room."

She wondered momentarily if that would be his only choice. They hadn't tested their chastity pact for a while. Could they take the next step?

She sighed and relaxed against him. "Point noted," she said. "Goodnight, Simon. I love you, strange magic and all."

"You're calling what I did strange?" he joked. "Night, Vi, love you, too."

She cleared her mind, letting only the sense of him fill her, then drifted to sleep, a sleep filled with blood red flowers and a world with two moons.

Looking at his watch, Simon saw that it was only four in the morning. He'd been drifting in and out of a sleep that was restless, dreaming of the world with two moons again, only this time he felt the magic he'd used earlier course through his veins. It was strong and enticing, leaving him wanting more just as Violet did. He rubbed his hand down his face, ridding himself of the last remnants of sleep, then glanced over at Violet. She was peacefully sleeping, her long blonde hair covering most of her face. Reaching over, he pushed it back to study her as he loved to do. Her eyes fluttered behind her closed lids, the thick lashes accented against the cream of her skin. There was a slight pink to her cheeks, and her lips curved softly, forming a subtle smile. He wondered what she was dreaming about, selfishly hoping it was him.

Gently, he moved his arm from under her and pulled away, rising out of the bed. She stirred, shifting to the place his body had lain, her lips dropping to a frown, brow furrowing momentarily before her features calmed and sleep swept her further under its spell again.

Running his hand through his hair, he grabbed his pants and moved from the room, not wanting to wake her. He knew she wouldn't sleep long. Neither were able to sleep without the other now unless necessary, and those nights were always restless for both of them. They were attuned to each other so much so now that when one rose the other would wake shortly after, noticing the absence even under a deep sleep.

Simon quietly closed the door of his apartment, hoping the noise didn't raise her. He needed some fresh air, their previous conversation still on his mind, her words running through his head. He couldn't make sense of why she'd said such a thing, but the words were there hanging before him, threatening to break his reliance on reality. He thought of the nightmare tree and the flowers it now possessed. She'd done that, and he'd watched with wonder as it had transformed, against all the laws of a sane mind.

He'd always had strange abilities, nothing as unique as what she'd done but enough to know he was different. Enough to use them to his advantage. His ability to read the truth in a person's words was particularly useful in negotiating strategies and had served him well.

He stopped and looked around, noticing he'd walked to the bar without realizing it. There were lights on inside, and he half wondered if Chelsea was still there tending to more than just the bar. Curious, he went in, ready to chastise her as Keary would have done but was surprised to find not Chelsea, but Keary sitting with a bottle and a shot glass.

"A little early to be drinking, isn't it, Keary?" he asked.

"Never too early when the whole world's gone to hell."

"Are we in that much peril? I thought my troubles were bad, but if that's the case, give me a shot, too," he replied, taking a seat at the bar.

"I've never known you to be a big drinker," Keary said, placing a shot glass in front of him. "Dulls the ability to think, I believe you said."

Simon laughed. "Something like that, however, right now dulling my mind would be a good thing."

Keary eyed him and set the bottle down, leaving the glass empty.

"What's going on, Simon?"

"You tell me. Who is Ren?"

Keary looked slightly thrown off then recovered. "Chelsea's cousin."

"Bullshit. Why is he staying with you and not Chelsea?"

"She doesn't have room—"

"She has a couch just like you do. What the hell is going on, Keary? And what does it have to do with me and Violet."

Keary took his shot, leaving Simon even more irritated that his own shot glass had yet to be filled.

"You've been acting strange ever since he arrived. There's something off about it, there's more to his appearance, more to him."

"The walk he took," Keary mumbled, "you bumped into him, didn't you?"

"Violet did at first."

"Dammit, I told him to stay where he was." Keary stopped and rubbed his hands over his face, something Simon knew he did in particularly challenging circumstances.

"Who do you think he is?" he finally asked Simon.

"It's not who I think he is that's the issue."

"Violet."

"Yes."

"Damn her instincts. She must have been a handful for her Council," he mumbled.

"What?"

"Nothing. Who does she think he is?"

Simon thought about putting it into words. It was insanity, and he still couldn't validate it, so in his mind, it couldn't be true. "This sounds mad, but she thinks he's..." He ran his hands through his hair. "Our son."

The shot glass fell from Keary's hand, the sound of its breaking, shattering the silence that followed Simon's last word and affirming it.

"How in the Fates did she come to that conclusion?" Keary said shakily.

"Don't tell me there's truth in her words, Keary? Fates?"

Keary ignored him, "How, Simon?"

Simon studied his friend; he'd been hoping Keary would laugh, validating the absurdity of the idea, but he hadn't.

"She thinks he looks like me."

"I'll give you that, but you and I have similarities, and we're not related. What else?"

"She said she feels it in her heart. There's something there that she can't explain."

"Hmmm, so she has a feeling, and that's enough for you?"

"I feel it, too, Keary. He's connected to us somehow. He's not here randomly. It has to do with us."

"Ok, but how does that make him who you think he is?"

"Who Violet thinks he is."

"I know you, Simon. You wouldn't have left her asleep to wander around if you weren't trying to figure her idea out, if you weren't believing her."

"I don't know what to believe anymore. All this, finding her, loving her...she has magic, Keary. Just like me. None of that is grounded in reality. It's something out of a fantasy book. And now Ren. He knew what she could do, knew what I felt, knew that lake has been calling me."

"Wait, what?" Keary's voice carried an edge of concern.

"The lake, there's always been something about it that draws me to it. I can coax something from it. Something dark, something Ren can sense, too."

Keary looked speechless, his face now wearing his concern.

"What is it he's not telling me?" Keary mumbled.

"So, there is a connection."

Keary didn't move, didn't deny it. He grabbed Simon's wrist.

"Please leave it be, Simon. Tell Violet to leave it. There are things going on that shouldn't be and if we dig too far into it, I don't know what will happen."

"Violet asked Ren who we were to him, and his answer was *everything*. Is that true?"

"Yes. His life depends on you, and I believe yours depends on him. That's why you need to just accept that he's here and move on. If you question too much, you jeopardize our future and your happiness. Trust me and leave it to fate."

Simon sighed and nodded in acceptance. Leaving things to fate was not something he ever did, but somehow, he understood that when it came to him and Violet, he was just going to have to leave things that way. Ren had something to do with their story, but it wasn't for them to know right now and maybe they never would.

"And what do you think fate would say about this?" Simon reached into his pocket and pulled out a ring, placing it on the bar.

"Is that what I think it is?" Keary asked.

Simon looked down at the ring. He'd had it for a few days now, not certain when he would ask her but knowing he would from the first day he had met her.

"Damn, Simon, you're going to ask her to marry you. Why didn't I see that coming?"

Simon watched as Keary's face revealed a myriad of expressions and wondered why happiness was the last.

"I'm happy for you, buddy," Keary said reluctantly.

"Are you sure about that? You hesitated."

"It's just fast," Keary responded hurriedly. "I should have expected this though."

"It is early, but it feels right."

"No, it is right. It makes sense, Simon. I am really happy for you. When do you plan on asking her?"

"Tonight, at the movie in the park."

"Oh, that's right, she's dragging you to that."

"It shouldn't be too bad. Besides, I imagine your ass will end up there, too. Paige is planning to go, and she likely will force you to go."

Keary rolled his eyes. Simon knew that sitting through an old movie outside was not Keary's ideal night nor was it his. Violet went every year though and was disappointed when he'd suggested otherwise. Now that he was planning to propose to her, it seemed more bearable.

"I figure if I ask tonight, then the town has a few days to get through the excitement before I'm surrounded by them at the charity event she's so excited about."

"The charity event," Keary said slowly.

"This weekend?" Simon said, surprised by Keary's reaction.

"The event. Of course. It's like a festival, that's what he's talking about. That's when it will happen. Damn, why didn't I think of that?"

"Keary?" Simon said as Keary ran from behind the bar, throwing his keys across the bar top.

"Lock up. I'm sure Violet will be looking for you soon

anyway. I..." Simon watched as he searched for words. "I have to go." Then he ran from the bar before Simon could say anything. Within seconds, his phone buzzed. Still shocked at Keary's abrupt exit, he looked down to see Violet's text asking where he'd wandered off to.

On my way back, he texted in response, his mind still working through the last few minutes. When he found no answer to Keary's actions, he shrugged, rose, and left the bar, heading back to the one thing in this world that did make sense...Violet.

Eleven

Keary was gone when Ren woke, leaving him to wander the small space Keary called home. It still seemed odd to be here; he kept expecting to wake and find everything as it had been. But he had woken, and the nightmare still had him in its clutches. He thought about his parents, wondered what they were going through, wondered what was happening in their time. Had his absence made a difference or had life simply continued.

He shook his head, concentrating on his surroundings, seeing things that were foreign to him but appeared as if they were everyday items in this world. The strange thing Keary had made coffee in, the round piece he had spoken to as if it were alive. He picked it up, studying it, looking for any sign of magic, remembering how Keary had asked it to play music, and it had. Jazz, Keary had called the music. Ren could still hear the smooth sound of the instruments overlaid upon each other and the rich voice that had accompanied it.

His mother had told him how wonderful the music of this world was, but he'd never truly understood until now. He picked up the device, trying to figure out how it worked. Technology. Something his parents had chosen not to bring to their world. Although they had marveled at the way humans created things to enhance their lives, they felt it had no place in their own world. His father had described technology as the human form of magic. While there was no true magic here, they used something his father had called science to create it in their own way.

Ren had asked why they hadn't adopted any of the human's magic for their people's lives and had been told they hadn't wanted to spoil the innocence of their way of life. There was nothing from this world that was necessary. They had magic to heal their people, to create food and water. Their people were happy and content. The only thing they had decided to change was adding running water, although his father said that was done at his mother's persuasion, and even in that, magic was still used.

"Don't drop that. I don't feel like ordering a new one," Keary said as he entered the apartment with two cups of coffee in hand. Ren put it down and eyed him. He was wearing a big grin which worried Ren who wasn't quite sure how to take it. He set the cups down then backed up, excitedly saying, "I've got it. The charity event. It's not the same as you described, but it's still kind of like a festival."

"When?"

"It starts tonight, but the celebration goes on for three more days, the last day holding the big event: concerts, food, dancing. It's a charity event to raise money. Violet started it years ago, and it's become an annual event."

"Three more days," Ren said. It seemed an eternity and too large of a time span with Tynan on the prowl. "Then three days from the time the spell breaks. That's a lot of days open for Tynan to strike."

"It is. But at least we'll have something to entertain us. He's proposing to her tonight. Why didn't you tell me he was going to do that? I know, I know, you can't give away the future." Keary went on, oblivious to the look of shock Ren was certain his face now held.

"No, that can't be."

"Well, it is. He just showed me the ring. It's a beauty."

The ring he'd never seen. His mother would tell him about it, losing herself in the memory as she described it each time. He never was told what happened to it, only that it was lost. His instinct told him it was part of the buried history with his uncle. Now he would finally be given the chance to see it, a piece of his parents' memory always lost to him.

"Hello?" Keary said, interrupting his thoughts. "The engagement?"

"No, that's not right. They got engaged the day of the festival, and they woke up the next morning. Could you have misheard?"

"No, it's happening tonight," Keary stated confidently.

Ren sat down, unsure of what to do next.

"So, it might be tonight then?"

"Does she sing at the celebration?" he asked, ignoring Keary's question. "Or tonight?"

"Not tonight. Tonight is only a movie in the park. She will sing on the final day though. It's tradition."

Ren ran his hands through his hair then looked back at Keary, "It's not tonight then. Something in her singing triggers her memory, I remember that distinctly from Mother's stories."

"Well, you said there were differences, changes from the way things happened. Maybe this is one of those differences."

"Maybe," Ren answered hesitantly.

"Look, I'm going to take a shower then we'll talk it through. We need to find out where Tynan is and what he's up to. We need a plan."

Keary went to take his shower, leaving Ren in thought. He

was lost, unsure of what his purpose here was, unsure of what to do next. Resting his head in his hands, he wondered what his father would do in this circumstance. Likely the opposite of what Ren was doing. His father was decisive and level headed, his emotions never standing in the way of what needed to be done unless it involved his mother. Ren had always resented his father for being what he considered overprotective, but now, he wondered if that was unfair. There was a history that belonged to his parents, a history that had left its scars and defined them both. His father loved his mother in a way that defied the rules of law and time. He saw that now, seeing them as Simon and Violet.

"Lost in thought just like your father used to get. Although he would never admit that his mind drifted to your mother," Keary said, coming back out of the bedroom to grab something he'd forgotten.

Ren smiled. "So I've heard."

Keary studied Ren for a moment. "What are they like now, Ren?"

He smiled, "Happy, in love, even after all these millennia. I always imagine that they'll be two dancing stars in the night sky when I ascend ... if I ascend."

"If you ascend?"

"Never mind, forget I said that. It's neither here nor there at the moment, and I've had enough lectures from you and my father."

Not ascending? Keary mouthed, eyes wide.

"Forget about it, Keary, we have more urgent matters to deal with."

"Like how you told them who you are? Why, Ren? Why even approach them?"

"I didn't. She approached me."

"And you said, hey by the way, I'm your son?"

Ren wanted to strike him with his power, but he held back even as his irritation grew.

"I'll be damned, you really do have all three powers," Keary said. "Your eyes—"

"Turn green when my emotions are high or so I've been told."

Keary sat down, looking as if the wind were knocked from him again.

"Look, I didn't tell them my identity. I simply encouraged her to use her power. I wanted to see what she could do."

"And?"

"Her innate abilities are active, and my guess is that his are as well. I could feel the Darkness rise in him in reaction to the lake. That's why nature reacts when she sings."

"Why did you go to the lake, Ren?" Keary asked, concerned.

"You sense it, don't you?" Ren asked, knowing that's why Keary had asked.

"There's something there, something Dark."

"There was something, but it's gone now. There's a trace of it still in the water."

"Tynan?"

"I think so, and something else." He wasn't about to mention the book; it was a key in his history that needed to be left to play its part.

"Wait, Tynan was here?"

"In a sense, but I can't explain why or how. You just have to trust me."

"Future knowledge again?"

Ren shook his head in agreement.

"Is he the reason that tree holds so much darkness?"

Ren thought about the question. The tree was his mother's creation, but it had been the result of Tynan's actions.

"In a way."

"Another thing you can't tell me?" Keary asked. "Am I to assume this will be a frequent response?"

Ren smiled. "I would get used to it if I were you."

Keary sighed. "Anything else happen at the lake that I

should know?"

"My mother made the tree bloom," he answered honestly.

"What?"

"I told her to do it. Wanted to see what she was capable of."

"You knew she'd do it, didn't you?"

"Aye, instinct told me she had the ability."

"Instinct? Is that how we're ruling these days?" Keary joked.

"My mother, yes, much to my father's irritation."

"I bet that drives him nuts."

"Quite regularly," Ren replied, laughing momentarily. Then, at the thought of his parents, he grew serious again.

"What am I supposed to do, Keary? Why am I here?" He stood and began pacing. "It's clear the Fates are changing things for some reason. They have powers, so why did I need to get pulled here and why to this spot?"

"First of all, their innate powers don't stand a chance against Tynan. I've seen what he can do, felt the insidiousness of his power. They'll need you to fight when the time comes."

Ren stopped pacing and looked at Keary.

"Second, you need to stop overthinking the Fates' plan. You are so much like your father it's uncanny."

"I'm nothing like my father, that's the problem. I'm too lost in the woods like my mother, living on instinct, hiding from my Dark powers. Trust me, I've heard it repeatedly."

Keary studied him for a moment.

"From whom? Your father or you? Because if I know Sinow, he sees what I see, an image of himself. The same restless pacing, the same questioning, always searching for a reason, a concrete answer to things." He paused. "Did you ever stop to think that you are the best of both your parents?"

Ren looked down at his hands.

"No need to answer, just think on it. I'm going to take my shower now. Don't break anything while I'm gone."

Ren didn't bother to look up, his mind now lost in thought. He sat there thinking on what Keary had said, thinking about his parents. Was Keary right? Had he been transferring his own feelings on to his father, hiding behind the powers he'd received from his mother to avoid seeing how like his father he was? Or was he hiding from his Dark heritage? Maybe his father had been right, he needed to embrace that side of him, own it. Even if he wanted to, he didn't know how. Calling his Dark power was overwhelming, it pushed every part of him aside and took over, dominant and consuming. He wished he'd taken the time to learn more from his father, to listen to him, to understand what he'd been trying to tell him, but he'd chosen to run from the situation, to disown his birthright, turn his back on the side of him that he had inherited from his father, distancing himself from him.

He didn't know how long he'd been lost in thought, but Keary returned faster than he'd expected, interrupting his thoughts then dragging Ren out to breakfast. When they were finished, they walked through town to what Keary called a town square, where he spotted Violet kneeling on the ground, her hands digging in the dirt, a basket of flowers next to her. For a moment, he mistook her for his mother then remembered she wasn't yet. This version of her had never knelt in the soil with him, encouraging the roots below to climb and flower in answer to their magic.

"Keary, Ren!" she said excitedly, spotting them. Standing, she brushed the dirt from her hands, wiping them on her pants, jeans as they called them here. He still couldn't get used to seeing his mother in pants, the image unfamiliar to him.

"What brings you up this way?" she asked, brushing a strand of hair from her eyes. It was the same lock that strayed from his mother's hair, the same lock he'd seen his father push from her face for as long as he could remember. His mother almost never wore her hair pulled back though. Once in a great while she would wear it weaved in a braid, but he'd been told it reminded her too much of Paige when she did so. Mostly, she wore it down, loose as his father liked it. Today, it was tied back high behind her head in a fashion he'd never before seen until his emergence in this world.

Keary looked from Violet to Ren like he was thinking things through. Then said, "This guy needs some time away from me, and I was thinking a day with you would be good."

Violet raised her eyebrow while Ren mouthed, *What?*

"Yes, I think time with you and Simon is exactly what he needs."

"Simon isn't here, Keary," she said.

"Ah, but he will be. That man can't go two hours without seeing you."

She laughed, her cheeks filling with color.

Ren wanted to kill Keary and felt his power stir at the thought of punishment. Why would he think it was smart to leave him here, risking exposure again?

"Come on, Ren, it'll be fun. Have you ever planted flowers?"

He wanted to laugh at the absurdity of his mother, a nature queen, asking if he'd planted before.

"More than you could imagine," he replied.

"All right then, I'll leave you to plant away," Keary said, leaving them.

"Come, I'm updating the flower beds, replacing the summer foliage with fall colors."

He followed her back to where she'd been when they'd arrived. She knelt down and patted the ground next to her.

"Why are you the only one planting? Do the people who own this space not maintain it?"

She looked at him with curiosity and smiled.

"That's what they pay me for."

He found it odd that someone would pay her to plant flowers in a common ground. At home, everyone tended to the crops and the natural growth that lived in their towns. His mother insisted they all know farming skills. He knew she secretly fed the land with her magic, but she still made it known they needed to own the process.

He sat with her through the morning planting, talking, laughing. No mention of the previous night was made, the time relaxed and calm. He watched as she tenderly planted each flower, respecting the life within. He had sat next to his mother, coaxing roots below the land's surface more times than he could count, but in this moment, he discovered he had never truly appreciated her connection to the land and how it had shaped her. It was part of her no matter where she was, memory or no memory. He had always known his mother was beautiful, but seeing her in this light, free of the burdens of her crown, free from the powers that ruled her, from the past that haunted her, her beauty radiated.

"Should I be concerned that you two are bonding over plants?" He heard his father's voice ask.

"Simon!" she said, jumping to her feet and hugging him.

"Apparently not," Ren said, standing as well.

"Ren has been helping me. He's really good at this. I am quite impressed."

"Where did you learn horticulture, Ren?" Simon asked him.

From my mother, he wanted to say, but after the previous night, he chose his words carefully. "It's in my blood. My family has been working with nature for generations."

Simon raised an eyebrow as if considering his answer and any meaning behind it.

"Did you come to feed me?" Violet asked, changing the subject.

"Why yes I did," he answered. "Am I to presume we'll have company?"

"You should be used to it, we usually have a chaperone," she said, teasing him.

He laughed, the words clearly had meaning to them both, but Ren didn't know why.

"Then the three of us it is."

Ren spent lunch with them, marveling at seeing his parents from a different vantage point, an outsider looking in. Both revealing a side of themselves that he'd never known, freed from the weight of prophecies and thrones. It fascinated him, but he also took in all of the intricate reminders of who they really were, the small pieces of their personalities that seemed to carry through, clinging to them as the pain of missing them reared its head.

He excused himself soon after they'd finished eating, afraid to spend too long with them for fear of slipping into a casual comfort as he had the prior night. He still wasn't certain what had overcome him in that moment, but there was no taking it back, and neither of them had mentioned it, a blessing he would gladly take. As he walked back to Keary's, he couldn't help but stop by the park, the lake calling to him. The afternoon sun draped the trees in a pinkish orange color, the effect then captured in reflection against the dark water of the lake. He could here bustling on the other side of the park, preparations he assumed for the movie later in the evening. He'd been told of movies but having never seeing one, was curious for the showing. Now, however, he tuned the noise out and concentrated on this side of the park, the trees providing a barrier to the commotion on the other side.

He fingered a red petal from one of the flowers Violet had grown the prior night, feeling her magic in a gentle layer atop it, his own power warming to the familiarity of it. He missed his mother, the softness of her voice, the warmth of her hugs, that ever encouraging, never judging, calming way she had about her. Perhaps she was the reason he identified with his nature and Light powers. She was his rock, the calming ocean in the fury of his father's powers, of his own Dark powers. Closing his eyes, he listened to his powers sensing the Light, then the nature and deep below, the Dark. He pushed aside the first two and welcomed the Darkness, letting it pull in the memories of his father. It swam through his veins, and he felt the shift in his eyes. Opening them, he looked at the tree, this time seeing the pain, the anger, the need for vengeance, the flower wilting in his fingers. His nature magic reacted, and he felt it flow, the flower returning to its full bloom but with a black edge that he watched trace the outside of the petals then find its home in the center changing it to a deep crimson shade of black. Startled, he jerked his hand back. He'd never had his Dark power interact with his other powers. He looked at his hand, studying it as if it might have changed.

"Why does it terrify me to be near you?" He heard a voice ask behind him.

Startled, he turned, quelling his magic and the urge to punish the voice's owner for trespassing on his moment of peace. He quickly let go of his Darkness, dropping it back in the lower layers of his power, letting the Light return to its lead place.

"You shouldn't sneak up on someone like that," he replied to the woman. He'd seen her at the bar the other night, watching, observing from a distance.

"Well now, that's strange. Why did the feeling disappear?" she asked.

He didn't respond.

"And what did you do to the flower?"

Not certain how to answer, he began walking away.

"It was magic, wasn't it?" He stopped and looked at her. She was too curious. He wondered what his father would have done to her, a mortal questioning a Dark Prince. She had no idea how lucky she was that his face and eyes were covered. The Dark tried to rise, and he was momentarily caught off guard by it then remembered the lake. Shifting his sight to the lake, he felt the draw of his power to it. He should have known better than to be so close to it.

“That was magic last night, wasn’t it? Creating the flowers on this tree where before it was bare?”

“Who are you?” he asked, turning back to her.

She took a step back, and he sensed the shiver of fear run through her.

“Someone who likes to solve mysteries,” she said, her voice quivering just enough for him to notice.

“Is that what you think this is?”

“For me it is.” She tipped her head in the direction of the tree. “Those petals appeared last night. I saw her grow them.” She stepped around the tree. “And the crevice that was here yesterday is gone now.” She turned back to him. “She did that, didn’t she?”

He walked over to where she stood, his Dark power going dormant again, his nature powers intrigued. She was right; the crack in the land where Tynan had escaped was gone. He leaned down and ran his hand along the land to find it completely healed.

“She shouldn’t have that power,” he whispered.

Then he stood and looked around, searching for any signs from the Fates, any sign to tell him what this meant.

“A month ago, that crack in the ground occurred, then suddenly from nowhere you show up.”

“A month?’ he said, knowing a month meant Tynan had escaped an entire moon cycle ago. What had he been doing all that time? Had he been watching, waiting, learning?

“You know what all of this means, don’t you? You know what caused it.”

She was starting to annoy him now.

“Not what. Who,” he said with authority. “And I would pray I were nowhere around here when he returns.”

“Who?” she asked.

“You ask too many questions. Who are you?”

“My name is Agent Abigail Lawson. I was sent here to find out the origin of that crack in the earth along with my team.”

"Team?"

"My agents."

Agents. Police? He studied her. No, police had uniforms like the Scian.

His father had said humans had levels of law. Perhaps government? *It doesn't matter*, he told himself.

"Abigail, leave this place," he said, walking away.

"I know it's magic, and I'll find out what's going on here."

He turned back to her again. "You mortals have your fairy tales. I know of them, princes and princesses, magic, happy endings. You want everything to be magical like the fairy tales you grew up on. Well, Abigail, it's not like that at all. You should leave before you find answers you don't want, before you find that happy endings don't exist."

He didn't wait, instead walking away, leaving her to answer her own questions. He didn't know why he'd become so angry, why he'd been so hard on her. She was simply a mortal attempting to find answers to things she didn't understand. Perhaps it was the remnants of the book's power or simply his mood.

He felt lost with no direction, no idea what he needed to do, and it frustrated him. Something needed to happen soon, he wasn't certain how much more he could take. His fingers twitched, a spark of arcane emitting from them. He picked his hand up, his fingers shaking slightly. Pre-ascension. Giving his hands a shake, he dropped them back down in hopes they would calm. He could not have his powers going rogue on him, not here and not now. Clenching his fists, he prayed his magic would settle. He was still some time away from his ascension, but the quirky tendencies a ruler's power had prior to his ascension had started a few moons ago. His mother had said it was normal, but he knew from his father's reaction that it was too soon. It shouldn't be happening yet, but it was. Being here and having this happen was a liability he couldn't afford. He just hoped it settled down in case a showdown with Tynan occurred, something he felt was inevitable. As he walked back to Keary's, he sensed a change in the air, subtle, but it was there. Something was about to happen, and he needed to be ready, they all did.

Twelve

When Keary had left Ren with Violet, he hadn't been certain where he was headed. Now as he stared at the nightmare tree with its blood red blooms, he realized this had been his destination all along. He didn't need to question from where the blooms had come. Ren had been with Violet and Simon in this very spot the previous night. She had used her magic and brought life to a tree that had never been anything but barren. He dropped his hand and looked at the lake, its black water eerily calm. He'd always been drawn to it, just as Simon had, since the day he'd arrived here. What was it about this lake, this spot, even the tree? He looked over to where the ground had opened, and the fissure was gone.

"Violet," he said as he walked over and bent to feel the ground, certain his eyes were playing a trick on him. It was healed, as if the opening had never existed. She had healed it. His mind followed where the opening had been, churning it all over. Tynan had been here; Ren had confirmed it.

"No," he told himself, he'd never truly confirmed it. He looked back at the lake; only Dark power would have drawn both of them. Tynan had caused the rupture in the land. He'd come through the opening, escaped. Escaped what?

Then the pieces slowly fell into place. The tree, the lake, the feel of Dark power. This had been Tynan's prison. Locked away below this spot. He'd escaped his prison, a prison in which he'd been trapped for nearly six thousand years.

Sinow hadn't killed him, he'd sentenced him to something worse, not an easy death but an eternity imprisoned in the depths of this world. It was a punishment fit for a madman but what else had Tynan done for Sinow to give him this sentence?

The tree held a clue, he felt it's connection somehow. It had bloomed at Violet's touch, and nothing bloomed this close to Dark power. In fact, now that he'd thought about it, he realized that this entire side of the park had always been barren; filled with brittle grass, no wild flowers, only weeds until closer to the tree line where it sprung back to life. He returned to the tree. It gave no feeling of Dark magic, it never had like the lake. He placed his hand on the trunk as if expecting to find the answers, but none came. They never did. Instead, as always, a feeling of deep melancholy washed over him. Closing his eyes, he opened himself to the gut-wrenching sadness that entered him. No one held their hand to it long enough to feel anything more, but he did, forcing himself to let it run its course until another sensation overcame him, pain mixed with anger. The anger stirred his blood, the pain wrenched like a knife through his insides. He heard himself suck in his breath but kept going until the agony of all three emotions was too much to bear. Pulling his hand back, he stumbled away from the tree, his breathing shallow and fast as his body came back to reality. The tree had been a vessel. Tynan's punishment tied into its existence, but the tree wasn't Sinow's doing. It was Violissa's. He had no doubt. What had happened after they returned? What had Tynan done?

The rest of the day, Keary spent trying to avoid any thoughts of the new developments in their situation until Ren finally wandered into the bar. He appeared as if his mind were adrift, and Keary whose own mind didn't think he could handle much more decided not to press him. Instead, they spent the remains of the afternoon together, Keary asking him questions but always mindful to steer clear of anything he knew Ren would consider off limits. Mainly, he asked about their world, the state of the realms, his brothers on the Councils. He was surprised to find that Cyric and Kanine were both still around having thought both would have surrendered themselves to the Fates by now. Most Council only served one king, stepping down close to the time the next in line ascended.

His phone buzzed, pulling him from his thoughts.

A brief *Where are you?* from Paige reminded him to check the time.

"Damn," he muttered. "We're late. The movie starts soon, and I promised Paige we'd go together. She gets nervous when she has to watch your parents by herself."

"I thought you weren't watching them anymore, they've been spending their days by themselves?"

"That's what we want them to believe, and in some respects, it's true. We still keep our eye on them. You were with them today."

"That's what that was about?" Ren asked.

"Of course. It gave me and Paige a break to have you babysit for us. Now come on before Paige has a conniption."

"What's a conniption?" Ren asked as they walked out of the apartment.

"I feel like a walking dictionary with you around."

"What's a—"

"Forget it," Keary said, frustrated. "Pull your hood up. It's night, but your eyes still glow. Freaky Lightbearer eyes. I don't know how any of you walk around with those things glowing all the time."

"Trust me, you get used to it," Ren responded, laughing as he pulled his hood in place.

They made their way to the park. He could sense Ren tense as they cut through the unused side of the park where the tree and lake stood and wondered if Ren could feel the pull of the lake just as he did. He relaxed as the air lightened upon their arrival to the other side, the tree line providing a barrier to the Darkness that now lie behind them.

Paige was set up on a blanket talking to Chelsea.

"Where are they?" he asked.

"Over there," Ren answered before they could speak.

Violet and Simon were sitting further back from everyone just near the tree line.

"Simon asked for privacy," Paige said.

"He's going to ask her to marry him," he said nonchalantly.

"What?" she and Chelsea asked in unison.

"Is that supposed to happen? Should that happen?" Paige asked Ren.

"Yes, and yes. It's fine. It means we're close to going home. I just can't figure out when. The events are changing."

"That can't be good," Chelsea commented.

"None of this is good," Ren muttered then sat next down to Paige.

Keary remained standing even after the movie started. He wasn't sure why, but he felt restless. His eyes kept drifting from Simon and Violet to Ren and Paige. There was something about the way he'd catch Ren looking at Paige that gave him pause. There was a bit of surprise and something else, fascination?

Keary shook his head; that had to be all it was. Fascination with a girl who had been dead long before he'd been born.

Paige laughed, her face filled with the same look he had seen on Ren. No, the Fates wouldn't be that harsh, and Ren wouldn't be so foolish.

He was about to say something when he noticed movement from the corner of his eye. He was drawn back to Simon and Violet. It had happened. He should have felt happy, a sense of joy should have washed over him, but instead he felt dread in his bones, a sense of foreboding that settled on him like an uncomfortable cloak.

"Ren," Keary's voice broke through Ren's thoughts.

When he'd sat next to Paige, he had done so for the vantage point it gave him to watch Simon and Violet. His eyes, however, hadn't strayed their way. There was something about Paige that nudged at him, a feeling he couldn't identify. When the movie had started, he had been amazed by the magic of it then Paige had reminded him of the technology that made it work. They ignored Chelsea's shush and continued chatting about it. She'd been telling him that she'd had the same reaction upon seeing one for the first time when Keary's voice drew his attention from her.

"Ren, look," Keary said again. "It's happened. He asked her."

Ren looked over to see Violet kissing Simon, the gleam of the ring on her finger the reason for the kiss.

"Now what?" Keary asked, but Ren ignored him, his senses heightening as a breeze tickled his skin. He slowly stood, blocking everyone out and listened to the world around them. Something was happening. The wind grew slightly in strength, sweeping across his skin, the air becoming heavy, the sky filling with clouds set in a pinkish hue as the white of the moon changed to maroon.

"It's happening," he said, his eyes moving back to the

couple. He recognized the hunger in Simon's eyes. Had seen it countless times. Thunder roared, the wind whipped, and the rain fell. Everyone around them moved, running for cover, but Violet stood, her hand out to catch the rain, her head stretched back to let the drops hit her face. In that moment, the clouds cleared, the moon's light streamed down to light her hair, its color now a brilliant white that sparkled against the raindrops in her hair.

"What was that?" Paige asked in a reverent tone.

"My mother," he said, smiling, "That's my mother, she feels nature's call."

"And so do you. Ren, your eyes, they're—" she started.

"Wow, whose eyes change color like that?" Cody asked; he must have joined them at some point, but Ren, whose attention had only been on Paige, couldn't remember when.

Ren brought his hand up and realized the wind had blown his hood back.

"A king with his parents' power," Keary answered.

"I'm not a king, Keary."

"Not yet, but you will be," he said, crossing his arms. "They look just like your mother's the first time I saw her."

"What are you guys talking about?" Cody asked.

Ren looked down at the ground and ran his hands through his hair, not sure what to say. Then he pulled his hood back over his head.

"You should own your powers, Ren. Your parents worked hard to make sure you were here to have them," Keary said, ignoring Cody and placing a hand on Ren's shoulder, not knowing how true his words were.

"I hate to break up the bonding moment, but look," Paige said.

Ren looked up to see Violet and Simon running through the rain laughing.

"They're going to his place," Ren stated.

"Then we should head back to my place," Keary responded.

"No. We go to Violet and Paige's."

"But—"

"Trust me, we head there. Cody, you and Chelsea head home."

"So, we go to my house and then what?" Paige asked.

"We wait. From this moment on, we wait."

Thirteen

As Paige paced for the hundredth time in front of them, Keary got up from the table saying, “Paige, enough coffee. You’re wearing a hole in the floor.”

She stopped, placing her mug on the table, and dropped into a seat across from Ren.

“I don’t think I can stand much more of this. When does it happen?”

Thunder shook the windows as the wind howled accompanied by a pounding rain that had been ceaseless since it started.

“It is happening,” Ren said. “They’ll awaken in the morning.”

“The morning?” Keary asked, looking at his phone. “That’s hours from now. I’m going to try to get some sleep. She’s all yours to babysit.”

He left the room, and Ren heard him rustling around on the couch in an attempt to get comfortable.

“Am I that bad?” Paige asked, peering over her cup.

"You do remind me a bit of a faina that has had too much sweet blossom," he replied, smiling.

"What's a faina?" she asked. "And what's a sweet blossom?"

Damn, Ren, he chastised himself for mentioning things only found in the Elvin territory.

"Nothing," he replied quickly.

She studied him then took another sip of her coffee, both hands wrapped tight around the mug as if she might drop it.

"Hmmm," he heard from her.

"What?"

"You're a man of many secrets, aren't you?"

He sighed. "It's important to maintain secrecy, the events of the future cannot be changed."

"Why do you sound so sad when you say that?"

"Do I?" he asked, not realizing he had.

"Yes, every time the future is mentioned. Ren, what happens to them? Is this not the end of their punishment?"

"I can't answer that, Paige."

"Fates, it's not." She put her mug back down. "They've gone through so much. That isn't fair."

"The Fates don't play fair, Paige. They have their own agenda."

"Do you trust them?"

"The Fates?" he asked, surprised by the question.

"Yes. After all they did, even the parts I don't know, do you trust them?"

He thought for a moment. It was a hard question to answer. "I do because my parents do. They will never question the Fates again and as so, I do not. My mother's faith runs so deep that she let Tynan bring me here, my father trusts her and, in turn, them."

"And you?"

"I trusted them enough to let Tynan take me. I don't, however, understand them or their ways. They've been hard on my parents. My parents thought it was over, that everything was on path, and now, the Fates have thrown them another curve. It was never over, their punishment continues."

"I'm sorry, I shouldn't have pushed. Let's talk about something else."

Raking his hands through his hair, he said, "It's all right, you didn't know. Yes, anything else would be better."

She fingered the chain around her neck. The stone. He remembered being told she was the key bearer, that she held it for all the years while they waited for his parents to awaken.

He was about to ask her to see it when she said softly, "Tell me about my father."

There was moisture in her eyes.

"How is he? I've always worried what would happen when he lost Mother and then me."

Ren thought about what he could say and realized there was nothing she didn't already know. She knew her father would outlive her, knew her fate as a mortal.

"He is well. There is a heaviness to his heart, but he lives for his queen now."

She sighed, understanding what his words meant.

"You know I can't have children. My doctor told me. There's something wrong inside, I'm not built the same as other women."

He wondered why she was telling him this.

"I suppose it's a blessing from the Fates. If I were to have children, and then they had children of their own and so on, I believe that would be harder on him. Having to bury so many people you love."

"Perhaps that is why the Fates do not give them families. Why they are taken from their families as soon as they are called," he said.

Her eyes drifted to her mug, and he took the moment to look at her. Her auburn hair was rich with color. In the light, he could see a blend of lighter browns with darker, a few with reddish tones brought out from time in the sun. Her skin, a soft cream, was unblemished with the exception of a few small freckles that peppered her nose, unnoticeable to most but him. She lifted her eyes, and their cerulean blue met his. He absently wondered if they sparkled brighter in the sunlight or the starlight. He noticed a slight pink rise in her cheeks and realized he was still staring at her. Dropping his eyes, he tried to think of something else to talk about but was at a loss, his mind trying to cope with the strange feeling in his gut.

Pull yourself together, Drostiren, he imagined his father saying, *you can't afford to get distracted.*

"Well, that was a useless nap," Keary said, thankfully interrupting his momentary awkwardness. "Is it morning yet?"

He heard a door open, and all three froze. From where he was sitting, Ren had a direct line to the front door, but Keary was in the way. Keary met his eyes then slowly turned.

"What the hell is going on in here? Did I miss a party invitation?" The tension left Ren's body, and he saw Keary relax.

"Cody!" Paige yelled. "Don't scare us like that?"

"Me? I come in here expecting everyone to be asleep, and you're all sitting around like you're playing an intense game of Dungeons & Dragons."

"What are you doing here, Cody?" Keary asked.

"I should ask why you're here so early in the morning. I couldn't sleep. That storm is miserable, I'm outta food, so I came to snag some grub since everything's closed. What are you three doing?"

Cody looked at Ren and gave him a curious look. "Cool contacts. I need a pair of those, might get a few more women with those eyes."

He nudged Keary and walked over to the counter, rummaging through the cabinets.

"I think you've already had enough girls, Cody. Is there anyone left in town?"

"Only you, Paige, and that's just a gross thought, like being with my sister. Where is my sister anyway?"

"With Simon."

"Shoulda figured."

The conversation continued, but after a while, Ren tuned it out, rising from the table and pacing as he lost himself in thought.

"Nervous?" he heard Cody ask, but something else caught his attention.

Ignoring Cody, he walked to the window. "The storm is over," he stated, looking out upon the calm that had settled on the debris from the storm. The pink of the sunrise was just beginning to tint the sky.

He looked over at Keary, then closing his eyes, he felt for it, the lingering magic of the spell lay upon the land like a dust covering. Beyond that, he felt something else, his parents.

"They're awake."

No one said a word, the three of them feeling the gravity of his words.

Cody, sensing the seriousness in Ren's voice, asked, "Should I ask why that sounds as heavy as it did?"

"No!" they all answered.

"What do we do with you, Ren?" Paige asked.

"You take me out of the equation." He drew up his hood. "I'm the last thing she needs to see when she walks through that door. And you," he pointed to Cody, "I still don't know your place here, but this is not where you need to be right now."

"Listen to him," Keary said, pulling Cody from the chair.

"Why are your eyes turning green?" Cody asked as Keary threw him toward Ren.

"Because she's coming, and her emotions are out of her control." His power was feeding off her emotions, and he could feel it rising.

Dragging Cody through the other doorway, Ren pushed him back so they were out of sight.

"Stay quiet and stay here no matter what happens or what you hear," Ren instructed him.

"You're worrying me, Ren. What's going to happen?"

The front door slammed open, and he heard his mother enter the house. He stayed hidden, trying to dim his powers as they reacted to her pain and confusion. Peering around the doorway, he took her in. The curse was sitting over her like a cloak, a black mist that clung to her. He could see it now that it had been activated, sense its poison in her veins, in the recesses of her mind. For the first time, he understood the true extent of it. Her hair was wildly strung around her face, her eyes, heavy with the mist only he could see, darted around as if she were locked inside trying to find an escape. In the corner of her eyes, a black essence lie in waiting.

His mother had never told him what it was like to be under the curse's control, to have it running rampant through her every thought and every move. Now he understood why. She was imprisoned, battling from within, ascending at times to a clarity then descending below the surface again, submerged by the curse. It had to be maddening. He watched as she yelled at Keary then turned on Paige. The slap she gave Paige sent a bolt through him, jarring his Dark code that yearned to punish the injustice. He clamped it down. Cody struggled to get through, but Ren had him pinned so he could only watch, using a spell to silence him. He couldn't take the chance that Cody would interrupt the moment. When she finally ran out of the room, he breathed a sigh of relief, hearing the slam of the door moments later.

Ren released Cody.

"What the hell? How did you do that? I couldn't talk! What's wrong with my sister?"

"Too many questions, Cody," Keary said curtly. "Paige, are you all right?"

She moved her hand to her bright red cheek, "Yes, I shouldn't have spoken to her."

"Would someone please tell me what's going on?" Cody asked.

Everyone ignored him, their attention drawn to Keary's phone which lie on the table lit with a new message. Keary slowly walked over and picked it up. "My king has summoned me," he said, holding the phone up to show them. "I have to go now."

He looked at Ren who nodded in agreement as another text appeared.

"Paige?" he asked.

"I'll be fine. Go."

He gave them one last look then left. Ren's heart raced. It had begun. Now if he only knew where and when Tynan would strike.

Fourteen

Sinow sat on the couch staring at the last text he'd sent Keary, trying to wrap his head around what had happened with Violissa while also trying to make sense of the sudden addition of Keary to this nightmare. Hearing the knock, he said, "Enter," knowing exactly who stood on the other side. He looked up and found Keary entering cautiously.

Keary looked exhausted and nervous. Was he waiting for punishment? One due him for living a lie these past twenty years and for the many indiscretions he'd had over those years. Sinow wouldn't forget but now wasn't the time for punishment. It was time for answers. He rose and walked over to his friend.

Sinow listened to Keary's story, his head spinning. Tynan had broken free and devastated their world while Sinow had been chasing Violissa down in a futile attempt to bring her home for hundreds of years. His mind drifted to his last mortal life that had ended. He'd wanted to fight for her one more time, knowing this one would be his last. Waking this time, he wasn't so certain. He was tired of chasing, tired of the fight. He wondered why the Fates had sent him here if not to torture him more. Now, listening to Keary, he wondered if he had made a mistake leaving to find her in the first place. He rested his head in his hands, unsure as to what to do now.

"There's something else," Keary said hesitantly.

Raising his head, Sinow asked, "More? How could it get any worse, Keary? Violissa has shut me out again, my brother has gone mad and destroyed our world, need I go on?"

"I know it looks bad, but—" He didn't have time to finish; the door to the apartment crashed open, and Cody came barreling in.

"What the hell did you do to my sister? I'll kill you if you hurt her!"

Sinow instinctively pinned Cody to the ground with the flick of his hand. Then he held the hand up and studied it as if seeing it for the first time.

"I have my innate powers?" he asked, looking at Keary. "I've never had any power before."

"And you've never had to deal with a brother before," Keary said, gesturing to Cody who was struggling to get up.

"No, I haven't. There's never been a brother."

"As I started to say, there's more."

"Do I want to know?"

Keary was thoughtful for a moment. "You need to know, but let's release him first."

Sinow released Cody who jumped up ready to fight again. Putting his hand up, Sinow blocked him with a magical wall.

"Boy does it feel good to have some power back."

"I wouldn't know," Keary muttered, walking closer to Cody. "Look, he can keep you like this all day, or you can calm down so we can talk."

Cody pounded on the invisible wall and demanded, "I want to know what you did to my sister!"

"First of all, she's not your sister, and second, I didn't do a thing to her. Now calm your ass down before I throw you out," Sinow commanded.

Cody stopped, and Sinow released him. "What do you mean she's not my sister? I remember the day our parents brought her home. I saw my mother carry her for nine months."

"Yet she looks nothing like you, and I would wager nothing like your parents," Sinow said.

"Wait, are you saying she was switched at birth or something?"

Sinow sat and rested his head in his hands, contemplating whether to simply kill him for his stupidity.

"Sit down, Cody. We have a story to tell you," Keary said.

"We do?" Sinow asked, looking up at Keary. "I don't think that's necessary."

"Wake up, Sinow. Look at him. Do you really think the Fates gave her a brother this lifetime for no reason? He looks just like one of her people. He's Cirillian."

Sinow studied Cody. "Why didn't I see that before? Keary, what's going on this time?"

"Let's fill him in, and then I'll tell you the rest." He walked to the fridge and pulled out two more beers. Placing them on the table, he gestured for Cody to sit. "You're going to need these."

As Keary went through the story, Sinow would interject occasionally. Mostly though, he tried to figure out what was going on. He ran through the events of this lifeline, trying to detect any major changes like the addition of Violet's brother. Each lifetime, although different in settings and experiences, followed mostly the same rules. He was always left parentless, always orphaned, always born in some part of Ireland. There were consistencies. What was different this time? Was the pattern changed?

"So, you want me to believe that you're from another world and that my sister is some kind of ruler?" He heard Cody ask.

"Not some kind, she is the ruler. Your sister is queen of one of two realms in our world," Sinow answered.

"And you?"

"I am king of the other realm."

Cody sat back in his chair. "So, when you two marry, you rule an entire world?"

"Yes," he said, looking back down at the beer in his hand. "If we marry."

"What do you need me to do?" Cody asked.

"Wait, you believe all this?" Keary asked.

"I don't know, but my sister...Violet has always been different, special. She always seemed like she belonged somewhere else, and she's always said she felt that way. You came along and seemed to complete her in a way I couldn't figure out until I heard your story. That and you body-slammed me back there without even touching me. That's not normal."

Sinow couldn't help but laugh, which felt good. It had been a long time since he had.

"What can I do to help?" Cody asked.

Sinow ran his hands through his hair and leaned back.

"Nothing. There's nothing either of you can do. I've tried everything. There's no way to break through to her."

"Remember how I said there was more?" Keary asked.

"Yes."

"Well, there is a way to get through to her."

That caught Sinow's attention. "Go on."

"We've been through this before."

"Keary, what are you talking about?"

"This isn't our first time here. We've done it before and succeeded."

Sinow leaned forward.

"Something has happened. I don't know all the details, but I do know that we made it home. You punished Tynan, and somehow, he escaped."

"Wait, he escaped? I didn't kill him? Why wouldn't I kill him?"

"I don't know, but you punished him instead, and he escaped his prison."

"How?"

"Not sure. But he's found a way to manipulate time. He wants to win this round," Keary said.

"Who is Tynan?" Cody asked.

"My brother...half-brother. The reason we're here in the first place."

Just the thought of Tynan made him want to kill him. "What did he do to make me punish him?"

"Did he do something good so you spared his life maybe?" Cody asked.

Sinow raised his eyebrow, and Keary let out a deep laugh.

"I don't understand."

"Death is a quick punishment, a blessing for anyone who is judged guilty. Punishment, true punishment, is reserved for the worst crimes. It usually involves a long, painful ending, one in which you pray the Fates take you."

"That's intense. Are you guys always this intense?"

"Depends on the day," Keary responded. "Sinow, I don't know why you didn't kill him, but at this point, it doesn't really matter."

"Wait, you said Tynan can manipulate time?"

"Yes, and now we're reliving this moment."

"This has already happened?"

"Mostly, apparently with some exceptions." He pointed to Cody.

"The brother. She never had a brother."

"And she didn't our first time through. There are other things that have changed, too."

"Why and how do you know all this?" Sinow asked.

"That I can't tell you. And I honestly don't know why except that perhaps the Fates struck a bargain with this world's god to help us."

Sinow looked at Cody. "What help does a brother provide?"

"Not sure but look at him, Sinow. You can't tell me you don't see the same thing I do."

"Hey, I'm right here. You can stop talking about me as if I'm not."

Sinow studied him. The brown hair and blue eyes of a Cirillian, but there was something else. The eyes were a little brighter, his build a bit bigger. He reminded Sinow of someone.

"Lightbearer," he said as it dawned on him. His eyes flew back to Keary. "He looks like a damned Lightbearer. I can even sense something different about him. What in the Fates is going on, Keary? Is he a future Lightbearer?"

"No, of that I'm sure."

Sinow rose and began to pace.

"Um, what's a Lightbearer? Something cool like you? 'Cause having super human powers like yours would be pretty cool. I bet I could pick up quite a few ladies that way."

Keary laughed. "Don't count on it."

Sinow tuned him out, trying once again to piece it all together. Tynan had turned back time. How? Where had he obtained the power to do such a thing? How had he been able to do any of the things he had done? There was a missing piece. He stopped pacing and raked his fingers through his hair. None of this made any sense, but he knew it was hard to make sense of anything the Fates did now.

"Keary, how do you know we've been through this before? How do you know about Tynan?"

Keary hesitated, then said, "Now that, I can't tell you. You just have to trust me."

Sinow could have forced Keary to tell him. Could have demanded it on his oath as a Darkbearer, but he knew if Keary wanted to keep the source to himself, there was a good reason.

"What do we do, Keary?"

"We let things happen the way they are supposed to happen and pray Tynan doesn't appear before we get through them."

Sinow clenched his hands, feeling his innate powers roll

through his fingers.

"That's the reason we have our innate powers this lifetime. To give us a fighting chance."

"You maybe," Cody said. "I saw what my sister looks like. She's a mess, there's no way she'll be any help to you if your brother shows up."

Sinow inhaled deeply, realizing he was right. Violissa was not herself, nor would she be in any state to temper her temporary insanity long enough to fight Tynan. Fight Tynan. The idea was ludicrous.

"Neither of us could face Tynan in our state. Innate powers are useless against a full powered..." He couldn't bring himself to say the word.

"King," Keary finished for him. "Even if he is a false one. Cody, you can do something to help. Go back to Violissa. Keep guard. If you see Tynan, you call me."

"How will I know him?"

"Aside from the terrifying feeling that will overcome you, he looks like Sinow."

"No, he does not, Keary."

"Yes, he does. You haven't seen him at full power. He's changed Sinow. We think he fooled us the entire time. Trust me, he looks very similar to you now."

Cody rose. "Will do. She'll be safe under my guard."

"Don't engage him, Cody, and don't look him in the eyes," Sinow instructed.

"Why? Will I turn to stone?" Cody joked.

"No, you'll go mad, or if you're lucky, you'll die."

Sinow could hear Cody swallow loudly before he turned and left the apartment.

"Tell me some good news, Keary. Anything would be welcome right about now."

"I'm here," Keary said, laughing.

"If that's the only good news, this is going to be a long day."

They lost themselves in conversation, the time apart fading

with the day.

Paige rested against the sink, staring out at the dark sky. Time was fleeing, and all she had to go on was hope. Ren had left to take a walk, and Cody was sleeping upstairs in her room. He'd returned from Sinow's all worked up from learning who they all really were. She had to laugh at his response to Ren when he first walked in. The description Keary had given him of Tynan also fit Ren so she couldn't blame Cody for tackling him. Well, attempting to tackle him. He'd been flat on the floor within seconds of the attempt, struggling to get up. Paige and Ren had been forced to explain who Ren was and why he was here before Cody had finally calmed down.

"Why is it I'm always stuck on the ground around you guys?" he had asked, brushing himself off. Then he'd studied Ren. "So, you're my nephew? You look my age. My head is starting to hurt. This has been a seriously weird day. I think I need a few more drinks."

Now, he was upstairs sleeping, the scene with Violissa his tipping point. She didn't know how he could sleep, but then his life didn't depend on the next hours' events.

Violissa had been here. She'd spoke to Paige, and Paige had witnessed firsthand the effects of the curse. The entire interaction had left her shaken with no help from Ren who had sensed Violissa coming and hidden with Cody. He was insistent on staying out of her sight when Paige could really have used the support.

"You did it on your own before, you can do it again," he had said. He was right, but it didn't make it any easier.

She watched as a cloud passed over the moon, throwing a cloak of black across her vision. Her mind stayed on Ren. When she'd told him that she didn't know what to think of him, she'd been truthful. She didn't know—when she thought of him, a mix of feelings rose: fear, sadness, curiosity, and something else she couldn't quite pinpoint. Or maybe she didn't want to name it, for naming it made it real. Drawing her eyes from the sky to stare at the sink below she tried to get him out of her mind so she could focus on the situation at hand, but it didn't help. Butterflies flitted in her stomach, and she cursed them. That was the feeling she didn't want to admit, the one that threw her fear into overdrive. Why did her body even think having a crush on her future king made any sense? It didn't. He was a figment of the future and she a ghost of his past. The two could never align, so she turned a deaf ear to her thoughts and drowned the butterflies with reality.

"Stop being foolish, Paige. We need to get through this first, or he won't even be born," she chided herself.

"Who won't be born?" Cody asked behind her, causing her to jump out of her skin.

"Don't sneak up on me like that, Cody!" she yelled, throwing a wet sponge at him.

He dodged it easily and proceeded to ignore her anger, wiping the sleep from his eyes and grabbing a soda from the fridge.

"Seriously, who won't be born?" he asked again.

"No one, just forget you heard that."

His eyes squinted as he studied her. "Don't tell me you like the new guy? Wow, Paige. That's just weird. I mean, he's your best friend's son and my nephew, which is strange in its own right. What are you thinking?"

"Really? That's the first worry? Not, hey you're dead, and he won't be born for another few eons?"

"Well, there's that, too. I was just going with the easy stuff, not the mind-blowing Dr. Who stuff."

"Forget it, Cody, and don't you dare tell anyone." She yawned and rubbed her eyes. "I'm sure that's not what it is anyway. My mind's a mess, I'm sure it's just mixing up feelings."

Cody looked at her, doubt in his eyes.

“Don’t tell anyone!” she said angrily.

“Ok, ok. My lips are sealed, but I have to tell you, Simon is a pretty intense guy, and I don’t think you having the hots for his son will go over too well.”

“I don’t have the...eerrgg!” She stormed from the room, slapping him on the head on her way out. It didn’t stop him from laughing, a sound she could hear the entire trip upstairs to her room where she buried her head under her pillow, wishing all of this were over and she were home, blissfully going through her life, naïve to the doings of her world’s royalty.

Fifteen

The moon shone bright enough to light the streets as Ren walked them. He had left Paige and Cody, needing time to think. He was tired of waiting and watching. Seeing things play out was harder than he'd imagined, seeing this version of his mother confront Paige had been the worst so far. From the shadows, he'd watched the woman who would one day raise him, a woman who was the gentlest person he knew, struggle to keep herself together. The curse had made her into something he didn't recognize. This wasn't his mother; she was someone else. He couldn't even bring himself to refer to her as his mother, his mind filling that title with her name only. His mother wasn't here, only the cursed shell of her existed. There were moments when her true self surfaced, but they were brief, the curse maintaining its grip on her. When she'd finally run back to her room, Paige had been shaken. Instead of rushing over to her like he'd wanted, he had stayed hidden, keeping Cody still beside him, and watching as she'd gathered her composure and her strength. There was more to her than he'd imagined, an inner strength about which he'd never been told.

When she'd finally pulled herself together, she had called Keary just as Ren had been told she'd done. He was thankful his mother had been patient in answering a curious boy's questions. Otherwise, he would be lost as to what to expect next, navigating the events blindly as they played out.

Leaving Paige and Cody gave him a much-needed break from the anticipation of being near Violissa. He knew there was nothing more to do until Keary spoke to her. He knew Keary was likely heading back to the house. They were two days in, and tomorrow was the final day, the day it would all change.

But where was Tynan? Why hadn't he shown himself? Worry gnawed at Ren. He could feel his powers ebbing and flowing with the effects of his coming ascension. They were unstable, and against Tynan, they would be useless. He hadn't even grasped a full understanding of his Dark powers. He wanted to kick himself for not listening to his father.

Stopping just outside the park, he felt the draw to the lake once again, the infected water reaching out to his powers even after the book had been gone for this long. Unknowingly, he had walked closer, close enough to see the figure knelt down at the edge, the hue of his innate power just slight enough for Ren to recognize him. It hadn't been visible before, but now that his father had awoken, Ren could feel it. He had always heard his parents' innate powers were stronger than any before them, and he could see that now. But was it enough to help him fight Tynan? Ren sensed they had both remained mortal, so he wasn't certain they would be much help, but he could see no other reason for the god of this world to allow the Fates to give them their innate powers.

"You feel its call as well," his father stated, pulling him from his thoughts. Ren hadn't remained far enough back to go unnoticed. Dark power could sense its own presence. He watched his father stand, seeing the familiarity in his posture, the proud way he held himself, the king in him always present.

"At first, I thought it stank of Tynan, but it has a different signature to it, older, more corrupt." His father faced him. "What was buried here?"

Ren felt that same feeling he always had when his father questioned him; even without his power, his father was intimidating. For a brief moment, he wondered why he thought of this man as his father but couldn't give the same title to Violissa. Something about the curse made it impossible for him to see her that way. But this man, this was his father, younger, unaware of what was to come, but still his father.

Ren didn't answer, not knowing what to say. If he lied, his father would sense it, but he couldn't tell the truth. No matter how badly he wanted to change what was coming to protect his mother, to keep her from Tynan's grasp, to keep them from the moment his father had made his mother give up that part of her that he knew longed to be set free, to run with the wind, to be one with the land again, always to return to the man she loved, it couldn't be changed.

His father studied him then walked to the tree, running his hands along the smooth ebony bark.

"And this...this holds Violissa's magic but a side of it I only saw during the war. It's heavy with pain, Ren. Why?"

Ren swallowed. "I can't tell you that."

His father looked back at him then moved closer to him.

"She said you were someone that you can't possibly be. Even with no memory, she felt it."

"Do you?" Ren dared ask, knowing he should walk away, knowing his father shouldn't know, that it could change everything. A part of him, however, missed his father and selfishly wanted to scream, *I am your son, please remember me* even though he had yet to exist in this time.

"Who are you?"

Reaching up, Ren dropped his hood, saying, "You already

know."

His father searched his eyes as if looking for something.

"His eyes were green. I saw them. In the vision I had when I was younger, there was a boy but he had eyes of green."

"My eyes were green. My innate powers are nature driven just as my mother's are. They changed when my powers grew, setting to the color of my Cirillian forefathers," Ren replied quietly.

"Who are you?" his father asked again, the disbelief evident in his voice.

Ren drew himself up taller and said, "I am Drostiren, named for both my grandfathers. My mother calls me Ren, but you... you call me by my birth name."

His father took a step back. "It can't be. She—"

"Comes around this time as long as everything happens just as it did six thousand years ago," Ren finished.

His father came closer, studying him as if seeing him for the first time.

"You look just like me, but why do I not sense full Dark power?"

Ren dropped his eyes. "I have yet to master my Dark powers."

"Master them? They come naturally to a Dark king."

I am not a Dark king, he thought but instead said, "It's a long story and one for which we have no time."

He looked up at the sky in an attempt to make out the time. One of his favorite parts of their story had been the Dream Realm, a place he had longed to see.

"You need to head back," Ren said. "Sleep calls to you."

"Trust me, I'm not tired."

"You will be."

"I'm not leaving. We need to talk," his father said. "I need to know what's going on and where Tynan is."

Ren sighed. "I'll worry about Tynan. You worry about my mother, for if you do not follow the steps as they originally played out, she will never have the strength to break through the spell, and I will cease to exist."

"Why are you even here, Ren?" his father asked, sounding just as he had the day Ren had been taken. It was strange to hear him use the nickname he had refused to use all of Ren's life.

"Because the Fates deemed it so."

"And you heed the Fates? I've learned they don't always lead you down the correct path."

Ren couldn't believe how blunt the words were. His parents never spoke ill of the Fates, afraid of risking their wrath, knowing the consequence.

"My mother took you both down the wrong path, and you allowed her."

His father took a step closer.

"You know it's true—"

"They have been punishing us for a thousand years."

"And they will continue to punish you until the day they let Tynan step back into our world and take me. No one crosses the Fates. My parents know this, and they continue to tread down a path that was unbound by their own foolishness and now trodden with eons of regret." He stopped, realizing he had said too much.

His father stared at him, his face hiding the emotion Ren knew stirred below.

"It continues?" he whispered.

"Yes," Ren replied honestly.

He watched as his father ran his hands through his hair then down his face.

"It gets worse?"

"I cannot say for fear of changing a past that holds my future."

"But the past is already changed. You are standing here talking to me."

"I cannot tell you."

"And Tynan? He brought you here? The Fates allowed this?"

"Yes, they spoke to my mother."

"And I didn't stop Tynan?"

"My mother would not allow it. The Fates have spoken. I am needed here."

"What did they do to her to cause her to be so obedient that she would give up her only son?"

To a monster, Ren wanted to add but stayed silent.

"What happens to her?" his father asked, the worry no longer hidden but plainly written on his face and in his eyes.

"I cannot say. Now you need to go back."

His father grabbed him by the shoulders.

"You will protect a future in which your own mother is affected so much that it changes who she is? You have the chance to save her from whatever lies ahead of her!" he yelled at Ren.

The frustration of having to do just that, the weight of all he was carrying exploded within him, and Ren felt the Darkness take over, a blast of power emitting from him as he screamed, "I know! Don't you think I carry that burden every time I look upon her!"

His father was thrown with the fury of Ren's power but caught himself before he collided with the trees. His hand still on the ground when he stopped, he stared at Ren.

"You are my son," he said, pulling himself up and walking back toward Ren. "You have the eyes of a Dark king now, and I see the aura. Why do you not remain in that power?" he asked as Ren felt his power shift, the Light coming back into the forefront.

"I feel more at one with my Light and nature powers."

"Hmmm, I'm surprised I let that happen."

"Trust me, you put up quite a fight."

They both laughed, the tension from earlier lifting.

His father's eyes softened. "You can save her from whatever it is." His voice held a tone of pleading.

"I can't save her. Nor can you. The Fates have their reasons for everything that happens to both of you. You spend your life trying to protect her, to save her, since the day Tynan cursed her to this world, and it won't stop. You never see that you can't always save her. Sometimes, she needs to save herself. She's stronger than any of us see."

Ren didn't care that he had said too much. The words had poured out from centuries of running them through his head. They were the words he had longed to say to his father but never had.

"Is she happy?"

"My mother?"

"Yes. Are we happy?"

"Even after all that's happened, there are no two people who love each other more than my parents."

His father smiled.

"You should go," Ren said, the heaviness of the moment returning. "She'll be calling you soon."

His father gave him a questioning look. "More you can't tell me?"

Ren laughed. "Wouldn't want to spoil it for you."

"Of course not." His father looked as if he wanted to say more but wasn't certain how to say it. He began walking away, then stopped and turning asked, "Do you know everything that happens in the next few hours?"

"All of it."

"Why?"

"It was my favorite story as a child. Your story. My mother would tell me parts of it every night, and there were times my father would join her. And when it was finished, I would make her start again. Your story is a powerful one; it transcends time, weathers storms, and outlasts all else. It's a love story like no other, and it was the one constant that defined my parents."

His father looked at him for a moment then gave a short nod and turned back to continue his walk home. Ren knew what awaited him, the Dream Realm, the one part of the story his father always liked to tell. Perhaps that was why it was Ren's favorite part. He prayed that event hadn't been changed as well.

Tynan stepped through the portal, its destination exactly where he'd anticipated. The morning sun spilled across the lake as he walked to the strange tree he'd noticed when he'd emerged from his prison. It had changed, red blossoms cascading from its branches. Drawn to it, he placed his hand on it, the mix of emotions from it filling him. Within the emotional residue, he felt Violissa's power. The tree was her creation, yet it looked nothing like her magic. He thought back to the night Sinow had imprisoned him, the memory singed in his mind had played countless times as he lay trapped below this world's surface. This was where he and Sinow had stood in those last moments; there had been no tree. Violissa had created it after the fact, taking her emotions and bringing something wretched to life with them. He bunched his fists thinking of her, then he put his hand back on the tree, drawing forth the sensations of pain and agony, desperation, humiliation. He let them fill him, his Darkness tantalized by it. He had caused those feelings, and the thought pleased him. He would bring her more pain this day, and she would suffer in her death as Sinow would be forced to watch, helpless, powerless to save her. The Darkness poured from him as the thoughts filled him, the blooms on the tree turning ebony, all life fading from them.

Dropping his hand, he calmed himself. He had to be patient, the timing had to be just right, and he couldn't let his excitement leave him out of control as it had back in the Lost Realm. There was a window of time that would be his chance to make the suffering perfect. It couldn't be too early, memories had to be intact, and hope needed to be on the horizon. That's when he would strike, that's when he would have maximum suffering.

His brother would pay for punishing him, pay for taking everything from him, pay for even being born. The realms were his, the throne was his, and nothing would steal that from him this time.

Sixteen

The tension in the house was thick, everyone on edge, Ren the only one who knew what was coming. He sat with Paige and Keary, the endless wait excruciating. Cody had left after sunrise to clean up and prepare for the charity events of the day, which included a performance by his band. He'd considered staying, but they had all talked him into leaving, knowing he wasn't part of the story, at least that's what Ren kept telling himself. He had a nagging suspicious he was wrong, and that Cody still had a part to play.

As the morning ticked by, the small talk died away, and the anticipation grew.

Finally, Paige stood, saying, "I can't take this anymore. Ren, it's almost the end. You said Keary's talk would change things, said it would convince her."

He tuned her out as the clock ticked closer to eleven, knowing everything happened at the last minute. Then he felt the stir of power.

"She's coming," he said, moving from view just as Violissa stopped short of the doorway looking at Paige and Keary. She looked more herself in that moment, but with the curse present he still couldn't bring himself to think of her as his mother. She was still only Violissa, the woman who would one day become the mother he knew so well.

"If I don't think about it, I can move," she said quietly. "I need...I need to go."

In this moment, the curse was silent, held at bay by her inner strength. Ren saw it just at the very corners of her eyes, trying to break through, searching for a way in. He had never appreciated his mother's strength more than in this moment. He wondered if his father ever realized its significance.

She ran out of the house, and they remained frozen in place.

"Go!" Ren shouted, waking them from their trance. "Go after her. You need to be there."

They didn't question him, running out to trail her with Ren following close behind. As they approached the apartment building, Ren stopped. He looked around.

"This is wrong," he said.

"What's wrong?" Keary asked.

"Nothing. Get in there, you're needed."

They both went in, leaving Ren. He knew what would happen, and he preferred to stay outside, on guard for Tynan. He took in the crowded street and sidewalks. The charity event was spread throughout the town. This was nothing like the story he'd been told, everything about it was different, and he felt on the defensive, with no idea if things would still play out the same.

A few minutes later, Violissa ran from the building, tears staining her cheeks. He heard people asking if she was all right as she ran through the crowd. Moments later, his father emerged.

Keary and Paige ran out.

"What now?" Keary asked. "That didn't go as planned. Was it supposed to go like that?"

His voice was raised as the noise from the crowded street increased in volume. Crowded street? He looked around again. Where had all these people come from?

"Violissa!" he heard his father's voice call.

Ren spotted him through the crowd. Then he sensed what had been bothering him, nudging at him the entire time, an undercurrent of Dark magic.

"Tynan," he muttered, turning in an attempt to catch sight of him. He didn't see or feel him anywhere. It was only the magic he could sense. What was he up to?

"Violissa. Please stop!"

Ren's attention was drawn back to his parents. His father had caught up with her.

"Come," Ren said, grabbing Paige and Keary, pulling them in his shift to land closer to his parents where he had seen a clear space.

"Whoa," Paige said, clinging to him, the effects of his shift disorienting her.

"You'll want to see this," Ren said, leaving his worry of Tynan aside for a moment and listening.

His father had begun speaking, and Ren listened as he opened himself up to her, revealing the true extent of his love. A moment to glimpse the man below the Dark king. As he heard the words, he was taken back to the memory of the first time his mother had told him this part of the story, the look on her face as she spoke, revealing the depths of her emotion to his words. Now, as his father spoke of his love, Ren realized the true power of it. He had always known his parents were in love but never had he understood the depths of it. Then, in an instant, it all turned disastrous as he had expected it would, his father walking away, leaving her frozen in place.

His memory stirred again.

"Then what happened, Mother? Father saved you and

brought you home?"

"Ha, nothing is that easy with your mother," his father had said, stepping into the room. "No, your mother left me broken hearted, ignoring my moment of weakness."

"I thought you had no weaknesses, Father?" Ren had asked, only now seeing the look that had passed between them.

"Everyone has a weakness, Drostiren, even the greatest of Dark kings," he had replied, kissing his wife on the head.

"Ren!" Paige yelled, bringing him back. He saw Keary running after his father, Violissa still standing in place. All around, the crowd thickened.

"Ren, what's going on?" Paige asked.

"Tynan," he replied, "The people aren't real."

Paige was jostled as more bodies filled the space, separating his parents.

"That felt real."

"It will. Tynan is manipulating the environment. Forcing their separation."

"But why? Why not just kill them if he's here?"

Ren swiveled, trying to find him but again, only feeling his magic. He was lying in wait somewhere.

"It's the game that thrills him. He likes to torment his victims."

He grabbed Paige's hand and headed to the side of the road. Memories filled his head as they pushed their way through.

"I wasn't refusing your father, Ren. I was frozen, fighting for my life. He just couldn't see it."

"The curse, Mama?"

"Yes, his words had woken the worst part of it. Triggering an effect that I had to fight. There was no one else who could help me. I had to find my way out by myself."

Ren stopped next to a bench and raised Paige onto it, joining her. He took in the situation as his father continued to move further from her. He should have turned back by now, but there were too many people.

"If your mother hadn't spoken as I walked away, I would have never turned back. She saved herself that day."

"No, you called me home, Sinow. You told me to find the strands of your magic, and they saved me just as much as I saved me."

His father was too far to hear her this time, the crowd too large and too loud. Ren spotted Cody close to Violissa, trying to make his way to her.

"Paige, I need you to call Cody."

"Now?"

"He's the closest to her. Tell him..." *Tell him what?* he thought. He had no idea what to do. It was all a mess. He wished he had his father's ability to stop time so he could think on what he needed to do.

"Ren, what do I tell him?"

Ren looked at Violissa, she had dropped to the ground and was curled in a ball, the pain of the curse too much to bear. He could see it like a mist clinging to her, encasing her, drowning her. He spied his father now almost back to the apartment, Keary unable to persuade him to stop. He had no way to hear her, no way to know she couldn't break free.

"When your mother sings, it stirs my soul. I could hear your mother's voice through thousands of others if I had to. It's like a call to my blood." Ren remembered his father telling him once.

"Tell him that she needs to sing."

"Sing?"

"Just tell him, Paige!"

She dialed the phone, and he saw Cody reach for his then bring it to his ear. He turned, trying to find Paige. Ren watched the confusion on his face turn to determination as he put the phone down and pushed through the crowd to reach his sister.

Ren knew he was right as another memory emerged.

"How did you get the portal open if you had no power?"

"We had our innate power, Ren."

"And your mother had her voice."

"You sang?" he had asked, giggling. "That sounds funny."

"Ah, Drostiren, that's because you have yet to see the power in your mother's voice."

"There's power in our voices?"

His father had laughed. "Not ours, hers," he had said, looking at his mother. "Your mother's voice is an amazing thing. It can soften even the hardest of hearts, win over anyone who hears her, bring tears to their eyes, but it can also calm the wind or enrage it, bring the trees to life, the roots to surface. Her voice is the voice of the, Fates Drostiren."

He had looked wide eyed at his mother whose cheeks were a deep pink.

"My voice enhances my nature gifts, Ren."

That was it, she needed to sing, but as he watched, he knew she needed more.

"It won't work," Ren said, watching Cody talk to Violissa who remained curled in her ball. "Her bond to him isn't Cirillian. She won't hear him; she won't listen to him."

"Then why did I do that?"

"Because he can draw her focus from her pain. You need to command your queen to sing. Her voice is the only thing that will stop my father and the only thing strong enough to pull her out from under the curse."

"She won't hear me."

"Yes, she will. Now call her, Paige. You are the daughter of her Keeper. Make her remember that."

Paige stared at him.

"You can do this. You have the power to save us all, Paige."

She drew her eyes from him and looked back at her queen. Cody was still trying to draw her out, and it was working. Paige drew a breath, and standing taller, yelled, "Violissa! You need to wake up and save yourself. Sing, Violissa!"

Nothing happened, but he noticed his father stop and turn, waiting for any sign of a reaction.

"Ren—"

"Keep trying."

"You need to sing, Violissa! As the daughter of your Keeper, the closest to any Council you have right now, I entreat you to sing. Call him back to you. Use your voice to break free!" Paige was screaming now, and Ren noticed the crowd had quieted. She had command of them all. Still, nothing changed. His father, after a few moments of watching, turned back to walking away, his shoulders slumped in defeat.

"Sinow!" he heard Keary say.

"Even her own people can't wake her, Keary," Sinow said. "It's no use, she doesn't want to be with me."

"She's fighting."

"I've been fighting longer."

Ren's attention was drawn back to Violissa.

"What is that?" Paige said as a soft melody filled the air.

"She heard you," he responded as it grew to a recognizable sound.

He saw his father pause again.

Her voice filled the air, everything stilled, everyone stopped to listen, even the Dark magic thickening the crowds seemed to calm. As her voice grew with strength, she slowly rose, the mist of the curse dissipating slightly. She was doing it, she was breaking through. He saw his father turn as the words of the song made it to his ears. Ren recognized the song, another memory interjecting.

He'd been young, just given permission to wander the castle on his own and stumbled across his parents alone.

"And why did we create this room again, Vi?" his father had asked, pulling her into his arms.

"Because every castle needs a ballroom."

"For the balls we will never have?"

She had laughed. "I suppose that's true, but we can use it."

"And when would that be?"

"Now," she had said, twirling out of his arms.

"Do you remember that night in the Banished Realm?" she had asked.

"I'll never forget it. You danced in the moonlight like the goddess you are, singing that song."

"And you danced with me."

"Aye, that I did."

She began to sing softly, her voice quiet and vulnerable. Ren had watched, amazed as his father had brought her against him and begun to dance, the two lost in a moment, the kind Ren had never been privy to, one that he would forever cherish.

Now as he watched, she slowly brought herself out of her curled position, his father turning to see, his attention finally drawn back to her. Her voice grew in strength as she sang, the words expressing the love she had for him, the love submerged beneath a curse she couldn't break. With each word, he felt the world around them respond. The clouds stood still, the breeze rose, blowing through his hair, the ground seemed to hum, all of it waking to her call. The curse fought back. For an instant, her voice cut off, and she stumbled backward, holding her head, leaning forward in pain.

"Vi!" Ren heard his father yell as he tried to get through. Then, as if feeling Tynan's magic, he stopped, looked around and met Ren's eyes. *Tynan*, he mouthed, and Ren nodded.

His father cast his innate power out against the pervasive cluster of fake people, and they disappeared, leaving only the townspeople present.

"Wait," he heard Keary say to his father. "She needs to fight it herself. Look at her."

Ren looked back over at her. She had put her hands out on the ground and started singing again, raising her head, the words coming out angry and powerful, the wind now whipping around them.

"She's pissed," Paige said.

"She's fighting," he replied. He sent his power out, feeling for any sign of Tynan, but nothing remained. He was nowhere around. Violissa's voice crescendoed, the ground rumbling in response as she slammed her hands out. That's when he saw the curse for what it really was. The mist blackened and took shape, forming an angry, iron colored cell around her.

"Fates, that's what she's been dealing with all this time?" he heard his father mutter.

She stumbled again, looking wildly around the cell, finally free internally from the curse. In seconds, she'd regained her composure, picking the song back up. There was a familiarity to her voice now, to her moves, to the gleam in her eyes accompanied by the growing smile. She was herself again. This was his mother. This was the woman whose calm, gentle nature had guided him from infancy and shaped the man he was today. This woman he recognized as her hand reached back, freeing the braid binding her locks, letting them fall loose like she'd always worn them. She drew her hands up as the song ended, flowers climbing the bars of the cell, their roots transforming the power of the curse, weakening it until it turned to ash. A gentle breeze picked up the ash and the flower petals, sending them drifting across the crowd.

Everything seemed to freeze again as his parents met each other's eyes. His father tentatively took a step forward, continuing until he was within reach of her.

"I remember," she said quietly. "All of it. Every lifetime. I remember that I loved you." She smiled, laughing slightly. "But I never truly forgot. I always loved you. Each lifetime, it was you who held my heart, you it ached for, you I searched for, you I needed." Her voice broke, and her lips quivered. "I am so sorry," she whispered. "I was in there, but it buried me. I thought I had time to fight it, I thought—"

His father didn't wait for her to finish; instead, cupping her face in his right hand, he leaned down and kissed her.

The ground quaked below them, a wave of violet cascading across them all then dissipating. The spell had broken.

Too caught up in the moment, Ren didn't notice Tynan until his father, sensing him first, moved, placing his mother behind him for protection. By then it was too late.

Seventeen

Pushing Violissa behind him, Sinow stared at Tynan. He was almost unrecognizable, no longer the same man he'd once called brother. His eyes were filled with madness and hatred, their black color pulling one in like an endless void that no mortal could have escaped. His hair hung thick with tangles as if it hadn't been combed in centuries. Tynan cracked his neck and took two steps toward them.

"That's close enough, Tynan."

"Brother," he spat, the hatred layering the word. His eyes moved to Violissa, and a wicked grin formed. "Violissa, looking young and fresh, unspoiled. What would you taste like now?"

"Enough!" Sinow commanded.

"You have no power here, Sinow. You're weak. What will you do? Who will protect your precious mate?"

"I will, Tynan. Leave them be," Ren said, stepping forward.

Tynan's head spun to Ren.

"Ren, this isn't your fight. Move back with Keary before he kills you." As Sinow said it, he remembered who Ren was. Looking at Tynan didn't kill Ren as it would a mortal; he hadn't even flinched when Tynan turned toward him.

"Ah, nephew. So, this is where you've been hiding."

"Nephew? Sinow," Violissa squeezed his arm, "he said nephew."

He squeezed her waist in answer, his hand still wrapped around it, holding her behind him.

"Always messing with my plans, aren't you!" Tynan yelled at the sky. "Not this time. This time I win! You're still exactly where I want you, nephew."

Sinow felt for his power, but it was minimal. His innate powers were present, part of them had been present throughout this human life. Now as he flexed his hands, he wondered if the Fates had meddled once again, giving them a fighting chance. Judging by Tynan's appearance, he didn't think it would be much of a fight; his innate powers would be futile against Tynan.

"No, Tynan. You don't win. You never win," Violissa said from behind him.

Sinow felt a stream of Light power from Ren as he threw a shield up around the mortals in proximity, pushing them far back. He sensed commotion but never drew his eyes from Tynan.

"As nice as this family reunion is, it's time for someone to die."

"Not today," Ren said, his eyes shifting black, a fog of gray growing from him.

"And you're going to stop me? Tell me, nephew, how close are you to ascending?" He sniffed the air. "I smell instability. I smell weakness."

Tynan let out a maniacal laugh and drew his own power, the air growing heavy, polluted, thick with black and red hues. Sinow called his powers again, but they refused to answer; it was like a slow leak of magic entering his system and nothing close to what he would need to even think of fighting Tynan in this state. He felt Violissa's hand on his shoulder and tried speaking to her in enaigne, but the connection wasn't there.

Tynan drew his hand, but before he could strike, Ren sent a bolt of magic at him, catching him off guard. He toppled, crashing across the road and into a building.

"Go!" Ren shouted, pointing behind them. Sinow looked to where a beacon of golden light shone from the park. The portal home.

"Take her and go. I'll—" He was interrupted as Tynan struck back. Ren was down, crushed below Tynan's magic. Tynan lifted him, throwing him into the corner of a building which collapsed when it met the force of his body.

"Sinow, we can't leave him."

"I know, I doubt he's fought someone this strong."

"He's fought you, he'll be fine," Keary said, coming behind them. "Let's go. The portal is waiting."

As Tynan and Ren continued their fight, the townspeople ran for cover, the ground beneath them buckling with the force of the battle. They were trapped in the middle of the commotion, and Sinow knew there would be innocents wounded or worse, killed.

"We can't leave them," he said.

Tynan roared, emerging from a crater where Ren had thrown him.

"I don't have any power, Sinow."

"Neither do I, not enough to help Ren."

Tynan shifted in front of them, Ren doing the same, planting himself across from Tynan, a shield for his parents.

"I won't let you hurt them."

"How sweet," Tynan growled. "Too bad you can't stop me. I'm done playing this game."

Tynan threw out a tentacle of magic that engulfed Ren, forcing him into the air. Ren struggled to free himself before Tynan flung him back to the ground, the tentacle sliding down the road, dragging Ren within it, chunks of asphalt breaking with the impact until the magic crashed him into the post office, the building toppling down upon him.

Sinow hit Tynan with every bit of power he could summon, but it did nothing.

"That's funny, brother. You know, you punished me, very creatively I might add. Cursed me to spend the last six thousand years locked away in the center of this abhorrent world. Trapped, listening to the mundane drabble of their pointless lives. But you made one mistake." His eyes bore into Sinow as he stepped closer.

"You locked me away in your timeline, attached me to your time in this space. I listened, I learned as your moments with Violissa repeated over and over."

Sinow felt Violissa's heart rate increase.

"You know what I learned? You are mortal," he whispered into Sinow's ear. "Until you pass through that portal, you can be killed."

Violissa squeezed his hand.

"I was planning to kill Violissa and watch you suffer before torturing you, but I've played that game, and I've grown bored. Now..."

Ren shifted, stumbling a bit, still recovering from the last attack.

"Now, I kill you."

Before anyone could react, Tynan grabbed Sinow, throwing him through the air. Sinow tried to stop himself with his powers, but the blast of Tynan's magic hit him in the chest first. He heard Violissa scream, and then the world went black.

The scream escaped Violissa as Tynan's magic poured into

Sinow. She'd been trying to call her power when Tynan grabbed Sinow, his hand slipping from hers as he was thrown into the air. He was struggling to fight back, but his power was minimal and against Tynan it was useless. She felt her nature powers respond to her fear as the scream broke free. She didn't know what happened around her after that, her only focus Sinow. Reaching him, she dropped to his side. There was no external damage, but she understood how their magic worked. Inside, he was bound to be in trauma. The trickle of blood from his mouth confirmed it.

"Sinow! Sinow!" she yelled, trying to wake him.

"Violissa, can you heal him?" Keary asked, running to them, his voice heavy with concern.

"No, I have no power."

"You just sent Tynan to hell with a scream," Paige said.

She glanced back to see the cavern that now lie where Tynan had been, vines climbing their way out. Or were they climbing in? She looked back at Sinow.

"Sinow, wake up. Please," she cried.

He grunted and rolled his head slightly, his eyes blinking open, filled with pain.

"Vi," he sputtered, more blood trickling from his mouth.

"There you are. Stay with me."

He grabbed her hand.

"We're going to heal you," she said.

"What can we do to help?" Cody said, coming up to them.

"Somebody get a medic!" she heard, looking over to see more people running over.

"Keep them away."

"But they can help."

"No, they can't. But," she looked at Ren, "you can."

He shook his head then she noticed he was shimmering slightly as if his skin was growing translucent in patches then coming back into focus with every wheezing breath Sinow took. She rose and grabbed Ren's shirt.

"If you are who I think you are, you can heal him. You have the power."

His skin grew hazy as he shook his head again sadly. "I can't, and you know I can't."

She bit back the sob. Not wanting to believe him. "Yes, you can. You have my power."

"Yes, but you know the rules."

She stumbled backwards, "No, no."

"Heal him, Ren!" Paige screamed.

"He can't," Violissa sobbed, dropping back to her knees over Sinow whose eyes had closed again. "We cannot heal once the Fates have claimed a person."

"Ren?" Paige said, fear in her voice. "What's happening?"

"He's dying, and—" Keary started.

"With him dies the son I won't have," Violissa finished, the tears rolling down her cheeks.

"Sinow?" she said softly, his hand dropping to the ground.

"No," Paige whimpered.

Violissa dropped her head on Sinow's chest, knowing Ren was gone along with his father. Paige's sobs filled the silence.

This was wrong. This was all wrong. She rose, backing away, not worrying about Tynan. She looked up at the sky and screamed. It was primal, it was unrestrained, coming from a place deep within her.

"You will not do this to us!" she yelled at the Fates. "I know you can hear me! I know you're watching, and I know their god can hear me, too! You will bring them back! This is not how it will end!"

Silence greeted her, but she wasn't done.

"Don't you ignore me! You will listen. I can bring him back, and you will let me! God of this world, let them hear me! Now!"

The ground rumbled, and the sky filled with small lightning strikes.

"That's better. Now, bring him back! Let me fix this, please," her voice broke. "Let me fix it, and I promise you I will never doubt you again. I will follow the path you lay before me unfaltering."

Sinow inhaled a pained breath, and Ren shimmered back into existence.

"Thank you," she said, running over to Sinow and noticing Paige racing to Ren out of the corner of her eye.

"Vi," Sinow whispered, reaching for her. He was still mortally wounded—she could see it in his eyes, hear it in his voice.

"I'm here," she said, grabbing his hand.

"The Fates said to stop screaming, they can hear you clearly," he said, coughing.

She laughed through her tears.

"You are one loud and demanding woman."

"They listened, didn't they?" she asked.

"For now, but there's not much time. Vi, I'm mortally wounded."

She wiped the blood from his chin. "You are not going to die." But she didn't know what she was going to do. She needed power then maybe she could heal him, maybe they would let her. But how did she get her power back? Ren. Ren would know.

Violissa looked at him, seeing only now the resemblance; he looked so much like Sinow that it hurt. His sharp blue eyes met hers. She vaguely recalled recognizing him when she was Violet, but now, she truly saw it.

"Tell me what happens. Tell me how I get my magic back."

"The future—" he started.

"Is gone. Everything is gone if he dies. Tell me how."

Ren swallowed. "The union ceremony then you summoned the voice of the elders. You brought your power and that of the Councils' back."

"But no one—"

"You did."

"Then that's what we do now."

"You can't summon them here, Mo...Violissa," he said.

"What is it?" Sinow asked, squeezing her hand.

"A ritual that summons all the former kings," Ren answered for her.

"No, you're right that won't work. Then we'll have to go with the ceremony and pray it's enough," she said in desperation.

"You both already have some power. There's a chance," Keary said.

"Yes, there's a chance," she returned, looking down at Sinow.

"Not quite the way I was hoping to marry you," he said softly.

"About as bad as the first time," Ren said. "I don't know if it will work."

"We try," Violissa said, wondering how the first time could have been worse. "To save you both, we try."

Ren saw the hope in his mother's eyes and didn't have the heart to tell her it was the summoning that had bought about her power. What did it matter anyway, there was no way their ancestors would hear her call from here. His father lay dying, pulled back from death but for how long? He wanted to run, to flee it all and let his mother figure it out. His parents always found a way. They were the strong ones not him. He could barely control his Dark powers.

His mother's eyes pleaded.

This is Ren's journey, not ours, his mother had said. The Fates had placed him here, pulled him from Tynan's clutches. Maybe this was why he was here.

"All right, we'll try," he finally said. "I can't perform the ceremony though. I don't know it. Even if I did, I doubt it would be right to marry my own parents."

Below his father coughed, blood trickling from his mouth. Ren felt the pull of his life-force draining just as his own was.

"Sinow, hold on please. We will fix this."

"Paige," Keary said suddenly, "You can perform the ritual."

"Me? No, I don't know it."

"Bullshit, Paige, I know your father. There's no way he didn't hand every piece of Keeper knowledge to you in case he died before another Keeper could be called."

"I...but—"

"Paige, it's ok. I need you to remember the ritual. You do know it, right?" Violissa asked.

"Yes," she said reluctantly. "Father made me promise not to say anything."

"Perform the ritual, Paige. This is the reason he taught you. The time has come to use your knowledge," Violissa said.

A determined look overcame Paige's face. "Ok, but I need the ceremonial knife and the binding cloth."

"Will this work?" Cody asked from behind her, holding out a small knife.

"Ouch, a pocket knife? That's going to hurt, but yes, it will work."

"And here, use my scarf," Violet's aunt said, stepping forward.

"Thank you, Aunt Emma."

"Something borrowed, something blue," she said as she handed the scarf to Paige.

"Those will work," Ren said.

"Vi," his father choked, barely audible.

"We need to move fast," she said. "I'm here, Sinow. It's time we get married."

"About time you said yes," he joked then groaned in pain as Keary helped sit him up. Too weak to sit on his own, Keary had to use his own body to prop him.

"We don't have much time," Ren said hurriedly, a strange pull making its way through his body. His father was fading quickly. They needed to start the ritual. "Paige, you need to begin, before it's too late."

She met his eyes, their cerulean blue filled with fear.

"You can do this," he told her.

"Ok," she said softly before taking a deep breath and beginning the ritual.

Ren watched as she hurried through the ceremony, every word exactly as her father had taught her. Every word as it should have been, as it had been the first time they'd been spoken. As she reached the cutting of the life and blood lines she flinched and apologized with each slice, her hands shaking the entire time. The pocket knife matched the movement of her shaking, leaving jagged lines.

The further into the ceremony, the more confident Paige's voice became, and the more blood flowed from his parents' wounds. He watched with anticipation, waiting for them to begin healing. When Paige finished, all eyes fixed on the scarf, the union cloth that should have dissipated with magic, yet it did not. Instead, it darkened with the crimson of their blood. Blood that dripped in spatters on the ground below.

"It didn't work," his mother said.

"I'm sorry. I—"

"No, Paige. It's not your fault," she replied as Keary lowered his father back down. She leaned closer to him. "Sinow?"

His eyes looked heavy, and Ren felt his own body becoming lighter, that pull stronger.

"Vi," he said, bringing his hand up, the scarf falling across him. He touched a strand of her hair, the same one Ren had seen him touch hundreds of times. His blood darkened it, but neither seemed to notice. "They're calling me home."

"No, no. Sinow, it will work. Just hang on."

"Shhh. I love you, Violissa, and I will wait for you as I always have. Keary, protect her. Whether you're here or back in our world, protect her," he said, his eyes never leaving hers. "Always waiting for you."

"No, Sinow." The tears fell from her face as his hand dropped to the ground.

Ren, however, didn't see the tears for darkness overcame

him as his father's hand fell, his body lightening entirely as it was pulled away by the Fates.

Eighteen

The vines wrapped tighter as they pulled Tynan down further from his prey. He struggled to free himself, to escape their hold but to no avail. They slid around him, encasing every inch of him, and the more he struggled, the tighter they wrapped. He tried using his powers, but they were silent. The Fates were interfering once again. He cursed them and Violissa with her damned Elvin gifts.

He needed to get back, needed to watch Sinow die, had waited a lifetime, cursing his weak self for missing his chance eons ago. This time, there had been no conscience, no doubt, no hesitation, no weakness. Tynan had struck Sinow with a killing blow, and there was no way to heal him, he'd felt it the instant his spell had hit his brother, seconds before the bitch had cast her spell and had her minions drag him here. But she was powerless. How had she done it?

She had been powerless when she escaped you last time,

fool, he scolded himself.

Should he have killed her instead? It didn't matter, kill one, you kill the other. The two couldn't survive without each other. He relaxed, he needn't struggle any longer, his brother was gone, he felt it to his core. He had finally done it, had finally won. His skin began to tingle, his body fading. His past now rewritten; his story now changed. He closed his eyes, letting out a celebratory laugh that reverberated through the ground that caged him. He was king now, the only king, the rightful one, and nothing would change that now. He faded, the vines collapsing as he was pulled away by time.

Ren blinked. Where was he? The chaos of the scene that had been before him was gone, now he stood alone in a field in a place that felt familiar yet unfamiliar. He walked, uncertain as to why he was here, why this time was different from the first time his father had died.

The meadow seemed to go on forever with no ending, no markers to let him know where he was.

"This is the Dream Realm, son." He heard his father's voice behind him.

"Father?" He turned, seeing not the younger man who had just died before him but the father he knew. His eyes deep with knowledge were usually rimmed with a subtle fear that Ren's powers sensed. Now, however, he could no longer detect the fear.

"Where are we? Where is Mother?"

"I believe it's a sort of limbo while things continue to play out. Your mother still lives because she continues to live in the time you left her."

"You died." It was a statement and a question, Ren unsure what the final outcome had been.

"So, it would seem." His father laughed. "All this time, I worried about your mother, never thinking I might be the one to go first."

"But then why are you the one I know, why aren't you the younger self?"

"So, you did go back. How far?"

"The human world."

His father's face dropped. "She was right. We're powerless."

"Yes."

He rubbed his face. "Tynan never fails to screw things up."

"And he succeeded this time."

His father looked beyond him, and Ren turned to see what he was looking at.

"This field lies in limbo between our two fates. That end is where my younger self lies, taken by the Fates and likely watching the turn of events. The other end is the mortal world, the living world."

"Life and death."

"Yes, and I believe we are here because our fates lie in the balance. We are both the future of the man behind that veil."

"He's not truly dead?"

"He is, but the Fates haven't made their final play. As your mother would say, there's still a player on the board."

"Mother."

"Aye, and if it's one thing I know, your mother is someone to be reckoned with. She's a fighter although it has taken me this long to realize how strong she truly is. She holds all of our fates in her hand, and I have no doubt she'll bring me back."

He thought of his mother and her ways, so soft and gentle, her eyes always seeing what he could not, sensing beyond his senses. Keary had always joked that she would have been locked away in what he called a madhouse had she been human. He smiled, thinking of her always wandering off, a stir in the air sparking her attention, the flap of a butterfly wing drawing her away.

"Yes, she'll be fine, won't she," he said quietly.

As he said it, he felt the pull again. His father looked at him, a strange sparkling filling his skin.

"I believe she's found a way," he said, smiling.

"Father, I—"

"I love you, son," his father said then disappeared.

The tug on Ren grew until he could no longer breathe, and everything went black again.

Sinow was gone. Again. In the unstable future, Violissa searched for him, running out of the castle, knowing she wouldn't find him but going anyway. He had disappeared briefly a short time before only to return again minutes later. Now he'd been gone longer, the strands of time increasing their chaotic dance all around her.

"Something is happening," he had told her when he'd returned that first time. "Things have gone wrong."

"Tynan?" she had asked.

"I think so."

"I felt your absence, Sinow. You were—"

"Dead," he had replied, his eyes holding a seriousness she hadn't seen since their return to their world. "You must have brought the younger version of me back."

"Ren. If you're in trouble, then he's in trouble. Sinow, what do we do?"

For the first time, she had felt completely lost. She always found a way, but this time she was a world and lifetimes away.

He had placed his hands on her arms, bringing her closer, the black of his eyes darkening, the Dark king coming through and taking control.

"Calm yourself, Violissa. You will find your way out of whatever is happening." His eyes had softened. "Just as you always have."

"If he's wounded you, then you're still mortal, Sinow. We don't even know if I'm with you."

"I have no doubt that you're there."

"But I was so young—"

"Everything we went through, you went through, happened when we were young."

He was right, it had all happened so long ago it seemed a lost memory, tucked away.

"Don't leave me again," she had said, leaning into him.

"I think that's out of my hands now," he had said softly, pulling her close and running his hand through her hair.

She could have stayed that way, safe in his arms, but then she had felt a burning in her hands. She had pulled back at the same time as she heard him mutter, "What the Fates?"

She couldn't draw her eyes from the searing jagged red marks that had appeared over her union scars.

"Vi," he had said, and she had finally forced herself to look up, her eyes catching his extended hand, the same jagged red marks on it.

"Fates, Sinow. They've performed the union ceremony. I'm trying to save you the same way we saved me."

"By bringing back our powers."

"It won't work. If you're still mortal, then we're not in our world. Their god won't allow it. There's no magic allowed there. It would take a miracle."

"The only way they'd know about the ceremony is if Drostiren told them."

"He's with them. That's why they said to let him go. He's saving them."

He had not answered, his eyes getting a far-off look.

"I don't think it worked," he had said, meeting her eyes. "Vi."

He had faded again, her heart breaking again, her world crashing around her. Now, she ran wildly through the castle until once outside she came to an abrupt stop. The world around her was in chaos. The ribbons of time had come unglued, all around her colors streamed out of control. Behind her the keep lifted away in pieces then disintegrated becoming a fine dust that rose to the sky, which she could no longer see because it was now draped in layers of hues. Ribbons surrounded her, closing in, creating a wind that blew her, pushing her back, her hair blowing wildly, whipping at her face. She stumbled, unsure of what to do as time unraveled before her eyes. Then, through the storm of streaming colors, she spotted one strand glowing a bright golden hue, standing apart from the others, but buried deep beyond. The strand called to her, the golden glow of magic drawing her in. Fates' magic, she thought, then slowly but confidently she reached her hand in through the ribbons of light against the force until she felt the strand, the magic in it tingling against her fingertips.

"Vi?" she heard Sinow's voice behind her at the same moment she felt his presence return. He was back, looking around, confused and patting his body to feel if he were really there.

"Sinow, I have to. She needs me, you need me." She gripped the strand tightly, and the world fell away.

"No!" Violissa cried, looking down at Sinow. He was gone. She had lost him again as the union had not worked, the Fates turning a blind eye to them. Blood stained the ground around his body, dripping from his wounds as well as hers. She felt defeated, weak, unwilling to move. She looked up at Ren to ask what had gone wrong, but he was no longer there. A sob escaped her throat, and she dropped her head onto Sinow's chest, not caring that his blood seeped into her hair and clothes. As the life drained from her, the tears flowed. She had lost everything. The man she loved, the son she would have raised, both ripped from her, and this time there was no doubt they were gone for good. The Fates had given them a second chance, had brought Sinow back once. They would not do it again. She lay there, feeling the blood drain from her and welcoming the death it would bring. Knowing it would bring her to the Fates and to Sinow.

"I've seen enough. Take her." She heard a man's voice boom. She recognized it, but in her sorrow gave it no heed.

"No, she's grieving."

"I don't care. Take her away now."

Hands grabbed her roughly and pulled her from Sinow.

"Sir, she's really bleeding."

"It can wait. I want them separated. Remove her from him and somebody cover that dead body. When you patch her up, I want her down at the office, and I want answers. I'm done waiting."

The callousness of his words triggered a fight instinct, and she began struggling to get back to Sinow as they dragged her away.

"No!" she screamed. "I won't leave him!"

"Let her go!" She heard Keary yell as hands gripped her tighter. She glanced over to see him tackled by two men who brought him to his knees and handcuffed him. Even then he still fought to get to her. Cody, who had also been fighting, lay sprawled out on the ground. The crowd around them erupted until gunshots fired, silencing them. It was out of control, but Violissa tuned it all out, her mind trying every which way to make sense of how she'd lost Sinow and how to get back to his side.

"Violissa," Keary called, meeting her eyes.

Pray, he mouthed.

Pray. In that moment, the word was powerful enough to focus her. She knew he didn't mean to pray to the Fates, understood on a deeper level that she needed to pray to the god of this world. Somehow, she realized that this god didn't like magic. The Fates were trying to intervene, waiting beyond his border to do so. This wasn't the Fates' doing.

This was his.

She stopped struggling, let herself go limp as she closed her eyes. She knew the god of this world, had given herself over to him in many lives, served him, worshipped him, prayed to him. So, in that moment she let the world around her fall away, and she prayed, feeling the calm that came with the spiritualism and closeness as her prayer was answered. In the darkness behind her eyes, she saw something sparkling just beyond her mind's reach. She urged it forward, welcoming the warmth of the radiant light. Magic, her mind registered as it reached out, and she opened herself to it as if grasping it in her hands. As she did, she felt herself drawn to the light then as she reached it, the light fell away, and darkness engulfed her.

Violissa breathed in as if her breath had been stolen from her.

"Vi?" she heard Sinow ask, his voice deep and strong, filled with worry.

She blinked her eyes open to see his face above hers. He had her in his arms, she could feel the safety of his embrace.

Bringing her hand up, she ran it along his jaw. "You're healed," she said, looking deep into his eyes. He gave her a curious look then his eyes filled with an understanding.

"What has she done?" he whispered.

Only then did she notice the subtle differences. His features matured, his eyes deeper with the wisdom and experience that living thousands of years brought. There was something else, something behind the strength and power, behind the knowledge, subtle yet distinct to her, something harbored there through lifetimes. Fear. Her mind briefly wondered what they had been through for fear to settle that deeply in him, in a Dark king, but it slipped away as he helped her up.

He studied her, smiling gently as if she were a child, but then she supposed she was to him.

"How did you know?" she asked.

"Your eyes. Their...brighter. They don't carry the burden of our past," he paused, "of our choices."

"Are we that unhappy?" she asked tentatively.

"No," he answered, smiling. "We are still very much in love. Further so than you can even imagine now." He brushed her hair back. "But time, the Fates have not always been kind, and the paths we have been forced to tread not always the easiest."

He must have seen her face drop with the thought.

"Don't fret. Our love saves us and heals us each time. And with time the way it is now, I'm hopeful we won't tread the same path," he said, gesturing behind her.

For the first time, she noticed the storm that surrounded them.

"Time is unwinding."

"You can see it, too?" he asked.

It was subtle, underneath the violent storm that seemed to encapsulate them. But she could see the colors, strands of time flowing chaotically.

"Yes, but I'm guessing with my full power it appears more vivid. Why am I here?" she asked, turning back to him.

"Because she needed to be there. The Fates work in ways we have never fully comprehended."

"She needs to save you for I could not."

His eyes searched hers. "You underestimate your strength." He laughed. "Just as I always have. No, you are the one who will save me, Violissa." He stepped closer to her. "When the time comes, don't stay quiet, Vi. Don't take the choice that I make for us. Fight back."

She had no idea what he was talking about.

"But you will," he seemed to answer her confusion, "if our path is not changed, then you will."

She felt a strange tug and yelped.

"She is calling you home," he said.

"To you."

He smiled and kissed her forehead. "Aye. Remember, I never stopped loving you. I will love you until my last breath."

"And beyond," she finished for him as the tug became stronger.

She let go and felt herself drawn away into the blackness once again.

Nineteen

Sinow took a deep, painful breath. The Fates had sent him back. He opened his eyes, expecting to see Violissa, but instead, slowly pushing himself up, pain searing through his body, he discovered a world of chaos. Violissa was on the ground with two officers standing over her, Keary was on his knees handcuffed, Cody sprawled on the ground, and Paige hysterical like all the others who had gathered. He heard a deep inhale and turned to see Ren who was patting his body, a look of relief in his eyes when they met Sinow's. Then it dawned on Sinow that Ren had disappeared when he had died, erased from existence.

Ren took in the scene before them, and his eyes followed a layer of fog that was rolling across the ground draping Violissa; Sinow noticed it as well. He tried to move, trying his best to get to her, but the pain was too great. They had brought him back, but he was still mortally wounded. He leaned back on his hands, breathing heavy from the exertion then noticed everyone had quieted down.

In the midst, a figure appeared.

"Fates," Ren muttered as a voice filled the air, sweet and delicate. A second figure appeared, her voice joining the first. Both had long white hair, gowns that flowed loosely down past their feet and vibrant emerald eyes.

"Get away!" Ren shouted. Everyone backed up. The two men with Violissa looked up at him then over at the agents.

"You need to get out before the four voices converge!" he shouted as a third figure emerged, throwing her voice out with the others.

"Get out now! Once the magic hits, you will be stuck, and you will die!"

"You will stay, grab the girl now!" the other agent yelled.

One of the men looked around, confused.

"Get out!" the female agent.screamed. He remembered vaguely seeing her around the town after the earthquake. His mind briefly registered a connection between the quake and Tynan's presence, but he let it go as the scene played out before him.

The confused agent ran, leaving the other behind, still debating whose command was to be heeded.

A fourth woman joined, her voice meeting the others. The sky darkened, and a stream of emerald light descended upon them, causing the final man to run, sliding under the descending field of magic just as it crashed into the ground, sending a quiver through the land.

Ren helped Sinow up, causing him to groan in pain. He leaned into Ren to help ease it.

"Sorry," Ren said, "but you're going to want to see this."

"What is it?" he asked, trying to stand as pain careened in waves throughout his body.

"They're summoning their queen," Ren replied, eyes fixated on the figures. "You have no idea how I dreamed of seeing this as a child."

Sinow looked out at the mist filled scene, his eyes heavy with the looming sleep. If he shut them, he knew they would never reopen. This was his final chance, and his life depended on whatever was happening in that mist. As the spirit-like women continued to sing, Sinow took in their features. Their straight hair glimmered stark white, their eyes shimmering sage like Violissa's. They reminded him of the shade in the Guardians' lair, Violissa's mother.

"Elvin," he said.

"Yes."

Sinow watched as the mist thickened, the clouds completely shielding the sun, but with their song's crescendo, the sky turned a golden color that he instinctively knew wasn't the sun, but instead knew to be Fates' magic.

With a thunder that shook the ground, the light funneled to the mist then dissipated, leaving a sparkling train around where Violissa now rose. The singers continued their song, oblivious to the motion in the middle of their formation.

Violissa stood, her back to him. She put her arm out and moved it around then her head lifted, and he could see she was surveying the scene. Finally, she turned his way, eyes locking instantly with his, eyes that shone deeper than they had, eyes illuminated with power, which carried something more. Her expression grew concerned as she took him in, as if seeing his injuries for the first time. Then her eyes took in the remainder of the chaos and landed finally on Ren. Her face lit then dropped, and he wondered what was going on in her mind until pain reared its head. The song continued, and Violissa tore her eyes from them. She turned and moved with the grace of someone who had carried her magic for lifetimes. Her moves made a dance that complemented that of the spirits, but with her movements, the world reacted. Grass erupted below their feet, forcing its way through the asphalt. The trees seemed to come alive, their leaves a frenzy of motion, a thundering coming from below where their roots lifted, seeming to cast a beat. The clouds turned an ominous gray, the sky darkening to match their mood. The natural world was answering her call, answering its queen.

Suddenly, the song ended with a crash of golden light. The spirits left, only a dust of gold remaining where they had stood.

Everything was still and quiet.

Violissa turned and walked over to Sinow. He was using every bit of strength to remain standing and hoped she was coming to heal him. Power poured from her eyes, but there was something different about their brightness. They bore a heaviness to them, a weight carried through time. Time and a past he had yet to discover, he realized as she placed a hand on his cheek and said softly, "So young." Her smile, sad, faltered slightly. "And free, unfettered by the chains of our past."

Her eyes searched his as if looking for something they could not find.

"She loves you. More than you know. More than she knows."

"Are you here to heal me?" he asked, still not quite believing what his mind was piecing together.

She shook her head sadly. "No, I am the conduit, the way to her powers. She must be the one to heal you." She looked down at the point Tynan had struck him. "And soon or we will lose you both again."

His face must have reflected his surprise at her words.

"He is you. If you die here, he no longer exists with me. Our timelines are distanced, but we are still as one. We must call her back before it's too late."

She pulled her bottom lip in, gnawing it just as she always did, the loose curl brushing the edge of her lips. He reached out and pushed the curl back, wondering how many times his future self had done that. With the movement, he noticed his wounds from the union ceremony had closed.

She caught his hand as he dropped it back down.

"When the time comes, if it still comes, don't make the

choice for her. She will agree, not understanding what it will do to you both. Don't take that path." Then before he could respond, she dropped his hand and moved to Ren.

"Ren."

"Mother."

She brought his head down and kissed his forehead, the movement throwing Sinow off balance slightly as Ren still held him.

"Your father and I love you, Ren."

"I'm not going back, am I?"

She shook her head. "No. Time is unraveling. The world has all but collapsed to the strain of it. Everyone is gone, pulled away in some stasis to await the settlement of time's flow. Only your father and I remain."

"But—"

"You must continue your path, Ren. Your work is not done. The Fates still need you. They need you," she said, gesturing to Sinow. "Past, present, and future are now interwoven and are key to your return."

She kissed his cheek and began walking away, stopping as if she remembered something then turned toward Paige, bringing her hand to her heart.

"Paige, my old friend," she said softly, her voice heavy with sadness, "I never imagined I would have the chance to see you again."

She walked tentatively toward Paige. Sinow grimaced as the pain deepened. He wanted Violissa to do what she needed to do to heal him before it was too late, but seeing her eyes fill with tears, he bit back the urge to pass out and watched the interaction.

She brought her hand out and hesitantly touched Paige's. Paige, as if understanding it all, took Violissa's hand and held it.

"There isn't a day that passes when I don't think of you. And not a day goes by that your father does not miss you dreadfully.

I told him it was all right to return to the Fates, to ease his burden, yet he is too loyal to his queen to do so. At least that was, before the unraveling." Her eyes drifted away, looking beyond them all. "Now they are all gone." She lingered on the last word then her stance changed, the queen returning.

"That is enough reminiscing. We need to bring her back." She glanced at Sinow. "We need her to save you."

She kissed Paige on the cheek. "You will forever be in my heart."

Then she turned toward Cody who lay sprawled on the ground still. It was only then that he noticed everyone else lay outside a shield. She must have thrown one up when the song ended.

She leaned down and lifted Cody's head.

"Hmm, you're new," she said, bringing him to his feet. "What are the Fates up to?" she asked. "Yes, you'll do fine. The heart of a Lightbearer." Smiling, she took his hand. "Yes, just fine. You play fiddle. That's exactly what she'll need. Weavers need a thread."

She waved a hand, and a violin appeared in Cody's hand. Cody looked speechless for once.

"You'll know when to use it. Paige, sing like your father taught you. You need to call your queen home, and you are the only one to do it," she said, walking away from them.

"What do I sing?" Paige asked nervously.

"You'll know."

With that she slammed her foot down, the ground quaking in response, the trees answering her signal and drumming a rhythm of their own, their roots reaching up with each pound. The shield fell, but everyone was too stunned to move.

"Sing, Paige. The life of your king depends upon it."

Paige began singing in what sounded like ancient Cirillian and seemed as surprised as everyone else at hearing the words come from her mouth. Whatever she was singing was working; the clouds thickened, covering the sun completely. She stopped her verse then Violissa picked up, her voice strong and confident, the power of it coursing through the air, tingling Sinow's skin. It was a voice that held centuries of experience and knowledge. As she sang, the sky darkened, the clouds becoming a heavy gray, the wind stirred, blowing through her hair and teasing the layers of the dress she'd awoken in.

A shimmering of gold accented the clouds then grew, spreading to encase Violissa. As it dissipated, he noticed the change. Instead of one voice, it was now layered with two voices singing in harmony. Two souls sharing one space. His Violissa had returned. The effect was captivating, the sound drifting through his conscious, pouring its way into his soul, lifting him, opening him. But to what?

The sky turned golden once again, and the future Violissa yielded to it. He felt her pull away, heard her voice fade as the verse ended. The golden light dimmed, and his eyes were drawn back to Violissa, his Violissa, who was leaning on her knees, unsure as to where she was now. Where had she been? Had she seen him in the future? Her eyes met his, and he knew she had. She surveyed him then took in her surroundings, Cody still playing wildly on his violin to a song Sinow was certain he had never before played.

Violissa stood, and out of the corner of his eye, Sinow spotted an agent draw his gun, his hand shaking. Sinow tried to move, but his wounds were too great. Violissa started singing, her voice assured and determined. The gun went off, and in his mind, he knew it would do no damage, but he instinctively lunged, Ren holding him back as the female agent jumped in front of the bullet's path. It all happened quickly, but in Sinow's eyes, he watched as it played out in slow motion, the bullet ripping into the woman's flesh then making its way through, hitting not Violissa but a prism of colors that had wrapped around her.

"She's weaving," Ren said, as if it were nothing unusual.

"Weaving," he stuttered, his mind moving past the scene

of the agents gathering around the wounded woman. Moving to what he knew of weaving, the magic of the Elvin. No one weaved anymore, not since the last Elvin, but Violissa was special, and she was Elvin. The colors seemed to drift from the violin, a spectrum of hues that dazzled the mind.

Ren pulled away. "You're going to have to bear it a few minutes on your own."

"Why?"

"I need to call my Light queen. She needs to heal you."

He stepped away, and Sinow grunted, taking on his own weight, teetering until he caught himself. The pain was excruciating, and his eyes grew heavier.

Violissa paused her singing, and Ren picked up. His voice, deep and filled with power, called to her, causing her to turn to him, returning his call with the answer of her voice. Back and forth, they sang all the while a blue aura of magic grew around her. They sang a final verse together then Ren stepped back. Violissa directed her words toward Sinow, her eyes piercing blue, meeting his. Then she pushed her Light magic to him. He felt it wash over him, seeping into his skin, tingling through his body, working its magic on his injuries. She was healing him. The blue filtered back to her, her hands drawing it away, the healing done, her eyes now changing to a deep sage, the sky above darkening with them.

"Ready?" she asked over the music as he stood taller, his healed body strong once again.

He nodded, and she drew her power, jumping into the air and landing with a force that sent the ground rolling beneath their feet, the sky opening above them. He didn't feel the movement however, his power pouring into him at that moment, knocking the breath from him. He stumbled then fell to his knees as the Darkness filled him once again, insinuating its way into his blood, his cells, every piece of him. He felt Violissa's power, the Light of it causing an instant reaction, and as his power flared, he felt the distinct familiarity of Keary's power then the new pattern of Ren's. His powers rose, and he closed his eyes, bracing himself as Violissa finished her song.

Ren watched with awe as his mother brought her full powers forth and returned his father's power, making him whole once again. He had seen her work her magic but never on this scale, never with the force she'd had now. He was still trying to contemplate how his mother, his actual mother, had been transported to this time. She was gone now, replaced with her younger self, but the essence of her lingered. It stirred a melancholy in him that the version of his mother he knew would be no longer. The woman in front of him, now an empty canvas to become the one who would take her place. It left so many questions. Would she be the same? He doubted it; too many events that had shaped her had now changed. Possibly those ahead of her as well. If she and his father returned home now at full power, they would destroy Tynan immediately, no need to hide behind the Banished Realm shield while Tynan reinforced his army.

Yet she would still love him the same, in that he had no doubt. This was his mother and would be going forward, just as the man on his knees next to him was his father. Now as he watched her standing there, waiting for his father to rise, he saw her as he had never seen her before. A queen as powerful as his father and every bit as intimidating.

His father rose, rolling his neck and clenching then unclenching his fists.

"Now that feels good," he said, his voice rich and deep. Ren could see the Darkness swirl around him. His mother shifted her stance, and Ren felt her draw her magic. She was unsure. Not certain his father was not being ruled by his power. Tension cut the air.

"Violissa."

She stood prouder, her face blank. "Sinow," she replied as Ren felt her shield herself.

His father cocked his head slightly.

"Really, Vi? I'm not sure that's the best way to great your new husband."

He took a step closer.

"I'm not sure I trust said husband."

"And have I ever done anything to cause you to doubt me?"

"Plenty."

"Ah, but that was all Tynan's doing, Violissa. Clear the cobwebs from your memory, and you will see the truth."

She faltered slightly, her magic dropping as he moved closer, slowly, step by step.

"Trust me, Vi."

Ren thought that would do it; he sensed no ill in his father's magic. It felt the same as it always did. He glanced at Keary who had freed himself from the cuffs and stood full powered, ready to help. Everyone else looked on, the woman who had been shot, now healed, his mother passing her healing magic to her during the song. Cody and Paige had backed away, Paige clearly affected as was everyone else by the Dark magic in the air. Everyone that was except Cody.

"Trust. That's always been your problem hasn't it, Violissa?" his father said, bringing Ren's attention back. "Trust. You don't trust me, you never did, you didn't trust your Council, and you don't trust yourself."

"That's enough, Sinow."

Ren couldn't tell if she was referring to his approaching proximity or his words.

"No, Vi. It's time you trusted me. What does your gut tell you?"

"I—"

"Exactly." He stopped a few feet from her. "You claim to love me, yet you need proof that I won't hurt you."

"I do love you, Sinow. I always have."

"Then trust me."

She hesitated, then lowered her power. To Ren's surprise, she dimmed it so that she was left defenseless. He was aware of their past up to now, the mistrust, the missteps taken, most caused by Tynan, so her action was unexpected. His father walked up to her, his Dark magic at full power, blanketing the two of them, surrounding her like a cape. She didn't flinch, her green eyes never leaving his, the intensity of the moment overwhelming. His father reached out and drew her close, their lips hovering for just a moment in anticipation before they finally kissed. Her power burst forth to meet his, both encasing them in a mixture of hues that turned a deep violet. The ground rumbled, and thunder boomed above them. Then the ground erupted, and Tynan burst through.

Ren tensed and threw a protective shield around the mortals closest to him. He felt Keary do the same, all of them moving far back to avoid the Darkness.

His parents were full power now; this would be their fight. His father had moved his mother to his side this time rather than behind him.

Tynan roared. "Damned Fates!" he screamed. "Always interfering!"

"That's enough, Tynan. You're done now," his father said, drawing his power.

"No, we're not," Tynan replied. He shifted to Paige, knocking Cody over and grabbing her by the throat.

"Tynan, let her go!" his mother screamed. Ren looked for an opening to attack but knew if he did anything Paige would be dead.

"Violissa, go," Paige said. "Look, the portal's still waiting. Go, tell my father—"

"Shut up!" Tynan shouted, squeezing Paige's throat tighter. Her face was filled with pain, masking the fear that had been there earlier.

Ren felt desperate to help her, his heart hammering so loud it threatened to burst. Tynan ripped the necklace from her throat, the gem now glowing a brilliant white. The portal key. He'd forgotten about it.

"You're not going anywhere without this." He threw Paige to the ground and dropped the gem, grinding it to pieces with his foot before his father's bolt of magic made it to him. The blast went straight through Tynan and hit a building that crumbled from the force.

"Looks like I get my way this time," Tynan said, fading then disappearing. The shattered gem beneath lay dormant and plain, the magic it once held now gone.

Daneele stared at the sky, the golden light of what could only be the portal reflected across the skyline, but no portal appeared in the Banished Realm. When he had sensed Violissa awaken, Daneele had ordered the signal be given, the others alerted to the occasion, the people gathering over the few days' time to witness the return of their king and queen. Now, they waited, all of them, their hearts high in hope, their nerves high in anticipation.

"Why has the sister portal not appeared?" Mackay asked.

"Keary said the Fates would direct them here with the stone. Why are they not here?"

"Perhaps, they haven't triggered the stone yet," he answered, hearing the doubt in his voice. The portal had shown outside the realm for far too long, and they all knew it.

"Something has happened," Kanine said, no one disagreeing.

Suddenly, the light in the sky faded, a sign that the portal was gone. Silence was all that could be heard as they all contemplated what it meant.

"Did he fail?" Cyric asked. "Did he not break the spell and

return without her?"

"Then he will die by Tynan's hand," Kanine answered.

A powerful force hit the barrier, pulling them all from their thoughts.

"Tynan," Daneele said as the barrier shook a second time.

"Then Sinow did not return," Cyric said, "Otherwise, Tynan would still be fighting or celebrating his victory."

"Then they both still live."

"Perhaps," Daneele answered, "but they did not return. We are left alone to fight Tynan."

The ground shook, the boundary trembling again under the attack.

"I don't believe it will be long before that fight begins," Kanine said. "Let's pray they are both still alive and that they have found each other."

"And find their way home quickly," Daneele finished, holding his breath as the fury of Tynan's attack grew. "Otherwise, they will have nothing to which to return."

Sinow watched as the color returned to Violissa's face, still holding her in his arms after his visit from the past version of his wife. Slowly, her eyes blinked as she drew in a long, calm breath.

"There you are," she said softly, her hand reaching up to touch his cheek.

He helped her stand, tipping her chin up to look in her eyes which were sparkling mysteriously.

"And where have you been?" he asked.

"Helping out an old friend," she said. "I saw you." She searched his eyes. "You were so young..."

"Unaware," he finished, knowing exactly what she wanted to say.

Her eyes looked out beyond to the changing timescape.

"Time has become more chaotic. I fear for them, Sinow. It should have settled. She has her power now."

"Then the Fates aren't satisfied yet, Vi. You know they play by their own rules."

She chewed her lip.

"Did you see Drostiren?"

She turned back to him. "Yes, I fear it will be the last time."

"Vi..." he hesitated. He knew what she thought, and he trusted her intuition. She sensed their reality fading, gone with a past that no longer held relevance. "I'm sorry," he said.

Her eyes darkened slightly. "I know. We both made choices, Sinow."

He took her hand, tracing her union scar. "But you were in no condition to make that choice. I forced it upon you. I should have—"

"Shhh." She brought her finger to his mouth, silencing him, tears shining within her eyes.

"It was what we both needed at the time, Sinow. I needed your strength in that moment, and that is what you gave me. It's what you've always given me."

"Is it, Vi? Have I been strong, or have I let my fear rule us, my insistence on burying the past divide us?"

She smiled then, leaning into him, kissed him. "There is nothing that can ever divide us. And your fear did not rule us, it only cloaked us, a burden carried by both of us enabled by our choice that day."

He pulled her close, nestling his face into her hair.

"The past is changing, Sinow. Perhaps it will erase our choice, erase the events that changed us both. Perhaps we will now live with the freedom in our hearts that we lost that day." She looked up at him. "I love you, Sinow. My love for you has only grown with each passing century."

Her eyes flickered to look beyond his shoulder then beyond his sight to something only she could see.

"The past is undone."

A crack filled the air like ice breaking, and he saw what she saw as the ribbons of time grew, swirling around them, closing in on them.

This was it, the end for them.

"And a beginning," she said.

In that moment, there was nothing but her, the fear that had taken shelter in his heart for so long chased away with the reality that the day had finally come. The man and the Dark king within finally at peace that there would no longer be a reason to fear. As the ribbons drew closer, he held her tight, never looking from her eyes.

"I love you, Violissa."

"And I love you, Sinow."

He felt the pull as his existence unraveled, the past claiming them both. There was no pain as their bodies turned to a sparkling dust that blended with the threads of color. Finally, after all time was erased, the ribbons faded, the land lie still once again, empty and awaiting its future. A slight shimmer of silver dust settled on the grass then, picked up by a soft breeze, scattered to the winds beyond.

Twenty

No one moved, all eyes fixed on the shattered gem, knowing what it meant, knowing they had no way home. No way to open the portal. Ren's eyes moved from the stone to where he knew the portal should still be. It had been there, brightly calling them the entire time, but now all that remained were the shimmering particles dispersed in the air, drifting away like specks of dust.

Ren didn't know what to do, too much had happened, the emotion of it all settling in. There was a new emptiness that had made its way to his heart, and he didn't have to question what it was. The parents he knew and loved were gone, the events changed so that the future was now empty, waiting to be reshaped. Everyone he knew, everything that made up his life now gone.

"Please tell me that wasn't our way home," his father said.

His mother who had walked to the fractured gem, dropped

to her knees in front of it.

"Yes, it was," she answered. "I felt the Fates' magic break when Tynan destroyed it."

Paige crawled over to her.

"It was our connection to the portal, and without it, the portal—"

"Is gone," Keary finished for her, his eyes following where Ren's had been.

"I'm so sorry," Paige whispered.

"It's not your fault, Paige," his father said, surprising him. Ren had expected those words from his mother. She remained silent, staring down at the gem, her eyes a misty green.

"That's enough. We need to talk now." Ren heard from behind him. He didn't bother to look, his father's expression said everything, and Ren was thankful his eyes stayed fixed on his mother, or the man would have died.

"Leave them be, Ethan," someone said then more voices filled the silence, all demanding they be left alone. Ren let the voices go so they became a distant buzz in the background. Somehow, he knew the five of them would be left in peace. His mother moved, her hand coming forth gently with a subtle slight of magic that brought the shattered pieces in the air before her.

"Can you fix it, Vi?" his father asked, hope deep in his voice.

"No. There is no magic left to it. The Fates' gift is gone, and I don't know how to bring it back."

She moved her hand, and the air around the fragments stirred. In her other hand appeared a small oval container. She guided the pieces until they gently landed in the container then she moved her hand over it, enclosing it with a matching lid. With one last movement, she made a chain for it. Finished, she lifted the locket, a shimmering green of her magic making its way down the chain, weaving through each section until it reached the locket. There it stayed, enveloping the locket, enchanting it.

She reached over and took Paige's hand, opening it then placing the locket in it.

"My queen?"

"Shhh," she said softly. She closed her hand around Paige's. "You have been my Keeper all these years. Filling in where your father could not reach. You will remain my Keeper until we return. The Fates chose you to carry this and so you shall."

"But I failed," Paige said, tears in her eyes.

"No, Paige. You did exactly as you were meant to." She turned and looked at Ren.

"We made it home the first time, didn't we?"

He gave a slight smile, and she turned back to Paige, brushing her hair back. "The Fates do not make mistakes, Paige. We are here for a reason this time."

"What do we do now?" Paige asked.

"We find a way home." His mother rose, leaning down to kiss Paige on the head. Ren caught a glimpse of his father's surprised face, surprise mixed with an element of admiration before she walked over to Ren.

She stood before him, and all he wanted in that moment was for her to take him in her arms like she'd done countless times when he was a child.

As if sensing his thoughts, her eyes grew sad. She took him in, her fingers reaching up to trace the details of his face. "He looks so much like you, Sinow," her eyes filled with love, and she smiled, "but your eyes—"

"I know," he replied, dropping his eyes. "They're not green."

She laughed, picking his chin up so that his eyes met hers.

"You have your grandfather's eyes."

Surprised, he said, "But you haven't met him yet."

She looked at him curiously then he realized he'd said yet.

"No, but I must have stared at his picture countless times wondering what he was like. After I discovered my heritage, I couldn't help but wonder about him when before he'd only been another king on the wall. His eyes were the fullest, the richest of the entire line. Like there was a story there that needed to be told. You have that twinkling his eyes carried as if to say life held so much more."

Ren looked down again, not certain what to say.

"We will get you home to them."

"They're gone."

"What?" his father asked.

"The gem, the portal," his mother answered for him.

"When it shattered, I felt them. I don't know how but I felt them pull away. She said I wouldn't be going back to them. She knew. Tynan has taken us too far from the path, and the future is now being rewritten," Ren said, meeting his father's eyes. His father ran his hands through his hair.

"We will get you home, and when we do, we will be on the other side, Ren."

"If the future is being rewritten, then why is Ren still here? And why isn't his memory changing?" Paige asked.

"Because the Fates aren't done with him, and they want him to remember," his mother answered.

Her eyes sparkled with hope, and her smile eased the pain in his heart. She raised herself on her tiptoes and kissed his forehead just as his version of her had done only minutes before. He took a deep breath, taking in the lilac scent that she'd always had and knowing that she was right. They were still alive in this time, and when he returned home, they would be there waiting for him. Their memories, their paths different this time, he hoped better this time, but they were still his parents.

She turned and walked over to his father.

"We need to find a way home," Keary said. "And standing here won't help."

"Then you need to go someplace to think it through," Cody said coming up to them. "Everyone!" he shouted. "We need to get these guys home. We can't help them by standing here. Let's do what we always do in times like this."

A murmur grew as people started shouting out what they

could bring, Chelsea telling everyone to meet at the bar. The crowd started thinning, it had moved well back once his father's power had returned, and thankfully, he had kept it at bay, avoiding eye contact.

"I think now's a good time for an explanation," the female agent said, approaching them.

Ren turned to see her shiver in fear as his father drew his attention to her. Her pulse raced as did everyone's behind her. Ren could sense it along with the urge to scream. He had also felt the permission his father granted lingering in the air.

"I'll talk to them," his mother said, coaxing his attention back to her. Ren felt the relief that flooded them all, as her calming spell settled on them.

"And I'll teach you how to dim your powers," Ren said to his father.

"Dim my powers? Why would I ever do that?" He looked at Keary who shrugged.

"Do I do that?" he asked Ren.

"You don't stay married to my mother unless you do. You would have killed half the population by now."

"I'm confused," Keary said.

"Let's just say you spend quite a bit of time in the villages."

"I do? Why would I do that? I'm a Dark king."

Ren sighed. "Because my mother does and, well, you never leave her side. Now let's dim those powers."

Sinow listened as Ren described how to quell his powers, but his mind was still on Ren's prior words.

You never leave her side. That's what Ren had said. There was something more to it, something in his voice, a weariness that spoke of his father's overprotective tendencies and his mother's resolve to allow them. What awaited them? What more did the Fates have in store for them?

He glanced over at Violissa, the woman for whom he'd given up everything, whom he had chased life after life, the woman for whom he would do it all again without hesitation. The thought of anything more happening to her terrified him. He watched as she spoke to the agents, her face stern but soft, her voice forceful yet gentle, she was a juxtaposition of everything that made her who she was. She was powerful enough to hold her own, yet delicate in so many ways. Had he overlooked her strength in Ren's timeline? Forgotten the two sides co-existed within her just as her powers did? Had fear truly taken the ability to see her true nature away?

"Sinow?" Keary asked. "Are you paying any attention?"

He dimmed his power just as Ren had instructed, and ignoring Keary, walked over to Violissa. To his wife. The woman he had fought for with all he'd had.

The agents paused and stepped back, Violissa turning to greet him with a smile. He'd forgotten how breathtaking she was when she smiled. His eyes never left hers as he came upon her and brushing her golden lock aside kissed her, pulling her into his arms. As she gave herself to him, he didn't care that the agents were there, that others could see their private moment. They'd waited too long for it, nearly lost it. They deserved their moment before the reality of their situation pulled them back, splitting them once again. Their future had been riven by Tynan's actions; he wouldn't allow the same to happen to their moment of happiness.

Violissa pulled her lips from his slowly as if savoring the kiss, then looked at him, searching his eyes. She brought her hand up from his chest where it lay and touched his lips, then brought her fingers up to trace his jawline.

"A moment," she said, reading the reason behind the unexpected kiss.

"Aye," he answered. "One for which I've waited lifetimes."

She smiled. "The first in a lifetime of moments." She paused, her smile fading. "I've missed you," she whispered.

He pulled her in, kissing her once again until he heard Keary teasing Ren. "And that doesn't bother you?"

"No," he answered, laughing. "I'm used to it."

Sinow dropped his head to lean against hers.

"What are we going to do?" she asked softly.

"What we always do. We find a way."

"A way home."

He kissed her head. "Yes, home."

She looked over at Ren. "You knew, didn't you?"

"I did, it's hard not to notice."

"He really does look like you. Fates, Sinow, that's our son." She brought her eyes back to his. "Ours. He's what we've both been fighting for."

And will continue to fight for, he wanted to answer but instead he took her hand and ran his finger along her fresh union scar. Jagged and rough, it was prominent, a visual sign of their love, the only scars either would ever carry. *Physical scars,* he corrected himself, thinking back on Ren's words again.

"Let's go find a way to get us all back home," he said, his mind too overwhelmed with the reality of it all to find the right words.

The next few hours were spent going through everything they could. Ren told them as much as he would offer, refusing many details on the grounds that they still could happen. Keary and Paige filled Violissa in on what had happened since she'd been sent to this realm, Sinow listening as they elaborated on pieces for which there had not been time earlier. All the while people filtered into the bar, bringing food and company to the quiet space, filling it with sounds to which he'd been familiar as Simon but not so as a Dark king, and he wondered how long it had taken his future self to grow accustomed to this kind of life.

"So, there's still something I don't understand," Paige said.

"Go ahead," Ren said, encouraging her, his voice holding a tone that gave Sinow pause until her question pulled his attention back.

"If Tynan could come back here in time, why not do it alone? Why not just come back and kill one of you while you were powerless? Why take the chance of bringing Ren?"

"He needed my blood to access the portal," Ren answered.

"But he had it. Why not just come back by himself?"

"Because that was too easy," Sinow answered. "And Dark kings," he cringed at the word in reference to Tynan, "we don't do things easy."

"I don't understand."

"Brining Ren would have yielded the maximum reward. He came here with the intention of killing Violissa, which would have crushed me, but killing her and having Ren die as a result...having me watch as he killed not only the woman I love, but the son we would have had, well that would have destroyed me."

Paige stared at him. "That's horrible."

"To a Dark king who is lost in madness. that is pleasure."

Paige was left speechless, her hands trembling. "Is that who you are?" she asked, standing.

"No, Paige. Don't judge me by my brother's actions."

"But you said that's pleasure. How? How could anyone take pleasure from that?"

She rose and walked away, leaving the bar. Only then did Sinow notice the room had grown quiet.

"I'd better go talk to her," Violissa said, her voice sad.

"No, let me," Ren said, standing. "I think I know a way to make it better."

He went after her, and they all stayed silent for a moment until Violissa said, "I want to hear what he tells her."

"Why? What difference does it make, Vi? She doesn't have

to like my powers. She has to fear them, they all do."

She chewed her bottom lip and looked at him. "I had forgotten that. I suppose this will take some getting used to?"

He couldn't help but smile; she looked so innocent in that moment. "I suppose."

"Still," she said hesitantly, looking back over to where Ren and Paige had walked out. "I feel like we need to see this."

She began to leave.

"Any reason, Vi?"

"Call it instinct," she answered and walked on through the doors that led behind the bar.

Sinow looked at Keary. "Instinct? And I'm supposed to take that as an answer?"

"I believe it's something you'll have to take as it is. From what I hear, your new queen does quite a bit on instinct."

"Instinct?" he said again, rising to follow her. "I don't do anything on instinct."

"Should make for an interesting marriage," Keary joked, catching up to him.

"Yes, it should."

They walked out, and he stood by Violissa who was looking on as Ren spoke to Paige.

"You've only seen one side of Dark magic, Paige," he was saying.

"And it's a terrible side. Why would the Fates even give Dark power if all it causes is pain and destruction?" she asked, her arms crossed.

"As my father said, you can't judge us all by Tynan's actions."

It was strange hearing himself referred to as a father, something to which he supposed he'd have to adjust.

"You see, the Fates blessed our world with these powers because they work in wonderful ways when yielded by rulers such as my parents. There are many facets to each power that you don't see."

He moved out from her side and raised his hands. "There

is a reason the Fates blessed the immortals with these specific powers, Paige, and you need to look at them differently to fully appreciate them."

"I don't know, Ren. Violissa's powers are so gentle. The Lightbearers are healers. There is no fear there, they cause no pain, they take it away."

Ren looked over at her and smiled. "I don't believe you've ever seen my mother angry."

Sinow snickered, and Violissa elbowed him.

"Watch," Ren said, moving his hands in the air. A wave of Light magic covered the sky in a blue mist that took form as he spoke. "My mother's magic is gentle, peaceful. It heals the soul and the body, calms the spirit. It is soft and delicate to the mortal eye."

The mist darkened to a deep blue. "But what you don't see is the force behind it, the strength it holds. To heal the body is to force it to go against its will, to coerce the cells to repair, to extract a poison or a virus, kill a disease, all of it influenced by the same drive that is found in Dark magic. Light power is life or death. If a healer is too fast, too reckless, the body will be traumatized, and the mortal will die."

He moved his hand, the arcane of his Light magic remaining in the sky before them, now a bright cerulean, the color of his eyes.

"My father's power," he said, a wave of Dark magic, red and black filling the sky next to the Light, "is not so discreet. It is violent, hard, cold some might say. It is terrifying to the mortal eye as it should be. Dark power at its essence is law, it is death, where Light defies law yet gives life. The two seem quite opposite, yet underneath, the Dark is a beauty that goes unappreciated."

The red mist brightened, wrapping around the night sky.

"It is protection, it is lifesaving. Dark kings, true Dark kings use their powers for their people."

Within the red hue formed the shape of a child and mother.

The red encased the shapes as the black mist surrounded it.

"The code that drives my father is the same as it was for the first in our line. Protect and defend. Kill only in that instance."

He moved his hand, and the mist drew back, the figures disappearing as the Dark magic danced with the Light magic, the two lighting up the night.

"My parents are different yet not so different, the two things that have always driven them is their love and their need to help their people."

The colors merged.

"Now, you throw in a bit of my mother's Elvin," a green mist of nature magic bled into the colors, the world around them sparkling with life as it answered his nature call, "and you get something truly incredible."

The three powers blended, a magnificent purple hue filling the sky. Everything around them seeming to soak it in. The stars sparkled lilac, the moon a deep violet.

Sinow released the breath he'd been holding.

"It's beautiful," Paige said, lifting her hand toward the sky.

Violissa squeezed his hand, and he looked over to see the tears in her eyes.

"There is a reason the Fates brought my parents together, Paige. The magic of our world needs balance, it always has. My parents are the balance." There was a tone of appreciation, and something else underlying it, something close to reverence. Sinow wondered what lie behind it.

"I'm sorry," Paige said softly. "My father always taught me that there was more to Dark power than we saw from Tynan, but...well, it's never been so close before now. I misjudged," she said turning to Sinow, "and I will never do so again."

"Paige, my power is to be feared and respected for what it is. It is not pretty, not flowers and rainbows."

He felt Violissa tense next to him.

"Sorry, Vi. I mean that in a good way. But you are right to fear it."

"Fear but not hate. Ren is right. All of the magic the Fates gave our world serves a purpose." She began walking toward the door. "Now, we should get back to finding a way home so that purpose can be restored."

Ren lingered for a moment, looking down at his hands before following her inside.

"He doesn't understand his powers yet," Violissa said, walking out to where Ren's magic lingered in the air.

He followed her, taking in her beauty as the violet remnants of the magic sparkled in her hair and eyes. He opened himself to Ren's magic, feeling the patterns of it, the strengths and subtle weaknesses.

"He doesn't understand his Dark power," he said, feeling the hesitation in it.

She gave him a puzzled look. "How do you know that?"

He moved behind her and picked up her hand then moved it through the violet. "The patterns don't carry the same strength. Do you feel it? The Light outweighs the Dark."

She moved her fingertips, the sparkles shimmering on her skin, and it was in that moment that he realized how close he was to her.

"I feel it. The nature side is as strong as the Dark."

"And nature is the weakest magic."

She glanced at him, her eyebrow raised.

"Don't give me that look," he said, laughing. "You know as well as I that it's a minor power. That's why the Elvin died out."

"The Elvin died out because your grandfather annihilated them."

He sighed. "Touché," he said, leaning against her. "The errors of my ancestors that I can't seem to shake."

She turned to face him, a maneuver that placed her in his arms. His heart quickened. "You are nothing like your grandfather, Sinow."

He smiled. "Perhaps not, but I still carry the burdens of the past, the consequences of the many men in my line who were not so lucky and lost themselves completely to the call of the power."

"Burdens of the past," she muttered, looking around at the barely visible specks of Ren's earlier demonstration, putting her hand out so that a few could settle in it. Looking back up, she met his eyes.

"Ren is the key," she said.

"To what?"

"To us." Her voice was filled with awe. "He is the reason for all of it. He is what we've been fighting for. He is where our path leads, the end of everything that defines us, the final piece of our prophecy. The end of it."

He searched her eyes, not sure he was following.

"The Fates joined us so that he could be born, Sinow. I've always thought it was us, that our union would be the merging of our powers, the balance the Fates desired with our prophecy."

"Ren holds all three powers, the balance isn't with our union, it's inside of him," he said, feeling the same wonder as shown on her face.

"He is where our path leads, the reason for everything we've gone through."

"And everything that lies ahead of us," he answered, "but that doesn't diminish what we have, Violissa."

"No, no it doesn't." Her eyes shone a bright emerald in the moonlight, and he lost himself in them. It felt so comfortable with her, as if they were old lovers who had already spent eternity together. He'd almost forgotten that he had only just found her again, that they'd only had their second kiss, that he'd never truly made love to her, only doing so through someone else's memories or through the Fates' manipulation.

As if thinking the same thing, her expression changed, and he saw the desire flash in her eyes, their color deepening, his own body reacting in response. He pulled her in, relishing the feel of her against him and kissed her, the previous conversation fading as he lost himself to her.

Violissa let herself go, her need for Sinow too great, the feel of his lips on hers, his body pressed against her, reminding her of why she had continued to fight against the curse that had torn her from him. All else faded away, and it was only the two of them. As his hands explored her body and hers made their way to his, she left the present and the future behind, content in this moment. She felt greedy as her kisses became more demanding, matching the need in his. Two thousand years of longing and finally they had found their beginning, their destiny, each other.

He drew back, breathless, but she pushed forward biting at his lip, drawing him back to her.

"Vi," he said between kisses. "Vi, we need to stop."

She paused, catching her breath, her heart pounding uncontrollably. His eyes were filled with need the same that was now coursing through her, so she didn't understand why he had stopped. Reaching her hand out from under his shirt, reveling in the feel of his muscles as she passed over them, she reached up and pulled him down, kissing him again.

He groaned and pulled her in tighter, his hands caressing her skin. Then he dropped his head, "Vi we need to stop. There's too much—"

"No, there's not, Sinow. There's only us."

He looked back up at her, drawing his hand along her cheek then along her loose curl.

"There's not only us. I wish there was, but there's more. There's home. There's Keary and Paige. Tynan is still loose. And then there is our son."

"Our son," she repeated, relaxing, her desire extinguished with his words. "We have a son."

"Amazingly. I wish I could remember conceiving him," he

said, winking.

"Or all the times before that one?" she asked, playfully dancing her fingers up his chest.

"Those, too," he said, laughing. "But for now, we need to wait."

She sighed. "Finding our way home comes first."

"Yes, and getting Ren back to our future, back to his destiny."

She chewed her lip. "How are we going to do that, Sinow?"

"I don't know, Vi, but we need to find a way soon. The longer we're here, the more our future changes."

"And the more vulnerable our Councils are."

"Yes. And the more at risk all of these people become."

She wondered what he meant, and he must have seen it in her eyes.

Laughing, he said, "If I don't get someplace where I can stop dimming my powers soon, I'm going to explode." He rolled his neck. "How do I do this all the time in our future?"

She could sense the strain it was causing him, could tell he wasn't comfortable. "That bad, huh?"

"It's like wearing shackles."

She cringed. "It is strange seeing your power dimmed." She traced her fingers over his chest seductively. "I kinda like the full powered Dark king."

"Do you now?" he said playfully, his power heightening.

A chill danced along her spine mixed with a flitter of butterflies in her stomach.

"We need to get home fast," he said, running his hands through her hair then moving a step closer so that his body was pressed against hers again. Her breath caught.

"One, two, three," he said, her heart picking up its beat again as he reached three. "Each time. I hope that never changes."

"I can't imagine it ever will," she answered, losing herself in his ebony eyes. She thought of his future self, the one who had looked at her the same way. "No, I'm sure it won't."

"And you're certain about that?"

"As certain as I am that your breath will always catch when our eyes meet."

He leaned in and kissed her again, the lust behind it changed to emotion, filled with the love he had carried for her all these lifetimes.

"Ahem," she heard Keary behind them.

Sinow pulled his mouth from hers and dropped his head, groaning.

"You'd think I'd be used to this after the whole Simon, Violet chaperone thing."

"Tell me you interrupted us because you've found a way home," Sinow muttered.

"And if I don't, is there punishment involved?" Keary asked.

"I've missed punishing you, so yes."

"Well damn, now I'm not so sure about having offered to come out here. It seemed the obvious choice at the time. Paige is in stress mode, and Ren, well it's just weird to separate your parents while they're locking lips. Wow, that still sounds weird."

"I'm guessing you haven't found a solution to our dilemma then?" Sinow said, his eyes never leaving Violissa's, his lips forming a coy smile. His relationship with Keary was unique; she sensed that it wasn't normal for a Dark king and his Council to be on such comfortable terms.

"You guessed right. It might help if our two rulers, current rulers, were involved."

"Doubtful," Sinow said. "But we'll come back anyway."

"Good, I'll just meet you inside."

Sinow rolled his neck and winked at her.

"I'll have to think on that punishment. Find something suitable."

"You're out of practice," Keary joked but stopped mid-track, sensing the rise in Dark power from Sinow. Keary's hands were gripped tight, and Violissa noticed a quiver in his legs. Sinow walked over to him, the air growing heavier, Violissa's own powers rising in response. Keary collapsed to his knees, and Sinow leaned down, whispering, "You're out of practice, Keary," before releasing him.

Violissa's powers calmed, but she didn't move. Sinow glanced up at her, his black eyes endless, then he turned and entered the building. She hoped for the sake of those inside that he quelled his powers before he met anyone in passing.

Keary rose, stretching his back out. "Damn, I haven't missed that," he said, glancing over at her. "You'll get used to it, Violissa. He's a bit moody at times. That was nothing compared to what it could have been." He went inside, leaving her to wonder just what else she'd have to adjust to now that she'd married a Dark king.

Everyone had moved to Keary's office by the time Violissa returned. She sat down on the couch next to Sinow, noting the Darkness had diminished.

"We thought it best to get away from everyone," Paige said, reading her mind. "You know this town, Violissa. Everyone comes together in times of crisis, and they know we're having one of those times. The bar is packed now."

Sinow ran his hands through his hair, and out of the corner of her eye, she spotted Ren doing the same. How alike they were. She couldn't help but smile.

"So, the stone holds no magic, the portal is gone, and Ren says you can only create a portal once you've passed through to this world and back again. Did I leave anything out?" Sinow said.

"Where was the portal centered, Ren?" she asked.

"Over the lake."

"Maybe we should have a look there, see if there's any sign left of it."

"The lake," Sinow said distantly. "That's where Tynan emerged, isn't it, Ren? The day the divot appeared, the day the water turned black. He emerged there." He stood up. "Didn't he, Ren?"

"Yes, the ground was riven with his escape just as your future now is."

"His escape?" Violissa asked. "He was imprisoned here. Why?"

Ren looked at her, and in that moment, she knew there was more that she would endure, knew from the sadness that filled his blue eyes as the tide fills an empty beach, that her path would remain painful and heartbreaking and that Tynan was somehow involved.

"I didn't kill him," Sinow said. "I punished him. Death is too good, too easy for the worst criminals."

A knock interrupted the heavy silence that had saturated the room. Chelsea peeked in. "I hate to interrupt, but those agents are here demanding to see the two of you."

"Tell them we can't talk," Sinow said.

"Ah, yeah, no that won't work. Cody's been trying to get them to leave for the past twenty minutes, and they're not budging."

"Dammit, we don't have time for this," Sinow complained.

Violissa placed her hand on his. "I'll go talk to them. It's better that way, perhaps even safer."

"She's right," Keary added in agreement.

She didn't wait for Sinow's response, following Chelsea out of the office instead. The further away she moved from Sinow's presence, the more the emptiness filled her, a longing that only he could fill. It was strange, she'd never felt it so strong before. Glancing down at the fresh union scar that now lie on her palm, she wondered if the union had anything to do with the strength of the sensation.

She put the thought aside as she approached the agents. It was then that it occurred to her that Tynan's prison break had been the impetus for their presence. Had they existed in her past life or were they new like Cody. She stopped short of reaching them. It hadn't occurred to her, but Cody was new. In no other life had a sibling existed. Rulers didn't have siblings so why would that change here? Cody was new but why? Had the Fates planned him? Had they known this would happen? Of course, they had, Ren was here.

Before she could think on it more, she heard, "Violet?"

She refocused, seeing the two agents, a male and a female standing in front of her. The man's arms were crossed, his eyes surveying her. She'd seen them both around town but had never interacted with either until today.

"Where's your boyfriend?" he asked.

"Her husband is right here," she heard Sinow behind her. She'd been so distracted with her thoughts she hadn't even noticed him.

You looked like you needed help, he said in enaigne, his voice like dark silk in her conscious. It was the first time they'd used enaigne since they'd been trapped here, and it felt good.

That feels nice, I've missed your voice in my mind, but are you sure you're not here just because you didn't want to be left out?

Maybe, but I'll never admit it, he returned playfully.

On the surface, he looked terrifying, his broad shoulders squared, arms crossed like the agent's, his eyes intensely on the edge of his power.

"Well then both of you can talk to us. We need to take you both in for questioning," the man said, a slight shake to his voice.

Violissa tried to place his name, but she wasn't certain she'd ever heard it. The two had shown up right after the quake she now knew had been Tynan. They'd then called backup, the place had been swarming with agents since, the area around the lake taped off while the team studied the unnatural events as she'd heard someone call them. They'd been shutting their investigation down or so she'd thought but around the time

Ren arrived, that had changed.

"I'm sorry but who are you exactly? I don't believe we've met," Sinow said, trying to maintain his human persona.

The female spoke up first, "I'm agent Abigail Lawson and this is my partner, Ethan Sanders. We're in charge of the investigation here, and the two of you are now at the center of it."

"There are too many questions here, and you both have the answers. Now, we're taking you both in," Ethan said, reaching out and grabbing Violissa's wrist. She felt the rise in power from Sinow before she saw it. The room darkened, and the agent backed up, dropping her arm. Fear filled the room.

"Touch her again, and you'll pray for a quick death," Sinow gritted. Violissa could feel him struggling to retain control.

Both agents had dropped their eyes, neither likely knowing instinctual fear had triggered the reaction.

"Are you threatening me, Mr. Black?" Ethan said, trying to force his eyes up. She wondered why he couldn't but then sensed the second layer of magic in the air. Ren. He was controlling them, knowing Sinow could easily kill. Violissa had heard the stories, the power of a Dark king's eyes, the ability to kill in seconds, but she'd never seen it. She swallowed, her heart pounding from the tension in the room, her Light power reacting to Sinow's.

Glancing back, she met Ren's eyes, they were a deep brown, the cusp of black. His Dark powers triggered with Sinow's rise. Keary stood further back toward the office, but she could see he was having trouble, his own powers answering his king's. She needed to de-escalate the situation and fast. She sent a calming spell out as Sinow answered the agent.

"I don't threaten."

Sinow, she said in enaigne, increasing her calming spell.

He turned to her, his eyes black with power.

These are not our people. They do not know our ways. If you hurt one, you will be hurting an innocent.

She knew their code, had never believed it based on his

grandfather's behaviors, so she was hoping she'd been wrong, praying what she'd been taught was true, that Dark kings and the Darkbearers had a code they strictly followed. The air lightened as the black in his eyes began to fade, the tension leaving the room. She heard the collective exhale as everyone began to breathe again.

"Who are you?" the female agent asked.

"Your worst nightmare," he answered, his eyes never leaving Violissa's. "If you touch her again, I will ensure you understand the true meaning of those words. You have been warned. I suggest you heed my warning or forfeit your life."

He walked away not waiting for a response. The two agents brought their heads up, finally released from Ren's spell.

"He threatened an officer. That's—"

"Ethan, leave it. I don't think he plays by our rules, does he, Violet?"

Violissa, Sinow called her in enaigne. It had the tone of a command, which irked her a little.

She turned back to the agents.

"You are correct. Don't push him. My husband is the law in our world."

"Will you tell us why you're here?" she asked. Violissa sensed no ill intent from her question.

"Perhaps. But we need time. This isn't the way things were supposed to happen." Or perhaps it was, she thought, her mind moving to Ren.

"We don't sit around and wait—"

"But we will this time, Ethan."

He stared at her and looked like he was going to say something but stopped before storming off.

"Looks like we both have volatile partners," she said to Violissa.

"And that's never a good thing."

"Look, I can hold him off a few more days, but then we need to get some answers. I have to report back to my superiors, and if I don't, they'll send someone else who hasn't witnessed the amazing events that took place today or been miraculously healed by some magical being."

"You took that bullet for me, Abigail. You didn't know what was going on or who we were, but you jumped in front anyway. You held him back when I needed the time to save my husband then you stopped his bullet.

"Foolishly, I might add, since it wouldn't have been more than a pin prick to me, but you still did it. You deserved to be healed, and your injury was only due to our being here."

"You're immune to bullets? Like superhuman?"

Violissa laughed. "No, it would have hit me and injured me for a brief second. I'm immortal not bulletproof," she said, winking. "I'll try to convince Sinow to answer your questions, but I can't make any promises," she continued as she walked away, leaving Abigail with wide eyes and hearing her say, "Who's Sinow?"

Watching his father, Ren could sense he needed to step in before someone was hurt. He felt the ire in the air the moment the agent grabbed his mother's hand. He sent a spell to force the two agents to look down, accidently sweeping the room with it.

"Ren?" Keary asked, feeling it. Ren gestured toward his parents.

"Ah."

He felt his mother's calming spell fill the room and relaxed. She knew, even this early in their relationship she understood how his father worked. The air lightened and shortly after, his father walked back to them. There was a slight pause in his step, and Ren wondered if he were speaking with his mother in enaigne. Whatever he'd said to her, she hadn't listened, remaining with the agents. Irritation flashed on his face. Ren laughed, his father eyeing him.

"You'll get used to it. She doesn't like being commanded to do anything."

His father didn't reply.

"What's going on over there?" Keary asked.

"They want to question us about what happened. I don't plan to be here long enough for that to happen."

His mother returned a few minutes later, and Ren could see the slight annoyance that remained in her demeanor.

"Sinow," she said quietly, approaching his father, "we're different, in every way, from our magic to our temperaments. We'll have to adjust, to get accustomed to one another, and it will take time. Don't command me, I promise you I won't obey. But if you let me go, be who I am, follow my instinct, I will always be by your side."

Out of curiosity, Ren watched his father's reaction. This was a side of his mother that was new. She was independent in many ways, but she'd always reminded him of a free spirit who had been bound, bound by prophecy and a man who loved her too much, too close to see that he was crushing her and that she was allowing him. Now here they were, two people unbound by the constraints of a path that had warped what would have been, and in his future had stolen a piece of both their spirits. Ren knew what his father would have said, knew his mother would never have bothered saying what she had. His father, too lost in her to notice Ren's voyeuristic moment, reached his hand up and let his finger linger on her loose curl. It was a move Ren had seen him do hundreds of times, but there was something different, something lighter to the way he did it now.

"I suppose I should apologize...but I'm as new at this as you are, Vi. I shouldn't have expected you to follow me. I have to remember that you're not Council, you're not mine to control. You're another ruler with her own ways, her own abilities, and a mind that works differently than mine." He sighed. "This is going to be hard, isn't it?"

She laughed and leaned up to kiss him. Ren looked away. So, this had been what they were like before he was born. Or, maybe it wasn't, maybe this was a result of the event change. He didn't know much of what had happened after their return to their world. He only knew that his mother had been powerless, and they'd been forced to wait until her powers returned before they could move forward, another event that likely would have shaped them. He could only imagine his father's angst at her vulnerability.

"Time is changing them," he muttered. "Changing their relationship to what it should have been."

"Before what?" Keary asked, startling Ren from his thoughts.

Ren looked at him, not sure what to say.

"You said it's changing them to what should have been. What happened to take them from this in the first place?" Keary crossed his arms, and Paige peeked her head around, waiting for his answer.

"Hey, have you guys figured anything out yet?" Cody asked, coming up behind Ren at just the right moment.

"No, although we've been sidetracked for a bit," Ren answered quickly as Keary glared at him. He wasn't sure he could keep the story from Keary much longer, especially with time changing as it was.

"We haven't gotten anywhere," his mother said, coming over to them, her hand in his father's.

"I don't get why it's so hard. Can't you just leave the same way you came here?" Cody asked.

"Trying to get rid of me already, Cody?" his mother joked.

"Not you, Violet, but maybe the big guy there. Ever since he got here, it's been nothing but hands all over you. Big brothers don't like that stuff," he joked, winking at her.

"Funny," his father replied.

"I could take you if it came down to it. You know that, right?" Cody said, moving around like he was fighting.

His father's eyes blackened, and Paige let out a whimper, moving behind Keary. She had implicit permission to be in his presence, but even then, the change in power level would be painful to her. Cody, however, didn't flinch. He stopped bouncing and put his hand on his hips, oblivious to the curiosity of every one of them.

"Is that it? Your eyes change. That's what makes you so terrifying?"

His father studied Cody then grabbed him. "Outside now," he commanded.

Cody started to talk, but Keary interrupted. "I would go, and Violissa, I would refrain from objecting."

She looked at Ren who nodded in agreement. He had a good idea why his father wanted Cody outside. It was the safest place to test his suspicion, the same suspicion Ren had had from the beginning.

"Paige, stay here and don't let anyone come out," Keary said to her. "It won't be safe."

"But—"

"Do as he says, Paige," his mother said as Sinow dragged Cody out the back door of the bar.

Ren followed them out, his father pushing Cody into the open area where Ren had shown Paige the three powers.

"You didn't respond, Cody," his father said.

"You didn't do anything, Simon," he replied.

His father gritted his teeth, "It's not Simon."

"Sinow, what's this about?" Violissa said. "He was just playing."

"It's not that, Vi."

"Then what is it?" she asked.

"Seriously, Simon. If you want to fight it out, I'm ready," Cody said, moving his neck left then right to stretch it. "I'm usually more of a lover than a fighter, but I can still take you."

"Shut up, Cody, and stand still. I'm not going to fight you although I should teach you a lesson for daring to confront a

Dark king."

Cody stopped moving, and then Ren felt the eclipse of Darkness. His father was drawing his full power, and Ren's own reacted, clawing from within to be released. He felt Keary's respond and noticed the aura around his mother brighten in reaction.

He was testing Cody. Cody, the brother who never was, the brother who should never have existed, stood silent, arms folded, eyebrows raised in question.

"Should I be feeling something? Aside from the slight chill that just ran down my spine? Have you seen what you look like? That's crazy. Really like something out of a movie, all those black wisps and those...are those tentacles? Holy shit, you're like a walking nightmare!"

"He's not affected," his father said, ignoring Cody's admiration. "Why isn't he affected?"

He looked over at Keary who shrugged.

"And Violet, you're glowing! That's so cool!"

"You can see that Cody?" she asked.

"Yeah, all three of you have some kind of mist around you like Mr. Bad-Ass here."

"Mortals can't see our auras," she said. "Sinow?"

He quelled his powers, but Ren answered for him.

"Lightbearer. Only a Council can survive what you just experienced."

"What's a Lightbearer? I keep hearing that word, but no one ever explains."

"Are you certain?" his father asked, ignoring Cody.

"Aren't you? You had your suspicions, otherwise you wouldn't have brought him out here."

"Heart of a Lightbearer. That's what you said, Vi."

"I did?"

"When your future self came through. That's what she said."

"She saw it, too," Ren said.

"But why? Why would the Fates...what purpose would it

serve?" she asked.

"Anyone mind telling me what you're talking about?" Cody asked.

"Ren, you said the Councils are intact, right?" his father asked.

"Yes, but every minute we remain here is another change in my history. We don't know what effect our being trapped here will have, and we don't know how long we'll be here. Significant events took place after your return. If any of that is lost—"

"Everything changes," his mother finished.

"So, we can presume that's our path," his father said.

"Not necessarily. We could find a way—"

"No, Vi. He's here by the Fates' design. The only reason they would need a Lightbearer, and one here with you is if you were to lose one."

"Lose one?"

"The balance must be kept," he said, his voice serious.

"I agree with Fath...Sinow. This does not bode well." Then his mind went further. "Keary and Cody would balance the Councils if there were no one left at home."

They all turned quickly to look at him.

"What? Why would you say that, Ren?" his mother asked.

Because I know the land is dying until you heal it. Because I know what Tynan is capable of, and I know the Councils are defenseless. That's what he wanted to say, but instead, he said, "I don't know."

"You don't know, or you won't say?" Keary asked.

"There are things I can't tell you, Keary."

"But if we're stuck here—"

"If we're stuck here, then it won't matter. It will have been re-written."

"Then it will make for a good tale," his father said. "One I will need to hear."

"I'm really confused," Cody said. "I have no idea what any of this means."

"It means nothing," his mother said, walking up to him and pricking him with a needle she'd made appear.

"Ouch!"

"He's still mortal," she said, holding up the finger with the blood pooling. "And he has no magic."

"He can stand in my presence with no permission and at full power, meeting my eyes, something that would have killed any mortal in seconds. Besides, magic and immortality aren't present until a Council is called. It's normal for him to still be mortal until then. It means something that he's here, Vi."

"It means nothing right now, Sinow," she said sadly before walking away back into the bar.

"What was that?" his father asked after she left.

"She's afraid," Cody answered unexpectedly. "Whatever you think I am and for whatever reason, she's afraid of what it means. What does it mean?"

"It means everyone we love is in mortal danger," his father replied. "Running away again," he muttered.

No one said anything, their minds all contemplating what awaited them now that the Fates were re-writing their future and Ren's past.

Twenty-One

Violissa didn't want to hear anymore. She couldn't fathom what Sinow was saying. That Cody, her human brother, was a Lightbearer and that she might lose one or more of her family. She felt overwhelmed by everything that had happened since she'd freed herself from the curse. People looked at her when she re-entered the bar, why were they still here? There were too many of them. She spotted the agents in the corner watching her. All eyes were on her, their stares boring into her. She needed to get away.

"Violissa?" she heard Paige say, but she didn't turn; instead, she ran out the door and down the street, not stopping until she came to the park which caused her to halt her sprint.

There was magic here, Dark twisted magic on the surface, but underneath, she sensed her magic. She was drawn, as she always had been, to the tree. Black and twisted, a few deep ruby flowers emphasizing its dark beauty, the rest now shriveled and dead. Had they died naturally or had something else caused their early demise? She walked over the ripped police tape and rested her hand on the tree just as she had done as Violet. This time, the magic stirred her blood, she felt the pain, the tragedy that lay behind its existence. It was her pain, her trauma, all of it belonged to her. As it crashed upon her, she sank to the ground, her head leaning against the bark, all thoughts of the transformed petals gone with the tide of emotion.

"Vi," Sinow said behind her.

"This tree is mine, Sinow. My grief, my experiences shaped it. My magic gave it life. What happens to us?" she asked, her voice breaking.

"I don't know," he said sadly.

She drew her breath and raised herself from the ground. His hand brushed her hair back, and she turned to face him, stepping toward him and away from the tree. Sinow wiped a tear from her cheek.

"What was the cost of my step from the prophecy's path?"

"I wish I knew. But both of us took that step, Violissa. We both made the decision to turn our back on our destiny."

"I took the first step, Sinow."

"And I let you. We are both to blame."

"If we make it home, what faces us? If we don't—"

"Death faces us," he finished. "Either way, we lose."

She leaned her head against his chest, feeling the solidness below, the security, the safety of him. He kissed her head, and she relaxed into his arms. It felt nice, lifting away her fear, her worry, bringing her a sense of security.

"Whatever happens, we have each other, Vi. I have no doubt that we love each other through it all. And if the future is changed, we will figure it out again, together."

"Together," she repeated. "It's going to be ok."

"It is, and we will find our way home when the Fates are ready to show us the way."

She looked up at him, losing herself in the depths of his

eyes. "The Fates. We trust the Fates, just like I promised them."

"Just as we did in Ren's lifeline," he added, running his finger through her curl. "I have to say, holding you in my arms feels really good."

"It does," she said, letting the world fall away as he kissed her. Butterflies skittered through her stomach again, and she felt her body react to his touch. He pulled her in closer, his hand skimming her back then moving into her hair. Every part of her wanted him as she parted her mouth to give his tongue entrance. He tasted of magic, and it stirred her core, the tingle of it passing to her lips.

Unable to resist, she moved her hand, feeling each muscle in his back, taut and firm. His hands explored her body, the light material of her dress giving it the feel his skin was touching hers. She silently thanked her future self for choosing the Elvin style dress out of which she had neglected to change. His touch was ecstasy, and she didn't want to stop; they'd waited an eternity. She felt the vibration of his phone as a text arrived and heard him groan, but neither of them stopped. Instead, her hands moved under his shirt and up over his warm skin, the muscles of his chest tightening as she explored. Moments later, his phone buzzed again, followed by another few frantic buzzes from her own.

Frustrated, he drew back from her lips and dropped his head against hers, catching his breath.

"You'd think after a thousand years they'd leave us to ourselves."

Breathless, she replied, "You'd think, but I do believe it was you who said we needed to wait earlier."

He gave her an irritated look then reached his hand down to where her phone had vibrated in the small pocket she'd created to hold it on her hip. His fingers lingered on her hip bone, a coy smile forming on his lips as she sucked in her breath.

He looked down at the phone. "Our chaperones are looking for us to return."

"Ugh, chaperones even now."

He laughed. "I'm not sure the ugh is a sound befitting a Light queen."

"I think you'd be surprised at what I do that's unbefitting a Light queen," she said seductively, her fingers skimming his chest. He groaned, a sound that touched some instinctual part of her. She pressed her hand to his chest and leaned in, initiating the kiss this time, her phone falling to the ground as he grabbed her hips and pulled her against him, his hands moving to her bottom, feeling the curves then scooping her closer. She could feel his desire, and it urged her on. His phone vibrated again and hers moved on the ground below, but they ignored both. As their passion grew, so did the intensity of their moves and something else. She felt the Darkness wrap around her ankles and climb. It wasn't the sensual feel of Sinow's magic but something insidious. He must have felt it, too, for he stopped and pulled her back from the lake. Letting her go, he stumbled back a few more steps.

"What is it?" she asked.

"I don't know, but it's corrupt. It's unlike any Dark magic I've felt before."

"I felt it, snaking around my legs."

He looked toward the lake. "Ren knows what it is."

"But he won't tell us."

"For fear of changing a future that no longer exists," he said, walking closer to the lake. "Tynan is connected to this, all of it." He put his hand out over the water, and she watched as a mist climbed from it toward his hand. Something nudged her, something instinctual, and she threw her nature powers toward it. The mist shrank, the water bubbled as if boiling below, black and angry, whatever it held struggling to free itself from her power.

Sinow looked at her, "It's like the Torathar."

"Only different, it reacts to my nature powers where the Torathar need both Light and nature. It's ancient, and it's not whole, Sinow." She increased her power, and the water stirred, the mist evaporating, leaving only clear water below. "That was only a trace of what was originally here."

"Your nature magic destroyed it without the Light? What is it?"

"I don't know, but did you see how it reacted when you drew close to it?" she asked.

"Yes, the Torathar fed from my power, harvesting strength from it. This was different, the other way, as if it were seeking my power out, not to feed from it but instead to feed me, to darken my magic."

"I wish I knew what all of this meant."

Running his hand through his hair, he replied, "So do I."

She was taken aback for a minute. She had forgotten how beautiful he was, a dark god, and he was hers, her husband, her mate.

He raised his eyebrow. "And where did your mind wander to, Vi?"

"Remembering how handsome you are."

"Did you forget?" he asked teasingly. "Because I never forgot how beautiful you were."

She blushed.

"That sounded really corny, didn't it?" he asked, giving her a sheepish grin. Was there any part of him she didn't love?

"I still love you, corny lines and all," she said, moving into his arms. His phone went off again and she sighed. "Reality calls."

"It keeps pulling us back, doesn't it?" he asked, brushing her stray lock from her cheek.

"So, it would seem. Will we ever get to be us?" *Be what we've longed for all these centuries*, she wanted to add.

"We will. If Ren is any indication, then we have plenty of us time. I promise you, Violissa, we will have it." He kissed her again, and she greedily took his kiss, pressing herself against him, savoring the closeness of his skin, his heartbeat below his shirt.

He dropped his head, kissing her neck, then took her face in his hands, his eyes full of an intensity that excited her.

"I've tasted you in the Dream Realm, I've tasted you through someone else's memories lifetime after lifetime, I have a hunger for you, Violissa, that centuries, even millennia apart could not quench. I will taste you again, and I won't wait much longer, regardless of what the Fates think or want."

She swallowed, her breath shallow with desire, his words settling in a part of her that had wanted him since her first breath. She felt the fire intensify, the flames licking at her self-control. She wanted to tell him to take her here, to not wait, to end her endless need, but she held back, knowing they needed to focus on the situation at hand and find a way home.

"Once again, we wait," she said softly.

"I believe the last time we had to wait was your call," he said playfully.

"And the time before was yours," she retorted.

"Hmmm, true but the first time was all you."

Her face must have reflected the sting the comment caused her, for he quickly said, "And I agreed, Vi. I didn't mean for that to come out harsh."

"It didn't, and you're right. I started this mess, and now we're both stuck cleaning it up."

"You're too hard on yourself. There were many factors that led us to this point, many players in the game besides you."

She smiled, loving how he was trying to make her feel better. Reaching up, she kissed him gently then whispered, "Let's go before we change our minds."

Sighing, he wrapped his arm around her waist, the touch sending tingles across her skin.

"My shift?"

"Sure," she answered as he shifted them. The feeling was exhilarating, the Dark power in his shift cascading over her like a thick velvety sheet. Her desire flared in response, and when they arrived seconds later, she had to hold on to him to catch her breath.

Chelsea and Paige both screamed upon their sudden arrival.

"My heart, where the hell did you two come from?" Chelsea complained, her hand over her heart.

"You shifted, didn't you?" Paige asked excitedly.

"Of course, I did," Sinow answered.

"Oh wow, I've always heard about it but it's even cooler to witness in person!"

Keary shrugged as Violissa laughed, giving Paige a big hug. "That's why you're my best friend. It's the little things."

They both laughed, and she felt the tension fade.

"What's so urgent that you had to harass us repeatedly?" Sinow asked, not bothering to hide his irritation.

"Tell them what you told us, Ren."

"We're not going back any time soon."

"How do you know that?" Sinow asked.

"Instinct. Like my mother, I listen to it."

"You want me to believe we're stuck here because you have a hunch?"

"Yes, but the signs all point to it. My mother said I wasn't going back yet because the Fates aren't done with me. And then there's Cody."

"We already discussed Cody," Sinow said. Violissa sensed the ire in his voice. "This is why we had to urgently return?"

"Wait, Sinow, this is where it gets good," Keary said.

"Good?" Paige asked, her voice sad. Violissa wasn't sure she wanted to know what was coming.

"The barrier protecting the Banished Realm will fail."

"Did it fail us before?"

"No, but it would have if Mother's powers hadn't returned. Tynan is tearing at it, and it's weak. It wouldn't have held more than a few moons if my parents had waited."

"He's right. We couldn't see the barrier without our powers, but we could hear the Torathar battering at it and feel Tynan bombarding it, trying to get through. Even before Paige and I left, we were suspicious that it was weakening."

"And I can guarantee Tynan has increased his attacks," Ren said

"You think he knows we're trapped here?" she asked.

"The portal had two sides. There's no way he didn't feel its magic, no way he didn't see it."

"If the barrier fails?" Sinow asked.

"Tynan will kill everyone in the Banished Realm."

"But Council are immortal," Violissa said, hearing her own doubt as she spoke the words.

"We had no power, all of us aging, some quickly. Cyric looked his age when I left. I don't know for certain that the immortality is gone, our lives remained long but age, time was catching up. I felt mortal, and although we never had sickness, we did bleed when wounded."

Violissa brought her hand to her mouth. For the second time today, they were discussing the death of her Council, and it hurt.

"Tynan is strong, stronger than you remember," Ren said, "and his one goal is to destroy everyone who is loyal to you."

"He hates me that much? What am I missing? Was he always set against me and I never saw it?"

Violissa saw the sadness in his eyes, a part of him still hoping, still loving his brother. Seeing his denial even after Tynan had nearly killed him, she wondered what they had been like as kids. Had they been close? She took his hand.

"Yes," she answered before the others could.

He turned to her. "You knew this?"

"I saw the snake in the grass for what it was, Sinow. I may have set the stage for all of this with my step off the path that day, but Tynan was there to ensure we never found our way back."

He walked away, running his hand through his hair. "I thought maybe he'd just gone mad after I punished him for sending you here, but he's been at it this entire time?"

He began pacing as he thought through it. "Orchestrating it all. They weren't mistakes, they weren't accidents. He played my struggle with my power, played my..."

She could see the anger building. He hadn't had time to think about Tynan, to digest what Tynan had done, but now as it sank in, she watched it taking hold, his Darkness rising.

"What did I miss, Violissa?"

"All of it." She thought back through their life in their world. Thought back to that first day. "It wasn't me," she said slowly, the meeting grove in her mind. "I wavered, but he pushed me." She met Sinow's eyes. "I was scared, terrified, determined the Fates wouldn't force my hand, determined I had free will...but that day, the moment I saw you, all of it was lost. I was in the Fates' trance."

"As was I."

"We would have kissed, and I would have known my heart was yours. But Tynan—"

"Tynan distracted us. He broke the spell, Vi. He was there at every weak moment. Manipulating, planning. None of it was coincidence." He looked heartbroken then covered it quickly, his eyes darkening. "He sent you here then waited for me to come after you. Waited for me to leave our world vulnerable. Then he destroyed it."

She looked over at Keary. "He hasn't, has he?"

Keary remained silent.

"Cirillia?" she asked, her voice cracking.

"Gone," he finally answered.

She felt the sob but refused to let it out; instead, only a small noise escaped.

"He laid waste to Cirillia first then turned to Tenebron. We saved who we could, but most of your people were lost."

She stumbled backwards with the weight of his words. Her people killed, slaughtered. It made her sick, but then it did something else. It made her angry, the Elvin in her fueled by

Sinow's increased Dark power. She caught his eye and knew instantly that her eyes had grown a deeper shade of green. She sensed his pulse increase.

Now that's a side of you I look forward to discovering, his voice said seductively in enaigne.

Not giving her a chance to respond, he turned to Ren and asked, "What happens in the Banished Realm to them...to us? Tynan's still alive, why? Why isn't he dead? Why wouldn't I have killed him for the atrocities?" Sinow asked.

"I can't tell you."

"What? You can tell me the realm barrier will fail, that he'll get through to kill everyone within it. You can tell me that history will be rewritten, but you can't tell me the past he's undone?"

"It's not the right time yet."

Sinow slammed his hand on the table nearest him. "When is the right time?"

Ren didn't flinch like Violissa had.

"Fine," Ren said calmly, but she could detect something stirring under the emotions of his Elvin blood. "When you, when they returned, it was over a moonspan before my mother found a way to bring back her powers. When they performed the ritual, my father brought the barrier down and fought Tynan. My mother obliterated the Torathar army he had amassed then they freed the realms and restored all he had destroyed."

Violissa exchanged looks with Sinow. Aside from the shock of learning Tynan had amassed an army of Torathar when she thought they were no more, something was missing from the story.

"I take it that was the abridged version, but is there something I'm missing here?" Keary asked for them all.

"What happened to Tynan? What did I...your father do to Tynan?"

Ren looked at Sinow. "Nothing, he escaped."

"And I chased him down?"

Ren hesitated. "No, he escaped to somewhere he couldn't be found."

Violissa could sense his discomfort. They were getting close to whatever it was he was hiding.

"Ren, there's no place we can't reach in our world," she said.

He remained silent, and Sinow's anger was evident.

"Where did he go, Ren?" Sinow demanded.

"I can't tell you." Ren's eyes were shifting, their blue deepening.

"You claim it doesn't matter, but on this you won't budge. What in the Fates happened, Ren!" Sinow shouted, the room overcome with the shadow of his mood.

"Things have changed but only so much. The events that shaped my parents, shaped my history can still happen!" he yelled back, his eyes now a shade of hunter green. "Everything that happened after my parents' return shaped them, changed them." He ran his hands through his hair. "No matter what, I can't undo that. Time won't undo that. I used to resent my father for keeping her close, for hovering, never letting her out of his sight, never allowing her to be free to roam the lands, to heed the call I know pulled at her Elvin blood every minute, but now I finally see it for what it was.

"The events that are coming made them who they were. My father tried to protect her, he did everything in his power to keep her safe, and in the end, he couldn't. In the end, it scarred them both, made him cage her, and forced her to let him. It wasn't done to hurt her, to hurt them, but it was done, and it was always there. My father loved my mother, loved her more than anything, and she loved him. They didn't get what you have now. Time."

He paused, his green eyes shifting to blue, the two colors dancing for position. "Maybe that really is what this is about. Time. The Fates are giving you what they could never give before, whatever their reasons. My parents didn't have it. They faced obstacle after obstacle, a realm to free, a brother to defeat, a world to fix, people to heal. They put it all before themselves and then...then they were hit again." His voice dropped. "Take what the Fates are giving you. Stop questioning what might be around the corner. Love her, keep her safe, but don't...don't do what he did and," he looked at Violissa, his eyes desperate, "don't let him. Stand up like you always do. Don't put your strength aside to seek his. Go, take the time they've given you both. We won't find a way home, not until they're ready to show it to us. Take it, my parents would have."

He left, the door closing behind him, a sound that echoed through the silent room, all eyes left staring at the spot where he had stood. No one said a word, he'd said it all, and there were no words left. She felt Sinow's fingers wrap around hers and drew her eyes from Ren's empty space. Sinow's eyes held an array of emotions, captivating her.

"When the time comes, don't make the choice for her. Don't take that path. That's what you said to me today," he said softly.

She didn't have to ask; she knew her future self had spoken those words.

"When the time comes, don't stay quiet. Don't take the choice I made for you. That's what you told me." She felt the tears behind her eyes. "We knew what it did to us, but we let it happen. Whatever it was, it was enough to change us both, to cause us to regret."

"So, what do we do now?" he asked.

"We do what we told ourselves to do," she said, smiling partially. "We do what Ren suggested."

"Take the time they've given us," he said.

"I think it's safe to say those of us left here think you should do that. You deserve it," Paige said.

He smiled and put his hand around Violissa's waist as he had earlier.

"I don't need to be told twice."

"Well technically that was twice," Cody joked.

Violissa couldn't help but laugh, the tension gone from her

body.

"Keary, you're in charge," Sinow said. "Don't call us, we'll call you when we're ready."

He didn't give Keary time to answer, shifting them on his last word.

Sinow shifted to Simon's apartment, but Violissa gave her surroundings no heed, her only focus Sinow. Ren's words were running through her heard. Who had she become? She didn't feel like someone who would have accepted the picture he'd drawn. What circumstances had diminished her spirit, her will? She backed from Sinow's arms, never leaving his eyes. Her will had never been her own, the Fates owning it, Tynan manipulating it.

"I'm taking it back," she said.

He raised his eyebrow. "And what would *that* be?"

"My will. They took it from me, from both of us, and it's been stolen from me at every turn. I acquiesce to the prophecy's first intent. I do love you, and I always will, but that's it. I won't be forced to follow the same path she did. I won't—"

"Vi, do we have a choice? We're on this path that they've orchestrated—"

"No, that Tynan orchestrated." She felt the falseness of the words as she said them.

Sinow took a moment as if thinking the same thing. "Maybe, maybe not. If the Fates continue to test us, perhaps he's part of the test."

"Another player in the prophecy," she said softly.

"Three players in a game we don't control."

"Sinow, I want my will back, I want my decisions to be mine."

He twisted her stray lock around his finger. "Maybe they

are, Vi. We don't know that they aren't. What if the Fates laid the path for us, and your will took us from it, then each decision we've made has taken us further from that path? Who's to say it wasn't the insistence of our free will that kept us from finding the way back?"

She shook her head. "No, there are too many places the Fates have been involved. Look at Ren. I let him come here, let Tynan take him. Why? The Fates wanted him here. We have no choice but to tread their path, Sinow."

He sighed. "Then where does that leave us, Vi?"

She bit her lip, thinking on his question. Then she took a step back. "I may not have free will over most of my life, but I will have it over this part," she said seductively.

Reaching her hand to her back, she released the clasps to her dress with her magic, her eyes never leaving his as it dropped to the floor. He drew in a breath, his eyes skimming the curves of her body. She felt the flush on her cheeks as his eyes moved back up to meet hers.

"I wonder how many times I've seen that," he said, his voice hoarse. "And if I still have the same reaction."

He walked to her, pulling his shirt off. "I can't imagine it would be any different."

Reaching his hand through her hair, he pulled her against him and kissed her. The feel of his skin against hers stoked the fire within, and her kisses became more demanding, his answering hers. The world fell away along with their fears of the future. All she needed was to know that future contained him. As he moved her to the bed, leaving their clothes scattered across the apartment, she felt her powers rise to meet his, the two engaging in a dance around their bodies, filling the space, pushing against the walls to escape. As she climaxed with him, it unleashed, shattering the windows and shaking the building foundation, the colors of their lovemaking lighting the sky.

Violissa lost count of how many times they took each other, but eventually, she lay content in Sinow's arms, the steady rhythm of his heart threatening to lull her to sleep. A smile formed on his lips as he kissed her head. She peeked up at him, cursing the unruly lock that draped across her eye.

Pushing it back, he laughed, saying, "Not ready for another round already, are you?"

"Hmmm, that's a possibility, but I was really just wondering if it was worth the last thousand years of torment I gave you."

"Well, you were quite wicked. I have to say I wondered at times if you were truly the daughter of a Light king. You have quite a Dark streak in you."

She sucked her lip in and chewed it, worrying at his words.

"That was worth every lifetime of hell you gave me, and I would go through it all again if it meant I could make love to you like this every night."

"And every day?" she asked sheepishly.

"You are insatiable, aren't you?"

Kissing his chest and shifting her body onto him, she seductively answered, "I have a lot of lost time to make up."

They made love again until she finally drifted off in his embrace.

The morning sun spilled through the curtains, the sunrise just high enough to send a pinkish glow across the shattered glass that lay scattered upon the floor.

Violissa stared at it, trying to remember when it had happened. She didn't remember anything but Sinow, his touch, his kisses, his body, everything that they'd done the prior night. She turned her head, feeling his arm across her back. His face, relaxed in sleep, was turned toward her. She lay there taking in the beauty of him, the strong jaw, the firm muscles defining his cheeks, the thick long black lashes that lined his closed eyelids, the bit of black hair that fell across his forehead. She wanted to touch him but didn't want to wake his peaceful slumber.

Quietly, she slipped out from under his arm, taking a moment when she rose to look at him. His powerful body stretched out before her sent a shiver of desire through her, and she yearned to touch him. He looked so content that she continued to restrain herself, walking instead across the floor, only remembering the broken glass as a shard penetrated her skin. She bit her lip at the small pin prick. Pulling the shard out, she wondered at the damage they'd caused the prior night. Most of the glass had been sent raining down on the street below but in the fury of their power, some had been pulled back in and strewn across the floor. Drawing her hand up, she repaired the windows and turned the glass fragments to dust, continuing her walk out of the room, her wound now healed.

She stretched, feeling complete for the first time she could remember. The sun was continuing its rise, and the beauty of it spoke to her through the now doorless balcony. Reaching down, she picked up Sinow's shirt, holding it to her face, taking in the scent of him and letting it fill her before putting it on. He was taller and broader than she, so it hung large on her frame, making her feel as a young child might. She cleared the remaining broken glass, leaving petals in her wake this time, then walked out on the balcony, the crisp morning air cooling her skin. There she stood, reveling in the birth of a new day, a new life, thinking on all that had happened the day before, her fingers absently running along her union scar. She was married, finally with the man she was destined to be with, finally free to love him as she always had. She saw that now; her heart and soul had always belonged to him. She'd pushed that knowledge away, buried it below a need to rebel, to control her own destiny. What if she'd succeeded? Would they have found each other? Would she ever have known what she had lost?

Her thoughts were interrupted when she heard Sinow run across the apartment and fling the door open, yelling her name.

"Dammit," he said, punching the wall, then dropping his

head to rest against the fractured plaster.

Sinow, she called to him in enaigne.

He turned, his face a mix of sheer pain and hope. She didn't need to ask, knew immediately what her absence upon waking had meant to him. Remembered how she had woken and run off each time she hadn't been dragged from him by angry villagers or witch hunters. She understood where his mind had gone and that her absence had ripped his heart in two again.

"I'm so sorry. I didn't think," she whispered as he came upon her and took her in his arms, kissing her with the passion of a man who had been separated from his love for centuries. It was desperate and ecstatic at once. His fingers laced through her hair as he tilted her head away from his, searching her eyes.

"You're here," he said quietly.

"I am, and I promise you, I will be here every time you wake. I'm not going anywhere again."

She felt heartbroken. What had he gone through each lifetime, losing her over and over again? She brushed her fingers along his face.

"I could get used to that," he said, the tension leaving his body, "especially if you greet me in this once in a while." He gestured to the shirt she'd donned.

"I can do that," she replied, smiling. She kissed him, feeling the need stir in her once again. The shirt wouldn't be on long, and she was content with that.

Twenty-Two

The day went by quickly, but Sinow took no notice. It was filled with Violissa. He'd been so certain she had left, so sure the cycle hadn't been broken, that he'd had a moment of weakness when he'd awoken to find her gone. She wasn't there, she never was when he would wake, he'd grown accustomed to that fact, and so he'd done the one thing he did every lifetime; he'd run after her.

The sound of her voice in his head had been nothing short of ecstasy. It had soothed his anger with himself for being so weak again and for having her witness it this time. She hadn't judged him. Instead, it was as if she understood completely. It was a moment between the two of understanding, of accepting their past, a moment just like they'd had in the Dream Realm, one of two people who knew the other's soul.

He had taken her again, his shirt draping her body hadn't helped his control any, and they'd made love right where she had stood. The rest of the day had been filled with the two of them catching up on a thousand years missed. A blend of lovemaking and talking. Neither wanting it to stop until finally, two days later, their hunger for food surpassed their hunger for each other.

Sinow sat across from Violissa with a carton of Chinese food, watching her cutely attempt to use the chopsticks for which he'd asked. She was sitting cross legged on the other end of the couch, her long, bare legs too much to remain covered by the ridiculously large T-shirt, the same one he'd found her in that first morning, her long locks spilled around her as she bit her lip, focusing on the noodle that refused to be tamed by her chopsticks. His heart swelled, and he wondered how he'd survived without her all those centuries. He'd never felt complete before now, as if half of his soul was missing and had only now been found. He laughed as the noodle won the battle, and she dropped her sticks in frustration.

"I do believe the Light queen has been bested by her lo mein."

She gave him an irritated look then joined his laughter. "I do believe you're right," she said, picking up the noodle with her fingers. "But not for long." She dropped the noodle into her mouth then licked her two fingers. He didn't know why but he found the action seductive, a surge of desire lighting in him.

She raised her eyebrow. "Should I avoid eating Chinese food any time you need to concentrate?"

He was about to answer when a knock interrupted his witty comeback.

"I thought I commanded them to let us be."

And he had. In fact, neither of them had picked up their phones in their time away. He had even blocked Keary from his mind. Irked, he rose and opened the door, only realizing after the fact that he was still shirtless and in his boxers.

"You could have put some clothes on for us," Keary joked, pushing his way in.

"You're lucky I have this much on," he replied, the anger evident in his voice.

"Good god, do they build you to look that perfect?" Paige muttered.

"Fates, Paige. Remember where you come from and who your creators are."

"Sorry."

"What are you doing here and why bring an entourage with you?" Sinow asked as Ren and Cody walked past him, Cody squeezing Sinow's biceps as he did.

"I think they did build him that way, Paige," Cody said. "I don't believe I've ever seen him go to the gym."

"We have a gym?" Sinow asked.

"What's a gym?" Ren added.

Sinow ran his hands through his hair in frustration.

"I'd tread carefully, Keary. Your king isn't very happy anymore," Violissa said.

"He was," Sinow mumbled.

"What's going on?" she asked them.

"Shouldn't you be more...covered?" Ren asked, looking away from her.

She blushed slightly.

"No, she shouldn't because none of you are supposed to be here," Sinow said, walking to the bedroom and grabbing a shirt for him and a blanket for Violissa.

"Are we being modest now?" she asked when he returned.

"In front of my subjects and my future son, yes," he quipped, pulling the shirt on.

"There's still something off about seeing you in those," Ren said, pointing to his boxers. "I don't believe I've ever seen your legs."

Sinow gave him a sharp look.

"I'll get used to it though," Ren said quickly, apparently used to Sinow's temper.

He wanted nothing more than to toss them all out.

"I think you should tell us why you're here before you all push him over the edge," Violissa said, attuned to his feelings better than he'd imagined.

"My job is to push him, Violissa. It's why he keeps me around," Keary answered.

"There are times I question why I keep you around," Sinow retorted. "Did you find a solution to getting home?"

"No," Paige answered nervously. He looked over at her. She'd positioned herself as far away from him as she could. He needed to work on quelling his Darkness better if he was going to be stuck here longer. Keary's presence didn't affect her as badly, but then Keary had always been different, more social than a Darkbearer should be. Sinow was glad the Fates had chosen him to come here rather than another of his Council. There may have been a trail of bodies if another had been sent. Darkbearers weren't known for their patience or sociability.

"Then what's going on?" Violissa asked, bringing his attention back.

"Your friends, the agents, have been hounding us. They want answers, and they want them from you two."

"They don't seem concerned with the rest of us and clearly didn't notice that Ren is a bad ass, too," Cody said. "We've stalled them enough. They want you both down at the station at two today, or they'll take you in themselves."

"Take us in?" Sinow asked. "This is ridiculous. Do they have any idea who they're dealing with?"

"No, Sinow, they don't," Violissa said. "Maybe we—"

"No, we don't have time for this, and they don't need to know anything about us."

"That's not the way they see it. We're lucky they haven't called in back up."

"Especially with the condition you left Main Street in," Cody added.

"What?" she asked, concern in her voice.

"Well, you kind of left a path of destruction. Between Ren

and Tynan fighting and you going all nature queen, it's a bit of a mess," Paige said.

"Yeah, there's an ancient ruin jungle feel to it," Cody added.

Violissa dropped her head in her hands and mumbled, "We need to clean that up."

"Why didn't you clean it up?" Sinow asked Keary.

Keary crossed his arms. "Well, we thought about it, but the sex storm the two of you brought down on the town the night before did little to help. I don't think I've ever seen ivy grow that fast. You can barely see the diner. Most of the businesses are open, but they're not happy. I'm surprised your food wasn't cursed."

Violissa's cheeks grew crimson, which Sinow found incredibly cute.

"We'll clean it up," she said.

"We will?" he asked, surprised. "I don't do clean up, Vi."

She furrowed her brow. "You don't?"

"No, that's what mortals are for and my Council, if necessary," he replied.

Ren snickered.

"Is there something funny about that?"

"Let's just say you will be doing it. It took a lot of hard work to rebuild the realms, or so I've been told. My father used magic as often as he could and was lucky my mother didn't make him do it by hand."

Sinow felt his jaw drop at the same time he saw Keary's drop.

"What did you do to me, woman?" he asked Violissa who shrugged.

"I believe that's what they call whipped in this world," Keary joked.

Sinow felt his eyes darken. "Do I need to punish you here?"

"It's been a few days. We're still a little out of practice," Keary dared. Sinow could have killed him, and his power rose in response until he heard Paige whimper.

"Let's save that for later," Violissa said. "Keary, stop

antagonizing your king before he takes the entire building down. I just fixed all of the windows."

"You did?" Sinow asked.

She laughed, a sound that teased his senses.

"You were asleep, I didn't want to wake you, and then, well it never came up."

That explained the flower petals he hadn't had time to ask her about.

"So, they want to talk to us. What time?" she asked.

"Two o'clock," Cody answered.

"Don't tell me you're considering this?" Sinow asked, stunned.

"What's the harm? They're curious."

"She's curious," Ren contributed.

Sinow wondered what he'd seen or if he'd spoken with the agents.

"Even more reason to ignore the request. We have better things to do with our time."

"Maybe you two do, but the rest of us are out of ideas. Might as well enjoy our time here. Maybe see the world," Keary said.

"I've seen it," Sinow answered.

"Just saying."

Sinow ran his hands through his hair.

"She's right," Ren said. "Talk to them, get them off your back so they go away. Right now, they're like an annoying bug you can't get rid of. Maybe answering their questions will resolve that."

"And say what?" Sinow asked.

"The truth," Violissa answered.

"That I can kill them without lifting a finger?" He rolled his neck, his irritation rising. "That they're lucky they have permission to look at me? That either of us could take this entire town down within seconds?"

"Paige and Cody, let them know we'll be there. Please give us some time to talk this through and get changed," Violissa said, ignoring his rebukes.

"Vi—"

"We will discuss it, Sinow," she cut him off, her voice firm, the emerald in her eyes deepening.

"That's our cue to go. My liege, my queen," Keary said, bowing sarcastically before scooting everyone out of the apartment. Sinow didn't pull his eyes from Violissa's. He crossed his arms and released the Dark he'd quelled the entire time.

Violissa rose, the blanket dropping, her lithe legs tempting him as she sauntered over to him. A fire rose in him, the need for her rearing its head.

"Sinow."

"I don't enjoy being disobeyed, Violissa."

"Since when am I someone you command?" she replied, caressing his arm, her sage eyes seductively pulling him in.

"You're not playing fair."

"And you're assuming you are my leader and not my equal. We're both rulers, Sinow, both used to getting our own way."

"Should we ask Ren who wins most of the time?"

She laughed. "I'm willing to bet it's me."

He relaxed his arms. "There's no reason those people need to know anything about us."

She leaned against his arms, her breasts, loose below the shirt, teasing him. "If we are truly trapped here as Ren says, then we need to get along with them. We don't know how long we'll be here, and if we don't cooperate, then we risk drawing even more attention to ourselves. Others will come, and we'll be drawn into a fight with them, an endless battle that will only cause destruction on their side and annoyance on ours."

"So, you'd turn into some kind of warrior queen?" he asked playfully. "That might be a sexy look for you."

"Sinow."

He lowered his arms and drew her in. "You're relentless, aren't you?"

"Stubborn I've been told."

He kissed her, the sweet taste of her lips lingering. "You win. I'll go, but I leave the minute they begin to annoy me."

"Deal. Now, I don't think it would be appropriate for me to go like this."

He meant to stay focused on her last comment, but the thought of dressing brought his mind to a dilemma.

"Vi, I don't think I can be in the presence of mortals much longer."

"That was an unexpected one-eighty," she said. "What's wrong?"

"My powers are tough to quell. Dark kings aren't designed to frolic with mortals. The longer I contain my power, the more it fights back. I need release, and there's no place here for that."

"So, you're like a ticking time bomb?"

"Pretty much."

She chewed her lip. "Is that normal? I mean, I don't have that issue."

"Because your powers are meant for mortal contact, you need them to heal. Mine are meant to punish, Vi. Mortals don't want to be in my presence."

"So, you punish people for power release?" Her face wore a horrified expression.

"No, we have a code, Violissa. You should know that. Only the guilty are punished. Sometimes, we keep them, those who deserve more lengthy punishments. I usually leave them to my Council."

"Keary?"

"Has a particular fondness for torture," he said nonchalantly, then seeing her expression added, "But nothing unnatural."

"Torture is natural?" she asked, her expression deepening. "And you?"

"Never really enjoyed the torture part, I prefer a quick but painful death."

She looked appalled.

"It's not like you think, Vi. We don't go around killing people every day."

"Then how do you release your pent-up power?"

"For me, I don't have to keep it under control when there are no mortals around. Like now. And when we were home, we would spar, or I would just torment my Council."

"You fight each other?"

"Of course. It's fun for me. I beat the crap out of them all. I don't think they like being my sparring partner though."

She laughed. "Here, I thought you were going to say something serious like an ancient Darkbearer ritual and all you do is fight each other like a bunch of kids?"

She was laughing hard now.

"We're not a bunch of kids, and it's not funny, it's serious training," he said defensively, causing her to laugh harder.

"Vi," he said, trying to reign her in although her laughter was surprisingly enjoyable.

"Ok, ok. I'm sorry. I'm sure when we get home, and I witness it, I'll understand better. Now, you need to shroud your powers until you find an outlet, kind of like Ren is?"

"Exactly."

"Then covering you might help like you did when we were home."

"Might help some, at least I wouldn't have to worry about permission nonstop."

"Why not wear a hoodie like his?"

Was she serious? "No."

"But it works for him."

"He's younger, and he's not a king yet. I'm not wearing a hoodie."

"Thor wore a hoodie and made it look good."

"Seriously, Violissa? I don't even want to continue the conversation after that."

"Sorry," she said, laughing. "Why not a cloak then? It works at home."

"And it fits in at home. It sticks out here."

"We stick out here, Sinow. Nothing we do will change that."

He sighed, and she must have sensed his frustration.

"All right, let's figure that out later. Now, as I said, this," she gestured to the shirt that draped her temptingly, "is not appropriate for going beyond this door."

"But it would be sexy."

Laughing, she said, "I need a shower."

"You need company in that shower," he said, kissing her neck.

"I do?"

"Definitely."

Sinow sat next to Violissa at the small table. To think they had the nerve to put him in an interrogation room, as if he were a common criminal. He pulled at the collar of the uncomfortable hoodie, feeling constrained in the covering. Violissa had won, he fit in better dressed like this although he felt like a fool. He was going to have to work on keeping his powers concealed better if they were to live here for however long the Fates insisted. He made a mental note to drag Keary out and find a secluded space to spar then thought maybe Ren should come as well. He was confounded by the boy—a son, his son but one who didn't accept his Dark powers. It required some thinking on, but as the male agent slammed a folder down on the table, he was drawn back to the issue at hand how to keep from killing the man.

"Is that necessary, Ethan?" the female asked.

He couldn't remember her name, hadn't paid much attention to either of them until they'd harassed Violissa two days ago. He felt his power rise at the thought.

Sinow, Violissa said in enaigne, her voice cool and calming in his head.

"Look, you don't want to be here anymore than we do," the woman said.

"Who are you again?" Sinow asked.

"I am agent Abigail Lawson, and this is my partner—"

"Ethan," Sinow finished.

"Agent Sanders," he said in return.

"Look, Ethan and Abigail," Sinow said, purposely enjoying the aura of annoyance from the man, "why should we answer any of your questions?"

"Because we can lock you up for a long time."

Abigail placed a hand on Ethan's arm. "What my partner is saying is that we are a division of Homeland Security. It's our job to keep this country safe from threats, and right now, you are perceived as a threat, a very dangerous one."

"We don't know anything about the two of you. Your records look spotless, you both lived separate successful lives, then one day you met and became inseparable," Ethan said calmly. "And suddenly things, unexplained things, start to happen. The earthquake, the fissure, the strange consistency of the lake. Did you know that every migration pattern in this area changed that day? No bird wanted to come close to this town, and some were even killing themselves to avoid it until a few days ago when you put on that show in the middle of town."

"That is weird," Sinow replied sarcastically, crossing his arms and leaning back.

"We saw what you two did. It was magic, dangerous magic that could hurt people."

Sinow leaned across the table. "My magic doesn't hurt people. It kills them."

The agents flinched, and he could smell their fear.

"Sinow," Violissa said, putting her hand on his and looking at him. "We'll answer your questions." Sinow felt his growl escape. "Even though my husband doesn't want to."

She'd called him her husband, and it disarmed him, sending a rush from his heart that doused the fire within.

"What do you want to know?"

"Who are you, really? We know what the files say," Ethan said, tossing the nearly empty folders on the table again. "Tell us what we don't know."

Sinow gripped the neck of his hoodie again.

"Just take it off," Violissa said then turned back to the agents. Sinow, agreeing with her that he'd be better off with no constraining clothing, made the thing disappear, not bothering to conceal his power.

Both agents shifted back in their seats, the female standing to move further away.

Violissa took a deep breath then began. "My true name is Violissa. I am queen of Cirillia, the ruling and only Light queen, and the last of the Elvin. Sinow, not Simon, is king of Tenebron and the ruling Dark king. We are not from this world, I don't believe our world is even in the same galaxy, but I don't know. It might be a different dimension of some sort."

They stared at her.

"You're aliens?"

Sinow laughed. "Not in the sense of the word as you usually use it. It might be easier to explain it this way, which is the way I learned it. The universe was created by a multitude of what you refer to as gods. Each branched off to create their own world, not many got along, power and tempers getting in the way, so most found their own corner of the universe to call home.

"Our gods, we call the Fates, were a group that decided multiple creators would make things more interesting, and so the group of them formed our world and created the three races, all of which were ruled by one king and one line of magic with which that king and only a sparse few were blessed. As far as I can tell, your god wanted his own world and created man. He disliked the idea of his creations having magic, and so your world exists without it."

"Our god is one of many and dislikes magic? How do you

know that?" Ethan asked.

"Partly from the history of our creation and the last from," Violissa hesitated, "well, call it instinct. I have a connection to him, we have an understanding."

Even Sinow looked at her on that one.

"Is she sane?" Ethan asked.

Sinow knew she was. What had Keary said? Her instinct drove her. "Completely," he replied. There wasn't a doubt in his mind that she'd spoken the truth.

Abigail started pacing. "So why are you here?"

"That's the question of the day, isn't it?" Ethan added, leaning in.

Sinow felt his angst growing at the man's move. Abigail stopped her pacing and shivered.

"And why do I fear you?" she said, daring to look in his eyes.

"Because you should." *And if you were in my world, looking at me would mean your instant death,* he thought.

"Why?" Ethan asked. "And doesn't that mean you're a threat to our nation?"

"Because my power isn't pretty and fanciful like Violissa's—"

"Fanciful?" Violissa asked, her eyes narrowing. "My magic is not fanciful."

He rolled his eyes. "You know what I mean. My magic is not meant for healing, it's not calming and peaceful." He turned back to the agents. "It's meant to punish. It's designed to kill, but I am not a threat to your nation or your world."

"And we simply take your word on this?"

"Yes," he said. "That's exactly what you do."

"Ok. Abigail, they've promised not to hurt anyone. Let's send that to the director, and we're finished here," Ethan said sarcastically.

Abigail shot him an annoyed look. Sinow lost his patience and stood, the feet of the metal chair causing a jarring sound in the awkward silence.

"I've had enough. We owe you no answers. We have no

interest in your world. It's dirty, polluted, petty, self-absorbed, and not worth my time. Permission revoked."

He felt the Darkness free itself and center on the man, he held back enough as to not kill him but released enough to teach him respect. Ethan grabbed his head and staggered back.

"What are you doing?" Abigail asked. She had moved back as far as she could, her back pinned against the wall in fear of the Dark power that permeated the room. "Stop now!" She drew her weapon, but he paid her no mind. Ethan crumbled to the ground.

"Sinow?" Violissa said.

The door slammed open, and more agents entered, their weapons drawn. They clustered at the doorway, their hands shaking. He could smell their fear.

Abigail fired then the other agents followed suit, their fear feeding Sinow. He slammed his hand out against the bullets, intending to turn them to ash, the drawn guns crumbling in their hands. Then he released his hold on Ethan. He would survive, he was annoying, but he wasn't guilty of any more than that, at least in this world.

Sinow, Violissa's voice whispered in his mind.

"Permission." He leaned down next to Ethan and said, "If I wanted to do harm to your world, everyone would already be dead." Then he shifted.

The room was silent, the agents didn't move, all of them looking to Violissa for an answer. Sinow had left her to clean up his mess. He had lost his temper and hurt the agent. Or had he really lost it? Maybe he hadn't. Maybe this was the Dark king establishing his place as the alpha. Violissa wasn't sure what to make of it, but she didn't have time to dwell on it.

She didn't know where to start but finally moved toward

Ethan.

"Don't move!" the one named Abigail shouted. Violissa ignored her and stooped down next to Ethan. She sent her senses out to feel for the injuries but found nothing physical. Sinow hadn't hurt him. She reached in and removed the Dark cobwebs that layered his head then sent a calming spell out to calm his heart and the fear. His breathing slowed, the tension leaving his body.

"Will he be ok?" Abigail asked. She had stooped next to Violissa, a worried look on her face.

"He'll be fine. Sinow didn't hurt him."

"How can you say that?"

"Because I'm a healer. There was no damage. If Sinow had wanted to hurt him, there would have been nothing left for me to heal. He would have been dead within seconds."

Violissa rose, the other agents staring at her, still unmoving. In front of them, bullets hung in the air, frozen. She walked around them, not knowing what to say. No one had the power to freeze motion. They could destroy something in motion, change its physical properties, and turn it into something else, or re-direct it but not stop it mid-air.

"Is that one of his powers?"

"No," she responded. "At least, it never was."

She reached out to touch one, and it moved slightly with her touch but didn't fall.

"How odd," she muttered.

"That's not normal?" one of them asked her.

"No, it's not. Not in the least."

She stood back, chewing her lip, then sent a spell at the bullets to release them. They clattered to the ground, and she turned back to Abigail and Ethan who was just rising, looking around with a perplexed expression.

"We're not a threat to any of you."

"After what he just did to me?" he asked, rubbing his temples.

"If he'd wanted you dead, he would have killed you. If he'd wanted to hurt you, I would not have been able to heal your mind. You believe me, don't you, Abigail?" she asked, knowing the agent did.

Abigail looked hesitantly to her partner. "Yes, but that doesn't mean anything. Our director wants answers. She wants to know what caused that mess at the park, she wants to know who you are, and what happened here the other day. We need to tell her something."

"Then tell her the truth."

"They'll have us take you—"

"No one can take us. This isn't some superhero movie where you can disable us with your technology or some magic rock that binds our powers. Now, I have taken an oath to not use our powers to interfere with everyday life in this world, but if you continue to engage my husband, he will judge you guilty and punish you."

"And that's supposed to help us trust you?" Ethan asked.

"No, it's meant to warn you. Now I'm done here," she shifted, not bothering to say anymore.

Following Sinow's shift, she found him outside the building, a cape draped over him to shield his mood. No one was around, and she wondered if those who'd been here had fled in fear when he'd shifted. She sighed and walked up to him, taking her fingers and lifting the edge of his hood, peering in to meet his black eyes. Seeing him this way brought the ache of homesickness, his cape a reminder of who they really were and the world to which they truly belonged. It was a look that took her back to better times but that stuck out in a land where they were lost, an endless search for home before them.

"A bit moody?" she asked playfully.

"Not funny, Violissa. Every part of me wanted to kill him, and he would have deserved it."

"If we'd been home?"

"Yes."

"But we're not and the part of you that follows your code knows that," she said softly, bringing his cape down to see his face. His eyes had softened to a rich brown, and she rested her hand on his cheek, feeling him lean into it as his eyes searched hers.

"I don't want to be here any longer, Vi. I need to get home. We need to get home." There was a sadness to his voice, a glimpse of the man she loved, the vulnerability he contained but rarely showed.

"We will, Sinow, but they're not ready to send us home yet. I don't know why, but we'll keep looking for a way home, and one day, they'll show us."

He took her face in his hands and pulled it gently forward, leaning his forehead into hers. Closing her eyes, she breathed in his scent, relishing his closeness.

"We have each other. For once, we're together in this fight, Sinow. We'll get through it, just as we always have, but this time together as one," she whispered, shifting to bring her lips to his, savoring the feel of his lips on hers.

"Let's go back," he said.

"Mmm hmm," she mumbled then remembered they had one more thing to do before they could return to the apartment. "But not yet."

She pulled away as he sighed. "What now? You're not dragging me back in there."

She laughed. "No, I promise. No more uncomfortable interrogations. We do, however, have some cleaning up to do."

"Hmmm, I suppose you're referring to the mess behind me?"

"It's quite a mess, isn't it?"

He smiled. "We did a little damage. I don't suppose you're going to let me out of fixing it, are you?"

"Not on your life. I clean, you clean."

Sighing, he turned to survey the damage that ran the length of the town. "All right, let's get this over with, and you are not to mention this to my Council when we return home. Dark kings do not repair things."

"They didn't before, but there's always room for change, and I believe we've set a few precedents, why not add another to the list," she replied, backing away.

"You are demanding, aren't you?"

"You've no idea. Now, let's get this over with so you can make love to me again."

She walked away, drawing her nature power as she heard him groan.

"You're torturous, you know that?"

Laughing, she began undoing the wilderness her magic had created as he drew his power. They worked as they walked quietly through town, and when they finished, she made one more demand with which he easily complied, shifting her back to the apartment to spend the rest of the day exploring their desires.

"I'm out of ideas," Keary said, interrupting the awkward silence that had filled the room. Ren looked up from the wood floor he'd been staring at, glad Keary had finally said what all of them were thinking.

"Keary's right," Paige said. "I think we have to face the fact that we're stuck here."

His father sighed but remained silent. It had been over a week since the gem had been broken, and they were nowhere closer to getting home.

"If that's the case, what's the plan now?" Cody asked.

"Why are you even part of this?" his father asked Cody.

"You need the entertainment?" Cody joked.

"I get enough of that from Keary."

"Then, Ren said I'm that Light thingy, so I stay."

"You're not a Lightbearer, Cody," his mother said.

“Well, whatever I am, I’m staying,” he replied, crossing his arms, his voice resonating with hurt.

She walked over to him then leaned up and kissed his cheek. “You’re part of the family, you can always stay.”

“And when we find our way home, Vi?”

She shot Sinow a look, then said curtly, “We’ll figure that out when the time comes.”

“Speaking of time,” Keary said. “We’ve got some time on our hands now. What do we do with ourselves?”

Ren thought of his situation and the parents he knew were no longer waiting for his return, their time gone, unraveled. What had happened in their final moments? Had they thought of him? Did they have regrets? Did they accept their fate, knowing he would help guide them to a new future?

“You put your affairs in order, take the time to leave things resolved in this world. My parents disappeared the day that portal opened, then stepped into a world that needed them too much for them to have time. Use what the Fates are now giving you to do the things they regretted never having time to do,” Ren said.

“Like what?” Paige asked, her eyes shining with curiosity.

“Like saying goodbye,” his mother answered.

Paige looked at her. “Oh, I didn’t think of that.”

“Leaving the bar for Chelsea to own,” Keary said.

“The shop,” his mother said to Paige.

“Donating my money,” his father said.

“That’s right,” Keary replied. “I forgot you’re loaded.”

“Loaded?” his mother asked.

“Loaded,” Keary added.

“How did you manage that?” she asked. “My human parents left me a small inheritance but not enough to make that same claim.”

“You learn a few things after so many lives, Vi. Remember, I had my memories intact after we were separated. I started to notice the patterns. I was always named Simon, always born in Ireland, then left an orphan when my parents died. The towns were patterned as well. They cycled back every four lives. Always the same towns in the same order. I was always successful and in one life I found a good man to be my lawyer, hired him to manage my money, to hold it in trust when I died, and to find the orphaned Simon in said town born the day of my death to which to gift the trust. He managed my money, grew it while I was young, then gave me access when I came of age. When he died, his son took over the business, then his son, and so on. A few hundred years later, and I've amassed a good deal of wealth."

Ren, knowing this bit of information, looked at the stunned faces. It was amusing.

"You told me you were successful, not rich."

"Simon told Violet, and now I'm adding the details."

"Seriously? That's your excuse for not telling me?"

"Ha! Violissa, we can make what we want, go where we want, and do whatever we want. We have no need for money. We rule an entire world for Fates' sake."

"It's the principle of it," she said, pouting.

"If you don't need to take it with you, and you don't take me, can you leave me some of that money?" Cody injected.

Ren's father eyed him. "No. But that does get me thinking. Maybe Ren's right. This is a chance to have resolution where before there was none."

"Think of the impact you could make with that money, Sinow. The lives. The charities."

He brought his phone out. "We need to see my lawyer, have everything put in place for our departure."

"And where is he?"

"New York City," Keary answered excitedly.

Ren couldn't keep from staring. He'd never seen anything like it, nor had his imagination come close to representing what stood before him. He marveled at the height of the buildings, the crowded streets, the noises and smells that overcame his senses. This was the city, something his father had attempted to describe, but with no reference with which to go by, Ren had failed to comprehend.

They'd driven in, a miserable experience in Ren's mind, being caged in such a small space for so many hours. His father thought it best to maintain the human façade and not startle anyone by shifting there. Of course, they were followed by the two agents who must have come to realize his parents couldn't be contained but could be tracked.

"I thought they didn't have magic in this world," he said to Paige who was walking with him. Sightseeing she had called it. They'd left Keary with Cody while his parents had headed to the lawyer's office. Ren still didn't quite understand what a lawyer was.

"They don't. It's called engineering."

"Not a form of magic?"

"No," she said, laughing. "It takes a long time to build something like this. With magic, I presume you could do it in a day."

"In moments," he said, staring down at the buildings below, "but why would we ever need to?"

He stepped back, still not comfortable with the height. Paige had insisted they see all the important spots as she referred to them. This one she called the Empire State Building, and it was both the worst and the best so far. It was decided that he didn't care much for heights, but he still couldn't help marvel at the building.

"I guess we wouldn't," she said, sounding disappointed.

"You would want something like this in our world?" he asked her as they finally made their way to the elevator.

"I don't know that I ever thought about it," she replied.

She remained quiet the rest of the way down, and he gave

her the silence. Finally, as they walked down the street, she said, "No, I suppose I wouldn't."

"Wouldn't what?" he asked, his mind having moved past the conversation, his eyes still taking everything in.

"I wouldn't want to spoil the innocence of our world with buildings like these. But it would make life a lot easier if we had at least some upgrades."

"Upgrades?"

"Things like running water, hot water, maybe a Starbucks. Is that asking too much?" she asked, cocking her eyebrow as she looked over at him.

"Maybe just a little," he joked.

They made their way to a park that dwarfed the one in the last town, then sat in the grass eating what Paige called a hot dog. She'd told him not to question the ingredients, and from the taste of it, he was glad he hadn't.

"How do humans eat this food?" he asked.

"You get used to it. It took me a while, especially when we moved to the states," she said, wiping her mouth with the back of her hand, a move at which he couldn't help but smile.

It felt good sitting next to her, spending time with her. It was comfortable and stirred that thing inside of him that he still couldn't identify. It was as if being with her made everything better, made it all right. She made him happy.

"Can I ask you something, Paige?"

"Sure."

"Why did you leave? Why did you go with Keary?" It was something he'd always wondered about her. A decision that would have been impossible for most, but one she had easily accepted, or so he'd been told.

"I don't know. The Fates said I needed to go, so I went."

He gave her a questioning look.

"What?" she asked.

"There's more to it than that."

She looked down at her lap then out across the park. He

took in the way the sun highlighted certain strands of her hair, making some more red toned, some golden.

"I suppose I wanted to do something special, to step out of the world I was stuck in, one I never really fit into. Everyone around me was special. My father was Keeper, my family Council, all revered even without their power. Then there was me. The strange, powerless, mortal child who didn't have a place with them and who had no place with the other mortals. I wanted to be something more than who I was destined to be there."

He didn't know quite what to say, the words she'd spoken nothing like he'd ever heard spoken about her. "Paige, you are special. You have no idea who you are, do you?"

She looked at him, her blue eyes sparkling in the sun.

"You risked your life, left everything you knew to blindly follow the Fates, never knowing if you'd return. You are known throughout the realms. The best friend to the queen, the woman who helped save the world. When my mother talks about you, she lights up the way she does when my father enters the room. If you don't believe you were special to everyone else, know that you held a place in her heart that remained to the day the Fates took her. You are so much more than you realize."

Her eyes glistened, and she looked away. "I guess I just don't see it yet."

"We do," he replied.

They sat in silence until he finally said they should head back. He wondered what she was thinking about and if it had anything to do with that nudging feeling he had that wouldn't dissipate and instead seemed to grow with each passing hour.

Twenty-Three

Sitting in the many windowed law office, Sinow felt Garrett staring at him as he signed the last document. As Simon, he had known Garrett all his life. Garret had stepped into his father's shoes and taken over as Simon's lawyer when his father finally retired. They weren't too far apart in age, and while Garret was groomed by his father, Simon had gotten to know him well.

He passed the pen to Violissa.

"Why do we have so many windows in this building again?" Sinow asked.

He had purchased the building in one of his former lives when he realized he was drawn to the city. The past few lives he had settled here from Ireland and built a life for himself. It made sense to have a place to hold official business, the rest of the building he leased out at discount to smaller upstarts and a few charity organizations that couldn't afford the pricey New

York rental rates.

“I believe that was your doing,” Garrett said, still eyeing him.

He knew there was a change; to anyone close to Simon, it would be easily recognizable. Garrett’s family had served him for centuries, never questioning that Simon looked the same each lifetime, never questioning the strange way the trust was passed to a new Simon each time, or the pattern of each birth and death. There were bound to be theories in the family about the situation, about Simon, but this was the first time any of them had seen him as a fully powered Sinow. It was also the first time steps to end the trust, to end the arrangement that had defined Garrett’s family, were being taken.

“So, you’ve thought this through, Simon? Seriously thought this through?”

“Yes.”

“You’ve been married two weeks, and you’re changing your will, changing your trust. A trust that’s been in place for centuries. And you don’t want me to add your wife to it but instead want to give it all away upon your death or if you disappear, which, in itself is an odd request.”

“I believe I’ve made that very clear, Garrett.”

Garrett moved from the window and leaned over the table in front of Violissa. “And you’re ok with this?”

She smiled. “I am. Trust me, I won’t need it.”

“But your children may.”

Why were humans so curious? “No, there will be no children to worry about here when we are gone,” she replied, sliding the last document back to Garrett.

“There has always been a final clause, Garrett. You know that. This just ensures certain people in our lives are included.”

Garrett gathered the forms and placed them back in the folder.

He sighed. “Fine. It’s your money. It has always been yours to make decisions on.”

“Exactly, and you and Erin will be set for the rest of your

lives."

"It's not about that, Simon. It's about the extreme nature of what you're doing."

Sinow stood as did Violissa.

"This doesn't seem right," Garrett said. Then he sighed. "How long are you in town?"

Sinow looked at Violissa who shrugged.

"I don't think we've decided yet."

"Well, in that case, you need to come out to the house for dinner."

Sinow started to protest.

"Eh, eh. Erin will have my neck if she doesn't get to see you, and she's chomping at the bit to meet the woman who finally stole your heart. Besides, she'll never believe how beautiful your new wife is if she doesn't see for herself."

"We'd be delighted," Violissa answered for him.

Vi, he said in enaigne. *What are you doing?*

Being social. Besides, it'll be nice to get away from our problems for a little while.

He wanted to fight her on it but knew Garrett would notice.

"We'll see you at five then," Garrett said, Sinow having missed all he had said.

Violissa, ever better attuned to interactions than he, said, "I don't know if we can make it by then. Will that give us enough time?"

"I tell you what. Make it seven. That will give you plenty of time."

"Seven it is," she said.

Garrett shook Sinow's hand, still giving him that appraising look, then turned to Violissa who leaned in and hugged him.

"It was so nice meeting you, Garrett. I'm looking forward to meeting your wife tonight. I'm sure she's just lovely."

Garrett gave Sinow a look. "How on earth did you catch someone this sweet and personable?"

Sinow laughed. "Fate I guess."

As they walked down the street after leaving the office, Sinow said, “You’re sneakier than you lead on, Vi.”

“I prefer the term coy.”

He laughed. “And why are we going to his house for dinner tonight?”

“Because he’s you’re friend—”

“Simon’s friend,” he corrected.

She shot him a dirty look. “Your friend. He’s curious, I think he knows more than you think, and he’s Tenebron.”

Sinow stopped walking and turned to her. “What?”

“You can’t see it? The brown eyes, black hair?”

“There are millions of people in this world with those traits, Violissa. You can’t be serious.”

“I am. Think about it. Just like the town, they all have Cirillian and Tenebron traits.”

“The doorman to my building has brown eyes and black hair. You’re telling me he’s one of mine?”

“No, don’t be silly. He’s just a regular man.”

Sinow felt the ire building with his frustration, the pedestrians around them walking a wider path.

“Then how do you know Garrett is Tenebron or any of the others for that matter?”

“Instinct.”

Laughing hard, he started walking away, saying, “This is crazy.”

“It’s a sense I get when I’m around them. Like...like home.”

He turned back and looked at her. She was serious, the green of her eyes a brilliant green.

“Ren feels it, too. I can tell.”

“Even if this were true, Vi, why would our people be here?”

“I don’t know, but so many things about this life are different. We know this from Ren. What if Ren isn’t the only thing the Fates did to help us, to guide us?”

“What good would having our people around us do?” As he said it, he realized he knew the answer. “Remind us of home, a support network from the Fates."

"They knew we would need people here, people who would believe us, people who would feel their connection to us grow when we woke."

"That would mean they knew this would happen," he stated.

They stared at each other, both knowing the power of his words.

"You think they knew this would happen?" she whispered as if saying the words aloud would bring the wrath of the Fates down upon them.

"Ren said we let him go, that you had been told to do so by one of the Fates. Why would they do that if they didn't know Tynan was going to bring him here?"

"They wanted him here. With us. That's why he didn't arrive with Tynan. They wanted him there exactly at that time and not with Tynan."

"They knew we'd be curious. They knew we'd need his help."

"Sinow, they've known all of this would happen."

"If you're right about Garrett, Vi, then they want us to go there tonight. That's why you accepted."

"I wonder if they knew I'd stray? Sinow, if that's the case—"

"It means all of this has been planned. None of it was unexpected. I wonder how much of that prophecy scroll the Fates kept from your Keeper."

They both stood there, neither willing to move, neither willing to talk for fear of admitting they'd both only been pawns in a game where will did not exist.

Ren stared at his parents. He couldn't believe what they were saying. To think the Fates had directed them down their path, a path in his lifeline that had left his mother abused and even murdered by his father's brother. His parents revered the Fates, never crossing them anymore, never speaking ill of them. Was this why? Had they figured this out as well?

"What you're saying is crazy," Keary said.

"Why? Think about it. Our lives have never been our own. They belong to the Fates," his father said.

"As does everyone's life."

"Not like ours," his mother said. "We were created for their desire. Split from the same soul she told me."

"The Mother Fate?" Ren asked before he caught himself.

"Who?" his father asked.

"Nothing."

"The Mother Fate?" his mother asked. He tried looking away, but she was too quick. "She's the Mother Fate. A true Fate? How do you know this, Ren?"

"You know I can't say. I shouldn't have said that." He wanted to kick himself.

"If she's a true Fate, then we're right. They're directing us down this path, writing the story for us," his father said.

"It doesn't change anything," Paige said. "Whether they're pulling the strings or not, we still need to move forward. You still have decisions to make, puzzles to solve, people to love. It all still remains."

"On their terms," Sinow said. "Do you have any idea what it's like to have no choice, Paige—"

"But you have choices. You always have," Ren interrupted, frustrated with it all. "Each time, a choice is made. She could have kissed you that day, you could have forced her. She could have broken off the sham union with Daneele when you told her the truth. You both could have given in at any time." He stood, angry at it all, forgetting where he was and that he wasn't home. "You could have stayed by her side that day, and you could have let him. You could have said no to whatever agreement you made that final day that changed it all, and you...you could have trusted her enough to not ask her." He stopped, his hands shaking as the pre-ascension power surged and ebbed in him.

They were staring at him, an uncomfortable silence falling upon them all. His mother stood and walked over to him, placing her hands on his, calming the tremors.

"What happens to us, Ren?"

Suddenly, none of it mattered, the only thing that seemed of importance was her, his gentle, loving mother. Something in him tripped, his Dark code taking over, Dark power rising, his eyes heavy with the black he knew had filled them. He needed to protect her. He needed to keep her from the fate that awaited her, and the only way was to tell his father.

As if she sensed this, she stepped back, allowing him to see them both.

"He hurts her. He takes her. He nearly kills her, he does kill her before they bring her back. Nothing you do can stop it, he hides her away where you can't reach her. He'll hurt her." He stopped, realizing only then that the room was black with his power and his father's.

"How does he hurt her?" his father asked through gritted teeth.

"You leave her side. She convinces you she'll be all right, but she's not. He'll steal her powers and her immortality then he'll steal her. He wants everything you have, your crown, your throne—"

"My queen."

"Sinow, it hasn't happened," his mother said, resting a hand on his arm. Ren could see the tension in the muscles below.

"But it will. Tell me the rest, Ren."

"I don't know it all. My parents never spoke of that time in their lives. It was forbidden to ask. What I gathered came from Keary or other Council. It was a forgotten time to my parents."

"What did Keary tell you?"

He ran his hands through his hair, his power calming enough to sense his mother's. She was shielding Paige and Cody from the Dark power that filled the room. He looked back up at his father whose black eyes were an endless cavern of terror. If he knew, he'd kill Tynan this time, ensuring his mother would never be hurt. Maybe this was his reason for being here.

"He steals her to the Hidden Realm. He has a way in." His mother took a step back. "I don't know what happened there, only that he hurts her—"

"How?"

"Sinow," his mother pleaded, fear in her voice.

"How?" his father demanded.

"He will abuse her for the moon she is locked away with him, beat her so badly that her body fails her." A crack split the air as his father's power erupted. "The rest I think you already know. You can infer just as I did."

The room went pitch-black, the air heavy. Paige whimpered in the corner. Then his father shifted, and the room lightened. He heard a massive explosion then everything froze. He and his mother stared at each other then she glanced around and gasped.

She waved a hand in front of Keary's face, but Ren knew he didn't see her.

"He can stop time. It effects everyone but those with royal blood. At least that's the theory. I've never actually seen it done at this level. I've heard he discovered the ability when he rescued you from Tynan."

She dropped her head. "That's why your father never leaves my side, isn't it?"

"Yes."

She walked past Keary who remained frozen and, opening the balcony doors, walked outside. Ren followed. All around, life was paused, the cars below stationary, people on the streets caught mid stride, the clouds above with no movement, awaiting their release.

"Fates, Ren, no one has ever had this power." Her voice carried a tone of admiration. "He doesn't even realize he's doing it, does he?"

Ren shook his head.

"Sinow has the power to stop time and," she paused, her brow furrowing, "Tynan has the ability to manipulate it."

"I don't think Tynan's comes naturally."

"Why is that?"

"Call it a hunch," he said, staring out at the scene, feeling her eyes on him.

"I should go to him," she said, thankfully not pushing the subject.

"No," he said instinctively. "No, he needs someone else."

Ren walked back and tapped Keary's chest, releasing him from the spell with the magic his father had taught him.

Keary looked around, confused.

"You were over there, Violissa, and...holy crap, why are Cody and Paige not moving?"

"My father's pissed, and his powers need release," Ren said, ignoring the question.

"And he did this?"

"Yes."

"Well, that's new."

"Keary, Ren thinks you can help better than I."

A look of sadness passed his face. "Sinow doesn't deal well with emotions, not to any fault of his own. Dark kings aren't meant to be emotional. They react to injustice and deal with it."

"Except when it comes to me," Violissa said.

"Bingo. There are too many other emotions, mortal emotions that conflict with the Dark king in him. When you were cast here, he was a wreck, finally shutting everyone out, letting the madness in."

"And when I was stolen?" she asked Ren, her eyes deep with worry.

"I've been told it nearly destroyed him."

She pointed out to the balcony where a thick gray fog was now covering the quiet stillness. "My oh my, we have one massively upset Dark king. He wants to punish, but he can't."

"What happens if he doesn't?"

"He'll destroy this entire city which goes against everything he stands for."

"I did this," she said quietly.

"Violissa?" Keary asked.

"I'm a weakness for him. I always have been."

Ren studied her, seeing the familiar side of his mother he hadn't yet seen in this version of her.

He was about to speak when Keary said, "I don't believe that for a moment. He's stronger with you, Violissa. Look around, you haven't made him weaker."

"But I—"

"Give him something more than Darkness and order to worry about. You allow him to be a man, and that conflicts him. It does not, however, make him weak."

"When did you become so wise?" she asked, smiling playfully.

"I've always been like this. Right, Ren?"

Ren shook his head to disagree, laughing. "An entirely new side of you, Keary. But," he added seriously, "he's right. My father once told me that being bound to my mother was frustrating and complicated, but she made him a better man, a better king."

"Need I go on?" Keary asked.

"No," she replied with a smile, her eyes filled with moisture. "But you do need to go talk to him or whatever it is you do to get him out of this mood."

"Annoy him," Keary responded. "Fires him up every time, and that's what he needs."

Keary closed his eyes, feeling for Sinow's shift trace then disappeared.

Ren was left alone with his mother, unsure what to do now. She looked over to where Cody was frozen standing guard in front of Paige.

"You protected them, didn't you?" he asked, only now

realizing what damage he and his father could have done to Paige. He had a suspicion that Cody would have been just fine, but Paige would have suffered. She walked over to them and knelt down next to Paige, brushing her hair back, the movement not disturbing Paige's stillness.

"I knew she wouldn't survive the Darkness," Violissa replied, "and I wasn't sure about Cody. What happens to her, Ren? Does she live?"

He thought about his mother and how she often talked about Paige, how she missed her friend. It was a loss she and Daneele carried together.

"She does. She marries a man from Cathal but will have no children."

"She served her purpose," his mother said sadly. "She's so much more than they see. She deserves better."

"She was happy to her last day, or so I've been told."

She rose, but Ren continued to stare at Paige, her blue eyes hidden mostly by her hands except a small sliver that showed between open fingers, fingers purposely separated to peek at the action. He couldn't help but chuckle, his mother doing a double take. He could feel her eyes appraising him as he tried to bury the stir he had in his chest.

"Ren," she said slowly.

He met her eyes. "It's nothing. I simply found it funny that she was so curious."

He ran his hand through his hair, feeling the jitters again as a pre-ascension shake passed through him.

She chewed her lip but then a massive boom broke the silence, a plume of dirt and dust rising from an area a few miles away. He took her in, wondering what was going through her mind. Was she thinking on all he had revealed or still pondering his response to Paige?

Not wanting to talk further about either subject, he said, "Keary has him occupied. We should go see. You've probably never seen them spar."

"I've fought Sinow. I know what he's like."

"Not the same."

She continued to stare out at the expanding dust cloud, the steady battle noises filling the air. Then her eyes turned back to him, dropping to his hands which he quickly tucked in his pockets.

"When is your ascension, Ren?"

"About fifty years."

Taking his hand, she said, "That's so far, why are you having the side effects so soon? I didn't have mine until—"

"Right before your ascension. I know, mine are too early. My mother, well you, think it's because I hold opposing powers."

"An internal battle?"

"Always."

Her face softened, and she smiled, bringing her hand up to brush his hair from his forehead.

"It'll be better once the ascension comes. Your full powers will rise and balance." He heard the worry in her voice, the same his mother's voice always carried when she spoke those words.

"You'll be king then, and all of it will come together."

Instinctually, he dropped his eyes, forgetting how intuitive she was. A crash could be heard outside, but she continued to stare at him.

"We should go see what's going on."

"Ren."

"Mother," he said, forgetting for a moment.

"Do we know?" she asked. Then she continued, "Of course we know. If I can tell now, I would have seen it then. But Ren, you can't seriously be contemplating it."

"This isn't the right time to discuss my ascension," he said angrily. "Let's go."

"You can't run from it, Ren."

"I don't want to talk about it." He felt the Dark rising in him. "Now let's go."

She crossed her arms over her chest, her eyes growing a shade richer.

"If you want to go so badly, then leave."

He stared at her, the Elvin in him reacting to his Darkness and her Elvin side. She had him cornered.

"I can't," he said reluctantly.

Her eyes softened, lightening a shade. "But I've seen you shift. All immortals shift, Ren."

"I can shift, but for some reason, I can't follow your shifts. I've only been able to shift because I've known where you were going. I had already been to the bar, Violet's house—"

"You can't follow our shift trace?"

"No, nor can I use enaigne with any of you, I've tried."

She furrowed her brow as another strike hit the ground and shook the building. It didn't appear to phase her.

"You're not connected to this timeline. Even after all that's happened, you're still aligned with your timeline." Her eyes grew sad, and he could tell she was figuring out the same thing he already had. If he were still on the same timeline and his world was gone then he too would fade away as his parents had. If that were the case, then it didn't matter whether or not he wanted to ascend, there would be a completely different version of him to take that step.

"You know that's not true," she said as if she had read his mind. "You will continue on, Ren. When we finally find a way home, you will step through that portal and wake up to exactly the same person you are today."

He wondered if she were right or if it were simply her hope talking. The building shook again.

"Which is why we will revisit the ascension discussion," she said.

Not giving him time to respond, she grabbed his hand and shifted.

Sinow's feet pummeled the ground as his shift landed. Dirt spewed from below him, but he took no note of it. He was lost to his Dark powers. They soared through him in response to his anger. He roared, looking for some outlet, some release of the Darkness before it broke free on its own and destroyed the city. Ren's words continued to play in his head, his mind filling in the pieces, knowing precisely what Ren had left out. Knowing Tynan had touched her, raped her, beaten her. Every crime his Dark code should have prevented him from doing. Every violation that went against everything Sinow stood for, and Tynan had done them all to his brother's mate.

"Leave me be, Keary," he growled, feeling Keary shift near him.

"So, you can wallow in misery until you decimate Central Park? No way. You need to let that power go, Sinow."

"No, now leave me."

The air around them was heavy, and the physical effects of his power were coating the surroundings in a black mist.

"You can't change the future, Sinow."

"And what do you expect me to do? Sit back and let her get hurt, let Tynan—"

"Yes, that's exactly what you will do."

Sinow felt his eyes darken, the thought of simply letting it happen fueling the fire.

"I will not sit idly by and let him hurt her," he gritted.

"So, what will you do? Keep her caged? Clip her wings and take her freedom? You already tried that in Ren's timeline and look where it got you." Keary paused but Sinow didn't respond. "You can't lock her away. It doesn't appear to have worked the first time. Do you really want to make her give up the part of herself that makes her who she is? From what I can tell, you both suffered because of it, lost a piece of yourselves. Do you want a wife you force to remain in your shadow? A son who resents you for it?"

Sinow stared at Keary, the ire rising.

"You can't change what's coming. You can't avoid it."

"I can kill Tynan."

"But you didn't. You punished him with a fate worse than death."

"This time I will kill him."

"It doesn't matter. He'll still take her before you can kill him, Sinow. The Fates have their reasons. What happens to Violissa serves a purpose. There is a reason it happens."

Keary waited for Sinow to respond, but Sinow couldn't, the thought of Tynan hurting her, touching her, too much to bear. His power overflowed, and he struck Keary with it, sending him soaring through the air.

Keary shifted in front of him.

"That's it. Let it loose, Sinow. Hit me."

Unable to control himself any more, he attacked Keary. They fought, volleying back and forth, earth and trees thrown in their wake. He didn't stop until he felt the anger drain, the Darkness fading. In that moment, he sensed Violissa's presence. He rammed Keary then shifted over him, pounding him into the ground.

"I yield. I yield." Keary coughed, his broken bones fusing. "Damn, did the union give you more power? I thought that was just a myth."

"Apparently not," Sinow said, offering a hand to help Keary up.

"Better?" Keary asked.

"Better but still not happy about it."

"Eh, you're a Dark king. Very little makes you happy."

"You boys made quite a mess," Violissa said, peering into the gap where they now stood. "I do hope you're planning to clean that up."

"You're the nature queen," Keary said, looking at her. "Isn't that your department?"

Violissa crossed her arms and frowned at him.

"I think that's a no," Sinow told him.

"Worth a try," he said, then shifted to where Violissa and Ren stood.

Sinow followed, looking around when he landed. Violissa eyed him.

"Trees?"

"Just be glad we're not home, or I would be in immense pain right now."

"You're that tied to the land?"

She shook her head. He hadn't realized the connection ran so deep.

"But not here, lucky for you."

"We'll fix it," he said, then realized he had no idea how to undue this damage. When they'd cleaned up the town after Tynan's mess, it had been easy. He rebuilt the stores and physical structures, and she restored the damage to the grounds.

"This isn't exactly Darkbearer territory," Ren said. "Let me."

He moved his hand out, and a wave of nature magic appeared but instead of drifting away to help the land it crested like a wave then collapsed, dissipating before them. He looked at his hand, a puzzled look on his face.

Violissa laid a hand on his arm. "I don't think you're allowed to impact anything we do with more than your words and your presence, that's why you can't follow us or speak to us with enaigne.

"Really? You can't?" Sinow asked, glad his mind was finally on something besides Tynan.

"So, it would appear," Ren replied.

"I'll take care of it," Violissa said. She brought her hand up, closed her eyes, and opened her mouth to sing.

"You don't need to sing," Ren said.

She closed her mouth and looked over at him.

"I always sing when I need to use my nature magic for something this big, and they made a pretty big mess," she said, shooting Sinow a look then peering down into the gaping hole closest to them. "It's the only way to bring my nature magic to full power."

"No. Our nature powers are instinctive. You can recreate this place with the same effort that you would coax a rose to bloom."

"And where did you learn that?" she asked, a bit of awe in her voice.

"My mother."

Violissa looked down at her hands. "I don't know how to do it without singing."

"Close your eyes, listen for the call of your nature magic then for the answering call from the land and let go."

Sinow could see the doubt in her eyes.

"Trust me. I've never had to sing to use my nature powers."

"But my voice—"

"Enhances your powers, reinforces the Light. But that's not necessary for something like this. In fact, it's not needed for most things."

Violissa's brow furrowed. "And I learned this on my own?"

Sinow noticed the slight hesitation before Ren answered her. "No, you had help. Now try it."

Another moment in time he wouldn't disclose. Sinow thought back to what they'd learned recently and decided that they'd learned enough. Ren was right; it was best to leave some things to be discovered. He wished they hadn't pressed Ren, wished he didn't know now what their future held.

Violissa put her hand out again and closed her eyes. Sinow felt her draw her nature power, his Dark power reacting to it but not in the same way it would to her Light power. Her nature magic was seductive to him, it stirred something, a connection between the two, and he wondered if the Elvin and his kin were more alike than they'd realized. The feel of her magic pulled him from his thoughts, and he watched as it spread as Ren's had, this time coursing through Central Park, a mist of emerald and jade cascading through the devastation. Glancing over at her, he took in the crystal green of her eyes as they shimmered with power then drew his eyes away to witness something most people in his world had never seen, the power of the Elvin.

The land rolled gently below his feet as it rose to fill the gaps he and Keary had created; felled trees lifted and mended, their leaves shivering in response. The dirt trodden grass below their feet shook itself loose and, turning a deep green, awoke to take its former shape. The sky cleared, the remaining haze of his Dark power fading as the sun's rays penetrated it, the clouds shedding their gray film and filling the sky in fluffy white powder puffs. All around them, the air lightened and nature spoke.

Violissa drew her power back, but they remained silent. She, too surprised at her actions to speak and he too impressed. Finally, Keary broke the silence. Placing a hand on Sinow's back, he said, "Yeah, I'd be worried. I think the Fates definitely skewed the power ratio to her favor."

Sinow elbowed him and heard Violissa laugh. He met her eyes which had softened, returning to the vibrant emerald he loved.

"I think we'd better give them a moment, Keary. I know that look all too well from my parents."

"You think you can find your way back. It's a long walk," Keary joked.

Ren shot him a look. "I can shift to places I've been," he grumbled then shifted.

"Give him a break, Keary. We both know how hard it is to have your power limited," Sinow said.

Keary shifted, leaving them alone.

"So, is this cleaning up after you thing going to be a regular part of our life together?" Violissa asked.

"Once we get home, no. For now, maybe," he said sheepishly, running his hand through his hair.

"You're better now?"

"Calmer, yes," he replied, moving closer to her. He ran his finger along her curl, enjoying the softness of it.

"One of those calming spells you use might come in handy next time."

"I'll remember that."

He dragged his eyes from the curl and met hers, the now lush sage color revealing the depths of her emotions.

"Sinow—"

"Don't Vi..." he started then thought back to what Keary had said. He searched her eyes. "I don't think I can handle speaking of it," he said honestly.

Her eyes grew sad. "There's no way to avoid it, Sinow. You know that; you know the way of the Fates."

He gripped his hand tight as the ire grew again.

"Sinow, whatever happens, nothing will change the way I feel about you. Nothing will diminish what we have."

"But it will. You heard what Ren said."

"Yes, but I didn't hear him say his parents, we, loved each other any less. We made sacrifices that we shouldn't have made, something that changed our relationship but not our love for one another."

"He resents me for whatever it was, Vi."

Her eyes held sadness as she brought her hand up to his chest.

"She told me not to make her take that path."

"Then when the time comes don't. You told me to stop you. So, I'm stopping you. Whatever happens, we don't make the same choice."

He closed his eyes, knowing in his heart what his future self had done, what he'd chosen to make them do, what she'd chosen to let him do. The same way she had made the choice for them to walk this path, and he had chosen to let her.

Feeling her lips on his, he pulled her in closer, returning her kiss, the need for her resurfacing. He lost himself momentarily before he remembered they were still in Central Park.

"Let's go back," he muttered between kisses.

"Not before you do something for me," she returned breathlessly.

"I can think of quite a few things to do to you, but this might not be an appropriate spot."

She laughed and lowered her head. "Not to me, for me." He noted the twinkle in her eyes as she brought them back up. "First, you need to unfreeze everyone."

"What?"

"Well, you seem to have stopped time." She pointed up to the sky, his eyes following. It was only then that he saw the clouds were static, a few birds stuck mid-flight under them.

"Did I do that?" he asked incredulously.

"Mmm hmm."

"How?"

"I was hoping you'd tell me. It's a pretty cool trick."

"I honestly have no idea, and I don't know how to break the spell. Wait, why aren't you frozen, Ren, and Keary? And how did I not notice that while you were healing things?"

"I don't know about that last part, but Ren says it doesn't affect royal blood, and he did something to unfreeze Keary."

"So, he knows I have this ability."

"It would appear so."

"Well," he said, pulling her close again and nuzzling her neck. "I believe this gives me a reason to make love to your right here, right now. No reason to go back to the apartment."

A flush filled her cheeks, urging his desire on. Not giving her a chance to reply, he kissed her, her body not protesting the move. Instead, she pressed in tighter against him, her heart beating a matching rhythm to his. He let the feel of her, the taste, the heat that rose in him drive his moves. Running his hand through her tangle of hair, he found the back of her dress. Thankful she was wearing human garb, he brought the zipper down, feeling the increase in her pulse, sensing the flare of desire that grew in her.

He gave himself over to his need and let the dress fall as her hands worked to remove his clothes.

Sinow, Keary broke through his pleasure.

Go away, he growled back.

Are you—

Leave us be, Keary—

Oh, good Fates, Sinow. You two aren't—

Goodbye, Keary, he said, cutting his enaigne off and bringing his focus back to the feel of Violissa's skin against his as they moved to the ground. They made love, the world around them oblivious, onlookers static, life frozen as their love deepened.

Violissa watched as Sinow pulled his shirt over his chest, her fingers clasping the top of her dress as her other hand brought the zipper back to its full position. She could have stayed in his arms for eternity, the feeling she had when they were so close was indescribable. She'd once read a book where the protagonist had described her lover as home, and that was probably the closest she could think of, but it still didn't feel like the right word. He was strength, safety, protection; he was a part of her, the other half of her soul.

His eyes followed her hands as they moved down her body, smoothing the material of her dress. She'd chosen it to look more businesslike for their meeting with Garret. It still felt odd to wear human clothes, the material fit to her body rather than flowing and sitting loosely like she preferred. He brought his eyes back up to meet hers and smiled coyly as her heart skipped. She felt her cheeks grow warm, and he laughed.

Walking over to her, he kissed her forehead. "Please never stop blushing."

"You like my pink cheeks?"

"I love your pink cheeks." He kissed her cheek as if to prove his point.

She sighed. "You need to set things right, Sinow, and we need to get back."

He leaned his head against hers. "We can't leave things like this? Think of all the great places I could make love to you."

"As tempting as that is, it might get a little awkward for Keary and Ren. Besides, I don't think the god of this world would appreciate us leaving his people like this. I'm certain he's already angry about it."

He looked at her, eyebrow raised.

"Don't question, just trust me," she replied with a smile.

"Fine. Any thoughts on how to undue my spell?"

"Not one." She had broken the spell on the bullets that day with the agents with a bit of effort, but this was a huge undertaking compared to that. She knew this had to be Sinow.

"That's what I was afraid of." He looked around, brow furrowed as he thought it through. She couldn't help but smile at how cute he looked. *Cute?* Violissa said to herself. *He's a Dark king. You've been human far too long.*

She watched as he rolled his neck then felt him draw his power, her blood stirring with its increasing presence. Then he put his hands out and swept them along the air in front of him, a burst of magic emitting from them. She felt it tickle her senses, it was gentle, non-invasive, lighter than other times he'd used his powers.

Within seconds, the clouds began to float by again, a subtle breeze drifted through her hair, and the silence was replaced with the busy hum of city life once more. Sinow looked down at his hands as if unsure that he'd just done what he had.

"That seemed easy," she said.

"Oddly so. Post union power?" he asked.

She shrugged. "I guess. They did say we'd have greater powers."

"Greater. Not new."

Violissa, Keary said in enaigne, *is it safe to talk now?*

She smiled. *Yes.*

Good, Sinow cut me off.

She raised an eyebrow. "Did you block Keary?" she asked.

He laughed. "Damn right I did. Poor timing."

Paige and Cody are moving again. Sinow broke the spell?

Yes, we'll be back in a moment, Keary.

"Wait, you're talking to Keary?"

"Yes, he..." At that moment, it dawned on her. She shouldn't be able to speak enaigne with Sinow's Council. A ruler only had ability to speak within his own Council.

Sinow stared at her, but she was as shocked as he.

Finally, he said, "Another perk of the union?"

She shrugged. "I guess so." Then she bit her lip, thinking. "If I can speak with your Council then you can speak with mine. This is incredible."

"I wonder what other new talents we gained from the union."

"I've no idea, but I have a feeling we're going to find out. How did Keary know?"

"Ren must have told him, and I have a feeling Ren knows what other powers we've gained."

"But I don't think he'll tell us," she said playfully.

"I would have to agree with you on that," he said, kissing her.

They returned to the apartment where they endured a chewing out from Paige who was furious at having been excluded from the action. One that continued until Keary finally dragged her and Ren out to eat. Sinow eyed Violissa when they left.

"Are we certain Daneele didn't marry a Tenebron?"

"Cirillians get upset, too, Sinow."

"Really?" he asked, pulling her close. "I thought it was only their queen."

"Now that would be a false assumption. Although I have been told my temper runs quite a bit hotter than others in my realm."

"A bit? There have been times when I wondered if you weren't a Dark queen in disguise."

She winked. "The Elvin in me can be a little temperamental."

"The Elvin in you could make a Darkbearer quiver, Vi."

Laughing, she replied, "That's not a good thing?"

"Maybe to a Light king but as luck would have it, you're married to a Dark king, and he finds that side of you quite irresistible."

Slipping her fingers up his chest playfully, she said, "Then I guess it's too bad we only have an hour left before we need to leave."

"That'll do just fine," he replied, kissing her neck.

As her body began to react to his call, she wondered how they'd ever make it to dinner on time.

The drive to Garrett's took an hour during which Sinow could barely keep his eyes on the road. Violissa looked stunning. He didn't know why that surprised him, she always looked beautiful. She had piled her hair in a loose style that left her wayward strand seductively grazing her cheek. Normally, he preferred her hair down, but tonight was an exception. His mind continued to wander to how he would enjoy taking it down later along with removing the dress she'd chosen to wear. The deep green of it accentuated her eyes which were rich with color; they'd remained that shade since they'd left. He'd been unable to resist making love to her again while she'd been getting ready. In his defense, she'd instigated it that time, those lush eyes seducing him, drawing him in as they always did. Who was he kidding, he'd take her every second he could if that were possible. He couldn't resist the need for her and wondered if that fire would ever wane. She shifted in her seat, the loose fabric of the dress moving to expose more of her thigh.

He swallowed ridiculously loud.

"Sinow, I know our powers give us a lot of advantages but driving with no eyes on the road isn't one of them," she said just as he heard a horn. He corrected his vision then the wheel, bringing the car back to their lane just in time.

"Sorry, I was distracted."

"I noticed," she said. "It's hard, isn't it?"

"What?"

"Keeping our desire at bay."

He glanced at her.

"Eyes. Road," she responded.

Laughing, he focused on the road, saying, "Having a hard time, too?"

"Yes, is it bad that I want you to pull the car over so that we can continue doing the things we did before we left?"

He gripped the steering wheel, turning the car into Garrett's long driveway.

"Fates, Vi. You make this difficult on a man."

"Why? Because I'm just as sexual as you are?"

He put the car in park and rested his head on the steering wheel. *Get a grip, Sinow,* he told himself. He turned to Violissa and started to speak but stopped when he saw that she was focused on something else.

"Wow, I don't think I've ever seen a house so large!"

He gave her a funny look. "Seriously Vi? You live in a castle, one hundred times this size, might I add."

"I know, but for a house it's huge. He must have a lot of wealthy clients," she said, exiting the car, her eyes still wide with wonder.

It made him smile, there was an innocence to her that was special. He imagined it was something that made her a rare ruler, one who found wonder in the small things others took for granted.

"I'm his only client."

"What?"

"I've paid Garrett and his family well, Vi. In return, I receive their loyalty, their secrecy, their only attention. It's served us all well for a very long time."

He knocked on the door, hesitant to go forward with this. Socializing wasn't something a Dark king did nor was it something with which he was comfortable. He glanced over at her. Her eyes were bright green now, and she wore an expression of childlike wonder.

"Who are you?" she whispered.

"There's more to me than you know, Vi. Just like I remember you telling me ages ago."

The door opened, interrupting their playful conversation.

"Simon, Violet," Garrett said, his eyes never leaving Sinow's.

They know, Violissa said. He turned quickly to look at her.

They know, Sinow.

"Simon?" Garrett asked. "Everything ok?"

He recovered quickly, saying, "I thought I heard Violet say something." He took Garrett's hand and shook it, sensing the tension in his grip. She was right, but it was to be expected, the two of them could try their hardest to look human, but their power was hard to hide. He'd been working with Ren to quell his magic and had gotten better at it. He could go out now without covering himself with a hood, but he still stood out as did Violissa.

Garrett stepped aside to let them in. His wife Erin stood behind him.

"Simon," she said hesitantly, her voice shaking slightly. "So nice to see you again."

She moved toward him, but he extended his hand instead. "Never one for hugs, were you?" she replied, shaking it.

Sinow felt Violissa's calming magic gently flow through him and sensed Erin relax.

"He may not be, but I am," Violissa said, greeting Erin with a hug. "It's so nice to meet you."

"You as well, Violet. My, Garrett was right. You are a rare

beauty."

"Thank you," she replied. "Your hair is such a beautiful shade." She picked up a piece of Erin's hair, studying it.

Sinow shot her a puzzled look.

"Thank you! I had it done a few days ago. I usually go a shade lighter, but this time I wanted a deeper red," Erin replied excitedly.

"I had no idea it wasn't your natural color." Violissa glanced coyly at Sinow.

"My stylist is terrific. She's the only one who can mask my natural color. If it weren't for her, I'd have a head of Garrett's hair."

"You don't say. Black is your natural color?"

"Yes, but it hasn't been that shade since before we were married," Garrett answered. "I like the red, but I miss her true color."

They had walked into the sitting room. Sinow watched as Violissa chatted with Erin, Erin's brown eyes growing excited when Violissa complemented a map Erin had framed.

"They're getting along well," Garrett said, handing him a glass of bourbon. "Your drink of choice."

He wished it would alleviate the stress he was feeling in this situation, but it wouldn't. He chugged it anyway.

"Wow, didn't expect that," Garrett exclaimed in response.

"Wait, you were born near Birr, Sinow?" Violissa asked.

Vi, remember who we are.

She turned to him, clearly not caring that Garrett and Erin were staring at her.

"How did that never come up?"

"I'm sure it did, Violet," he said stressing her human name.

"I was born near Kinnity."

That caught his attention. Kinnity was close, how had they never met before now?

"Well, this is fascinating," Erin started.

"Where were you born before that?" she asked, ignoring

Erin.

"What's going on, Vi?"

She turned back to the map which he now saw was an antique map of Ireland.

"I was born here in my previous life." She brought her hand up to where the town lie on the map, too close to where he'd been born that lifetime.

Now he was curious. He stood and moved closer to her, pointing to the town of his prior birth.

"Would either of you mind telling me what's going on?" Garrett asked.

"Instinct," Sinow replied, knowing that's what was driving Violissa.

"Erin, I'm sorry. I promise I will replace this."

She brought her hand up and using her magic shattered the glass, freeing the map which to Erin's horror she slammed down on the closest side table, moving the glasses of alcohol out of the way with her power.

"Where before that?"

He listed each town until the pattern re-started. As he did, a green light burned into the map for each one, all the lights forming a pattern. She went through her birthplaces, a blue sparkle appearing in each, the pattern interwoven with his.

"It's a pattern," she said.

"That was priceless," Erin stuttered.

"That was magic," he heard Garrett say, but his attention remained fixed on Violissa.

"This life returned me to the original town near Birr, which is the only one that doesn't fit the pattern," he told her, putting his finger on the spot. "It's further east. Why didn't I see that?"

"But my original birthplace, here, just outside of Kinnity again, does fit the pattern." She brought her hand over the map, and the lights spread in lines. All the lines converging slightly north of Birr.

"What is that?" she asked.

He thought about the town and surrounding area. The convergence was north of the town. What was north of the town?

"A lake," he said, meeting her eyes. "There's a lake behind the town."

She gnawed her lip, her eyes sparkling brightly, then grabbed the map and ran from the room.

"Where is she going? Simon, what's going on?" Garrett asked, the concern overflowing in his voice.

"I think we're about to witness how instinct drives my wife."

Quickly, he followed her toward the back of the house out the deck doors. She had the map in the air, stretching it into a world map, her magic adding the missing content. It rotated, the lights shining over Ireland. She pushed the map out into the yard, looked back at him, then leapt off the balcony to run after it. He shook his head, smiling broadly.

"Can you explain what's going on? Please, Simon," Garrett pleaded.

Not drawing his eyes from Violissa, he said. "You were right, Garrett. I would venture a guess that your family has had suspicions for a while now. My name is Sinow, not Simon, and my wife Violissa is about to show you the beauty of nature magic. So, sit back and enjoy the show."

The magical world rotated, the lighted towns shimmering in the night sky. The moon's beam shone down upon her golden hair giving her a star-like quality. He was mesmerized. The rotation sped up, the world shifting then folding itself multiple times in various directions so that finally only Ireland shone to them once again. The lights reached toward each other to illuminate the town in which he'd been born this life, a brilliant purple hue filling its spot. She brought her hand up and gently tapped it, causing it to spin, revealing another section of the map at exactly a ninety-degree angle, the purple beaming through at a forty-five-degree angle. He jumped the deck rail and walked over to her only then realizing he recognized the shape.

"New York State," he said.

"And that," she answered, pointing to the beacon. "That is my lake."

He looked at her, speechless.

"The two are connected, and I would bet with all the magic that went into placing our births—"

"That there's magic in the Irish lake." He had no doubt she was right. Running his hand through his hair, he called Keary.

Keary!

Everything all right?

Just come to us, and I'll explain. Dim your power.

He refocused and saw Garrett and Erin had moved closer. Keary shifted in, and they both jumped, Erin screaming.

Keary laughed then caught himself as Sinow threw him a look.

"Sorry," he said, putting his hands up.

"Keary?" Garrett asked.

"Hey, Garrett, Erin. Nice to see you both. Guessing they filled you in for some yet to be seen reason?"

"No, we haven't. Violissa found a link to the lake from the town. I need you to get the others ready. We're heading to Ireland."

"That's unexpected. Do I want to ask?"

"Probably not. Even if you did, I don't think I could answer. We'll head out in the morning."

"And how do you expect to do that?" Violissa asked.

"We'll shift."

"With the others? Remember Ren can't follow our shifts."

"We're strong enough to take all of them at once, Vi."

"And where shall we go?"

"Uncle Pat's," Keary answered.

"Just shift in unannounced and scare them half to death? Surprise, don't mind us we're just immortals from another world who you've thought were someone else all this time?"

"She has a point," Garrett said.

Sinow had to grab his power before it rose at the intrusion. He felt Violissa's calming spell increase, realizing she'd been casting it this entire time to calm Garrett and Erin.

"You can't go without letting them know. Even if you can appear out of thin air. Your aunt will flip, especially if you bring others without warning her."

Sinow rubbed his temples. "How do you propose we go about this then, Violissa?" He was growing agitated, the confines of human life aggravating him.

"We fly."

"You must be out of your mind. You want to put two Dark kings, one ascending at that, and a Darkbearer in a metal tube for seven hours!"

"Not the wisest decision, Violissa," Keary added.

"Ren is not a Dark king; his other powers keep that side of him tame. I'll sit between you and Keary to keep you both calm, and Ren can sit on the other side of you. There's no way he has Light blood and doesn't know how to weave a calming spell." She put her hands on her hips as if ready to take his argument, but he had none.

"Keary call Simon's Uncle Pat and Aunt Maeve. You're much better at pretending to be human than Sinow is."

"I've had enough practice," he muttered, pulling out his phone.

"Sinow, you call your assistant and get her to book us a flight."

"Simon's assistant," he replied.

"They'll know," Garrett said. "Your uncle and aunt will know you've changed. Just as we did. You're different."

"Terrifying," Erin added.

"Good. We'll deal with that when we get there."

He pulled his phone out and heard Keary talking to Simon's aunt.

"Yes, Simon's here. No, he's not ignoring you. He's a bit... preoccupied with his new wife."

They could all hear the screaming on the other side as she chewed Keary out. Sinow had to laugh. The woman was a spitfire, and he knew she was erupting because no one had told her—Simon hadn't invited her. Keary held the phone out and mouthed, "You owe me."

"Let me guess, your aunt has black hair and brown eyes to go along with her Tenebron temper?"

He shot her a look. "Simon's aunt," he grouched, knowing she was right. Dammit, she was always right about abstract things. He thought about the town he'd grown up in this life, they all fit the Tenebron mold with a few exceptions who were dead ringers for Cirillians.

"That's why I'm calling. We're flying over." The voice through the phone took on an excited tone.

"That's exactly it. See Violi...Violet is from the homelands, too, and they wanted to have a traditional Irish wedding with our family."

"What?" both he and Violissa said.

Keary put his hand over the phone. "What else was I going to say?"

"A wedding?" Erin said.

"That's funny," Garrett added. "I know your aunt. The entire town will be there."

Sinow put his head in his hands then felt Violissa's hand on his arm. "It'll be fine," she said. "A real wedding might be nice. The first was a bit rushed and emotional."

"We don't have time for this, Vi."

"Maybe we do, Sinow. We don't know that we'll find anything when we get there."

Keary walked back to them. "We're all set. She's pissed at you, but I can guarantee your wedding will be planned out by the time we get there."

"I'm going to kill you."

"Consider it payback for all the times you punished me when you were moody. I'm going to have fun watching you squirm around your family."

"Simon's family. Now you two go fill these two in while I call Simon's assistant."

He turned from them, not giving them a choice and made the call.

When he finally hung up, Sinow stayed outside, trying to wrap his head around everything. His assistant was arranging travel, and he had given her Paige's cell phone to get details from her and Cody. Ren was a different story. All of them had passports, all being dual citizens had kept their passports current. Ren didn't exist in this world. He had no identity, no passport, no human name. Sinow had been forced to give him a name and an age that fit his appearance. Now they had to figure out how to make him a passport. Violissa was making things challenging by not shifting there, but perhaps she was right. It would be difficult to explain shifting into a crowd or in front of someone.

He ran his hands over his face. What were the Fates up to? He still wasn't clear why Ren was here, why they had let Tynan strand them, what the point of all of it was. They needed to get back, they needed to right things. What point was there to keeping them here? The only saving grace was that every day they remained in this world was another day Tynan couldn't touch Violissa. His mind wandered back to what Ren had told them, the Darkness threatened to rise in response, but he kept it at bay. He wouldn't let Tynan take her this time, no matter how many times they told him it needed to happen. It didn't matter to him if it changed their future, didn't matter if it meant whatever revelation came from it wouldn't happen. He would keep her safe. The words from her future self came back to him. He had kept her close in that life, and it had still happened, then he had tied her to him, never leaving her side. What had it done to them both? What had it done to Ren?

He looked back at the house. He could see Violissa through the windows. She was laughing, bringing food to the table with Erin while Keary talked with Garrett. Her golden hair slipped forward, and she nudged it back with her shoulder before finally tucking it behind her ear after she'd emptied her hands of the plates she'd carried. It had come lose when she'd been working with the map. He smiled as her stubborn curl slipped back to her cheek before she turned her back to him. Sighing, he spread his fingers through his hair, putting thoughts of Tynan aside. It wouldn't do to dwell on it; he had enough to worry about. Walking back across the porch, he stood in the doorway unnoticed. If Violissa sensed his presence, she didn't let on.

"So, all this time you've been trapped in our world?" Erin asked Violissa as both laid plates out. Sinow knew Erin was an entertainer. He was certain she'd set the dining room prior to the visit, but with the events turning as they had, she had decided the kitchen table was the best place.

"Yes. I've been here a thousand years."

"That long?" Garrett asked. Sinow could see the wheels turning in his head.

"Don't over-think it, Garrett," he said.

"How can I not? You know, I told my father you looked like your benefactor. He said the same thing. Said there'd been others in the family who suspected witchcraft, magic, call it what you will. We were right all along. Every benefactor going back to the first was you, planning for the next life."

"After a few of Violissa's rejections, I realized it was going to be a longer journey than I'd anticipated. It made sense to live comfortably. It worked fine until longevity became more prominent, and your family grew suspicious. None of you ever questioned me though, and all of you kept quiet."

"My family was always loyal to you. We weren't going to cause you trouble. You made my ancestors who they were. You made me who I am today."

“By the way, I texted your assistant to let her know Garrett and Erin are coming with us,” Keary said.

“What? No, we don’t need any more—”

“Yes, you do! You and Keary can’t hide the fact that you’ve changed. Your appearance is—”

“Terrifying,” Erin interrupted, repeating the same description she’d given him earlier.

“Yes, and you have something about you that’s off, something I now see is power. You even carry yourselves different. You need me to diffuse the situation, to stop the minds that will become suspicious of you at first sight,” Garrett said.

Sinow crossed his arms and looked at Violissa. “And you agreed to this?”

“Yes, it makes sense, and after the trauma I put them through tonight, they need a vacation. Oh, by the way,” she said, turning to Erin. “I owe you this.”

She moved her hands, and the framed map appeared in the exact shape it had been in prior to their visit. She handed it to Erin who stared at it with amazement.

“Told you I’d replace it, good as new.”

The rest of the evening they spent talking and eating, answering questions about their world and the life they’d left. Sinow relaxed as time drifted by, having Violissa by his side helped calm him. He let her do most of the talking, and by the time they had left, he was comfortable with having Erin and Garrett accompany them.

That night, he held Violissa in his arms, her steady breaths slowing as sleep took her away. He was reminded of the night they’d spent in her room as Violet and Simon, that same deep-seated feeling of contentment filled him. She was his, and this was how they were meant to be, together. No matter what happened, no matter where they were, they were connected, their hearts and souls now one and nothing would change that.

They left the next day, Sinow and Keary relieved that his assistant had found a private plane to fly them. Violissa had asked why Sinow hadn't thought of that prior, but he had explained that he had never flown private. Simon had always been too concerned about the extra impact on the environment, and he'd been too frugal to waste the money. First class had always suited his needs. Violissa smiled, thinking of Sinow being environmentally friendly then wondered if that had only been a Simon trait.

The flight was a thrill to her, she'd never flown in a private plane before, and she felt like a child on Christmas morning. She spent most of the flight with Paige, excitedly touching everything, tasting the snacks and drinks, and gaping out the windows. The rest of the trip she spent weaving calming spells. Although not surrounded by people, containing a Dark king and his Darkbearer in a tin can, as Sinow called it, for so many hours was testing to their control. The environment was too volatile to risk their power spilling over.

Now, as they stood in the small town after what seemed the never-ending car ride from Shannon Airport, she had a jolt of nerves. This was Sinow's world, people he knew, a place he'd been without her. She laughed at herself for being so foolish, it was a small Irish village, not Tenebron.

As if he sensed her apprehension, he squeezed her hand.

"All right, everyone ready?" Keary asked as they approached what looked to be their uncle's bar, the second story harboring the inn for which their aunt cared. Simon's uncle and aunt. It was hard to keep their human lives separate from their immortal lives, confusing, at times, even throwing them into a bit of an identity crisis.

Keary opened the door and walked in first.

"Keary!" Violissa heard a woman yell. She dropped Sinow's hand and urged him in. The woman stopped short of Keary, looking him up and down then doing the same to Sinow.

"What have you two done?" she muttered.

"I told you they were into dark magic, mam," a man's voice said from somewhere. Violissa assumed it was Uncle Pat.

"It's nothing," Sinow said. "It's just been a while."

"Too long," Garrett said, stepping in with Erin behind him. Violissa stayed where she was, waiting for the tension to break.

"Garrett, Erin," Aunt Maeve exclaimed, hugging them both.

She put her hands on her rounded hips and studied Sinow, her brown eyes appraising him.

"You're moodier, more brooding than the last time we saw you. Both of you. And there's something else..."

Violissa stepped in, feeling the time was right and knowing she would be a distraction. She put her hand on Sinow's arm and peeked around him, aware that her presence, her Light power helped dim the Dark aura Sinow held.

"Oh my," Maeve said, her hand coming to her mouth.

"Fae," the girl behind her said. Violissa saw that she was younger, perhaps twenty. Simon's cousin Claire, her black hair and brown eyes mirroring her mother's and father's. "Where did you find a lost fairy, cousin?" she asked.

"Saints alive, but you are a beauty," his aunt said.

Violissa smiled and walked forward to greet her.

"Thank you. It's so good to meet you. I've heard so much about all of you." She hugged the woman, kissing her cheek.

"She's sweet and beautiful, Simon. Definitely Fae," his cousin said.

"I do hope you don't mind our intrusion," Violissa said. "I know it was sudden."

"Think nothing of it, you're family now." She picked up Violissa's hand then looked over at Sinow, flinching slightly in reaction to his power. "Where's the ring? You didn't get her a ring?"

Sinow's expression stayed static, but Violissa knew he was cringing. They'd been asked the same thing in New York a few times, and she could tell it was starting to wear on him. Rings weren't tradition in their world not in the same way they were here. They weren't exchanged in a union ceremony, there was no engagement ring. Instead, a family ring was handed down to each king to present to his new wife on their wedding night. Sinow had no ring to give her. If it still existed, it was in Tynan's hands, locked away in their world.

Thinking quickly, she remembered the engagement ring Simon had presented to her. She'd taken it off after they had woken, never able to wear it, the curse too strong when she'd tried to pick it up. Momentarily she wondered if she'd had the strength to in her first life. Had the curse woven deeper in her this time around?

"There is no ring," Sinow answered.

"No wedding ring," she corrected, calling her power and reaching it out to summon the ring. She didn't know if that were possible, but then she felt the weight in her pocket when she'd commanded it to appear there. "We didn't have time and wanted to wait for the Irish ceremony to exchange them."

Vi?

She pulled it out from her pocket. "I took this off for the flight. Flying always makes my fingers swell," she said, putting the ring on her finger, the feel of it welcoming as if she'd subconsciously missed it.

She glanced over at Sinow and smiled as his human family gathered to admire the ring.

Impressive.

Before she could answer, they were all dragged in further, introductions then made when Cody, Ren, and Paige entered behind her. The explanation that Ren was Violissa's cousin went over as well as the one about Cody being her brother. She was used to shock about the latter, they looked nothing alike, and in fact, Cody and Paige looked more like siblings. Ren's appearance was too similar to Sinow's to make it believable, but they stuck with it even through the gaping stares.

"Fae," she heard Claire whisper again.

The day progressed, and after the initial shock of Sinow and Keary's intimidating appearance there was much bustle with townsfolk coming in to say hello and meet the new beauty who had stolen Simon's heart. The final assessment was that Simon had grown broodier in America, and the Irish air would do him good. With that, Violissa made the suggestion that he show them around town, an excuse to get away so they could investigate the lake.

"Why don't you four go? Cody and I can stay here and chat," Paige said.

"We can?" Cody asked.

"It was a long flight, and I'm tired, Cody. You were telling me the same thing on the drive here."

"I was?"

Violissa spied the slight kick she gave him and bit back the laugh.

"Oh yeah, I was. She's right. You guys go."

Sinow shrugged. "Ok then. We'll be back."

They left the inn and walked down the street, Sinow and Keary greeting a few people as they walked. He turned down an alley then said, "Ready? Keary bring Ren. Let's see if I remember this place well enough."

He shifted, and Violissa followed, landing next to him in a field. To her east lie rolling hills shadowed by the passing clouds, trees standing proud in the distance, and to her right a lake twice the size as the one in her town. She drew in a breath at the beauty of it.

"Feels a bit like Tenebron," Ren said.

"Does it?" She had never truly seen Sinow's land and had never attributed the beautiful setting before her to the realm, her own biases coloring her beliefs of what it should look like.

"Aye, it does," Sinow replied. "I never noticed that."

"I did," Keary said sadly. "It's been a long time since we've seen the mountains of home."

"It won't be much longer," Sinow said, walking to the lake.

Violissa remained where she was, closing her eyes to listen to the land speak.

"I don't feel anything," she heard Sinow say.

"Nor do I. There's no magic here, no link to our world, Violissa," Keary added.

"You sense it, don't you?" she whispered to Ren who had moved next to her.

"Yes, it's subtle, but there's something."

"Vi?" She heard Sinow say.

She opened her eyes and noticed his subtle reaction. Her eyes were bright with nature magic; she could feel it.

"We are where the Fates want us. There's magic here in the land." She walked up to the water's edge and ran her fingers through it. "Yes, there's something here."

"Can you call it?"

"No, it will be evident when the Fates are ready."

"That's not a lot to go on, Violissa," Keary said. "We're supposed to just wait around for whatever it is you sense?"

"Yes," Ren answered for her. "I trust her instinct implicitly as does my father."

Sinow looked at her as she rose from the water's edge. "Your nature gifts feed your instinct."

She smiled, but it was Ren who spoke for her again.

"It is a trait of the Elvin. A link between them and the world around them, a way of seeing things others do not," he said.

Violissa turned to him. He had said it with the confidence of someone who had first-hand knowledge, of someone who had learned this from the source.

As if realizing his mistake, he dropped his gaze.

Did you catch that? Sinow asked her in enaigne.

Yes. The Elvin are alive, Sinow. She wanted to look over at Ren. She wanted to question him, but she knew Ren would avoid them, knew it was something he felt he couldn't share, so instead she said, "We should return and wait until the Fates signal it is time."

Wait again? Why do I feel like there's a lot of waiting that goes on in my life with you? Sinow joked.

When they returned, Cody and Paige were chatting away with Claire and Pat. Maeve was on the phone with someone, her laugh carrying through the room.

"Have a nice walk?" Claire asked.

"It's a wonderful town. Simon and Keary did a nice job as tour guides," Violissa responded.

"Well, you all may want to sit for a moment. Your aunt is talking to our Aunt Emma, Simon," Paige said.

"Why would she be doing that?" Simon asked.

"You know your aunt," Pat replied. "She's insistent. Wanted to make sure your Violet came from a good Irish family."

Sinow ran his hand over his face. Violissa could feel his frustration growing.

"They've been talking since you left and seem to be hitting it off. Last I heard, Aunt Emma will be booking a flight to come to the wedding," Paige continued, trying her best to keep the smile from her face.

Violissa sat, not sure what else to do.

"Oh, this is fun," Keary said, rubbing Sinow's shoulders. Sinow looked like he wanted to murder him, his fists curled tightly so that the whites of his knuckles showed.

"Why would she do that?" Violissa asked.

"Said you didn't have a real wedding there. That it was rushed. She wants to see you walk down the aisle," his aunt said, joining them. Violissa hadn't realized she'd hung up from the call. "At first, I thought you'd rushed the wedding because you'd gone and gotten her pregnant, Simon. Was about to hunt you down and give you a piece of my mind...all the good Catholic upbringing you were given. But then she explained you were just too eager to wait."

"Good thing, too. You know how she is, Simon. She would have dragged you back here by your ear like the old days."

"I believe that was Keary most of the time," he replied curtly.

Keary rubbed his ear. "Yeah, that was my ear she grabbed, Uncle Pat. I can still feel that grip."

"This just keeps getting more and more interesting," Ren muttered.

"You've no idea," Sinow said. He met Violissa's eyes.

Vi, I don't think I can take much more of this.

I don't think we have a choice.

"Anyone else need a strong drink?" Garrett asked from the other side of the bar. Violissa had forgotten they were there.

This can't get any worse, can it? Sinow said to her.

The door to the inn opened, distracting them all.

"Well, well. You two are hard to track down."

Violissa stared at the agents as they stepped through the door, then dropped her head to the bar in frustration.

Yes, I believe it can, she replied.

Violissa sat with Sinow, looking over the view from the back of the inn. There was a small patio with several padded chairs and a wooden porch swing. The spot was quaint, his aunt adding it a few years earlier. He had imagined it would be someplace Violissa would appreciate, especially in the summer when the flowers were in bloom. The others had gone to bed, the pub closed for the evening. Violissa snuggled up against him, a blanket wrapped around her legs to keep the fall chill at bay.

"My aunt will be here tomorrow," she said. "I have a strange feeling she won't be alone."

"She'll bring others?"

"Violet was close to most of the people in town, Sinow. It's a tight knit community, and most of them have family here. It'll be an excuse for them to travel."

"When is the wedding again?"

"In a few days. Strange, isn't it? We're getting married again but still not in our land, in our world, with our people."

"Our true family," he said, meeting her eyes. He reached over and brushed her curl back. She closed her eyes at his touch, as if feeling the same stir within her that always rose for him when he touched her.

The sound of the back door opening drew him from their moment.

"Mind if we join you?" Claire asked.

"Why not? We seem to have an entourage wherever we go now," Sinow replied.

Claire, Pat, and Maeve sat around them. They all seemed on edge.

"Look, I've been nominated to speak for the family, so I'll come right out and say it," Claire said. "None of us knows what it is, but we all know you're different. Mam thinks you've joined a satanic cult and that Violet here lured you in. She's also suspicious that you may be doing drugs. Da, well Da doesn't know what to think. And me, well, I think she's a fae creature who has seduced you and is feeding off your soul."

Sinow couldn't help but laugh and noticed Violissa was working hard not to.

"I'm slightly offended that I've been made the bad guy in all this," she said playfully.

"No offense, Violet, but you are a little too beautiful not to be up to something."

"Fair enough, I suppose."

"What's happened to you, Simon?" his aunt asked.

Sinow met Violissa's eyes; they were sparkling against the evening backdrop.

What do we do, Sinow?

This is getting ridiculous, Vi. Too many humans involved.

I know, but they deserve to know the truth. They're your family regardless of whether they were Simon's or not.

"Are you two done staring at each other?" Pat asked. "Your aunt asked you a question."

Sinow felt a surge of Darkness but kept it at bay.

"Sorry, we were discussing something," Violissa answered. They gave her a funny look. "We'll tell you."

"Against my better judgment," Sinow added.

"But it's a long story, one that begins eons ago with a prophecy."

Sinow noticed movement and saw Paige and Cody sneak out from the corner of his eye. Cody didn't know their full story, and Paige was the curious type, so he let them be as Violissa continued.

"That prophecy bound the heart and soul of two future rulers of our world, rulers whose realms were natural enemies. The union of these two rulers would finally bring a peace their lands had never known and bring down a magic barrier that separated their realms.

"Millennia later, the prince and princess were born. Both grew to be powerful in their own magic, he in the Dark power that ruled his line and she in the Light and nature magic that ruled hers. When the day finally came for the two to meet, the princess hesitated. You see, she knew deep down that this man owned her heart, but she was stubborn, foolishly thinking she could give herself free will. Her hesitation cost them everything. The prince had a half-brother who coveted his throne, and he seized the chance to cause them strife."

Sinow listened to her weave their tale, noticing others had stepped out to hear it, including the agents. He had thought everyone had gone to bed, but apparently there were more restless sleepers than just he and Violissa. He let it go, instead listening to the melodic rise and fall of Violissa's voice, mesmerized by it. As she wove the tale of their love, he realized that it was just that, a love story. He'd loved her through it all just as she'd loved him. He had loved her long before their path had become unbound, long before he'd ever laid eyes upon her. He remembered even as a child standing at the ravine, the very edge of the boundary, and looking beyond the magic that separated them, far into her realm, wondering what his future queen was like, longing for her even then but not recognizing the feeling for what it was at the time.

"Wait, he lost her?" the female agent asked. Sinow thought her name was Abigail, but he'd been too annoyed with their constant presence to remember. "Then what happened?"

"She was lost for a very long time. Her memories stolen, so she had nothing to tell her who she was." Violissa's gaze slipped beyond her audience as if lost in some memory. "Nothing but the dreams and the constant pain in her heart to let her know something was amiss."

She went quiet for a moment, and they gave her the silence. Then she quickly refocused as if the pain of her memories hadn't pulled her away. "The next part of the story I don't know, for it is the king's story.

She met his eyes and all else fell away. Compelled by the magic of her voice, Sinow said, "He too was lost, lost in his own pain, his own madness, unable to find her for centuries. Until he finally gave everything up to find her, leaving all that he was, all he had ever known behind. Knowing none of it mattered without her for she was now his everything, she was all he was. Through every lifetime that he found her and lost her again, he clung to that thought. It kept him sane, it kept him fighting until the day he finally gave up and discovered it had always been her spell to break and not his. He couldn't save her no matter how he tried, couldn't keep her safe no matter how he fought the truth."

A single tear rolled down Violissa's cheek. "But you did," she said. "You held my heart and kept it safe all those centuries."

He wanted to stop time in that moment, to take her in his arms and kiss her, but instead he refrained, feeling her brush his mind.

I love you, too, she told him, a slight smile forming.

"What happened to them?"

"He finally found her," she replied. "Woke her from a nightmare in which she'd been trapped, freed her from her cursed mind, pulled her out from the hell in which she'd descended."

"But you're still here," his aunt said, finally understanding.

"Maeve, what are you talking about?" Pat said.

"You're the two in the story?" Claire asked.

"Yes, Sinow's brother has us trapped here with no way home."

"Sinow?"

"That's me," he said. "And Violissa is Violet's true name."

"But I still call her Violet," Cody interjected.

"Wait, are you like them, too?"

"No, human. At least, we think. These three are from their world though."

Paige gave a guilty smile and a slight wave. "Sorry, Violissa, I've heard your story hundreds of times but hearing it from you was something I couldn't miss."

"You have power, too, Paige?" Claire asked, confusion in her eyes.

"No, I'm mortal. Keary and Ren are the only others with power."

"Mortal? You mean to tell me you're immortal as well as magical?" Pat asked.

"Wait, so are Keary and Ren related to you, Simon?" Claire asked.

"There's no way I'd claim Keary as blood," Sinow joked.

"And no way I'd want to be claimed. I'm enough of a handful, add the madness that runs through your family, and you'd be in trouble."

Sinow couldn't help but chuckle.

"Then Ren is another brother? He has to be related to you."

"That's a bit of a long story."

His aunt crossed her arms.

"I'm their son," Ren said.

Looks of confusion covered their faces.

"I said it was a long story," Sinow said.

"To simplify," Paige said, "Tynan dragged him from the future so he could kill Violissa and force Sinow to watch as Ren faded from existence, too."

The confused looks changed to ones of horror.

"I know, I had the same reaction, don't ask and just go with it."

His aunt turned back and studied him, then Violissa.

"You expect us to believe all this?"

"You easily believed I had joined a devil worshipping cult."

"That was easier than this," she replied.

"Your aunt is right. Do you have any proof?" his uncle said.

"You don't want me to use my powers as proof," he responded.

"Why?"

"Because you'd die," he answered bluntly.

Just then, something cold and wet hit his hand. He looked down and watched as a snowflake melted. Another landed next to it, then another.

He heard the astounded gasps.

"Snow? Mam, it's snowing," Claire said, the large flakes laying upon her ebony hair.

The snow fell harder, but it remained gentle and calm, accumulating on the trees and ground.

"It never snows this early. Were they calling for snow?"

"No, Maeve, it's too warm."

She cried out, "The trees, Claire, look, the trees." The closest tree, including his aunt's favorite, all began to bloom beautiful, pink blossoms that stood in contrast to the white snow below.

Violissa, what are you doing?

Giving them proof.

You know you don't have to give them anything.

I know, but a little wonder once in a while is good for the soul.

He shook his head and watched as his human family, Simon's family, walked in the snow, their hands outstretched to catch the larger-than-life flakes. Unlike a typical snowstorm, the temperature hadn't dropped yet the snow stuck, refusing to melt.

"Show off," Keary teased her. "Is this what we have to look forward to?"

"Get used to it, Keary," Ren said, laughing.

"This is you?" his aunt asked. "You're doing this?"

Violissa's eyes shimmered, and to Sinow's surprise, their emerald color reflected on the falling flakes. When she raised her hand, the flakes froze midair. She rose from her seat and studied the snow in front of her.

"I've always loved snow. In my realm, it only snows in the towns closest to the Sacred Groves. It's a sight to see. The fields, layered in white, untouched and pure, the trees hidden, reluctantly quieted in their new covering. My Council would tease me for spending so much time just sitting and watching nature cleanse itself, losing myself in the peace that I could only find there." She seemed lost in memory. "Nature is ever constant, ever changing, it speaks to us always but not many hear her. The only time they notice is during the hush of a new fallen snow when she is silenced, sleeping for a brief moment in time before she reawakens."

Delicately, she touched a flake, and he watched in wonder as it transformed, swirling to become a fragile white flower petal.

All of the flakes followed suit as the moon broke through the clouds above. It sparkled in her hair, the strands shimmering magically. He felt a gentle breeze as it picked up the closest petals, setting all the others in motion. The ones held by the breeze fluttered around Violissa, weaving in her hair. The moonlight became more intense, the breeze seeming to pick up its beam, encasing her in it, transforming her into the queen that she was, her clothing stretching then flowing to a soft lilac gown that fluttered in the breeze. No one moved, no one spoke, all too transfixed on her.

She tilted her head to the moon and smiled, a subtle thank you leaving her lips, the moonbeam dancing along her skin in diamond-like sparkles. She was every bit the nature queen in this world as she was in theirs, the god of this world embracing her as if she were part of it. In the silence, he walked over to her, leaned down and kissed her, not concerned that others were watching. She tasted of nature magic, a richer, seductive taste than when her Light magic was present. His Dark power answered, heeding its call. He pulled back and her eyes, now a deep sage, met is.

"I believe that should answer your questions. If not, the others can answer," he said, not leaving her eyes.

He wanted her, the emotions crashing within him: love, desire, need mingling with the rise of his power as it yearned to meet hers. Not waiting for a response, he held her tight and shifted.

No one moved. Ren knew this reaction. Even though his mother spent much of her time with their people, she rarely used her powers in this way. Instead, they were subtle, a strengthening of the crops here, a reviving of a dying tree there, healing was the most obvious way she used her powers; she preferred to be reserved with them, never one for the attention.

He also knew where his father was taking her. It didn't bother him, it hadn't bothered him for a very long time. This was who they were. Two people drawn to each, unablc to keep apart, unable to deny their need for one another. They truly were two halves of the same soul. He had recognized that early on, and nothing would change it.

He stepped away from the others as Keary began answering the flood of questions. The aunt was talking about a sister. Ren guessed it must have been Simon's mother. He paused, never considering the impact the curse had on those around his parents when they were here.

"She died for what? Would she have lived if your gods hadn't sent him here?" she asked sadly.

"Likely but none can know for sure," Keary said.

"In none of their lives did they have parents who survived," Ren said, turning back to look at them. "The Fates can be callous at times, but perhaps they weren't. Your sister wasn't meant to have children, was she?"

"Well, no. She was infertile or so they said."

"Aye, then the Fates blessed her with a child she never would have had. If I would venture a guess, she wasn't meant to live, it wasn't in the plans, and so your god allowed my father's rebirth through her. She played a role in an event that shapes my world, for if my father had never been sent here, never been allowed to follow my mother life to life, never been reborn each life, our world would have died, and I would not be here talking to you."

He didn't wait for her response but turned and walked away. The talking continued, but he tuned it out, looking out to the direction where the lake was. He was about to shift to it when he sensed Paige.

"Where are you going, Ren?"

He looked at her, noticing how the moonlight caught in her blue eyes, giving them a glimmering quality that was mesmerizing.

"I don't belong here, Paige. These are not my people, they don't know me. It's not my place to be here." Her expression grew sad momentarily. "I don't belong here either." She looked back at the others. "I'm not really certain where I belong."

He saw her in a different light from how his mother had always described her. She wasn't the self-assured, confident woman he had always imagined. She was lost, not part of the human world yet not part of the world his parents knew. She had no power, no immortality, she was a mortal yet not a human. He wondered if she'd felt as an outsider before she'd left on this journey. The daughter of a Council, how would others have seen her? How did she see herself?

Unconsciously, he brushed a strand of her hair from her eye. She was a bit like him, a child of two worlds, not clear which to call home. He dropped his hand quickly and lowered his gaze.

"Ren?"

Ren didn't know what he was doing, but when he looked back up, he caught Keary's gaze. It was intense, and Ren knew what it meant. He'd been scolded by enough Darkbearers in his lifetime. He took Paige's arm, saying, "Come," and shifted to the lake away from Keary's stern warning eyes. Paige teetered when they arrived.

"Wow," she said quietly. "That was so much better than Keary's shift. I still feel like vomiting but not nearly to the same degree."

He laughed and tried to focus on the land rather than the strange mix of feelings she was causing in him.

"It's beautiful," she said.

"It reminds me of home," he answered.

"It does?"

He pulled his eyes from the rolling hills to look over at her. Her eyes held a certain desperation, a longing. He had forgotten she had never seen home, all she had ever known was the

Banished Realm, a flat, undistinguished part of their world. She'd never seen her true home but the call of it still filled her veins as it did all their people.

"Aye, it does. The northern land of Cirillia is like this with its rolling hills and green fields of wildflowers, the likes I have yet to see in this world. They reach up toward the sky as if to touch the Fates, yet unable. The trees in the Sacred Groves almost succeed. They run the course from Cirillia over into Tenebron then reach the mountains in my father's land, white peaked mountains that seem endless until they flow south into valleys and fields that could envy Cirillia.

"The ravine separates both lands, a seemingly endless river lying within that flows to the top of the Sacred Groves then appears to stop until it returns miles north, winding its way through the Elvin enclave. If you climb to the peak of Cirillia, past the castle, you enter a valley that is breathtaking at dawn and sunset."

He stopped, pulling himself out from his trance only realizing he'd said too much when he saw her face.

"The Elvin?"

He cursed himself for the slip.

"They're alive?"

He nodded, knowing it was too late to hide it now. "I shouldn't have said that. You mustn't say anything to them. They cannot know."

"The Elvin," she repeated, her mind working it through. She inhaled sharply. "That's what she discovers, isn't it?" She brought her hand to her chest. "That's why Tynan has to take her, she discovers them." Her eyes grew sad. "A means to an end," she whispered.

"The Fates have their reasons for everything even if their ways aren't the kindest."

"There's no other way? Can't you tell her how to find them and spare her the pain?"

"It's not my place, and in my lifeline, that event, well it

changes everything."

"But what if you're here to reset their path? What if your lifeline no longer exists?"

Her eyes searched his, pleading for him to alter the future he so desperately wanted to change. He shook his head sadly. "I don't believe that's why I'm here, Paige. It's not up to me to redirect their path, only the Fates have that power. I learned from my parents that you can't run from your destiny, and if that's the future the Fates want for my parents, then they will face it again, and I will let them. She must discover the Elvin on her own and follow the steps to get there. I have already told them more than they should know."

She dropped her eyes, but he lifted her chin with his finger so she could not look away.

"My parents would not change that event, Paige. Even with what it cost them, they would say the path must be followed as the Fates lay it before them. I would venture that if you asked them now, before any of it has happened, their answer would be the same. They know the cost of stepping from their destiny. They know the price of an unbound prophecy, and they won't risk their lives, or our world being riven any more than they already have."

"Then why are you here if not to change the future?"

"I wish I knew the answer, but the Fates haven't shown me yet." He let his finger fall from her chin and looked out at the lake, the stillness of the water calming him.

"Ren," she said, bringing his attention back to her. "What happens to me in all this?"

"You live a long, happy life."

"No, what happens to me? Do I ever belong anywhere?"

He smiled. "No, you are unique, Paige." *Just as I am,* he thought. Neither of them fitting the mold, neither knowing which side of themselves to listen to. That sensation drifted through him again.

"Do you feel that?" she asked softly.

He furrowed his brow, not understanding what the Fates were doing. He had the strangest desire to kiss her. This woman he had known his entire life through stories and memories. A woman he'd never met but knew as well as if he'd been raised with her by his side. A woman who had died thousands of years before his birth and would do so again.

"What does it mean, Ren?"

"Nothing, it means nothing," he said. "It can't mean anything, Paige. Six thousand years separate us, and there is no way to change that regardless of what happens to my parents."

"Then you did feel it," she said shyly. "So, it won't hurt if I do this then."

She leaned up and kissed him before he could react. He had wanted to push her away, to stop it, but he couldn't. It felt too right. When the kiss finally ended, they both stood, unmoving. He dropped his head, his forehead touching hers.

"Maybe that's why you're still here," she whispered.

"No, Paige. No. This can't happen. You marry Colin—"

"Am I happy?"

"I think so. That's what I'm told."

"Maybe I marry Colin in that lifeline—"

"Paige, we can't do this. Time separates us, history separates us. This will lead to nothing but hurt. You and I shouldn't have even met."

"But we did, Ren. And we both felt that."

He backed away and ran his hands through his hair. He'd studied mating, knew how every king found his mate and the sensation he'd had every time he'd been alone with Paige matched the description. What did it mean? Was he destined to be the final king, his mate lost in time where he couldn't reach her?

He shook his head, he was taking this too far and needed to step away.

"We should go," he said, trying to avoid her eyes.

"Really?" She crossed her arms.

"You're stubborn, Paige. Let's drop this and go back."

"I may be stubborn but you're avoiding."

He looked at her, his irritation growing. "This can't be, and you know it."

She continued to stand there.

"You can't even tolerate being around my power."

"I was just fine that night you showed it to me."

He caught his breath, she was right, she hadn't even flinched when he'd drawn his power. It was his father's power she couldn't tolerate.

"Who are you trying to convince, Ren?"

He walked back over and kissed her, letting his Dark power rise, waiting for the fear but sensing none. There was no reaction to it, as if she hadn't even noticed. She paused, muttering, "And then there's the whole my best friend is your mother thing. That's awkward, isn't it?"

"Now who's trying to do the convincing?" he mumbled.

He went back to kissing her, wondering how he would ever stop and how he could ever leave her in the past when the time came to return to his life.

This is bad, Keary thought as he watched Ren shift with Paige. His attention was pulled back to the conversation, but his mind wandered until he finally gave up and looked for them. He couldn't follow Ren's shift, and he couldn't sense Paige since she was Cirillian. After checking the inn, making sure to avoid his king's room, knowing exactly what he and Violissa were doing, he took a chance and shifted to the lake, finding them exactly how he'd feared he would.

"Fates you two," he said, stomping over to them as they guiltily separated from one another. "It's bad enough having your parents all over each other but this too?"

He started to say more when he noticed Ren's black eyes, the power calling to his own. He looked from Ren to Paige then back again. Paige couldn't tolerate Dark power from anyone else, so there could be only one answer to what was happening.

"No, the Fates wouldn't be that cruel," he muttered, meeting Ren's eyes and watching as they slid to a vibrant blue again.

"I've found the Fates to be plenty cruel, Keary," he said, the brevity heavy in his voice.

"You two can't be," Keary said. "You—"

"We know," Paige said. "We've been through them all. We even covered the best friend's son weirdness although that's the least of the issues."

Keary didn't know what to say. The only reason Paige would tolerate only Ren's power was if she were his mate. But that didn't make sense and what it meant for Ren and for the future of their world was devastating. Without his mate, there would be no heir. Keary dragged his hands across his face; he felt as if he were back with Sinow when Violissa was trapped here, once again worrying about an heir and the future of their world.

"So, here's what we're going to do," he finally said. "You two keep away from each other. The last thing Sinow and Violissa need to be worrying about is this. We need to find a way home and then we can worry about this." He swept his hand up and down in front of them to indicate he meant the two of them.

"How is that supposed to make this better?" Ren asked.

"I don't know if there is a way to make this better. You both know that."

Ren sighed. "Yes, we do."

"I oughta punish you for even thinking of kissing her," Keary said, crossing his arms. "And you, you wait until this gets back to your father," he said to Paige. "Sinow is going to flip," he muttered.

He walked over and took Paige's hand. "Damn Fates, always meddling with things. Come on, he needs to concentrate on that lake, and you need to get your mind on something else."

She started to protest, but Keary shifted, dragging her with him.

"Keary!" she yelled, stumbling from the effects of the shift when they landed in the inn.

"Paige, leave it. This can't happen."

"You don't think I know that? I've been fighting this since he came here, but nothing I do makes it go away." She slumped against the wall, the fight gone from her. "I don't know what to do, Keary. It's not like I can just turn this feeling off."

He sighed. "Let's focus on getting home and then worry about this."

"But if we're home, then I've already lost him. I'll be dead long before he's even born."

"You're already dead in his world, Paige. You're a ghost to him, a memory he's gleaned from his mother and your father, from me."

Her blue eyes grew watery as she rubbed her arms. "I know."

He wanted to tell her to go talk to Violissa, but Violissa already had too much on her mind. Besides, she and Sinow had yet to emerge, so it was safe to say she was preoccupied. Against every Dark instinct, he took her in his arms and hugged her. She was family, the little sister he had to protect but couldn't.

"Thanks, Keary." She sniffed against his shirt.

"Just don't leave a mark," he joked, feeling her relax. "We'll figure it out, Paige. The Fates have their reasons. We just have to have faith in them."

He didn't know whether he was trying to convince her or himself as he spoke the words.

Twenty-Four

As the next few days passed, the Fates remained silent. Keary wondered if they were staying quiet or if they just couldn't be heard over the cacophony of voices emanating from the inn. Violissa's human family, which should have only comprised of her aunt, extended to many friends in the town who hadn't wanted to miss something magical. The inn was overfilled and well beyond anything Sinow was capable of tolerating. Keary noticed a constant calming spell blanketed him now and was thankful Violissa was keen to his king's discomfort.

Where did Sinow wander off to? he asked Violissa in enaigne. They'd realized quickly that the union had added this new ability, allowing the crossing of enaigne for the first time in their history. It was a strange feeling—touching Violissa's mind was a completely different experience: light, calming even, compared to that which he was accustomed. There had been times when Sinow was lost to the Darkness, when speaking to him had felt like wading through thick vines that tangled in his own mind.

To escape, she answered. *He's not far. I can still sense his presence.*

I'll find him, he replied. He could sense Sinow as well. Darkbearers were in tune with their king just as he was to them. He didn't feel too far from them, but he was no longer at the inn.

Keary watched Violissa for a few moments. She was in her element, talking, laughing, enjoying the company of the filled room. She was so unlike Sinow he wondered how they would manage with the differences. But of course, they would. Ren was proof of that. He looked over to where Ren sat brooding in the corner. Ren, on the other hand, was a mix of his parents, at times right by Violissa's side, talking as if he'd known these people his entire life, and other times, distancing himself as if the Dark in him had risen to disagree with what the Light had him doing. He was a dichotomy between the two dominant powers he held, and Keary could only imagine the internal battles that plagued him. Ren's gaze was fixated on something, and Keary followed it, spying Paige laughing with Aunt Emma about something.

He sighed, noticing Violissa's eyes flicker toward Ren then follow his line of sight to Paige. Her face grew sad for a fraction of a second then was masked with a smile as her eyes drew back to the person to whom she was speaking. So, she knew. Of course, she did. She had a sixth sense, instinct as she called it, which gave her the ability to notice things that others overlooked.

Not wanting to think on the Ren and Paige dilemma anymore, he left the bar and walked out to the patio in search of Sinow. He walked past the few people who were occupying the space until he was alone, then closed his eyes and felt for his king, shifting once he located him. He found Sinow by the lake, staring off into the distance.

"What is it with this lake?" he muttered. Even with no Fates' magic, Sinow and Ren were drawn to it.

Keary wondered if Violissa felt the same pull they did or if it was their Dark blood.

"Keary."

"Hiding, are we?"

"Too many people, Keary. I don't know how Violissa stands it."

"I'd venture she enjoys it and that you'll need to get used to it."

"Possibly."

Keary caught a glimmer in Sinow's hand as he turned the wedding band he'd bought for Violissa in his fingers. Claire had insisted they have bands and had dragged Sinow out to get them. He only chose the one for Violissa and only to get Claire off his back. Keary had accompanied as had Ren to provide the calming spell that Keary credited to Claire's survival. He knew Sinow would have killed her had Ren not been there. He'd not been happy about the ordeal.

"I want to be home, Keary," he said.

"I know, we all want that."

"This isn't right, it's not where we need to be. Living a farce, pretending we're human, preparing for a human wedding." He looked down at the ring. "A wedding ring? If we were home, Violissa would have my mother's ring just as she should, not this."

"I must say, you need to work on your acting skills if you're pretending to be human. You're doing a pretty shitty job of it."

Sinow laughed. "Violissa thought we should put our troubles aside and just be husband and wife, enjoy the wedding without the baggage."

"She's going to be a handful for you, Sinow, challenging every norm and everything that makes you a Dark king."

"Aye, she will. She already is. I'd even say she always has."

"And yet you still lover her?" he asked jokingly.

"Shut up, Keary."

Keary smiled. He'd missed Sinow more than he'd realized, and it felt nice to be back with his friend, pushing his buttons. In that regard, he thought he and Violissa might be very similar.

They stood in silence a few minutes before Sinow said, "When do they send us a sign? It's been a month since Tynan shattered the stone to the portal. We've been here over a week. If they keep us here any longer, Tynan will break through that barrier, and we won't be there to stop him."

To save our people, our family, Keary thought, knowing Sinow was thinking the same.

"This sounds like a Violissa conversation. She's the optimistic one with that annoying Light mind of hers."

"And she'd tell me to have faith," he said, laughing.

"Aye, and to trust the Fates," Keary added.

Sinow's smile faded. "I don't trust the Fates, Keary."

"But your future self does. Ren does, and Violissa promised them she would trust them now."

"I never did. I can't, Keary. They've done nothing but punish us, and they will continue to punish us. How can I trust them when I know what will happen to her? They will let him hurt her, Keary." His voice broke, and Keary felt his pain.

Keary sighed. He'd seen Sinow at his best and worst, he'd seen him broken, but he wondered what Violissa's absence did to him in the future. He knew his friend too well; he analyzed, studied, obsessed, and his mind would have played out every possible thing Tynan would do to her, he already was, and it had yet to happen. No wonder his future self never left her side; he'd likely driven himself to madness while she was gone.

"There's nothing we can do, Sinow." His mind slipped to Ren and Paige. Nothing to be done. Everything was out of their control, all of it now in the hands of the Fates. "We are being forced to let it all play out."

"Pawns in their game," Sinow said quietly.

Keary felt the warm calming sensation that he'd come to

recognize with Violissa's shift, the air filling with the scent of lilac that always accompanied her.

"What are you two up to?" she asked.

"Just talking," Sinow said, greeting her with a kiss.

"Talking or worrying?" she asked, running her fingers along his jaw, the tension still held there.

Keary had to admit she was in tune with Sinow's moods. It gave him hope that she could temper the Dark king within, keep him balanced and far beyond the madness that lay in wait within him.

"One thing you'll find about your new husband, Violissa, is that his mind never stops working."

"It's called thinking, Keary. You might want to try it."

"It's called over-thinking, Sinow, and I try at all costs to avoid it."

Violissa giggled. "You're a worrywart, as they say in this world."

"Ha! Yes, he is, and he will drive your free-spirited arse crazy, Violissa, so be prepared!"

"Don't make me hurt you," Sinow sneered.

Violissa studied him for a moment then said, "I still love you, worries and all."

"That's a relief since you're stuck with me for eternity."

"And that's my sign to go. Sinow, remember what I said, let it lie, there's nothing to be done."

"Is that why you're out here? Trying to rush the Fates?"

"No, trying to find a way home."

"Sinow, they will show us the way when it's time. We need to have faith in them."

"And there it is," Keary said, gesturing to Violissa. "The forever present optimism and belief in the Fates."

Violissa shot him an irritated look.

"I mean that in the best possible way, my queen."

"Now you've annoyed her, Keary. I'd run while you have the chance. You haven't experienced what it's like to be on her bad side."

Violissa couldn't hold her face and ended up smiling at his comment.

"That's why I don't fear her like I do you, Sinow. But I'll take the hint and leave you two to do whatever it is you need to do."

He winked at Violissa who blushed slightly then shifted back to the inn, ready to drown his anxiety in shots of whiskey that would burn away before they even came close to hitting his blood stream.

Twenty-Five

A red glow from the setting sun filled the room, leaving strands of Violissa's hair a lush bronze, but it did nothing to hide the stress Paige saw reflected in her eyes. Claire was fluffing out the skirt to the overly large wedding dress they'd made her get, and Paige had to admit that even with Violissa's beauty there was no saving it from being entirely too ostentatious for anyone close to Violissa's nature.

"Claire, why don't you go down and make sure everything is set outside? I'm sure your mother could use a hand," Paige suggested.

Claire stepped back, smiling at Violissa with approval. "I can do that. I think it's perfect, just like I always wanted. A princess dress fit for a...oh, I guess we should call it a queen dress instead."

"Thank you, Claire, it's beautiful," Violissa said with a smile, but Paige knew her well enough now to detect the sadness it held. Claire left, and Violissa turned back to the mirror, biting her lip.

"Second thoughts?" Paige teased.

Laughing, Violissa walked over to the bed, and after a few moments of struggle managed to sit down, her skirt puffing high in front of her. She let out an exasperated laugh.

"Other than the fact that this dress is entirely not your style, what's wrong, Violissa?"

"It's really not me at all, is it?"

"Not even close. How did you let her talk you into this?" Paige asked, sitting down next to her after pushing piles of material out of the way.

"Them, not just her. Our aunt, his aunt, Claire, the dress shop owner, I could go on. They all seemed to think I needed a dress from centuries ago. In fact, I remember wearing these back then, and they weren't the least bit comfortable then or now!"

Paige laughed. "It's not just the dress, is it, Violissa?"

She leaned her head on Paige's shoulder.

"What are we doing, Paige?" Her friend's voice cracked. "I asked Sinow to play human for just a little while, to take the time the Fates were giving us and live like normal people, live like a regular married couple. But we're not normal, this isn't us, it's a life we'll never have."

Paige said nothing. She was right. This was a façade hiding the inevitable, a moment in time to avoid the terrible things that awaited them. She wrapped her arms around her friend.

"I want to go home, Paige. This isn't right to be here, acting like everything is fine when our people are hurting, when our friends and family are trying to survive, thinking they've lost us, lost any hope of living. It's not fair to them."

Resting her head atop Violissa's, she asked, "Did anyone ever ask the two of you what was fair? You've both suffered and will continue to suffer, stop worrying about what's going on in our world and take this chance, Violissa. Even if for only this one night, be happy, you are getting married after all."

"Again." She sniffed.

"How many times is this now?"

"Three I suppose. I wonder if we ever had a true wedding our first time around?"

"You didn't like my version of your marriage vows?" Paige joked.

Violissa turned her palm over, and Paige noticed the scar for the first time.

"Oh, Violissa, I'm so sorry! I really botched it, so much so that the scar is still there."

"Shhh, Paige, the scar is meant to be there. It's a permanent sign of our love and will never fade."

"Really? I wish someone had told me that. I would have made the lines straighter." She cringed inwardly at the jagged edges. "I'm sure my father did a much better job the first time."

"It's fine, Paige," she said, staring at the scar.

"It's not fine, or you wouldn't look so sad."

Violissa ran her finger along the union scar.

"This is what all of it was for," she said softly. "All the struggle, all the emotion, the pain, all for this."

"Would you do it all again?"

"In a heartbeat," she answered unwaveringly.

"Then stop sitting here pouting and let's finish getting you ready. You've got a handsome king waiting out there for you." Paige stood and pulled her up. "First, you really need to do something about that dress."

The door opened, and Keary entered. He was dressed in a black tux and looked quite handsome, something Paige would have said if he hadn't noticed the dress first.

"Are women always this slow? Violissa, what in the Fates are you wearing?" he asked, laughing. "You know he loves you and all, but I can't guarantee he won't get a good laugh out of that dress."

Violissa crossed her arms and pouted.

"We were just about to fix that when you interrupted," Paige said to him.

"When did Claire rope you into this?" he asked, picking up a piece of the endless material.

"When we went ring shopping for Sinow's band. Oh, I need to give that to you," she said, trying to cross the room but tripping as her feet tangled in her skirt hoop.

She remained on the floor, looking up, blowing a thick piece of hair that had fallen from the tight updo Claire had given her before Paige could stop her.

Keary helped her up. "I have to admit this is the first time I've seen you defeated, Violissa. If I'd known it was this easy, I would have told Sinow to curse you into one of these gowns during the war. We'd have won in no time."

She yanked her arm from his as he laughed. "You're not helping, Keary."

"You know if my mother were here, she would have made the perfect dress for you," Paige said quietly.

"Really?"

"Yes, she loves to sew. In fact, she's been sewing since I can remember."

"What would your mother have made for me, Paige? Describe it to me."

Paige thought about her mother, remembering how she would sit on the bench outside their house or in front of the fire, cloth strewn around her feet, her delicate hands sewing rapid stitches. She had always added touches to clothing that said something about the future wearer, little details here and there.

"Well, she would do away with that massive bottom, fix the top with smaller sleeves, cut here for the chest." As she spoke, she noticed the dress changing to fit her description. Violissa was creating it with her magic and Paige's words.

She stood back, looking at the final product, amazed at the transformation.

"It's missing something," she said. *What would Mother add?*

"Turn around for me." Then she saw it. The dress was beautiful, but it didn't say anything about Violissa.

"Lower the back, now lighten the material on the skirt so it flows easily and add stitching, flowers and butterflies to lightly layer the material in whatever color you choose.

Violissa smiled as she followed Paige's instructions. "You know me too well, Paige."

"Wow, that looks amazing, but we need to do something about your hair."

Violissa shook her head, and her hair broke free, tumbling in loose curls down her back.

"Sinow likes it loose," she said softly.

"Wait, make me a clip with whatever you want on it."

Violissa opened her hand and a delicate clip appeared with purple and green gems that shaped the flowers engraved within it.

Paige took the clip, pulled just a bit of her hair back, enough to add an extra touch of elegance, then stood back to admire their work.

Violissa turned to view her reflection in the mirror. "Paige, it's lovely."

"Women are so complicated," Keary joked.

Violissa ignored him, taking Paige's hands and saying, "I look forward to meeting your mother. She must truly be special."

"You do?" Paige asked. "But I thought..."

Violissa gave her a queer look.

"I thought my father...well he broke his vow, and my mother was part of it."

"And you thought I would punish them?"

"Well, yes."

"Paige, I know your father well. He is my Keeper, the closest of my Council. If he broke his vow, it was only because the

Fates deemed it be so. There was a purpose to it, a reason for him to fall in love with your mother."

She brushed a strand of Paige's hair from her cheek. "That reason was you, Paige."

"Me? I'm no one special, Violissa. I haven't done anything."

"You saved me."

"No, that was Keary and Sinow and you. I was no help."

"You pushed me to talk to Violissa, Paige," Keary said. "It was you who opened Sinow's eyes to the mistake he was making. You are the reason he ran after her."

"But I...that—"

"Was you saving me. You are special, Paige. You have a purpose although I'm not certain that's all of it."

"What do you mean?"

She smiled. "My future son is in love with you. I think your reason for being here might be bigger than any of us thought."

Paige didn't know what to say; she suddenly grew nervous. "I, but, he—"

"Shhh," Violissa said, putting her finger to Paige's lips. "I see more than you think I do, and there is no one I'd rather have him love than you." She sighed. "That does leave us in quite a predicament, but it's one we'll need to figure out later. Right now, I have a husband waiting to marry me again."

With that, she walked away, stopping momentarily in front of Keary to adjust his bowtie and say, "You look quite handsome, Keary."

Then she was gone. Paige met Keary's eyes. "Did you tell her?"

"No. She's driven by things we can't see, Paige. I'm beginning to think serving as her Council is going to be quite unpredictable."

"It will be," Violissa yelled from down the hall. "Now get out here. You two lead, not me."

Keary gestured to let Paige out of the room, a wicked grin on his face.

"This should be fun." He laughed.

"Can it, Keary," she retorted.

The ceremony was to be held behind the inn, the patio and surrounding yard decorated with white lights and flowers. As Paige walked out with Keary, her arm in his, she spotted Sinow waiting at the end of the makeshift aisle. He was shifting his feet, pulling at the collar of his tux. She couldn't believe they'd gotten him to wear it but seeing him in it, she was happy he had. He was terrifyingly handsome; she couldn't get over how amazing he looked in it.

"Take it in, Paige, you will never get the chance to see your king this vulnerable or nervous again. He's a mess with all these people around," Keary whispered to her.

"Are you sure it isn't wedding jitters? I mean he is getting married again."

She felt Keary shrug. "Maybe some of that, too. If that's the case, then he's even worse off than I thought. Although it may simply be the monkey suit they forced us to wear."

She smiled, it was cute to think he, a Dark king, the most powerful man in their world and this one, was nervous about marrying the woman he loved. Her gaze slipped to his right, and she caught her breath. Ren stood next to Sinow, the mirror image of him in so many ways but for those piercing blue eyes. Eyes that held her gaze and a look of adoration she'd never seen directed toward her. He gave a slight smile, and she blushed. She felt like the only woman in the world when he looked at her like that, and she felt her heart flutter.

"Stop making googly eyes at Ren and watch the magic happen," Keary said as they approached Sinow. She looked to Sinow again and witnessed the change in his expression. His eyes softened, filling with the love he had for Violissa.

As Keary walked her to the bride's side, he whispered, "Now that's a man in love," then walked over to stand in his place as best man. Absently, she wondered if he'd meant Sinow or Ren, then scolded herself and turned her attention to Sinow whose eyes never left Violissa's. It was intense the way they looked at each other, as if the world had disappeared and only the two of them existed. Violissa looked stunning, everything about her screamed beautiful goddess, and as she reached Sinow, Paige realized that's what they were, a god and his goddess, beings worlds apart from everyone else in their presence. No one even came close, no one that was, except Ren. Ren, about whom she shouldn't be thinking, about whom she couldn't be thinking. He was an impossibility she could never overcome. Reluctantly, her eyes drifted to him, her heart leaping. His eyes were a deeper shade of blue, and he looked away as if caught doing something wrong. She smiled at the thought. *Stop it, Paige,* she chastised herself. Pulling her eyes and mind from him, she let the drone of the priest's voice steal her thoughts, praying they would stay away.

While Violissa had been upstairs, forced to play the part of the nervous bride, Sinow had paced the bar, tugging at his bowtie, feeling constricted by its presence.

"You keep adjusting that thing, and it'll break," Claire said, coming down the stairs. She wore a green dress that swept the ground, the straps entirely too thin, revealing too much skin. He had the urge to cover her but then remembered she wasn't truly his cousin and that the urge was left over from his time as Simon. She approached him, clearly forgetting for the moment that he'd changed, and straightened the bowtie. Then, as if suddenly remembering, she backed up, her hand shaking. She looked at him.

"I hate this. I know you're not Simon, I know you're different, but you're still family. You're still my older cousin. I don't like fearing you."

She pouted like she always had when they were children, and he couldn't help but smile.

"I can't do anything to change that feeling, it's instinctual, and it's there to protect you."

"But can't you turn it off?"

"No," he laughed, "it's turned down as much as I can tolerate but be thankful you have permission to be in my presence."

"Do I want to know why?"

He shook his head. "Probably not."

Sighing, she walked away.

"You'll get used to it, or so Paige says."

She turned back to look at him. "I hope so. Even if you are different, we still miss you, I miss you. We're family, and we'll always be family no matter who you are. Now, stop pacing and come on or your bride will bump into you when she comes out."

"And that's a bad thing?"

"Of course, it is. Bad luck, remember? And you two don't need any more of that," she teased him before opening the door and holding it for him.

"You dress up pretty well col ceathrar," she said, referring to him as she had always done by the Irish word for cousin.

"Aye, as do you, Claire."

"You're not nervous, are you?" she joked as they walked out.

"Dark kings don't get nervous."

"Then why do you keep fidgeting?"

"You know I could kill you for that, right?"

He heard her swallow then let out a nervous giggle. "Not really, right?"

He looked over at her as she stopped walking. "I wouldn't test it," he replied with a wink then continued toward his spot where Ren stood pacing his own path into the grass.

"Simon, that's not funny." He heard her say, her use of his

human name not bothering him this day.

"Tormenting the mortals?" Ren asked as he approached.

"Nothing better to do I suppose."

They stood quietly for a few moments his power stirred by the presence of so many mortals around him. He was having a hard time keeping the Darkness at bay and hoped Violissa wouldn't be long. Thankfully, Ren seemed attuned to the ire and continued to layer a calming spell around him. Unfortunately, it didn't have as strong an affect as Violissa's; he could feel the undertone of Ren's Dark magic in it.

The priest, sensing Sinow's power, kept his distance, moving another step back. Sinow was aware they'd had to convince him to partake in the ceremony, reminding him of the many favors and tithes they had given the church. As both their mortal families were Catholic and Violissa had done her fair time in nunneries over the centuries, it had been determined that the wedding would be performed by a priest; however, since neither worshipped in this world now, the ceremony was abridged and catered to suit them. If the family had not been so involved in the church the man would likely have called the Vatican on Sinow by now.

"You were always a frightening child," he said to Sinow as they were waiting.

"Now, I'm your worst nightmare," Sinow joked, a comment that didn't go over too well as the priest took a few more steps back.

In an attempt to take his mind off the rising Darkness and the surroundings, he asked Ren, "Isn't this strange to you?"

"Being stuck in another realm, surrounded by mortals, living with my parents before they even conceive me?"

"Well, if you put it that way, then I'd guess watching your parents get married isn't that strange after all," he replied with a smile.

"It's a little strange," Ren returned, laughing.

Sinow would have kept talking, but Keary and Paige walked

out at that moment, drawing his attention from the conversation. He heard Ren inhale and absently wondered at the reaction until his eyes met Violissa's, and he was lost watching her move down the aisle. Seeing her calmed him completely. She was breathtaking, and he couldn't tear his eyes from her.

You make a tux look really sexy, she said in enaigne.

He gave her a coy smile. *Dare I say you are the most stunning thing in this country? No, I take it back, in this world. And that I will enjoy having you take this annoying suit off of me when this is over?*

When she reached him, he couldn't help himself and kissed her, not caring that mortals surrounded them. Nothing else mattered but her in that moment. Then the priest interrupted, and it took every bit of his strength not to punish him for it. By the time they'd exchanged rings and gotten to the kiss again, Sinow was to his breaking point. He was tired of pretending to be something he wasn't, he wanted to set his powers free, he wanted to take Violissa someplace private and make love to her.

Much to his dismay, none of that happened.

When Paige had walked down the aisle with Keary, Ren couldn't take his eyes from her. She looked beautiful, her hair braided then pulled loosely back, strands of it gently touching her cheeks and neck. It was the first time he'd seen her with her hair up. Her eyes were a vibrant blue, the descending sun casting a glow to them that stopped his heart. He met her eyes and couldn't help but smile. *Fates, what is wrong with me,* he thought. He wanted to be walking next to her in Keary's place, wanted to be the one holding her arm, feeling her next to him. *Stop it, Ren,* he told himself. *It's not meant to be.*

Her eyes moved back to his father, whose power he sensed

increase. Looking beyond Paige, he saw the reason: his mother. She looked incredible, more like his mother than she had recently, always forced to wear human clothing. He looked over at his father who looked completely lost, his nerves now settled. Ren smiled, these were the parents he knew, lost in each other, the world around them non-existent. This was what he loved about them, their love for each other. It went beyond anything he knew he would ever feel, beyond anything anyone would experience. It was a constant, and it never faded, never diminished. The look he saw on his father's face at that moment, the intense love in his eyes, was the same look he'd seen countless times when his father had looked at his mother. It went deeper than words could explain, and it was theirs alone.

His mother arrived to stand in front of his father, never breaking eye contact, never faltering at the weight of the stare, then they did what he knew they couldn't avoid doing, they kissed. He felt the heat of it, the passion that layered the air. His eyes drifted to Paige, a longing in his heart to be close to her, to kiss her again. Then it was gone, the ceremony began, the constant calming spell now emitted from his mother, taking the edge off his father. When it was finished, they kissed again, but this time, Ren sensed something different, an undercurrent in the air, subtle but present.

"Vi?" He heard his father ask.

Her eyes drifted to Ren's, and he knew she'd felt it, too. How he wished his enaigne worked with them. She put her hand to her lips then walked away from his father, past the priest who had moved even further from them at the end of the ceremony, too scared of his father to remain closer. Ren watched as his mother stopped and, closing her eyes, tilted her head up toward the sky. No one moved, a hush had settled across the land. He listened, opening his senses to the natural world as she was, feeling his eyes turn the color of hers. There was a change to the air, it cooled, the wind picking up slightly. Opening his eyes, he looked over at her, feeling the ancient power and recognizing it for what it was, seeing the frost spreading from her feet. She knelt down to touch it then watched as it spread forward in the direction of the lake before lifting with the wind, the icy flakes funneling around her in a sudden rush then fading with the breeze. The world around them re-awakened, the magic gone but the sign there.

"What was that?" his father asked.

"Cainbae," he replied, although the question wasn't directed toward him.

His father and mother looked at him.

"Explain," his father commanded.

"It's a connection my mother has to realm borders. It is very rare and only her mother before her had the gift. It allows her access to lands blocked by Fates' magic or in this case, the magic of other gods."

His father looked at his mother questioningly. She glanced down at her hands.

"I've never—"

"No, you don't discover it until Tynan takes you."

He felt his father's power rise at the mention of Tynan, the humans around them moving further back from his presence.

"Does that mean she found a way to get home?" Paige asked.

"No," he replied, continuing to look at his mother. "That wasn't full cainbae. It was a sign."

"A sign of what and from whom?" his father asked.

"Their god," his mother replied, having felt the same thing Ren had. "He has granted his permission; he has let the Fates in to help guide us home."

"Why now?" Keary asked. "What's a wedding have to do with us getting home?"

"I don't know, but I think we needed to do it, to show respect to this world's traditions perhaps."

"Or to seal the prophecy in this world, under the blessing of this world's god. By doing so, the prophecy is bound on both sides, the path's course set right," his father said.

"But that can't be so, the path is still unbound when you return," Ren said, although his father's words settled in him.

"Maybe not. Time has changed, history has changed. We're on a new branch of the prophecy now, one tangled with this world even more so than it was. Tynan changed everything, Ren. Our future no longer exists as it did in your timeline."

"Maybe." He wasn't certain he agreed with his father, but it gave him hope, which was something he hadn't had since arriving here.

His mother approached him, laying her hand on his cheek. "You feel the land as I do. Your eyes reveal it," she said as he felt his eyes shifting to blue again, his nature powers receding. "Whatever this is, you and I are the only ones who can feel it. If it's a sign or something more, we need to be ready to follow whatever it is they need us to do."

He took her hands. "No, whatever it is you need to do. I am not the key to this, you are mother. I will listen for the signs, but you will be the one to follow them."

She reached her hands to tilt his head down and kissed his forehead as she'd done so often when he was young.

"Now what?" his father asked.

"Now you two celebrate your union while I go to the lake to look around."

"I should go, too," she said.

"No, Vi. He's right. Let him go."

"I'll accompany him," Keary said.

Ren shifted before anyone could respond.

"Escaping from the strange combination of mortal and immortal your parents are juggling with or being in Paige's presence?" Keary asked when he shifted next to Ren.

Ren wasn't really sure why he'd left, feeling like he needed to be here instead. He walked around the edge of the lake.

"I'm not completely sure, maybe a little of both, maybe something else."

"Well, I can tell you, your parents are just as confused about how to act in these new surroundings as you are. Sinow especially is on edge. One wrong move and he's bound to lose it, this entire town will be buried in Dark power."

"Do you think he's right?"

"About what?"

"Do you think this changes everything? That this change in the path changes the future, rewrites the next chapter?"

Keary sighed. "I don't know. After what you told us, I pray it does."

Ren knelt down, finally finding that for which he'd been looking.

"Regardless," he said, feeling the stiff grass below his fingertips. "One thing I know for certain is that everything is about to change."

Keary knelt down next to him, touching the grass. "It's frozen."

"The connection has been made. The Fates have given us their first sign. Now we wait. The game has begun again, and I suspect it's going to be quite an adventure."

Ren remained after Keary left, reluctant to return. Keary was right on both fronts. Seeing his parents like this, seeing them outside their normal roles, acting and living as mortals was a strange experience. It had given him a deeper appreciation of them as people, not simply the two people he had put on a pedestal since an early age, untouchable with endless power. Now they were forced to be vulnerable, living day to day with no control, confined to live within the constraints of mortal life.

His mind wandered to Paige, the second reason he had left. Since the kiss, his eyes had been opened. He understood what had happened, saw the truth of it. He had found his mate and now with this recent event, he was closer to losing her. Keary was right, the Fates were cruel. They'd been cruel to his parents, why did he think he'd be spared? He would be forced to leave Paige, to return to his own timeline and take the throne, a throne he didn't want, and live a life he now no longer wanted. Running his hand through his hair, he wondered what even awaited him upon his return. In his heart, he knew his parents were gone, he'd felt the tear in his link to them that day. Was there anything left? Would he return to see this version of his parents or would he return to nothing, a time that no longer existed? Perhaps that's why he'd been drawn to Paige. If she were his mate and he were returning to nothing, then it would make no difference if he lost her in the past, for he would have no future. The Fates were cruel indeed.

He stayed a little longer before heading back. The night ran long, his mother socializing as she always did, ensuring no one was left out, blessing them all with her presence. She lit up the area, as she always had. His father mostly stayed back, observing, his eyes following her, his occasional smile revealing the adoration he felt for her. Keary stayed with him, his mother and Paige returning to them here and there. Toward the end of the evening, Ren stood with Paige, quietly enjoying her company when his parents and Keary joined them followed by Cody who had clearly had one too many drinks.

"So, you're officially married now. What happens next?" Cody asked.

"You go to bed and sleep off the hangover you'll have in the morning," Paige joked.

He shot her a playful look. "I might sleep off a hangover, but I'm not going to bed yet." He winked. "I'm still trying to determine who's keeping me company until I'm ready to sleep."

"Cody," his mother scolded. "Really?"

"Get it out of your system now, Cody. When the Fates bring you into the fold, you're cut off," Keary said, laughing.

"You're joking, right?" he questioned, looking at Ren's parents.

They both shook their heads, knowing it indeed was no joke. If Cody were a Lightbearer, his desires would be curtailed, abstinence replacing them.

"That's my cue," he said quickly, running off toward a group of townspeople.

His mother laughed. "You two are mean, and he's not a Lightbearer."

"Keep telling yourself that, Vi. I'll get a big I told you so when it happens," his father said, pulling her into his arms. "I think it's time we take our leave."

Paige yawned. "I don't think they'll miss any of us. I'm pretty tired, too."

"Goodnight," his mother said before his father shifted them away.

"I'm going to keep an eye on the lad so he doesn't do anything stupid," Keary said, leaving Ren with Paige.

"I'll walk you back to your room, if you don't mind the company," Ren said to her, not sure why he suddenly felt nervous.

"That would be nice."

They chatted on the way, Paige commenting on the ceremony and how beautiful his mother had looked. When they arrived outside her door, he couldn't help but ask, "Are we going to talk about what happened the other day?"

Her eyes grew sad, and he knew instantly it had been the wrong question. "No, I don't think we should, Ren. We need to leave it in the past." She gave a weary laugh. "Just like me. I'm a figment of your history and you a future I don't think I would have even fathomed. Thousands of years separate us."

"The Fates have their reasons, Paige."

"That's what everyone says about everything, but the Fates aren't always kind, and this isn't kind. I'm in love with you,

Ren, and the thought of it hurts so bad that I can't think about it. We need to leave our kiss to that day, and I need to leave my thoughts of you there as well."

"Paige—"

"No, it can't be, Ren, and you know the truth of it as well as I do."

She turned, opening her door to go in, but he grabbed her wrist and pulled her back where she landed in his arms. He kissed her, and she melted into it, kissing him passionately as if it were the last kiss they would ever have. Then she pulled away, closing the door behind her, leaving him struggling with emotions that brought his Elvin side to the surface. He leaned his head on the door, listening to the wind that now howled outside, trying to calm the fury down, praying to the Fates that the kiss wouldn't be their last.

Twenty-Six

Sinow woke, cursing the Fates for his inability to sleep through another night. It had been several days since the wedding ceremony, and neither he nor Violissa had been sleeping well, both too anxious about their unknown future. So, it was no surprise to him that the room was pitch black when he woke. What did surprise him was that Violissa was gone; she was nowhere in the room. Throwing out his power, he felt her outside.

Vi, he said gently, brushing her mind.

No answer followed.

Violissa?

Still no answer. He rose from the bed, pulled on a pair of pants, then shifted to where he'd sensed her. He found her walking, still naked, in the direction of the lake. She was staring vacantly ahead, her eyes a vibrant green.

"Violissa?"

She continued walking as if he weren't there.

"Vi?" he tried again with no success. He waved his hand in front of her, but her sight never wavered. That's when he noticed the hint of golden light around her eyes.

"Fates' magic," he whispered, as she walked by him. Something was happening. He closed his eyes and sent his senses out to explore. Flowing past Violissa and the power she was emanating, he found it, a minute magic unlike either of theirs, unlike Ren's, coming from the direction of the lake.

Keary! he called.

Yes, my liege, Keary answered sleepily, knowing his king's command needed an immediate response.

Something is happening. Gather the others. I think it's time. Meet me at the lake.

There was no need to explain further; Keary would obey without question.

Violissa had continued walking, so he caught up with her, conjuring a light gown and draping her in it, as he knew the others would soon see her. The move did nothing to sway her steady footfalls. She'd made it halfway to the lake, already walking through the town. He followed her, knowing there was no sense in trying to talk to her; she was under the Fates' spell, and nothing he did would break it.

It was a painful walk, having her there but not present, unaware that she had walked the two miles out of town to reach the lake, her bare feet ripping then healing as they passed stony ground. He winced at each rip but knew she'd heal and was thankful she didn't appear to feel anything. When they finally reached the lake, she approached the waterline then stopped, standing in place, in silence.

The others were already there, having shifted, so he walked over to them.

"What's going on, Sinow?" Paige asked.

"I don't know. She's being controlled by something and doesn't seem aware of what she's doing."

He glanced over to where she remained frozen in place, waiting for something to awaken her.

"The Fates?" Ren asked.

"I think so. Her eyes, there's a golden tone to them that feels like Fates' magic."

"We're going home?" Paige asked, her voice a mix of hope and sadness, and Sinow wondered at the reaction momentarily before letting it go.

"Perhaps," he replied.

"We've got company," Keary said, gesturing to the two agents walking toward them with Garrett and Erin.

Sinow's power flared, a growl slipping from him. Paige backed away in fear, and he sensed Ren throw a shield around her.

"I'll take care of them," Cody said. "I'm not part of this. You make sure my sister stays safe." He moved to confront the others, whose numbers were growing as everyone was too curious to remain at the inn.

"They woke when Keary was waking us all up," Paige explained.

"Nosy humans. They have no place here," Sinow grumbled.

Just then, Violissa began to sing, her song a blend of a command and a chant. Sinow turned to look at her, but she hadn't moved, her voice the only sign she was awake. He looked over at Ren whose eyes had widened, his face filled with awe.

"What's she doing, Ren?"

"She's summoning her Council."

"What?"

"They are sworn to answer her call, it's instinctual, and they cannot disobey," he said slowly, turning to Sinow.

"How..." he heard Keary start, but Violissa stopped, and they were all drawn to her. She lifted her head, her hands pulling away from her body, then she slammed her foot down and opened her palms. The world around them erupted, the ground rumbled, the trees swayed to an invisible wind, and the lake began to sparkle. A line of frost ran from her feet and spread to the water. They all stood silent, unable to draw their eyes from her.

She turned and walked away from the lake, her hips swaying to a beat only she could hear. Then she began singing, turning back to the lake, her voice, layered with power, light like silk, gently cascading across the space. As her voice strengthened, the command becoming more evident, the natural world answered. The trees lifted their roots to cast a beat to her call, the lake water churned, and the wind blew. Above them, the sky darkened. The more she sang, the more her command went unanswered, the more demanding her voice became.

Then, the water shifted, swirling, pulling up in droplets until the lake was drained, the water hanging as if a rainstorm had frozen in place as the frost spread through it.

"Do you hear that?" Keary asked.

"They're answering her call," Ren said, the disbelief apparent in his voice.

Sinow heard it, too, a low chant, barely audible but growing. As if she heard it, her moves grew more forceful as did her voice. Her arms swept across the ground as her back arched in a graceful curve. The nightgown he'd covered her in, changing to a lilac gown, the material loose and flowing in the style she had worn at home. His heart raced. Would they finally be sent home? Finally be able to leave this world and take back their realms?

The voices were growing louder but stopped as she paused her song briefly before belting out a distinct command, one that even he knew required answering. A man's voice answered in song.

"Father," Paige whispered shakily.

"She's calling her Keeper," Ren said.

Violissa answered, followed by a verse from Daneele. The two volleyed back and forth for several verses, and as they did, the water droplets shifted, connecting then spreading to form a sheet of frosted water.

The other voices joined in, and the sheet quivered, the trees drumming faster, the air thickening, the world around them growing increasingly chaotic until the wall of water stretched and shimmered, the frost clearing to reveal their world, illuminated by torchlight against a night sky. The song ended, the world settled, the clouds dissipated. Illuminated by the backdrop of the full moon, Sinow saw Violissa fall.

He shifted to catch her, unable to take his eyes from the view into their world. The clouds moved from the moons, and he saw both Councils peering back at him, old, withered, tired faces but ones he knew to be theirs.

"Sinow?" Violissa asked wearily, sitting up.

"Shhh, look, Vi."

She looked up at the view and gasped.

"Did I—"

"Yes," he said, helping her stand. Both Councils moved closer to the window.

"Sinow? Violissa?"

She gripped his arm, swaying slightly. "How?" she asked, searching his eyes for an answer.

His focus moved from everyone to her, the shakiness, the teetering, the quiver in her voice. He placed his hands on her face; her skin felt too warm.

"Vi? Are you okay?" he asked.

"I don't know," she whispered. "I don't remember anything. I don't know how I got here."

"I can't feel it. It's some sort of boundary," Keary said, talking to another Council.

"Vi, we may not have much time. We need to figure out what the Fates want us to do and why they called you to do that," he said, pointing to the window into their world.

She drew in a breath, standing straighter. "I'll be fine, I was just thrown off." She still felt flush, her cheeks revealing the slight pink. She reached up and kissed him, saying, "I'm fine."

Taking her hand, they walked to the window.

"You have no idea how good it is to see you both."

It took Sinow a minute to recognize the voice as the man looked ancient.

"Cyric?"

"Yes, my liege."

Slowly, he identified each of them. Time had caught up with them, and to some, it had not been kind.

"We thought you both lost to us. When the portal closed, we had no way to tell if you were still alive."

"Save Daneele who insisted he could still feel you, my queen."

"The link between Keeper and queen is strong," Ren muttered.

As if just noticing him, Sinow noted the confused looks.

"We are trapped here. Tynan destroyed the key to the portal," he said.

"Tynan? But he's been relentlessly attacking the boundary. How could he have found his way there?"

"He didn't, his future self did. It's a very long story. One we can share when we get home."

He moved his hand toward the window, but it went right through, the action causing a ripple across their image.

"It's not solid," Keary said. "None of us can feel it."

"The cainbae," Ren said. Sinow could hear the reluctance in his voice. This was a piece to their future.

"You said the cainbae was a connection to the realm borders."

"Yes, it is what gives her control over certain barriers, including this one."

"Control enough to let us through?" Sinow asked.

"No, the cainbae only opens one barrier, and it is not this one." There was more to the story, but he knew Ren would not tell them even with their future path completely eroded. "This isn't a true barrier but a window into our world."

"Sinow, did Tynan bring company when he came to trap you?" Cyric asked.

"Yes, he brought me," Ren answered for him. "In true Dark king fashion, he thought I would make a more effective punishment."

"Kill Violissa, and as so, your son dies," Daneele said, no one questioning what he had said.

"The similarities are unbelievable," he heard Mackay mutter.

"We will discuss this more when we are home. Violissa, can you open the connection to our world so that we may go home?"

"No, like Ren said, it's only a window. I don't believe that's why they had me call it."

Voices came from every direction.

"Silence!" Sinow boomed. "Why do you say that, Violissa?"

"It's not time yet."

He stared at her, confounded. "Try," he commanded, frustrated by her answer.

"She already has," Ren said defensively. He bent down and touched the grass. "It's cold and brittle. You saw the frost freeze the lake water. She used the connection, and this is all the Fates will allow."

"Then what was the point?" he asked, frustration filling him.

Just then, a massive boom could be heard from their world. Sinow noticed cracks in the sky. The barrier was failing.

"Because they need help, and we can't get to them. This opening was given to us to help them," Violissa said, reaching her hand up and watching as it went through the window as his had. "I just don't know how we can help if I can't even touch the thing that separates us."

"You can. It took you a while to get used to it, but when you first discovered the ability, you were singing," Ren said. "Of course, that was before you knew you could use your nature gifts without your Light magic."

"My voice enhances my nature gifts but is only necessary in certain circumstances. That's what you said."

"That was one of those circumstances, just like this is."

"Calling a mirror into our world," she said absently.

She picked up her hand and hummed a tune. This time the window didn't yield. He could see the pressure her hand made on the invisible barrier, a thin line of frost spilling out around it.

"Can you get through, Violissa?" Cyric asked.

"No, Ren is right, the Fates have given us all the access they will allow."

The Councils looked defeated.

"So, we're stuck here still?" Paige asked.

Sinow noticed Daneele's face fill with sadness before he masked it quickly. There was a quiet sob from behind them, and Sinow noticed a woman standing off to the side, trying to go unnoticed.

"Mama," Paige whispered.

Violissa turned to look, her eyes growing sad. "We have to be able to do something. The Fates have their reasons for everything, including this."

Another hit shook the Council, the torches around them flickering with the impact. Sinow watched as several fractures split across the boundary. Violissa started walking away, mumbling as she paced. He had to smile at how she reminded him of himself. Then she turned abruptly.

"That's it. Power."

"Power?" he asked.

"Yes, they're powerless, defenseless against Tynan. If we can get their power back, they stand a chance."

"Even with our power, we can't fight him, Violissa, not without the two of you," Kanine said. "He's too strong, too corrupt."

"He's right," Ren said, "but it would give them a chance. A chance to protect the people, to hide them until you return. It gives hope."

"We'll take any hope we can get."

"Vi, how are we going to get their power back to them? We

don't have that ability, and even if we did, we're divided in separate worlds," Sinow asked, finding it hard to believe they were even having the conversation.

"The same way I did before. Ren, you said in your timeline I brought the Council's power back when mine returned. This time, I brought Keary's back and opened the way for yours to return, Sinow."

"Go on."

"Ren, how did I do it before? It wasn't only the union ceremony, was it? You said there was another piece."

"You summoned the voice of the elders."

"The voice of the elders?" Sinow asked, his mind vaguely remembering the phrase from when he was dying.

"That's a myth," Daneele said.

"He's right no one ever—" Cyric started.

"Until my mother."

They all stared at him.

"But you had father's blood coursing through you that day which allowed you to call the Dark power. You don't have that now."

"No," she said, her eyes lifting to meet Sinow's, "but I could have that power and direct it."

"I don't like the sound of that," Sinow said, "nor do I like that look, Violissa."

"Hear me out."

"I'm not certain I want to hear you out." The excited look in her eyes worried him.

"During the union, our blood mixed. What if there's a trace of Dark blood still in me?"

"It wouldn't be enough to call their powers," Ren said.

"But we don't know that for sure, Ren."

"I'm not following, Vi. There's no way to get their powers back."

"I agree, Violissa," Cyric said.

She chewed her bottom lip, and her eyes darkened a shade.

Sinow could tell she was getting frustrated.

"Just let me finish," she said. "Please."

"Let her," Daneele said.

She threw a grateful look to him, and Sinow wondered if he was the one who always stood up for her different approach to things.

"I can invoke the voice, but can I awake our ancestors? Do I need to?" She began pacing again while she spoke. "Maybe that's not the way it will work this time. The Fates have brought us here. They led me here for a reason. I know they'll listen." She stopped pacing and turned back to them. "I can perform the same ritual but use it to transfer our powers through this window and to the Councils."

"Wait, I'm not following, Violissa. You want to wake our ancestors and have them do what?" Sinow asked, trying to piece together what she was saying.

"No, there wouldn't be a way I can call our ancestors here, but I don't think I need to. We have our powers now. I don't need help getting mine back like it sounds like I did in our last life. They were necessary that day." She looked to Ren, and he nodded. "I don't think the powers of the Council can be called the same way mine were that day either. They've been stolen. I think I need to restore them, fill them once again by acting as a conduit and sending forth what we can replenish to them."

He stared at her, still not completely following. "It sounds like you want to harness our powers and then send them, somehow, through the barrier to our Councils?"

"There's a trace of Fates' magic still in me. I can feel it, that's how they led me here. It should give me the ability to send everything we have through my connection to this barrier. I don't need the elders because I already have the Fates." On her final word, a sparkle of gold shimmered around her iris, validating her claim. "My magic will restore itself, as will yours, once you give me what you can to transfer to them," she continued.

The Councils both erupted, a chorus of confusion and fear.

"Silence!" Sinow said. Violissa was winning him over, but he still had his doubts. "Violissa, there's no way I can give you my powers."

"A trace of your power still exists in me as well. Give me what you can, and I promise that small bit I have will help me contain it until I can transfer it to them."

He backed up, running his hand through his hair. "That's madness. First, to think you can transfer enough power to them with only our existing power and second to think you can hold my Darkness within you and not have it destroy you."

"Maybe she's not mad," Ren said. "I hold all three powers—"

"By birth, Ren. My power would crush her, and you of all people should understand that."

"And you of all people should trust her. I know my mother well enough to know that if she thinks this will work, it will."

Sinow stared at him, not sure what to say. He looked at the Councils. Daneele nodded his head in agreement. "You think this will work?" Sinow asked him.

"I trust my queen, especially when she's this adamant."

He glanced back at Violissa and sighed. "What do you need?"

Smiling, she said, "I need your hands, then I need you to give me everything."

"You promise me you'll be fine?" he asked her.

"No, but I promise you I won't leave you."

Reluctantly, he put his hands out over hers. Ren stepped back and yelled, "Everyone, back now. Keary, help me shield them."

Together with Paige and Cody, they herded those who had followed them back as far as they could then he felt the protective shields go up.

Violissa's eyes never left his.

"Tell me when you're ready."

"As ready as I'll ever be." She glanced over to the Councils. "Once I have enough power, I'll call the Fates for help to guide the power to you. I don't know what will happen then."

They all nodded, concern still reflected on their faces, then motioned the people who had gathered in their world back farther than they already were. When they'd finished, they lined up in Council formation, two rows awaiting their place to serve their king and queen once again.

"Ready," she said, her eyes now a crystal emerald.

Sinow called his power forth and let it engulf them both, watching as Violissa opened herself to it, as if she were making space for it, her eyes becoming a color on the cusp of black, the green of the deepest forests. His power settled on her then sank into her as she did something no immortal would ever contemplate doing: allowing the invasion of an opposing power to fill her body.

He started to pull back, to harness the Darkness, but she squeezed his hands.

No, she called to him, the Dark magic heavy in the feel of her voice. *More.*

Vi, it will corrupt you.

No, it's not enough yet.

He furrowed his brow, concerned for her sanity, for her health, but followed her lead and released his hold on his magic, watching as it cascaded through her. On and on, he sent it out until for the first time in his life, he felt drained, knowing he'd given her all he could. As if she sensed the same, she released her grip on his hands, closing her eyes to the funnel of black that surrounded her.

He stepped back, feeling his power replenish as he watched her disappear in what he'd given her. She was lost in a cloud of black until suddenly, in a long sweeping arc, it plunged into her, seeping into her skin and disappearing from the air. He held his breath and stepped further back. The air was still; in fact, everything had stilled to await her move. A line of ebony drew from her roots, coloring her wayward curl. Then, like a wave of night, it spread, leaving her hair black as a raven.

She took a breath, her eyes still closed, and began to sing, her voice rich and magical, calling to the sky, to the Fates who lie on the other side of the window. Her eyes opened as black as his for a brief moment until the emerald replaced it, her hair remaining the shade of coal, enhancing the vibrant crystal green of her Elvin eyes. He couldn't believe what he was seeing, couldn't understand how she was containing the amount of Dark magic he'd given her and how it wasn't screaming to be released.

Her song continued, and he moved over with Ren and the others. "Should I be concerned, Ren?"

Ren seemed as shaken as he. "I don't know. I had no idea that was her intent."

Sinow watched as she moved gracefully, the world around her and through the window into their world coming to life and answering her summons. "I thought you said she could hold my power."

"I didn't realize she would take so much."

Sinow dragged his eyes from her and looked at Ren whose eyes reflected the fear he held in his heart. The ground shook, and the sky seemed to come to life, lightning tearing through it, thunder screaming in its wake, the torches in the other world reaching to touch the lightning, the moons streaming their light in full intensity upon the Councils. Violissa reached her hand to the ground, a line of frost spreading from her fingertips, and with a sprightly spin, she lifted herself and slammed both hands against the window to their world, the frost climbing from the ground to reach that which was spreading downward to meet it. Pulling her hands back, the frost seemed to surround her. She threw her head back, a thick stream of arcane magic pouring from her body through the frosted window, the frost receding as it encased the magic that fled her body. The blue funnel poured into her Council, all of them buckling from the intensity. She spun, the arcane blue cutting from her but continuing its flow to the Lightbearers. Drawing her hands up the sides of her body, her voice intensifying with the storm around them, Sinow felt the Dark magic as she commanded it to make its way to his Council. Unlike the Light power, it needed no link to find its mark. It ripped through the barrier and into his Council, all of them crumbling in pain from the force. All the while, Violissa's song continued, the words filled with the Darkness of the magic that now held her until finally it softened, the Dark magic depleted.

She stumbled back, finishing her final note, the world calming, the last of the Dark magic settling in his Darkbearers. Sinow went to her, catching her as she tumbled, all energy drained from her, the ebony of her locks receding, the gold taking its rightful place once again. He looked beyond into their world and watched as the Councils slowly rose, their age falling away, their youth returning with the return of their power.

"You did it, Vi," he said, steadying her. "It worked."

Only then did he notice how weak she felt, notice the tremble of her muscles. He held her closer, supporting her, remembering that same weakness when the Fates had released her from their spell, only now it had worsened.

"It worked," she replied wearily.

Ren ran over and brought his hands to her face, Sinow sensing the healing power he was trying to use.

"I can't heal her," he said, moving back.

"You can't influence your past with your magic, Ren. I'll be fine Ren."

Ren looked at Sinow, doubt and worry in his eyes. She tried to stand on her own but wobbled then leaned upon his chest again.

"I just need to rest."

"Will she be all right?" Kanine asked, the others all wearing worried looks that matched Ren's.

"I'll be fine. You need to don your cloaks for the sake of the mortals, or Ren and I will need to do some healing here."

His Council did as she suggested, and Sinow helped her move closer to the window.

"Now what?" he asked, noticing Daneele's attention drawing to where Paige stood. He looked over to see her with tears in her eyes. They were all back to their true form, a version of her father she'd never witnessed.

"Go, Daneele," he said gently. Daneele looked at him questioningly, and Sinow nudged his head toward Paige.

"He's right, Daneele, go see her. I don't know how much longer the Fates will allow the window to remain open. She needs to see her mother as well," Violissa urged.

Daneele gave a slight bow, then went toward where Paige was standing, a woman joining her, tears staining her cheeks. She didn't seem fazed by Daneele's new appearance as Paige was, and Sinow wondered how long they'd known each other before he'd finally given in to his feelings for her.

He drew his attention from the reunion and back to the Councils.

"You have what you need to fight Tynan," he told them.

"We have hope," Cyric replied as Keary walked over to them.

"Damn, it's nice to see you all looking like old times again," he joked as a loud crash could be heard from the west of where the Council stood. The window quivered with the force.

"I pray it is enough," Brom said.

"Maybe you need more," Violissa said absently, her eyes wandering to Paige and her mother.

"Vi, what are you thinking?"

Her eyes flickered to the ground, the moons still bright enough to see the brittle grass that lay at the Councils' feet.

"The balance needs to be completely restored, and then they have hope."

"Balance of all three powers," Ren said.

"Yes."

"And how do you do that?" Kanine asked.

She looked back over to Paige. "I think I have an idea. Paige," she called.

Paige turned, her mother lowering her eyes and dropping

to the ground. Sinow had given her permission the moment she'd approached Paige, but she didn't know that. Violissa let his hand go and stepped away shakily.

"Vi," he said, reaching to steady her, worry nagging at him, "there's nothing more you can do, and you need to rest." His power had been restored, and he felt fine, so why was she still weak? He wondered if the residue of Fates' power and his magic was causing a disturbance within her.

"I'm fine, Sinow. I need to do one more thing."

"Is she always this stubborn?" Kanine asked.

"You've no idea," Ren answered for them all.

Sinow watched Violissa talk to Paige and her mother, not certain as to what she was doing and part of him leery of knowing what her plan was. It was then that he noticed the subtle pink on the horizon, the rising sun which he remembered Keary saying would only rise for a mere few minutes at the most. His eyes wandered to the moons which had been full in the sky earlier but now were sinking low in their descent. Had they risen to meet Violissa's call? He couldn't fathom how that could have been so let the thought go as he heard Paige's voice, beautiful and strong with a fullness it hadn't had the last time he'd heard her. She seemed surprised, stopping and bringing her hand up to her mouth.

Sinow looked to Ren who didn't seem surprised but wore a look of pride and something else Sinow suspiciously recognized.

Ren, having felt Sinow's eyes on him, quickly changed his expression, saying, "Her queen has returned, and the true beauty of her voice can now be heard. A Light ruler's connection to the people enhances their voices."

Paige began to sing again, her mother joining, then Violissa joining. The sound like magic on his ears, filling the air with a sensation that was unexplainable and one he knew he'd never forget, the true sound of Cirillia. Paige and her mother stopped their part, and Violissa continued hers, stepping away from them. The words of the song a goodbye to those loved fit with the situation as they all were well aware the connection between the two worlds would soon fade.

Paige and her mother added harmony in parts, but Sinow's eyes couldn't be dragged from Violissa as he felt her nature power increase, the green of her eyes growing rich with the depth of her Elvin heritage, a subtle emerald layer of magic coating the ground around her and spreading through to their world, feeding the grass and, although he couldn't see it in the cover of night, bringing their world back to life as far as she could reach. The nature magic grew, the green seeming to rise from her, the Dark in him responding as if it were calling him. He held his power at bay as hers increased, her eyes shining so brightly now that they cast their light out around her within the rich sage hue of her power.

"Ren, what's she doing?" he asked, the worry returning at the amount of power he sensed her drawing.

"I've no idea, but I think the sun may be her target. I've heard the story all my life, but never did I imagine I'd get to see her do it," he muttered.

As he said the last word, she pushed her power forward. It weaved its way through the land in a blaze of green that flashed so brightly they all had to look away. Then it sank into the horizon forcing itself up under the sun which had begun sinking back to its slumber. For a moment, it looked as if the sun would win then the green grew in brightness, the sun moving higher just enough for them to know it would continue its journey. Everyone watched as her power coerced it onward to its home in the sky. Only then did he notice she'd stopped singing, his attention sweeping back to where she lay on the ground.

The Councils turned back as he ran to her, picking her up. Her eyes were barely open, but the smile on her face said she knew what she'd done and what she'd given them.

"Sinow? Is she all right?" Daneele asked amongst the other voices.

He didn't have an answer, the green of her eyes a faint hue

that appeared translucent, all sign of the Fates' magic and her own now gone.

"The connection is fading," Kanine said. "She's given all she was meant to."

Sinow looked up at them. "Goodbye, my friends. Fates be with you. We will find our way back to you."

"We will," Violissa said weakly before he felt her body go limp. Sinow took her in his arms as the window to their world faded. The others looked sadly out as the Fates separated them once again, none knowing if Violissa would awake.

"Vi? Vi, wake up," he said softly, but in his heart, he knew she'd gone too far. He could feel it as he held her limp body; the power in her was silent. She'd given everything to their Councils even when it might not have been enough.

"Violissa, what have you done?" he whispered, bringing his face into her hair and praying that it had been worth it.

Twenty-Seven

Watching the steady breathing rhythm that ebbed and flowed as Violissa lay still on the bed, Sinow felt powerless, once again severed by the Fates from being able to help the woman he loved. Severed from any ability to even see what she was fighting. It had been days. He'd lost count after the first three days of endlessly waiting, watching for any sign of her to emerge. They took shifts but mainly it was he who stayed by her side, refusing to leave her, afraid if he did the Fates would take her completely from him this time. Over and over, he ran the scene, finding the places he should have stopped her, should have forced her to leave things as they were, should have heeded the signs that glaringly told him something was wrong, that she'd pushed herself too far. It was all he could do.

As his mind wandered back to the events of that day once more, his eyes slowly closed, and his breathing steadied to match hers, his head tipping as sleep took him.

He woke, the darkness of night encasing him. His eyes adjusted to see the forest around him, the mist that curled around its floor, the moonlight now streaming in, lighting the surroundings enough to add a fairytale essence to them. Moonlight that fell from two moons.

"The Dream Realm," he said, his eyes drawn to a figure far into the woods. Moving closer, he watched the young girl, golden curls peeking from beneath her ivory cape. He couldn't move, his body frozen as he watched her reach her hands out to the moonbeam, the southern moon answering, wrapping its light around her hand then up to her face, illuminating the emerald eyes. She giggled then skipped further into the woods, stopping at what appeared to be the edge of a ravine. His heart leapt—it was his ravine but on the Cirillian side.

She peered over, the moonlight following, a light breeze pushing her cape down, her curls tumbling free.

"One day, I will meet the prince on the other side, won't I?" She looked in the direction of his castle. "He lives over there, you know. I can see it, his keep." She shuddered visibly, her face taking on a more mature look, then in a whisper said, "Will he love me as I fear I already do him?"

When no answer came, her face grew childlike again, and she giggled. "You're talking to the wind, Violissa. Of course, you'll receive no answer. What would your Council say if they heard you asking the wind for answers?"

She drifted away, the image fading like a thinning smoke. He rubbed his eyes, wondering if he'd gone mad then, finally able to move forward, took another few steps. The forest before him changed once again, lighting as if the sun were streaming down between the trees. This time, an older version of her came running through the forest, her hands lifting her skirts, her hair streaming behind her as she laughed. Her features were younger than when they'd first met, more like those of a teenager, likely before her hundredth year. She laughed then stopped, catching her breath and peering behind her. A swarm of butterflies skirted around her, dancing in her hair and along her skin. She held her hand out, and they settled on her arm, their wings flitting gently.

"I don't think they'll find me here. Thank you for helping."

Their wings beat in unison before they flew off, two remaining on her hand.

"Go on then, you've done your part. Helped me escape another day's lessons."

They stayed, their wings stopping, spanned out to reveal their beauty.

"Don't give me that look. I don't need to learn Tenebron history. Our history is boring enough, but that's the worst."

She looked away, as if just noticing where she was. "Where have you led me?"

They flew from her hand, but she didn't seem to notice. Instead, she took a few steps further, looking down to the ravine below. "I've been here before," she said quietly. "But only once." She shivered as she had done as a young girl. "I don't remember liking it here much. Too close to the Darkness," she whispered, taking a step back. But then she stopped and turned to the direction of his castle. Sinow heard the intake of her breath. "You're over there, aren't you?" She stepped forward, tentatively. "Do you feel it like I do? Do I call to you the way you do to me?"

His breathing increased. He remembered that day, the memory coming back to him. He'd felt her there, felt the words without hearing them. "Yes," he had answered, not understanding why, never knowing she was standing far south of where he was standing, unseen in the tree line just as he would have been to her.

Her head dropped, and she turned away from the ravine. "If you do, then wait for me," she said barely loud enough for him to hear. "I cannot, I will not," her eyes raised, and he could see the deep sage they had become, "be forced to live the life they want. I will not let their words direct my actions, and I will not marry you when they want me to."

Again, the vision faded, pulling her away in a drift of smoke, the woods returning amid the moonlight again.

"She was determined to make her own path," he heard his father's voice behind him.

"Father?" he said, turning in surprise.

"My son," he returned, smiling. "You've come a long way since the day I left the throne to you."

"A throne that I've lost, a people I've let down, a realm that no longer belongs to me."

"Aye, you've made missteps but ones that were not of your making, ones that you could not avoid. The path she sent you both down that day led you to this point, my son, but it was one she was destined to make and one that has now led her here."

"Destined to make? But the prophecy—"

"Is not all that it seems. You have questions, but those questions will be addressed in the future and are not ones I can answer for you."

Sinow wanted to question him more, but he understood by his father's tone that regardless of how he pushed for answers, none would come. Instead, he asked, "How are you here?"

"The Fates rewarded me for my unquestioning faith in the prophecy."

"They made you one of them."

"In some ways, yes. I do not sit among the original Fates, but I am one of the lucky few who were chosen to take a seat in their Council."

Sinow didn't know what to say. His father had been a good king, a good father, a fair ruler who had shaped their realm into what it was when Sinow took the throne. He had picked it up from the squander that Sinow's grandfather had left and brought it back to the way it had been when his forefathers had ruled.

"You deserve it, Father."

His father gave him a slight tip of the head, the only response

Sinow knew he would get. Once a Dark king, always a Dark king. He sighed then looked out beyond into the forest.

"Where are we and what am I seeing?" he asked as another image appeared; this time, the forest opened to reveal a small open space with a stream running through it.

"We are in Violissa's dreams. Her memories play before you."

Violissa appeared, dropping in front of the stream and scooping the water to her mouth. He recognized the time immediately. Her hair strewn about messily, face smeared with char remnants, her dress dirty and caked with mud at the bottom hems could only mean this was their war. Even in such disarray, she was achingly beautiful. He watched as she peered into the stream, reaching her fingers out to the image, her face growing sad.

"Why am I seeing memories?"

"It is her mind's way of strengthening her, her heart calling to wake her, her mind protecting her."

"But why does she need to be wakened? What's wrong with her?" he asked as a butterfly flitted to Violissa, brushing its wings against her cheek.

"When she gave power to the Councils, she gave them everything, digging deep into her core, draining even her innate powers. If she'd held onto her Elvin gifts, she would have recovered immediately, her Light gifts replenishing, the Elvin gifts protecting the core she'd left empty, but she exhausted them to bring back the sun in an attempt to restore the balance. Everything she had to offer she gave."

"But her core has been empty before. Tynan takes it in the future, Ren told us what happens."

He watched as she spoke to the butterfly.

"I know," she said. "I look a mess." Its wings flapped in response. "Yes, more than a mess," she replied, laughing. "I don't know what to do. He's lost to the Darkness, lost to me."

Her eyes filled with tears, tears he never knew she had for

him back then.

"I don't know how to pull him out, to bring him back to me."

The butterfly rose then hung in the air above her as if waiting for her to do something.

"I can't," she said. "I've put us on this path, and now I can't free us from it."

She looked back at the water in the stream, spreading her fingers along the surface. "But I need to try, don't I?" She leaned forward on her knees and looked into the water. "If he can't find his way out, then I'll just have to lead him. You can do this, Violissa. You are a Light Queen. You are the daughter of the Elvin," she said, rising. "You are a child of the prophecy, and your other half is waiting for you."

She brushed her hands down her skirts, smoothing the material as if doing so would soothe her nerves. "I can do this. I am his other half and his soul mate." She looked up to the sky. "I know I refused to admit that before, but I admit that now. I will no longer deny my feelings, nor will I deny that I was wrong to rebuke what you offered me. Help me through this, help me free him from the Darkness, and I promise you I will take my place by his side and rule alongside him for eternity."

Taking a deep breath, she looked to her left where he assumed Tenebron lie. The image grew hazy, and her form drifted away in the haze as it had done previously.

"She loved me even then," he said, forgetting momentarily that his father was there.

"Did you ever doubt that she did?"

He laughed. "Yes, I did just as she doubted my love for her. Why am I here?"

"You need to know that she fights to return to you, just as she always has, now and in your future life. Her love for you is what drives her each time she has been in peril. It is stronger than either of you realize. Even at her weakest, when your brother stole everything, it was you she clung to, you that kept her living. Remember that, Sinow, no matter what happens she can never be broken because your love strengthens her. That is what you gained in the union, that is what enhances your powers."

He looked down at his hands, closing and opening them. "Yet here I am again unable to help her."

"You don't need to help her, Sinow. She is stronger than you know, than you've ever given her credit for. Even now, she is fighting her way back. Her mind recalling the memories, each one a reminder of what drives her, each one rebuilding her strength, readying her for the return of her powers."

"Will that be long?"

"That I do not know. It depends on her, but it will be difficult once they do return. You need to be warned that it will not be gentle. Our core powers are tied to our very existence, they run through the blood in our veins, through each breath that we take, each thought we have guided by them. They are insinuated in our bodies as much as they are in our lives, a part of us from which we cannot part, for returning to them takes strength that even Violissa may not have."

"What are you saying?"

"Their return may be too much for her. They may take her to a state equal to one similar to being overcome by the Darkness or they may destroy her, wiping away her immortality in the process and stripping away her essence."

Sinow looked at his father, his eyes wide with disbelief. "I don't understand. She survived their return here, and she survives them when they return in our future."

"Aye, she did, but the conditions were set for both returns. While here, your powers were never fully taken, your innate powers still present, your true powers locked away while your core remained intact. They were simply dormant, asleep from the Fates' spell. When they returned, the core was awakened. When Tynan takes her, it is true that he takes her power down to the core, leaving her stripped of even her innate abilities, but the foundation remains. Her Elvin powers are not contained in her core, they are part of her, they live and breathe in her. When her powers were returned, the Elvin power was the foundation, their true extent, those blessed through the ascension were returned first, a buffer for her core, the Fate given powers layering it, readying it for her Light power to return."

"She gave everything, every part of her Elvin powers exhausted, didn't she?"

"Yes, sending every bit of it to the rebirth of the sun."

"Did it even make a difference? Did the sun fully rise after all she gave? Can the Councils even fight Tynan for all she gave of herself to them?" he asked angrily. "Was it even worth all of this?"

"No, it will not rise any more than it did prior to that day. The Darkness tilts the balance too much. The sun remained high for the day but descended never to fully rise again after night fell."

"Then it wasn't worth it. There was no reason for any of it."

"There was hope."

"They can't defeat Tynan on hope."

"Perhaps not, but they can fight him with it. They can be the men they were before all of this happened. They can stand in defense of the people left in that realm. They can proudly fight for what is right with the abilities with which they were blessed. That is what she gave them. The sun may have set once again, but for just a moment, those people saw the true power of a queen lost to them. They were given validation to what they've been holding on to for centuries."

"It's not enough," he said.

"It is enough for them."

Sinow looked back to where Violissa had been, the forest empty now, another memory having played out while he and his father were talking. He ran his hands through his hair.

"What do I do now?"

"You wait for her, and when she wakes, you guide her just as she guided you that day from out of the Darkness. You be the rock she will need, the strength she will not have just as you will do in your future life and will continue to do through eternity. You are two halves of the same soul, Sinow. Her half will be calling for you, and you must heed its call."

His father placed a hand on his shoulder. "Have faith, Sinow, the path is unbound, but it will come to an end and at its end will stand the fruits of your struggle, the reason for it all."

"Ren."

His father smiled. "There is a reason for everything the Fates do, Sinow." Upon the last word, he disappeared, only a silver dust left in his wake.

Sinow looked back at the woods where Violissa had been. Another memory had taken shape. The woods changed to reveal Violissa curled up on the forest floor. He heard crying, knowing instantly it was hers. She lifted her head slowly, and he took in the bruises that lined her face and arms, the skin torn in places, the deep circles, the gaunt look to her too thin frame. His heart broke, and he instinctively understood he was seeing a memory she hadn't yet had, one gleaned from her future self, somehow left in her subconscious but one her heart felt needed to be called forth. Her thin cheeks were layered with tears, and she looked hopeless, the brightness her eyes usually carried gone, the color lost and replaced with an iridescent tint of color. She rubbed her tears away with the back of her hands and began to hum a sad tune. Behind her an extremely large butterfly drifted, it's wings gray like the forest around it. He watched as it drifted closer then moved so she could see it. He watched the interaction, Violissa speaking to the creature, unsure of its intent.

She started singing, her voice shaky and low, the creature moving away from her and putting what looked like paws up. They seemed to stop mid-air as if bumping against an invisible barrier. She stopped singing and looked at it questioningly until it gestured for her to keep singing. She said something to it then started again, this time her voice stronger, hopeful.

Placing her hand next to the creature's, she drew back quickly as if frightened by what she'd felt, then placed it back, spreading her fingers out against the invisible barrier. Her voice grew louder and more confident, and then he heard his own voice answer her call. He was searching for her. He watched the scene play out, his attention drawing from her to the world around her, one she couldn't see. The world awoke at her voice as if it were hearing her call as well. Colors more vibrant than any he'd seen burst forth, tree leaves that shook free of the gray muted hue to reveal a deep maroon. The creature now joined by more with colors that awoke the visual senses as the surroundings did. She was doing this, she had power when no power should have existed within her. Elvin power. His ears tuned back to the song, the sound grabbing his soul, filling him with the same love she was sending his future self. What was she telling him? The words were filled with the essence of home. She was home, not home in Cirillia but in her Elvin home. She was in the Lost Realm, and her Elvin roots were still within her. Her love for him was still there, protected as were her Elvin powers, both buried deeper than Tynan could reach.

The image faded, the sound of her song lingering in the air then changing as another memory was stirred. This time, he could see nothing but could hear her singing a song that seemed familiar, one that drew him back to his own memory. Violissa placing her hand on his chest that night in her castle, binding their hearts with her words. He brought his hand over his heart, he'd never realized that's what she had done until today, the feel of the song upon his skin and through into his heart tingling with the memory and the sweet sound of the song. This memory wasn't only for her but also for him as if she sensed him there, knew he needed that connection, felt his soul there with her.

"I love you, Vi," he said, not knowing if she could hear him or not.

The dream world faded, and he woke, his head jerking up in

response. He looked around, eyeing the bed where Violissa lie, the familiarities of the room. He leaned forward on his knees and wiped his face with his hands. She was trapped in her own mind, fighting to survive and awaiting the return of her powers, leaving him in a state in which he was all too familiar, waiting.

Twenty-Eight

Paige peeked into the room, not wanting to disturb Sinow if he were sleeping, but as with each time she'd come, he was sitting in the same chair, pulled close to the bed, eyes on Violissa, watching each breath she took. Silently, she cursed the Fates for putting him in the situation again and for taking Violissa from them when they'd just gotten her back. It was frustrating, and Paige didn't like being frustrated. Pushing her hair back behind her ear, she opened the door, Sinow's eyes never leaving Violissa as he addressed her, "Paige."

"I've come to relieve you, Sinow. You've been up here since last night, and the day is almost over. Go down and eat something."

"I don't need to eat," he returned.

"Yes, you do, and you need to get out of this room, get some fresh air."

"And if she wakes—"

“I will let you know immediately. Go,” she said as his eyes finally met hers. They were a light brown, no sign of his power to be seen, the man in him taking over.

“Go. I promise if she even moves a finger, I will let you know.”

He looked back at Violissa then sighed. Rising from the chair with a stretch, he said, “I suppose it wouldn’t hurt. I am a bit hungry.”

“Good because your aunt and everyone in town has been cooking, so the place is loaded with food.”

“With people, too?”

She smiled. “No, you’re safe to go down. Keary sent them all home. It’s only Keary, Ren, and Cody along with a few family.”

He rolled his eyes. “That’s enough to make it miserable. Maybe I should stay.”

She walked over to him and pulled his arm in an attempt to move him. Unfortunately, he was built like a wall, and her efforts did nothing but tire her. She crossed her arms as he laughed.

“Ok, ok. I’ll go,” he said. “You’re as obstinate as Violissa.” Saying her name brought a sadness to his eyes that he quickly replaced, their color darkening, a chill crossing her neck.

“Thank you, Paige. Let me kno—”

“I will, now go eat and clear your head.”

He took one last look at Violissa then left the room, the door closing softly behind him. Paige walked over to the window and opened the curtains. “No wonder you’re not getting better. He keeps the light out all the time.”

Then she walked back to Violissa, adjusted her blankets, and pushed her hair back, combing it out with her fingers. “Where are you, Violissa? You need to come back to us.”

Ren had told her what he knew about Sinow’s behavior when Violissa had been taken by Tynan, what little he had gleaned from Keary in the future. It hadn’t been pretty and taken with what Keary had told her about how distant he’d become when she was trapped here, it worried her. What if Violissa didn't wake up? There were so many consequences that she didn't care to dwell on it. Sighing, she took Sinow's place in the chair next to the bed and held her friend's hand. As the day drew on, she settled in, pulling out the book she'd brought and losing herself in the imaginary world, escaping her reality for just a moment to make living in it a little easier. The worry about Violissa, the anxiety about her growing love for Ren, the constant feeling of longing she had to see her parents again, all falling away.

She didn't know how long she'd been lost to her surroundings when a slight vibration yanked her back to reality. Lowering the book, she looked at Violissa. She hadn't moved, but Paige swore she'd felt something. She leaned closer to the bed. "Violissa?" she said, not expecting an answer as none ever came when she spoke the name.

"Geez, Paige, you spooked yourself. Maybe Stephen King wasn't the best choice for light reading," she said to herself, leaning down to pick up the book which had slipped from her lap. When she came up, she scooted back in the chair in alarm. A bluish light was seeping from Violissa's skin. Paige rose from the chair and backed away.

"Sinow," she said, her voice squeaking at not nearly the volume for which she was attempting. She was about to run for the door to get him when the light streamed out around the room in beams, Violissa's body rising from the bed which had begun shaking. The light beams connected, pouring the bluish hue across Paige's skin. She put her hand out and marveled at the sparkling color her hands now appeared. "Whoa, I really need to get Sinow."

Before she could move, the light flared with power, the force drawing her sight, the scream escaping her throat before the pain coursed through her.

Sinow felt the power right before Paige's scream bled from the second level. Not looking at the others, he dropped his drink and shifted to the room, feeling Keary and Ren right behind him.

"Fates," he muttered. The room was filled with Light power, his own powers rising to meet it, begging for release to fight against it. Violissa's body floated above the bed, her hair streaming around her head like a halo, her eyes still closed. Paige was huddled in the corner, her hands over her face. He could hear her cries, ones filled with pain. "Ren, get her out of here. The power is too intense."

Ren didn't argue, he ran to Paige, scooped her up and shifted, leaving Sinow and Keary. He could feel Keary's power struggling against the onslaught of Light magic that overwhelmed the space.

"Go, Keary. You can't do anything here, and her power will only taunt yours. You'll do nothing but cause more damage."

"What are you going to do, Sinow? She's tearing the place apart, and I don't even think she's aware that she's doing it."

The room shook as he said it, pieces of the ceiling scattering down around them.

"I need to get her out of here before she brings the place down."

Violissa's head tilted back, and a blood curdling scream filled the room. His heart leapt, his pulse quickening. "The power is too much for her. Go, Keary, now."

He didn't look back to see if Keary obeyed his command; instead, he pushed his way toward her, the strength of the Light power that was trying to find its way back to her core causing a barrier he had to fight to reach her, his own power rebelling, clawing its way out to defend itself from its opposite. Finally close enough, he grabbed her, pulling her body in against his, the Light so extreme it burned his skin. Shifting, he landed outside the lake, far enough away from town for the others to remain safe.

Light power poured across the space, the lake water turning vibrant blue. Sinow stumbled back as another wave of power poured from her. The water behind them grew rough, the trees across the field bent with force. Was this what their magic was like when unleashed with no vessel to keep it in check? If Light magic was this destructive, he couldn't imagine what his Dark power would do. He pushed against the force of it, his power screaming to break free in response to the Light, the feel of it burning against his skin.

"Violissa!" he yelled.

He could barely see her, a vortex of magic surrounded her; grass, stone, and dirt swirling within it. Her hair whipped around her head, back arching in pain. With all his strength, he made his way through the wind and debris until he found her. He grabbed her face, ignoring the storm around them, forcing her to look at him.

"Violissa! You need to gain control!"

"I can't," she mouthed, her voice inaudible against the noise. Her eyes focused on him; they were mesmerizing in a terrifying way. The green splintered amongst an array of blue hues that shifted constantly.

"It hurts," she said as a tear slipped from her eye, a brilliant emerald drop that slowly slid down her cheek.

What was it his father had said? She would need his strength.

"You can. Let me help, Vi. Let me be whatever you need to get through this."

Her hand reached out and grabbed his arm, breaking it with the force, but he didn't flinch, the bone repairing immediately. Beneath her hand, he felt a pull at his power. She was pulling it out, trying to coax it free. He wanted to question but refrained. He'd told her to take what she needed, and this was how she'd answered. He let go of his hold on his power, and it roared out in response.

She teetered but held tight to him. Around them the two powers warred against each other, but he never drew his eyes from hers. Their color was shifting, the green trying to take dominance, but each time a wave of Light power would crash against him, and the blue would dominate. The powers in her were fighting just as the powers around them were.

His mind wandered back to the memory of her singing, bruised and battered in the forest, Elvin magic bringing the world to life around her. She had no power, her core drained, her innate powers gone yet magic remained. It didn't exist in her core, it existed within her, flowing freely, that's what his father had told him. And currently, she was trying to control it, to clamp it down, to box it in so that it couldn't run free. It was the Elvin in her that wanted his own power released. That part of her needed his Dark magic.

"Violissa, you have to stop. Don't try to control it. I was wrong, we were wrong, let go but let go of your nature magic first," he told her.

Fear filled her eyes.

"Listen to me, Vi. You need to free it. Your nature magic isn't housed in your core, it needs to run free. If you try to contain it, you'll die, your Light powers will burn you up."

That's what his father had meant. The two powers that lived in her worked differently and needed to fill her in different ways. The Elvin was her base, it was what defined her and enhanced the Light, but it also tempered the Light.

"Trust me," he said against the raging storm, unsure that she'd heard anything he'd said.

Her eyes grew calm, and she let go of his arms and closed her eyes. He felt the rush of her nature powers, sensual and warm, as they took their place in the storm. Looking up, he watched as the green of their magic danced with his power, the two blending then separating. They were compatible, all the eons his ancestors had spent fighting hers, and they were more similar than anyone had ever fathomed.

The green darkened in shade as it pulled free, encasing the arcane of the Light power, calming it, settling against it, the coolness of the Light bringing out the vibrant emerald of the nature. He saw it so clearly now, the nature, the juncture between the other two powers. All three in harmony for just that moment.

He dropped his eyes to look at Violissa again, her eyes opening to meet his, their dark beauty calling to him. They were forest green. almost black, alluring and seductive. The world awoke, the storm calming at the same moment. The sky clouded over with thunder clouds, the vortex around them settling to a breeze that ran through her hair, straight hair that now shone nearly white, the Elvin queen ready to conquer but to conquer what? For an instant, he felt it, the Darkness that ran through her blood, the part of her heritage that made her volatile that drove her instinct, her reckless free spirit, the half of her that owned him, all of him.

She turned her eyes upward, stretching her arm forth, opening her hand to summon her Light power, to rein it in, her nature magic filling the space as he drew his powers back. The blue of her Light power calmed, drifting to her as her nature power harnessed it. The world settled around them, the sky opening once again, the sun shining upon her now golden curls. Her eyes dropped to him, a mesmerizing cerulean blue that was now vibrantly exchanging place with the emerald, fading to let it take hold.

"Hi," she said shyly.

"Hi," he returned, smiling, happy she was back.

"You're here, you stayed with me."

He brought his hand up and caressed her cheek, pushing her stray curl back.

"I will always be here, Violissa. No matter what happens, I will be here, I will always be on the other side of whatever it is that separates us."

She smiled, her eyes glittering as they filled with tears.

"I love you, too," she said.

He searched her eyes. "You felt me there?"

"On the other side," she replied.

Holding her face in both hands, he pulled her to him, his lips meeting hers. Kissing her filled him, reminding him of how he'd missed her and how deeply he loved her. He dropped his head, forehead touching hers.

"So, should I expect you to keep testing me like this?"

Laughing, she ran her hand through his hair, then brought her lips to his again.

"Always," she said as he lost himself to her touch. He brought her in, tight enough to feel her heartbeat quicken. Just as he thought there was no going back, that he would make love to her right there and then, she pulled away, her breath ragged.

"What else did I do?" she asked as he kissed her neck, trying to continue, his need for her too great to put aside.

"Sinow, the trees are bent, the ground torn asunder. I did that, didn't I?"

The question gave him pause. He sighed and brought his head up, seeing then the worry in her eyes.

"You make it very difficult on a man, Violissa," he said, rolling his neck and flexing his hands to focus himself.

"Sorry," she said, her eyes reflecting her guilt.

"We've got all of eternity, right?"

"Right."

She looked around, then cast her magic out, the ground below healing, the trees standing upright again.

"Did I destroy the inn?"

"You did some damage, but..." he paused, thinking of Paige.

"What? Sinow, what did I do?"

"Paige."

It was all he needed to say. She brought her hand to her mouth in fear, then shifted, leaving him wondering how everything had changed so quickly once again.

The world had been a blur of pain and burning until Sinow had brought her back, helping Violissa understand how to rein in the tidal wave of Light magic that had crashed into her unsuspecting body. He'd guided her, knowing before she that her nature powers would pave the way to leading her Light power home, to restoring her core. He'd known because he'd been there, the memory returning to her as he said the words. The other side. That's where he'd been, watching as her mind played out the memories that filled her heart, that gave her strength, that woke the power within her, the sleeping spirit.

There was a memory she shouldn't have had, one that didn't belong to her, not yet at least. A painful memory that left the burden of what was to come weighing upon her soul, an imprint from her future self. But why had it been left? Simply for that moment, for Sinow to watch it and see what she should have seen as it played in her conscious? That her Elvin gifts, her nature powers, were truly who she was, a part of her that ran through her like the blood that flowed through her beating heart, as much a part of her as every breath that filled her lungs. It did not need containment like Light power or Dark power. It was unique and inseparable from its bearer. How had she never seen that before now? How had Sinow seen it before she had?

The thoughts fled as she lost herself to his touch, to the feel of his lips upon hers, his body against hers. She could have stayed in his arms for the remains of the day and longer, for eternity but for the fleeting thought that there was more. That was why she'd stopped him, why she'd pushed aside her need for him and questioned the true impact of her loss of control. When he'd said Paige's name, she'd remembered the scream that had broken through her consciousness, ripped through the pain that had blocked everything else out.

Leaving him, she shifted to the inn, feeling him shift behind her but running instead to the back of the inn, sensing Paige in the kitchen where Sinow's human family would gather on Sundays to eat. She threw open the door and looked hurriedly around, the faces turning to her in concern. Her eyes locked on Ren who averted them and looked down at his lap where Paige was curled up, a cloth covering her eyes.

"You didn't heal her?" she heard Sinow ask.

"I couldn't," Ren answered sadly. "I tried everything, but my power won't work on her."

"You can't physically influence your past," Violissa said, kneeling down next to Paige and taking her hand.

"Paige, I'm so, so sorry," she said, her voice breaking to the reality that she'd hurt her best friend, caused her immense pain.

Paige squeezed her hand.

"You can heal her, Vi, right?"

"Yes," she answered, having already sent her senses out to determine the damage. Slowly, she removed the cloth from Paige's face, thankful they had wrapped it in cling wrap first to avoid it sticking to the wounds.

"I tried to calm the burn as much as I could, but she needs a hospital," she heard the local doctor say. They must have called him while she was off fighting her own battles.

"It's ok, I'll take care of her. What did you give her for the pain?" she asked, looking at the burns on Paige's face and eyes.

"Norofen is all I had," he replied. "She needs to go to the hospital, Violet, it's too bad for us to treat here."

"She's got it, Galen," she heard Sinow say calmly. "This is what she does."

She tuned everything else out and focused on the wounds. They were third degree, and it was a wonder Paige hadn't passed out from the pain. It showed how strong she was. Knowing it would take her a while to repair the tissue, she sat on the floor, afraid to have Ren move her, assuming he'd kept her there with that same fear. Every movement would bring her more pain. Bringing her hands up, she closed her eyes and focused on the deepest wounds, starting from the inside out. Her power had burned through Paige's retinas, blinding her. She healed the deeper layers of tissues around the eyes first, slowly and painfully rebuilding layer upon layer, then moved to the damage in her eyes. She lost track of the world around her. The deeper the damage, the longer the healing. Thankfully, there was no damage to any of her bone structure, but the eyes were delicate, and if not healed in just the right way at just the right timing, she could do more damage to them and be forced to start from the beginning.

Finally, she moved to the outer skin, repairing the soft skin that framed Paige's face. When she finished, she sat back, stretching her neck, the stiffness setting in from the intensity of using her healing gift and sitting in one position for such a long period of time. Paige brought her hand up to her face, slowly sitting and blinking her eyes repeatedly.

"I can see again, Violissa. The pain is gone, and" she felt the new skin, "it's all gone." She bent down and hugged Violissa. "Thank you."

"I'm so sorry, Paige. I never meant to hurt you."

Paige drew back and gave her a stern look. "Stop. You didn't know."

"But I hurt you," she replied.

"I will say I know the risk I take hanging out with your husband, but I didn't expect you to be the one to beat me up," she said, laughing.

Violissa's face must have reflected the guilt that statement caused her, for Paige said quickly, "I'm joking, Violissa."

Violissa felt Sinow move closer to her and saw his hand extended to help her up. She took it, looking into his eyes.

"Paige is right, Vi. You had no control over what happened.

I don't even think you were awake yet. You healed her, and everything is ok now."

She wanted to kiss him for making her feel better but didn't think the timing was right.

"You know," Ren said with a bit of amusement in his voice, "you have the ability to heal much faster than that."

"What do you mean?" Violissa asked. "If you heal too fast, you risk making it worse or killing the mortal."

"For your Council, yes. I probably shouldn't tell you this, but since things are completely out of sequence now anyway, you can heal an entire town full of people at once with your power."

She stared at him in disbelief.

"You discover it when you take back the realms. There are too many wounded for the Councils to take care of on their own without losing some, so you figure out a way to circumvent the rules."

"Circumvent the rules? Why does that sound like my queen?" Sinow joked.

She jabbed him in the arm. "It goes against code to risk a mortal's life. No one would ever try doing what he's saying."

"No one but you no doubt," Sinow said. "That sounds exactly like something you would do."

"I'll teach you just as you taught me," Ren said.

"Do you think you could do something about the half of the inn that seems to be missing first?" Uncle Pat asked.

They all laughed, the seriousness of the situation dissolving, all of them relieved Violissa had returned, and Paige had not been permanently injured.

Later that evening as Violissa lay in Sinow's arms, she heard him say, "Your powers are curious, Vi."

"How so?" she asked, kissing his chest.

"There are layers to your magic, each part having its own place within you, each working with the other half. The two parts living in harmony."

"Do you suppose Ren is the same way?"

"I don't know. He holds three powers that don't play well together, and he has yet to master one of them. Perhaps when he ascends, he'll finally find his way."

She picked herself up to look at him then said, "He doesn't want to ascend."

"Doesn't want to ascend?" he asked, his eyes darkening in response to the thought. "What prince doesn't want to ascend?"

"Ours," she replied.

"That's nonsense, Violissa. He doesn't have a choice."

"Apparently, he thinks he does, and he's made up his mind."

"And you've spoken to him about this enough to know?"

She sighed. "Not long enough, but it appears it's a sore subject with our future selves."

He stared at the ceiling; she could tell he was thinking on what she'd said.

"There's no sense in worrying about it yet, Sinow. We have a lifetime to figure out how to persuade him to follow his destiny. At least we know what we have to look forward to."

He brought his eyes back to hers. "That doesn't help, but I suppose there's nothing we can do about it yet. I still think if he can master his Dark power, it will give him more confidence. Enough perhaps to dissuade him from avoiding his ascension. I can't believe I'm even saying those words," he muttered.

"Let's not dwell on it. Tomorrow is another day," she said, running her hand along his body.

"Are you trying to distract me, Violissa?" he asked coyly.

"I believe they call it redirection," she replied as she brought herself on top of him.

"You're quite good at it."

"Imagine how good I'll be in a few thousand years."

"I'm in trouble, aren't I?" he answered, drawing her in. She let the worries of Ren's ascension go as he did the same and immersed herself in the pleasure that followed, a state where only she and Sinow existed and the rest of the world with its troubles fell away.

Twenty-Nine

Violissa sat on the patio swing, having left Sinow sleeping soundly. She had no doubt he'd wake soon and find her. They were so in sync with each other now it was inevitable. It had been two days since she'd awoken from her deep slumber. She breathed in the cool night air, the stars in the sky above twinkling against the dark night canvas. Feeling a stir in the air, she looked over to see Ren who looked surprised to see her there. She patted the seat next to her, indicating her desire for him to sit next to her.

"You're up late," he said, sitting and causing the swing to sway slightly.

"Couldn't sleep."

He looked around. "And father's not here with you?"

Violissa studied him, wondering how much of his parents' emotional burden he had carried and for how long. *Our burden*, she thought.

"I am my own person, Ren. Sinow does not need to follow me."

"Not yet," he grumbled.

Sighing, she said, "You truly resent your father, don't you?"

He looked down at his hands, "I love my father, but I hate what he's done to my mother, to you. I know the call of our Elvin blood, the call to be alone as it speaks to you, to sit quietly amongst the forest life or to lie in the fields listening to the breeze amongst the flowers. I know how the babble of the creeks call to your soul because they call to mine."

He paused, and Violissa sensed Sinow. Her eyes met his, but he stayed aside, not wanting Ren to see him.

"My father took that from her, he will take it from you, his fear of losing you too great for him to fight. A curse of the Fates, of the prophecy. You are the one thing he cannot live without."

"Did you ever think that perhaps your mother..." She shook her head. "No, that *I* wanted that? I'm a strong woman, Ren, and nothing Sinow says could make me give up my freedom or quiet the call of nature in my blood."

"You say that now because things haven't happened to change him, to drive that fear in him."

She picked up his chin and forced him to look from his hands to her. "Nothing has happened yet to change me either. He watches her, protects her because that is who he is, and she allows it because she needs him. Ren, they made an agreement. I have no doubt in my mind that in that moment two people who needed each other made the decision to change who they were. She needed him to be that person as much as he needed to be it. Ren, your father and I both need each other. You can see it as a weakness, or you can see it as a strength. The two of us complement each other because of our differences. Whatever we agreed upon after those events was necessary for both of us to carry on."

He searched her eyes, possibly looking for some sign of doubt, but she would give him none. She knew in her heart she was right, knew from speaking to Sinow's future self that the fault did not lie entirely in his hands.

"I suppose I never looked at it that way, always assumed she acquiesced, that he didn't give her any say."

"I wonder if you underestimated me."

He laughed. "I may have."

She looked over to where Sinow stood, no longer hidden.

Ren, noticing his presence, said, "I'm sorry. You would never talk about it, even the mention of that time would risk your wrath. I was left guessing, piecing it together, and I suppose I took your response as one that spoke for both of you but at your command. Mother never stood up, never challenged your reaction or pushed back when you stayed by her side." Ren ran his hand through his hair. "I blamed you, and you took the blame, never defending yourself, never arguing your case."

Sensing his regret, Sinow said, "I took it because I loved you, Ren. There was no reason to defend my actions and no reason for your mother to defend hers. I know myself enough to be certain of that."

"But I can't tell them now."

Violissa smiled. "You just did."

She kissed his cheek. "Now that we have that out of the way, let's discuss why you really came out here at three in the morning."

"I could ask you the same thing."

"And you know the answer both of us would give. Why are you restless, Ren?"

He dropped his gaze again, and Violissa sensed his hesitation then noticed the slight tremor in his fingers.

"The ascension," she said as Sinow took a seat in the chair nearest them.

"Don't," Ren said, moving to get up.

Sinow shot him a look, and he sat back down, scared of his father even at this stage.

"I heard you intend to avoid taking the throne," he said, his eyes never leaving Ren's, their hue darkening.

"Don't lecture me, I've heard it already from both of you, especially you."

Violissa sensed the Dark in him rise with a hint of Elvin. Both looked set to pounce, and she wondered if this was exactly what happened in their future. She was ready to step in when Sinow did something surprising. He calmed, his eyes lightening.

"We're not your parents yet, Ren. You don't have to defend your decision."

Ren's expression turned to one of suspicion.

"I'm guessing I haven't given you time to explain? I have a tendency to let the Dark guide my reaction to things," he continued.

Her heart swelled. This was the man she loved, and in that moment, she fell further in love with him. She wondered if this was how it had been in her future, falling deeper in love with him every day.

"You don't really like to talk about it, at least not with me."

"Then let's talk," Violissa said, following Sinow's lead.

Ren looked back and forth between them.

"Is it the power, Ren?" Sinow asked.

Ren stayed silent for a moment before saying, "Partly." He sighed. "My parents are better fit to rule. It suits them. The people adore my mother, respect my father. The people need them and—"

"You need them," she finished for him.

She looked at Sinow, the reason for Ren's hesitation becoming evident.

"My parents need to continue their rule."

"Ren," she said, putting her hand over his. "You are the first king blessed with both parents. The only one to have a mother and two parents who raised you together."

"No wonder our mothers are always taken from us," Sinow said. "My father was distant, a Dark king rarely shows emotion."

"But one with a wife, one whose heart is bound like yours would be different," she finished for him. "You don't want to ascend because it means you lose us."

"And you lose each other," Ren finished.

Sinow rose and started pacing. Violissa could tell he was thinking on something.

"Ren, all kings go through what you are experiencing. They must all let go of their fathers."

"Dark kings keep their distance for a reason, Violissa. Emotion weakens them, it's the struggle that's present in me every waking moment. Saying goodbye to my father was hard but not hard enough to question my ascension."

"But Light kings are different. They show emotion, they don't keep their distance because it's not an issue with our power."

Then there's more to this than we see, he said only to her.

"Ren, what else is it you fear?"

"I don't fear anything," he said softly. "Fear is weakness."

"That's me talking. But as you are not only a Dark king, I'm guessing your other powers don't question fear as mine do."

"That's it," Violissa said. "The power. Remember right before my ascension, Sinow? Remember my fear?"

"That you would lose a part of yourself to the ascension."

She smiled; he did remember. "Yes. Ren, it's normal to feel scared."

"I'm not afraid," he said forcefully. "I don't want to ascend."

He rose, and she knew they'd struck a chord.

"You don't want the Dark power," Sinow stated bluntly.

Ren looked up at him, eyes a deep blue.

"No, I don't." His shoulders relaxed as if a weight he'd been carrying had shifted. "I don't want it. I'm not you. I will never be you. I will never be the king you are, and you hate that."

Sinow didn't flinch. "Do I? Or perhaps I dislike you turning your back on your potential. You have three powers running through you, Ren. Only your mother comes close to understanding what that's like. You have the potential to be greater than both of us but not until you accept the Darkness in you."

"I won't."

"Why not? Because of your other powers?"

"I don't know." He was starting to fidget like he wanted to escape. Sinow was cornering him.

"You do know. You just wouldn't tell your father because he would have pushed you, challenged you."

Then she pieced it together, she had been right. Ren was just like her, but it wasn't the ascension he feared, it was what the ascension would bring.

"You're afraid your Dark power will overtake the other powers when you ascend. That you'll lose control of it and lose your Light and nature magic. That's why you won't ascend," she said.

Ren gaped at her, but Sinow didn't give him a chance to stop the momentum. "That's it? You're afraid of losing yourself to the Dark?"

"You don't know what it's like—"

"I don't? I may not have your other powers, but I know damn well what it's like to fear the Darkness. I know what it's like to lose yourself to it, to claw your way back from under it."

Ren ran his hands through his hair. "I know you do, but all you know is Dark magic. You don't know the cool, calm feel of the Light or the rich depth of the nature. The Dark is invading, it takes over everything."

"And you're afraid you'll lose those powers, but that won't happen. I had two ascensions, Ren, you will have three."

"It won't help. The Dark will overtake..."

"No, it won't, Ren," Sinow interrupted. "The three powers are compatible. I never realized until that night you showed us all three. The Dark and Elvin complement each other, the Dark brings out the strength in the Elvin, it draws on the emotional side of the magic while the Elvin feeds off the very qualities you fear from my power."

"But the Light—"

"The Light is the balance," Violissa said, meeting Sinow's eyes.

"Exactly. Without the Light, the other powers are volatile, especially combined. Dark magic is unstable, easily triggered, ready to send its owner into madness at any moment. The Elvin, emotion driven, eruptible. The Light calms, soothing the fire of the other two," he said, his eyes never leaving hers. "Without the calming of the Light, I would have been lost long ago. Violissa balances me. Her effect on me is external, but you," he turned to look at Ren, "you have it built in. Your Dark power can never overcome the qualities of Light. They were meant to be one within you. Your nature power is the bridge between the two, compatible with both sides."

Ren's eyes lightened to a brighter blue as Sinow's words sank in but quickly grew to a rich navy, on the cusp of black.

"You're wrong. There's no balance. She held all three, and it nearly killed her. Light and Dark are not meant to be one," Ren said, his hands trembling, a black mist beginning to form. Sinow's powers rose, his eyes blackening in response, the two feeding off each other.

"You can't compare what Violissa experienced to what you will. She was not made to hold Dark power, you were."

The air around them grew heavy.

"I will not ascend, I will not take the throne. I am not a Dark king, and I will not let the Darkness destroy the Light in me. I will not let it destroy me like it wants to."

He shifted, leaving them both staring at his empty space, wondering what had happened.

Violissa bit her lip, thinking about how to calm Sinow. His

power was raging, blanketing the patio; she felt the Darkness on his skin and saw it reflected in his eyes. She was partially fascinated by seeing both he and Ren respond to each other's powers. It was as if the Darkness in one fueled the other. Shaking her head to clear her thoughts, she walked over to Sinow and, skimming her hands up his shirt, kissed his neck. She felt the Darkness abate.

"He's conflicted, Sinow."

"He's stubborn. Fates, Vi, he's not even my son yet, and already, I'm frustrated with him. He's like a loose cannon. He has no control, no idea which power is active and when."

She ran her lips along his cheek then to over to his lips. His hands gripped her waist, and he relaxed more.

"You're sneaky," he murmured.

"I'm calming."

"You are not calming at the moment."

He pulled her in tighter, and she felt the need in him rise.

"Sorry, it was the first thing I could think of doing."

"I'm not complaining, but you do make it difficult to think."

She laughed and drew back to look at him.

"He's got multiple issues. He fears your power, his ascension tremors have hit him early, and then there's us. He fears for his parents."

"Do you really think that's part of it or is he using it to mask the fear of his Dark power?"

"I do. But I wonder how much of it is his fear or our fear projected on him."

"What do you mean?"

"Think about it, Sinow. We're at the infancy of our relationship, and I can't fathom losing you again. Imagine how that will feel thousands of years in the future when we know our end is imminent, when the birth of our son signals the countdown to our end."

Brushing her curl back, he said, "After I've experienced losing you a second time," he sighed, "I imagine I wouldn't hide my frustration very well."

"No, I have a feeling you wouldn't. He's not as worried about losing us as he is about us losing each other."

He rested his forehead against hers. "We're quite a dysfunctional family, aren't we?"

She pressed her face into his chest.

"What are we going to do, Vi? He has to ascend."

"We don't even know if his timeline exists anymore, Sinow. He may return to find there's nothing to which to ascend. He may wake up in our timeline with no memory of any of this."

"You go entirely too deep sometimes, Violissa, you know that, right?"

She laughed and picked her head up to peek at him.

Kissing her forehead, he said, "Let's just help him the best we can and assume the future of our world depends upon it. Well, that and us finding a way home."

His lips moved down her face, brushing her cheek then found her mouth. She reveled in the taste of him, the Dark magic still fresh on his skin.

"Let's go back to bed," he mumbled.

"Only if you promise we won't be sleeping."

"I can definitely promise there will be no sleeping for either of us," he answered confidently.

She grew warm, his touch increasing her arousal before he pulled her in closer and shifted, the Dark essence of his shift encasing her as it always did.

Keeping to his promise, neither slept when they returned to their room.

The forest floor was cool, but Ren paid it no heed. In reality, it wasn't a forest like he remembered from home but a patch of trees that stood in the distance from the lake. He'd shifted to the spot, thinking it would help clear his mind. It hadn't. The thoughts kept circling like vultures, diving down to their prey, fighting each other for dominance then soaring back up to circle again. His parents were right, he didn't want to lose them, and the thought of them losing each other killed him. They were constants to him and to each other. A world without them would be a lesser one. He had thought if he could avoid taking the throne they would be forced to stay, forced to remain in their world.

A beetle lumbered across his leg, its bulky body wobbling to and fro. Maybe he was a fool, thinking he could force the hand of the Fates even knowing the punishments his parents had endured for doing so. The beetle made its way to the ground and scurried away.

He thought about his father. He was different here, his temperament yet to be tested, his fear yet to take its permanent place in his heart. Was he right? Would the Dark power in Ren balance with the Light when he ascended? Even if he refused the throne, the true ascension, the Fates gift of his full powers would still come, they could not be refused. He was scared, scared of what the Darkness would do to him, knowing what it had done to his father, and worse to his great grandfather and his uncle. Scared, not a word to be muttered in his father's presence. "Dark kings fear nothing," his father's motto ran through his head. "There is nothing in this world that can harm a Dark king," he had told Ren when he was young.

Except their own power, Ren thought.

Standing, he breathed in the scent of the trees once more before shifting back to the inn. The patio was empty, his parents returning to their room, although Ren knew them well enough to know they weren't sleeping.

He rolled his neck and looked out into the night sky. It would not be dawn for some time, but he didn't want to go back to his room, knew sleep was beyond his reach. Not understanding why, he found himself in front of Paige's door. Softly, he knocked, hoping he wouldn't rouse anyone else's curiosity. He wanted to see her, somehow knowing her smile would make it better. He was about to knock again when the door cracked open, and she peered through the opening, her blue eyes distinct against the backdrop of the lightless room.

"Ren?" she said, her voice filled with surprise.

"I couldn't sleep. I—" He felt nervous, which he hated.

She smiled. "I was having a tough time sleeping, too."

She opened the door further, and he couldn't help but grin at the clothes she wore. Pajamas, someone had called them. Dozens of funny little snowmen filled the material.

"Not the typical garb from home, huh?" she asked, seeing his reaction.

"Still getting used to it."

"Do you often see women in their night clothes?" she asked softly, letting him enter her room.

"No, can't say that I do."

Her shoulders relaxed, and he wondered if she'd been jealous of the thought. Suddenly, he had the urge to kiss her again, but he remembered what she'd said the other night.

"I shouldn't have come," he said at the memory of how torn she'd been. "I should go."

"Don't," she replied, surprising him.

"But the other night."

"I know, but I could use the company, and I don't think I'm ready to say goodbye to you yet."

He closed the door behind him, the soft white moonlight illuminated the room so he could see her silhouette, her eyes shining brightly. Taking his hand, he weaved his fingers in her hair, pulling her lips to his. It felt wonderful to kiss her again, the worries of the evening lifting away. She was enough to let him escape it all for just a little while, the reality of all that encompassed his world disappearing. He stayed with her until dawn, talking, laughing, letting everything else go but her company. As the sun began its ascent, she finally drifted off in his arms, the soft movement of her breathing calming him as he pulled the blanket up over her arm, her pajamas too thin to keep the pre-dawn chill from her skin. He lay there, feeling her heartbeat, wondering how he would ever return without her now that he had found her. Wondering how one could bring a ghost back from the past.

Thirty

The rift in the boundary was thick, the shape resembling a long lightning strike.

"The damage is growing worse," Mackay said.

"The attacks are stronger," Daneele replied, studying this new crack. Since Violissa had brought their power back, they were diligently watching the boundary, finally able to see what they'd been blind to for too long. The smaller cracks they'd been able to repair, but that was all. Without power on both sides of the shield, the larger damage was beyond their reach. Tynan's strikes had become more frequent, stronger, as if he knew the Fates had interfered and given them leverage.

Daneele scratched his beard. "We can't repair this one," he said, sensing Cyric shift behind him.

"Fates, he's breaking through," Cyric said as another rain of magic could be seen pummeling the boundary. The fracture grew, long vines streaming from it, the damage intensifying.

Daneele could see the angry black essence seeping through.

"Can you fix it?' he heard Maggie say behind him, her eyes searching the sky to find what only he and the others could see.

"Maggie? What are you doing here?"

"I begged Brom to bring me. You've been gone for days now, and I thought a visit and some fresh tea would be nice." She held up the metal canister, tea dripping from the lip. She'd been experimenting with different plants to flavor the tea, reminding him of Violissa yet again.

"Sorry, Daneele. She's persuasive. I didn't realize this had appeared," Brom said, gesturing to the fracture.

"It's all right. Maggie," he said moving away with her, "as much as I miss you, you shouldn't be here. It's safer in the village."

"I don't want to be in the village, Daneele. My place is with you, it always has been."

He brushed a loose hair back from her eye and sighed. "You're a stubborn woman."

"I know, that's why you love me," she replied, reaching up to quickly kiss him.

Another blast hit the boundary, and he heard a loud crack, his eyes flying upward.

"Oh, that's not good," Cyric mumbled.

The crack spread, long fingers stretching from it, filling the boundary shield. Within moments, it shattered.

Lightbearers! Cyric shouted, summoning them all, Daneele knowing Kanine was doing the same to the Darkbearers. All of them shifting in to face the threat that lie on the other side. They all drew their power, Cyric aiming his to the shattered fragments of the boundary transforming them to sand before they fell.

Daneele's heart raced. Maggie. He pushed her away with his power. It was too late to shift her, the ground buckling as Torathar ripped through the tree line beyond where the village lie. With a whoosh of magic, he flung her back up and behind a fresh mound of sand that had accumulated. She'd be safe as long as she remained hidden from Tynan's sight. Then, he turned to stand side by side with his brothers.

"So, I have a question that's been bugging me," Cody said, pulling a chair up next to Sinow. They were all sitting around drinking, Sinow and Keary looking enviously on as the effects of the alcohol took hold of Cody and a few of the others. Erin had already had one too many, her head propped on Garrett's shoulder, sound asleep.

"What is it, Cody?" he asked.

"If you can tell when bad stuff is happening, why isn't your Spidey sense tingling non-stop. I mean there's bad stuff going on in this world all the time."

"Spidey sense?" Ren asked.

"Don't ask," he said, wishing Cody would go away. Sometimes, he asked too many questions.

"Cody has a point. Why isn't this world triggering your powers? And why not take care of all the nonsense we have to deal with?"

He stared at the agent, Abigail, trying not to kill her for adding to the annoyance. He tolerated their constant presence, but he preferred them silently watching. If he had a choice, he'd have sent them both packing, but they were under orders to observe.

"We can't use our powers here. Not for anything unrelated to us," Violissa said, as he felt the coolness of her calming spell wrap around him.

"Why not?"

"Because that's the deal. Your god allowed us to have our powers, to let the Fates step in to help us, but only if we stay out of his business. We can fix or heal damage we have inadvertently caused, like the damage in town when Tynan attacked us, but that is the limit of what he will tolerate."

"You can't seriously expect us to believe that," the other agent said.

"Why do you two think you're part of this conversation?" Sinow asked.

"Our world, we get to ask questions."

"Even if they were allowed to interfere, our power doesn't work that way," Ren interjected. "He's only attuned to people from his realm, his power."

They stared at Ren, and Sinow could sense they're confusion.

"We can't sense humans, and he can't sense my mother's people. There's no reason to have that ability in our world."

"You can sense Cirillians?" Sinow asked him.

"Yes, I'm aware of both our people."

Sinow looked at Violissa who didn't seem surprised.

"He's meant to rule both realms, Sinow."

"Yes, he is," he mumbled, thinking.

"I don't—" Cody started, but Sinow, who was done with the questions, put his hand up, silencing his words.

"Sinow?" Violissa said as if to ask why Cody was now mute.

"Ren, you can sense when a Tenebron has committed a crime?" he asked, disregarding her for the moment.

"Yes."

"Even when you're only drawing from your Light power?"

"Well, yes," he answered slowly.

Sinow rose, releasing Cody from the spell.

"That wasn't fair," he said, but Sinow ignored him.

If Ren could sense his people, then his Dark power was present constantly, and he didn't realize it. Sinow had a hunch. He looked over at Violissa.

"Vi, when you fought the Torathar when we were younger, how did you do it?"

She chewed her lip. "I blended my powers."

"Ren, come with me. Violissa, Keary, you too. Everyone else

stay here if you want to stay alive."

He grabbed Ren and shifted outside, well beyond the inn.

"What are we doing?" Ren asked.

"Helping you."

Ren's eyes shone bright against the night backdrop, a reminder to Sinow of how strongly Ren favored his Light power. He needed to push Ren out of that comfort. With all he'd learned about the three powers lately, he had a hunch they worked much differently than any of them had thought. He wasn't certain he was right, but it was worth the try.

"What's going on, Sinow?" Violissa asked when she arrived. Keary shifted in with Cody and Paige in tow.

Sinow turned and grabbed him. "I said no mortals."

"Sinow, it's my fault. They wanted to come, and Paige is one of us," Violissa said.

"As is Cody," Keary grunted. "I thought we established that."

Violissa shot Keary a dirty look, still adamant that Cody was a mere human, and Sinow dropped him only noticing then the shield Violissa had placed around Paige to protect her.

"Fine. Keep them back. Violissa, drop your shield. Keary, you shield her instead. I'll need Violissa's help."

"Ren," he said, as the others moved back. "Draw your Dark power."

"I know what you're doing. It won't work. My Dark power is too unstable. I can't control it well enough to live in it."

"That's not what I want, and you need to stop trying to control it. I'm sure you've heard that from me before."

"Many times."

"Draw your power," Sinow said, calling his own forth.

"Look, my father tried this."

Sinow hit him with a blast of magic.

"I'm not your father yet. I am your opponent." He stepped closer to Ren. "Your enemy. And I will not hesitate to hurt you."

He felt Ren's power respond, witnessed his eyes darken, the blue changing to a deep brown.

"Draw your power, Ren."

"I can't control it," he whispered.

"You don't need to." Sinow slammed his hands into Ren's chest, sending him stumbling backwards. He felt the change in the air as Ren balanced himself, the Dark power coiled out from him, and Ren's demeanor changed as the Darkness took over.

"Good," Sinow said. "Now hold it there. Violissa."

She moved forward, not questioning his intention.

"I can't do this. It's too unstable," Ren pleaded.

"You will do this," Sinow commanded. "Keary, drop the shield from Paige."

"What?"

"No," Ren said, straining to keep his power under control.

"Do it."

"She'll be hurt," Ren said.

"Not if you let go. My power will hurt her but yours doesn't."

Ren's face showed his surprise.

"Keary!" He revoked permission, and Paige cried out as Keary dropped his shield.

"Sinow?" Violissa said, her voice carrying the concern he saw reflected on Ren's face.

"Let your control go, and your power will overshadow mine. She won't feel anything but yours." He had purposely restrained his power in an attempt to not truly hurt Paige, knowing Ren's code would insist he protect her, protect an innocent. And somehow, in the back of his mind, he understood Ren's power wouldn't harm her, his mind not fully piecing together why that would be.

"Ren," Violissa said, looking back at Paige. "Do it, she's in pain."

He slowed his breathing and closed his eyes. Sinow saw the tension leave his body, saw the black aura deepen, and felt the Dark penetrate the surrounding area. He was powerful. Paige's breathing relaxed, and Sinow sensed her pain diminish. Ren's eyes opened, their now black irises glaring at Sinow.

"Now, Violissa, you do the rest, work your magic."

"Draw your nature magic, Ren."

"I can't draw them at once. You need to shield her."

"No," Sinow said, crossing his arms. "You will keep your Dark power present and at full height, or she will feel the effects of mine."

Ren growled. "What are you doing?"

"Waking your potential. You have more than you know, Ren. Your parents saw it, we see it. Now step into it. Draw your nature magic like Violissa said to do."

Sinow felt the change in the air; the trees in the distance rustled their leaves, and the wind howled around them. Ren stumbled back a few steps, straining to keep the two powers in check.

"Don't control them. Dark and nature are compatible. They feed off each other."

It took a few moments, but finally Ren relaxed, and the air changed, tingling against his skin as if filled with static electricity.

"Now, slowly let your Light magic in," Violissa instructed. "Very slowly."

"That's an invitation for war inside my body," Ren replied worriedly.

"No, they will find balance," she answered.

"Do it, Ren."

Ren's face filled with fear, his Dark powers abating slightly until he heard Paige whimper. Sinow had not dropped his own power nor had he given Paige's permission back. Ren's Dark power rose again, but this time, Sinow noticed his nature powers rise to meet them. They were coordinated now.

"Do it, Ren," he commanded again.

Ren stilled, and Sinow felt the subtle addition of Light power, his own powers reacting to it.

Sinow, Violissa said softly. *I think we should back up.*

The Light power climbed, and as it did, the air became more charged. Ren's eyes began changing, a kaleidoscope of hues that reminded Sinow of Violissa's right before her ascension.

Keary, shield her again, just in case, he called to Keary as he also granted Paige permission.

They backed up, the Light pouring out of Ren now, flickering in and out of the Dark aura that surrounded him like a loose bulb, the blue hue finally penetrating it. The Dark swirled around the Light as a green hue reached out to join the colors surrounding Ren, reminding him of when Violissa's powers had returned and confirming his suspicion.

"Relax, Ren, and don't try to control any of it. This is what you were meant for," Violissa instructed as Ren's worried eyes met hers.

The force of his magic grew, pushing them back further, the hues now reaching up to the sky above them as well as outward. Violissa grabbed Sinow's hand, and he moved her closer to him as they watched Ren's transformation.

The ground rumbled, lightning tore through the sky, the wind pounding against Sinow. All the while the colors swirled, faster and faster until with one last flare, they poured across the land then crashed back into Ren. Things quieted, the world growing still. The force of the magic had left Ren on his knees. His head bent, he brought his hands out to the ground, pushing one knee up then lifting his head.

When he opened his eyes, Violissa gasped. Looking back at them were no longer the cerulean blue of her people but a blend of all three powers. Ren's eyes were now a vibrant hue of purple that shone through the night.

Magic stirred like electricity pulsing through Ren, power unlike anything he'd experienced even with his full Dark powers drawn. From the reaction of the others, he had changed physically, he just couldn't tell how. He stood, flexing his hands and rolling his neck. The Darkness in him danced with the Light, the two bound by the nature that vacillated between both, all three powers working as one.

He looked at his father. "How did you know to do that?"

"I didn't. It was just a hunch. I did nothing more than push you."

"But you've tried doing that before, and this never happened."

"No, your father pushed you before. I have yet to carry the same emotions, the same connection to you. Our feelings for each other here are not the same as they will be. You have yet to resent me, to mistrust me. Without that extra layer between us, you were able to do what we were trying to do in your timeline."

"What happens when you use your magic now, Ren?" his mother asked.

"Let's see." He looked over at Keary, feeling his eyes darken.

"Oh no, why am I always the test puppet?" he yelled as he rose in the air, then catapulted into the trees. The trees threw him back to the ground which softened unexpectedly and pulled him far below from their sight. The magic coursed through Ren at a low hum as he directed it, never raising a hand. It felt good, no fear of the Darkness that had always taunted him; instead, the blend of powers was welcoming. He looked to his father and could see from his expression that he was impressed.

"You were too gentle on him."

Several minutes later, Keary crawled through the ground, spitting dirt from his mouth. Ren's eyes grew brighter, and the debris lifted from Keary, his wounds healing quicker.

"All three present," his mother said. "Can you use them separately?"

"Yes." The aura around him dimmed, and he felt his eyes transition to blue again.

"Can you still feel them all?"

"All three," he answered, flexing his hands. "All awake and in harmony."

The feeling was ecstasy, and for the first time, he felt as one with his powers.

"Now you are ready to ascend," his father said, crossing his arms and smiling. At that moment, Ren understood it all. His father was correct; he was ready now. This had been the reason for his presence here, to achieve what could not be achieved at home, to open him to the true knowledge of his powers. For once, he did feel ready. Looking at his future parents, he saw them in a different light. They would be fine returning to the Fates when he took the throne. Their love strong enough to conquer whatever faced them, and he would finally be ready to let them go. He glanced down at his hands, about to tell them all of this, but before he could respond, his mother doubled over, letting out a wounded cry.

"Vi?" his father said, turning toward her in concern. Stopping short, he clenched his hands and groaned, stumbling back from her slightly. Ren saw Keary stepping back as if someone had punched him.

His mother, her breaths short and pained, crumbled to the ground, letting out a sob.

"No," Ren said, not feeling their pain but understanding precisely what was causing it.

Another sob escaped his mother, and she buried her head in her hands. His father dropped to his knees, his hands stretched in an effort to reach her.

"Vi," he croaked as Ren watched another wave of pain hit him.

"What's wrong?" Paige whispered, fear layered in her face. How did he explain it? How could he tell her that with each death they felt, his parents were being gripped with pain as the connection to their Council was severed? That as each of them was torn from their world, they felt the loss to the core. He couldn't help them, he could do nothing but watch, the connection of Council to king not yet present in him but even separated by worlds strong in his parents. Keary had fallen to his knees, his pain only a sensation of loss, but the knowledge bringing him to his knees.

His father, having made his way to his mother, held her in his arms as every death hit him, their bodies crumbling each time another Council fell. Ren met Paige's eyes, the crystal blue of them glimmering under the tears that filled them. A cry escaped her, and the tears fell. She had figured it out. He went to her and pulled her in his arms, holding her tight with each cry that racked her body, putting his own sadness aside.

"Ren?" Cody asked softly, his eyes pleading for explanation. He saw the others peering out, some coming out to see what had happened.

His mother let out a sob that shook the ground, storm clouds rolled in, and the sky rained down upon them with the tears that fell from her eyes. His father's power spilled out around them, but Ren shielded Paige and the others.

"Cody, make sure they all stay inside," he said sadly. "There is nothing to do, nothing that can be done.

He looked over at his parents. The waves of pain had stopped with the final death, his father held his mother tight, his face buried in her hair. He brought his head up, his eye meeting Ren's, eyes black with pain, riddled with the need for vengeance. The Dark king in him ready to kill, ready to punish for the death of their family. Vengeance to be laid upon Tynan for every life he had stolen from them.

Tynan walked through the field littered with the bodies of the once revered Councils. Even with their powers, they had died as any other mortal men, easily. He had stolen their immortality, using the spell his future self had revealed in the book. With only their powers left, it had been more fun that way, giving them hope, a false one. Their powers were no match for Tynan, and they had been easily defeated, one by one, falling at his feet. All but one Darkbearer who had slipped away as the battle began favoring Tynan. Sent away in hope but Tynan would find him. It was only a matter of time, and the hunt would be worth the wait.

He kicked Cyric's body and knelt down next to it. "You were never a match for me, old man."

He stood, letting out a shrill laugh, the sound echoing through the land. Turning, he spotted the village in the distance, imagining the people all cowering in fear knowing their precious Council had been defeated, his Torathar standing guard, awaiting his command. He hadn't decided if he'd kill them one by one or give them to the Torathar to play with. Maybe he'd save a few of the young ones for his own pleasure.

He licked his lips in anticipation, feeling the need for flesh rise in him when a noise distracted him. He turned to his left to see a woman lying across one of the bodies, crying. Who would be foolish enough to dare come this close to him?

He moved nearer to her, the woman taking no notice, her cries irritating to his ears. He grabbed her by the arm and yanked her up, her arm snapping then loosening from its socket. She screamed in pain then her expression hardened. He had given her permission, his curiosity piqued, curious that anyone would be so foolish. Who was she crying over? He kicked the body with his foot, rolling it over. Daneele, Violissa's Keeper.

"Not so proud any longer are you, Keeper?"

"Don't you touch him!" she screamed.

He studied her, such fire in those blue eyes. Her auburn hair–touched in slight places with gray, the only thing betraying her age.

"Did you care for him?" he asked.

Her eyes answered for her. "Well, well, did some of our beloved Council stray?"

He couldn't help but laugh. "Not so perfect either," he said absently, staring into her terrified eyes.

Bored, he looked back at the village, still gripping her broken arm. "I think it's time to have some fun. Too bad you won't be able to enjoy it with me," he said, never looking back at her even as she struggled in his grip. He squeezed his other hand and heard her dying gasp as her skull collapsed, then he carelessly threw her to the ground next to Daneele, unaware of her vacant eyes staring blankly at him as he walked away to deliver punishment to the remaining traitors of the Banished Realm.

Thirty-One

Morning came, an unwanted visitor reminding Sinow that time moves on even when you beg it not to. He sat with Violissa in his arms, staring out at the world but seeing nothing. His mind still reeling, his Dark power still attempting to shroud his heart from the pain. Violissa had said nothing since the event, crying in his arms until there was nothing left in her. She'd drifted off to sleep, clinging to him as if by letting go she would lose him, too. Keary had sat with them through the night, staring blankly off as Sinow had. Every once in a while, he'd catch Sinow's eye, but the loss they both bore was too much to continue contact, and so both let their eyes drift once more. While he and Violissa had felt each loss, experienced the rip in connection, the pain of it, Keary was blessed to only feel each absence, if that was any blessing at all.

Ren joined them at some point, having taken Paige to her room. Paige, inconsolable, may not have felt the physical pain, but her loss was great. She didn't have to be told her father was gone. It was evident, and all of them knew that with the fall of the Councils, the people were slaughtered, her mother lost with them. It was heartbreaking.

All of them remained in silence, disregarding the food and drinks that Cody and Claire had brought. The others giving them space he assumed because Cody had insisted they do so. Sinow felt numb inside, never realizing the link to his Council, his family, ran so deep. He'd felt it return when Violissa had brought their power back but had not noticed the emptiness of being without that connection until now. Now that they were gone, it was palpable. Part of him wished she'd left them powerless, wished he hadn't felt each death, wished he'd remained oblivious.

Cody came back and sat across from them, rubbing his hands together against the morning dampness. The movement seemed to wake them all, drawing their stares back in, refocusing them.

Finally, Ren broke the silence. "Are they all gone?"

It was a fair question, one that needed to be addressed. This was his future as well as theirs. The Councils were his family, too.

"I can still feel one connection aside from Keary, but with the distance, I can't tell who it is," Sinow answered slowly.

Violissa picked her head up from his chest, her eyes, a deep sage, bore the pain she felt. Even after so many tears, she looked beautiful but in a fragile way, one that called to the protector in him.

"I feel none," she whispered.

Ren looked at him. "The Councils are unbalanced save for here."

"How do you figure that?" Keary asked. "I'm the only one here."

"Unless you count Cody."

"Who would have been called by the Fates if that were the

case," Sinow said.

"The Fates won't call a Lightbearer here. They have no domain here, and that would go beyond what this world's god has permitted."

"It makes no difference," Violissa said. "The others are gone, the one left behind will be hunted down and killed. Tynan will not allow him to live."

"I'm sorry." Sinow turned to the voice and saw several of the mortals standing in the doorway. "You lost your teams, I can't imagine what that feels like," Abigail said.

She was being sincere, he knew it, but he also wanted to be left alone. This wasn't their business. They couldn't possibly know what he and the others were going through.

"They were more than that. They were family, friends, the ones who raised us, taught us," Violissa said, her voice calming him. "And with their deaths come the deaths of all those they were protecting, innocents who stand no chance against Tynan and who will suffer horribly."

"I'm so sorry," she said again. "We can't fathom, and we won't. We're not powerful like you, but for what it's worth, we're all here for you when you need us."

"All of us," Garrett said before walking back inside. Erin came over behind their seat and wrapped her arms around Violissa.

"You can't get through this by yourselves. Remember we're here." She kissed Violissa's cheek then gave Sinow a quick hug.

"You scare the hell out of me, but you're still like family."

With that, she ran back to the door Garrett was holding for her. Garrett gave him one last glance then followed her inside.

Sinow glanced at Violissa who was looking down at his hand, tracing his union scar.

"Maybe that is the reason they're all here," she said softly. "A family to support us, people to help us through this."

"What happens now?" Cody asked.

Ren leaned forward in his seat, rubbing his hand across his

face. "We move forward. There's nothing else we can do but grieve and move forward."

"There's still hope," Violissa added. "We lost..." her voice cracked. "We lost most of them, but someone remains. Our hope. Even if we can't make it home, he may have a chance."

"Vi, he stands no chance against Tynan."

He expected her to argue, but instead, her eyes began to sparkle, the emerald brilliantly shining, power flowing from them.

"Vi?"

"Something's happening." She looked in the direction of the lake then stood. All of them stood as well, the heavy depression falling from their shoulder.

When Ren's eyes transitioned to the same shade as Violissa's, she said to him, "You feel it, too."

"Yes, the lake."

"The lake. Something beckons," she said, then shifted, Ren following.

"What just happened?" asked Cody.

Sinow looked over at Keary. "I no longer question."

"Should we get Paige?"

"No, Violissa would have said something. Let's find out what she's discovered first."

"And him?" Keary gestured to Cody.

"Bring him." Sinow shifted.

Violissa was standing at the water's edge where a dusting of frost layered the lake.

"They are calling her again," Ren told him, pointing to the frost.

She brought her hand up as if feeling for something.

"Your voice draws the cainbae," Ren said.

"Something else is happening in our world, isn't it?" Keary asked.

"It would appear so," he responded.

"She has to sing?"

"Yes, her voice draws the connection between realms."

"That's how she found her way from the Lost Realm," he stated, seeing it clearly now after the memory he'd witnessed.

"Yes, she found the barrier and sang. You heard her. She called you through a boundary that should have been impenetrable, and you answered her call."

"Nothing can separate our love," she said absently, then she began to hum, bringing her hand up. He watched as it met an unseen force this time, frost spreading from her fingers, the layer on the lake rising to meet it, then fanning out to encompass the window to their realm. Drawing her hand back, she continued to hum, the frost fading to reveal their world. Encompassed in black, he could make out barely anything until a passing cloud cleared the moons, their light bringing life to the grove before them.

"The meeting grove," Violissa said, moving next to him. He didn't question how she knew; he had no reason to do so.

"Sinow? Violissa?" He heard before he saw Mackay come closer to the opening, trying to touch it to no avail.

"It's not a portal, simply a window," Ren said sadly.

Mackay looked exhausted, his face marred with blood and dirt.

"The others—" he said.

"We know. We felt it," Sinow answered.

"I wanted to stay and fight, but Kanine and Cyric insisted I go, to hide just in case so you'd have help finding your way home. The others all stayed behind. They told Daneele to go, too, but something distracted him, and he didn't get out in time. I made it out just after Tynan brought the barrier down and shifted in. The people ... I fear for the people. They had gathered all in one place after the portal faded, too fearful of Tynan's attacks to leave our protection once our power returned."

"They're all dead now," Violissa said.

"I think so. I've been running from Tynan ever since. Trying to reach you. Dimming my power so he can't sense me as easily.

He's been hunting me but can't seem to sense me here."

"You're in the meeting grove?"

"Yes, it was untouched, unlike the rest of the realms."

"The Fates?" Sinow asked Violissa.

She chewed her lip. "Maybe. They seem to be insinuating themselves in certain places."

"Helping you when they can," Ren said. "There's no point in keeping it from you any longer. They interfere where they can. Tynan was part of it all, but they lost control of him. He went beyond the path they'd set in place for him, forcing their hand."

They all stared at him.

"The game, once started, cannot be stopped even if it bounds out of control. The players are already in place," Violissa said.

"Exactly what you told me a long time ago. It's one of the only things you told me from that time," Ren said.

"And now they've lost complete control," Sinow said.

"What do we do, Sinow?" Violissa asked.

He'll kill Mackay. He can't stay there forever, she added in enaigne.

I do what I should have done the first time; I kill him. This ends now.

"I want you to heighten your power," Sinow told Mackay.

"But he'll find me—"

"Exactly."

Mackay stared at him.

"Sinow, I don't understand. He's vulnerable as he is, but if Tynan finds him, he'll kill him," Violissa argued, confused by Sinow's instruction.

"Not if I capture him first."

"But how?"

"Frilairm," Keary answered. "A blood summoning."

"You're going to attempt to summon him through Frilairm?" Mackay asked.

"Yes, with Violissa's help."

"I'll gladly help, but it would be nice to know what in the Fates you're all talking about. Sinow, what is a blood summoning?"

"It's the call of our blood to one another," Ren answered. "The king's blood can summon his heir. It's a control, a way to restrain a wild prince or put one in his place. I've only ever studied it, never seen it performed."

"Felt it performed. If I had used it on you, you'd have felt it."

"How, and if it's father to son, then how would it work on Tynan?" Violissa asked, clearly still not following the conversation.

"The summons is done by drawing king's blood," Sinow said. "His heir feels the call, a pull in his own blood, and cannot resist, he must appear before the king or the king forces his appearance. My father would use it on Tynan, would rip him from wherever he was hiding. Tynan hated it. It's not a pleasant experience.

"With me as king, true descendent, I should be able to summon Tynan to me. He shares my blood, and I am his king, so it should work the same. I don't know why I didn't think of it before. I draw him through the barrier and kill him before he can kill Mackay."

She chewed her lip, thinking on what he had said. "Provided it works," she said, "provided you can bring him here. Otherwise, we watch him slaughter Mackay."

"Preferably that doesn't happen," Mackay said. He stood taller, prouder, "But I will take the chance for my king."

"But won't Ren be affected as well?" Violissa asked, concern in her voice.

"I don't believe so," Sinow replied. "The summons is directed to a specific person."

He could see her thinking through it. "Sinow why do you think I can help?"

"Because you control this window into the realm. It reacts to you. Somehow, you are the key to it."

Violissa stared at Sinow; she didn't completely understand what it was he was planning to do, the blood summoning foreign to her. Now, he was talking about using her as a conduit between the realms. She thought about what she'd done before; she had been a conduit, sending power to feed their Councils through the barrier that separated them, but that had been with the help of the Fates.

"I don't think I can do that again. The Fates allowed it before," she protested.

"And they'll allow it again," Sinow replied.

"The cainbae," Ren said, "is your connection between worlds with or without the Fates."

She furrowed her brow, thinking on it. "The cainbae will allow him to do this ritual?"

"Yes, you control the window with it. The frost is the key, once you see it, you'll know the connection is there. You can be the bridge for him to do what he needs to do. Trust yourself, Mother."

He had called her mother, the word slipping out before he caught himself. Smiling, she nodded in acceptance.

"Ren, once Violissa creates a link for me to summon Tynan, if she removes her hand from the barrier will that connection remain?"

"It should as long as she wills it to," he replied.

"All right then. Let's do this," Sinow said, the authority heavy in his voice. "Keary, Ren, make sure there are no foolish onlookers anywhere in this area. There will be a fight, I've no doubt, and I want no one hurt. Cody, go with them and stay close to Ren so he can shield you just in case."

The three of them moved quickly to follow his orders.

"Violissa, when I draw my blood, I want your hand on mine,

rest it on the barrier. When you feel the connection, let go then back away, this is my fight." He waited for her nod of agreement, then turned back to Mackay. "If this works, it will rid you of him. I don't know when or if we will be allowed to return. It will be up to you to find any survivors, to rebuild—"

"Rebuilding will not be possible without the two of you. You both know that," Mackay said bravely. "I am all there is left, and our world is too vast for me to repair alone. I will find who I can, free those I can, and wait for your return."

Sinow looked as if he wanted to argue, but they both knew what Mackay had said was true. They'd been taught from an early age of the need for Dark and Light in their word, that they provided a necessary balance. Their world was dying without that balance, without Violissa's power. There was no doubt, with the balance returned, she could heal the damage. From here, however, she was helpless to do anything more than she had.

"Right, then draw your power." Sinow stepped back. There were no sappy goodbyes for Darkbearers. Mackay straightened his back and drew his power. She watched as his eyes darkened. Tynan appeared within seconds across the field.

"Well, well," he started to say before noticing the window with her and Sinow. At the same moment, Sinow sliced his inner arm, letting the blood flow. As it dripped, it froze midstream. Violissa slammed her hand against his, pushing them both into the barrier. She hummed, calling her connection to it, and the frost appeared immediately.

Sinow's power flared, and she felt the Darkness as it strengthened, sensed the intent of it.

"What are you up to, brother?" Tynan asked, walking slowly up to the barrier. The word brother came out thick with venom.

"Teaching you a lesson," Sinow answered. His blood spread along the frost, the droplets rising then with a sudden force seeping through the barrier to freeze midair before Tynan.

"No," Tynan said, backing away. He tried to shift, Violissa

could see the attempt, but the summoning was working.

The blood began pulling back. Violissa removed her hand, willing Sinow's connection to remain, quietly continuing to hum. She watched as the droplets flew back toward Sinow's arm, the blood in the frost flowering back as well, but stopping short of pooling back into the wound, waiting instead below his extended arm, hanging in stasis.

Tynan screamed in rage, his body warping in a strange way as if it were shifting upon itself. It stretched and lengthened toward Sinow who had pulled his hand back from the barrier. Tynan's body morphed to a long stream, a blur of movement that crashed into the barrier slowly, painfully pouring through it toward Sinow, heeding his summons no matter how hard Tynan tried to resist.

As his body seeped through to where Sinow stood, Tynan's angry roar could be heard providing the backdrop to what could only have been a horrifically painful reconstruction of his body across from where Sinow stood. Violissa swallowed, forcing the bile back down as her stomach lurched at the sight.

Finally, Tynan's body and features became clear. He stumbled back, clearly disarmed by Sinow's powerful move.

The blood filled back into Sinow's wound, which healed quickly, and she stopped her humming. Power swirled around him, dark ebony and red hues that cascaded far beyond where he stood, blackening out the light. Tynan regained his composure, and the same layers of Dark magic swept from him through the air. The Dark feel settled over her skin, a mix of Sinow's strength and security with a tainted corrupt layer, the effect sending chills through her.

The sky darkened as their power intensified, the ground rumbling below as it seeped into it, the grass withering. Violissa held her breath. Two Dark kings stood before her, two kings vying for control. The fate of everyone's lives depended upon the winner. Violissa knew the history Ren had told them was in Sinow's mind, weighing on him just as the death of his Council was. There would be no punishment but death for Tynan this time. He would take no chance, and she could sense his need for vengeance.

"I've been a bad boy, haven't I, brother?" Tynan snarled. He looked over at Violissa. "I hear we get to have some fun soon, Violissa. I've been told you're quite tasty although I was warned you get a bit distracting. I'll wait. We can play after I've killed Sinow." His eyes bore into her, never leaving her as he spoke. "You've made it easy for me, brother, bringing me to you. Now, I can get rid of you once and for all, then claim everything you hold dear. She belongs to me just as everything of yours does."

Sinow glanced over at her, and she tore her eyes from the madness in Tynan's to meet his. An understanding passed between them; things would be different this life. Tynan would lay no hand on her. This was the end of his threat to them, to their love, to their son, to the prophecy.

She drew in a breath and nodded her agreement, one neither would come to regret as they had the last one. She severed her tie to the cainbae, the window to their world closing for perhaps the last time, then Sinow struck. There was no hesitation, no talk, no attempt to rein Tynan in. The punishment would be swift and deadly. Tynan went flying, the land buckling below as he scraped it trying to stop himself. The fight had begun.

As she watched, she wondered if they'd looked this way when she'd watched them fighting in Ren's timeline. They were two gods battling for ultimate power. She couldn't pull her eyes from them. They were everywhere seemingly at once, their movements too fast to track. Only when one hit the other hard enough did they separate. At one point, Sinow landed with enough force to knock half the forest from its roots, sending it well across from the lake, at least a mile past where it had stood. Tynan shifted to attack again, but Sinow caught him as he landed, flinging him into the air. Shifting to where Tynan peaked in the sky, he pounded him back down. Tynan was flung into a distant hill, demolishing it with his impact.

Will it ever end? she wondered. The two seemed equal in strength. What if there were no winner? They couldn't keep fighting forever. The air grew thicker, the clouds heavier above them, blocking the sun out completely. She sensed the change of power in the air. Sinow, she knew the feel of his magic, it stirred her blood. He was calling his power again, digging deeper, increasing it. There was a flicker of movement then a crash as the water from the lake exited its bed, Tynan's body forcing its abrupt exile.

Sinow shifted, and before Tynan could counter, Violissa saw what could only be binding. It was horrifying to watch. Magic-infused chains surrounded his body, entering in spots then exiting in others. The chain moved in a fluid motion weaving its way through Tynan's body. He struggled to get up, glaring at Sinow. Under the venomous eyes, Violissa could see the pain, pain Tynan would never show.

It was over. Now all that remained was Sinow's punishment. How would he sentence his brother, knowing all the pain he had caused in their past life, knowing he'd handed his own death sentence to their Councils, to their families, to every innocent mortal throughout their world? Violissa looked at Sinow, seeing for the first time the Dark king he truly was, this man who held her heart but also held terrifying powers, the kind that made up the worst of nightmares. His eyes were blacker than an endless night, a swirl of black fog enveloped him, and she watched as it extended to long tendrils that spread across the ground around him. She held her breath, a shiver running down her spine as the oppressiveness of his power infected the air.

Sinow brought his hand up, Tynan raised from the ground with the movement, hanging before him. He struggled to break free, but it was futile, his powers had been bound by his true king. Then he said the one thing that sealed his fate.

"You won't stop me. I always find a way to return. I will always come for you, brother. Everything you are is mine." He spat the words, the vitriol in them palpable.

Violissa knew Sinow had the power to kill him, it was an instinctual knowledge, but there was no doubt. She didn't think he would do anything but kill Tynan this time so, as she watched Sinow's response she wasn't surprised.

He spoke no words, only drew his powers in. They hit him like a wave crashing to the shore. He let them settle in him, feeding the ire. Tynan stopped moving, fear finally reflected on his face in that final moment. The true extent of Sinow's power now evident.

"Brother?" he whispered.

Sinow threw his arms out and with a cry of rage sent all of his magic tearing into Tynan. The sheer force of Darkness seemed to suck any remaining light from the world around them. Engulfed in blackness, Violissa could see nothing but she could hear the current of his magic as it flowed from him. Flickers of red appeared in the dark then she felt the power hit its mark. Tynan screamed, but it was stifled quickly as Sinow's power tore him apart. In seconds, Violissa could feel the shift in balance. Sinow stopped the flow of magic and Violissa watched as ribbon-like black strands dissipated in the air around them, the light of the moon breaking through in long silver streams. Flakes of ash fell like a light snow where Tynan had once been.

Violissa wasn't quite sure what to do. She stood, eyes drawn to Sinow who had dropped his hands and now stood silently staring at the ash as it landed on the ground around him. After several minutes, she felt a hand on her arm.

"Go to him," Keary said, his eyes heavy with the sadness they carried for his friend.

"Don't you think you would be better to go?"

"No, he needs you. He doesn't need a jokester trying to lift his spirits. He needs someone to reassure him, to comfort him. He needs you."

Keary walked away, and Violissa turned her eyes toward Sinow once more. He hadn't moved, so she took the first step and began walking over to him, the ash swirling at her feet with every step closer she drew, the only remaining reminder of Tynan's previous existence. Not knowing quite how to help, she did the only thing she knew to do and wrapped her arms around his waist, resting her head against his back. She stayed quiet even as she felt his hand rest upon hers, felt the tension flee his muscles.

Finally breaking the silence, he said, "He was my brother, Vi."

Her heart ached for him. Even after all he had done, Tynan was still his brother, someone he'd once loved, someone a part of him still loved.

"Do you regret killing him?" she asked.

"No," he answered curtly. "I may not remember all that he did in Ren's lifeline, but I know what he did, and I know what he would have done to you. He was guilty of crimes against our people in this lifeline, and of..." he drifted off, the pain of speaking the words too great.

"Murdering our Councils," she finished for him, her voice breaking as she said it.

His head dropped, and she pressed further into him, feeling his heartbeat. She rested her cheek against his back where she remained, quietly letting him grieve, all the while holding in her own grief that was resurfacing knowing one of them needed to be strong in this moment. Finally, sensing his mood shift slightly, she loosened her hold on him and began walking away thinking he needed space to resolve the mix of emotions assailing him, but as she went to move away, he held tight to her hand, pulling her back in front of him. Softly, she lifted his face, his eyes a muted brown looked back at her, the sadness in them evident in their shade. She watched as his demeanor changed before her eyes, the king stepping in to compensate for the current weakness it sensed in the man. His eyes deepened to the cusp of black, the tension filling his muscles as he stood taller. She wondered how many times she had watched this transformation, her eyes searching his but finding no evidence of the sadness with which he had just grappled.

"Sinow," she said, meaning to affirm to him that his feelings were reasonable and necessary.

"Tynan has been punished, his sentence was fair and warranted. He can't hurt you now."

"And your Council?"

She noted the pain that surfaced momentarily before he caught it.

"Will be mourned in due time. I have two Council left," he paused, his eyes softening slightly. "Yours is completely gone. You need to mourn, Vi, and not worry about me."

"I have mourned, and you need me, Sinow."

He smiled slightly. "I do, but you need me as well." He took her hand and traced the union scar. "We need each other, but you mustn't put my needs above yours. I have the Darkness to lean on. I'm fine now."

"You have the Darkness to mask your pain, Sinow."

"As I always have," he replied, eyes now a deep ebony. "Tynan is dead. Now we move forward, but first you need more time to finish mourning, and then there's Paige. She needs you more than I right now."

Paige. In all that had happened, she hadn't had time to think about Paige. She had lost both her father and mother, a loss that went deeper than Violissa could imagine.

"Yes, Paige." She looked toward the town then back at him. A gentle breeze blew her hair, sending her wayward curl across her face. He moved it back, saying, "We'll make it through this. We've made it through every trial the Fates have given us."

"I promised the Fates I would have faith in them, Sinow, that I would follow their path unquestioningly, but this..." She swallowed the tears back, afraid to open the floodgate she knew would break. "This is too much," she whispered.

He brought her in tight against him, holding her as if letting go would bring his world crashing down. There they remained, holding each other in silence, neither willing to move and face the reality that awaited them outside the comfort of their arms.

Eventually, Sinow kissed her head saying, "Let's go back."

Both knew the others were in pain as well. Keary, Paige, and Ren had all lost their family, all were suffering. Vengeance had been paid, but it did little to allay the heartache. She looked up at him. "We'll be all right, all of us."

He kissed her, and she momentarily lost herself in his kiss. Reality, the grief it held, the pain, all disappearing for that brief moment. She took her hand and brushed it along his cheek.

"Let's go," she said quietly.

They shifted back to the inn where they found the townsfolk gathered. All went silent when they arrived, the looks on their faces evidence they knew what had occurred. Keary and Ren sat at the bar with their hands around drinks in which they stared, searching for an answer to what had happened. Sinow sat down next to Keary, and his uncle dropped a glass in front of him. Violissa walked up to Ren and watched as Sinow raised an eyebrow in question at the move.

"Scotch, my best bottle," his uncle said, filling the glass.

"Where's Paige?" Violissa asked.

"She came down for a few moments but went back up," Ren answered. "She's a mess. Said she needed more time alone."

Violissa glanced over at Sinow.

Go, he told her, knowing exactly what she wanted to do. She gave him a sad smile, then headed out of the bar toward their rooms.

She found Paige in her room lying on her bed, her back to the door. Violissa remained silent, knowing her words would do nothing to alleviate her friend's pain. Instead, she crawled into bed next to Paige and wrapped her arms around her. There she stayed as Paige shed her tears, holding her, comforting her as best she could, letting her tears fall silently.

Sinow stayed at the bar with Keary and Ren until two bottles of scotch were gone. His uncle, giving up after he could drink no more, finally saw himself to bed. Looking longingly at the empty bottles Sinow wished it could have numbed the pain, but alcohol burned right through the three of them, powerless against the magic they contained that snuffed out its potency.

Needing to be alone he left the others and walked outside, finding a bench his aunt had added years ago under a tall oak tree. Simon's aunt, not his. He rubbed his face at the complexity of their lives now. Tynan having complicated everything, creating a new life for them all. *Well, not all of us*, he thought, the sadness returning.

It was hard to believe most of his Council were gone. They had been his family, his brothers, men who had deserved a better death. He had avenged them. Tynan was dead. Violissa was safe. There would no longer be the threat of him hurting her, their future now irrevocably changed. Tynan had started them down this new path toward an unknown future and now they were forced to follow it, for better or worse.

Tynan. His emotions were conflicted when he thought of his brother. Staring at his hands he opened himself to those emotions, a mix of anger, satisfaction, and sadness. The Darkness in him driving the satisfaction, its punishment served, the crimes avenged but the anger belonged to both parts of him. Anger, hatred for what Tynan had done and what he would have done, what he had done to Violissa in Ren's timeline. He squeezed his hands tightly as the Darkness surfaced, feeling his eyes darken with the reaction. It was over and his Violissa would never suffer by Tynan's hand. He couldn't take back the deaths of their Councils, the loss of all the people Tynan had murdered, but at least she was safe. Relaxing he opened himself to the grief that lie below the other feelings. It wasn't there for the others, that was a wrenching pain that hit him in waves if he allowed it in, one that he knew would take time to abate. This was different and was reserved for Tynan, the brother he'd once been. They'd been close at one time and Sinow had never stopped loving his brother, he saw that now, saw the mistake he had made in doing so, in continuing to have trust in him, continuing to need that relationship even though Tynan had pushed it away. He'd been blind, his emotions blinding him to the betrayal. The more he thought on it, the more the sadness dissipated, hardening his emotions, the anger taking its place. Tynan had deserved his punishment, deserved the death served to him. Yes, he had loved Tynan, but it had been a mistake that had cost him greatly. He'd been soft to it in Ren's lifetime but not this time.

The hint of lilac stirred his senses and he looked up to see Violissa coming toward him. Her eyes carried the burden of her loss even if the rest of her remained beautifully tranquil.

"Paige?" he asked as she sat down next to him and leaned her head on his shoulder.

"Sleeping finally."

He moved his arm around her and pulled her in closer. "Did you cast a calming spell?"

"No, she needs to grieve Sinow, without my interference. Delaying her grief will only make it harder on her when she does have to face reality."

"And you?"

"And me what?"

"When will you continue to mourn, Violissa?"

She sighed, "I'm done crying Sinow. I grieved yesterday. Now, like you I need to be strong. I'm fine Sinow."

He pulled away from her and looked at her, knowing she was lying. She was hiding her emotions, locking them away to stay strong but that wasn't her. He knew her too well now to think she was truly fine.

"Only one of us needs to hide behind our power."

"I need to be strong. People are counting on me."

"And who would those people be? Paige? She's tough; she's strong enough to support herself."

"Ren..."

"Is old enough and he has his Dark powers to balance his emotions."

"You..."

"I am a Dark king Violissa. It takes a lot to break me." He briefly thought of the future Ren had told them about. "Only losing you would completely break me."

He took his finger and moved her wandering curl back.

"When do you have time to grieve if you're worrying about all of us?"

"Maybe worrying about you helps me grieve."

"Or maybe it lets you hide your grief. Vi, let go. You lost everything you've ever known and now it's over. Like you said about Paige, you need to own your grief."

Her eyes welled and she bit her lip. "I didn't lose you," she whispered, a tear spilling down her cheek.

"Then hold onto that just as I am holding on to the fact that I still have you and that you're safe."

She laid her head against his chest and he felt the wetness from her tears soak into his shirt as she finally let it all out, the emotions of the latest events with Tynan, of confirmation from Mackay that indeed her Council was gone, all of it flowing from her. He held her tight until the sun came up and her tears finally stopped, her quivering sobs quieting. All the while he held back, his own sorrow inviting the Darkness in to subdue it. Eventually, she lifted her head and looked at him, her tear-stained cheeks only adding to her beauty, giving it a sense of fragility.

"What do we do now?" she asked, her voice slightly raspy from crying.

He wiped her cheeks and gave her a small smile. "We mourn,

we remember, we honor, then we find a way home."

Her eyes darkened to a forest green.

"There is no home Sinow. We've lost it all."

"We need to return Violissa. To pick up the pieces. To..." he hesitated not wanting to say the words. "Rebuild our Councils and let the Fates call forth our new Dark and Lightbearers."

Her eyes lightened slightly, the tears slipping back in, their color quickly returning to a deep sage, her expression changing.

"No, Sinow. Our world is dying, and it won't last much longer."

"Why would you say that?"

"I sensed it when I fed the sun but didn't mention it because I thought we would be home in time. Our world needed our return, it needed the balance of power. Tynan leeched the world of magic so badly that it left an incurable scar."

"A scar only an Elvin queen could fix," he finished. "The sun rose that day never to rise to its full height again," he mumbled. "That's what my father told me when you were locked away in your memories awaiting your power."

"There will be no rebuilding, the damage he has done is permanent now that we've been locked here for so long. Our window to save it is gone and our world is lost."

Her words hung in the silence that followed, a heaviness settled in the air. Sinow didn't know what to say, the revelations devastating. Tynan had stolen everything from them.

"He finally succeeded. He won after all, didn't he?"

"No," she replied. "We still have each other. We still have Ren."

He thought about what she'd said. "Why do we still have Ren?" he asked.

"Because he's our son, our love continues even after all of this Sinow."

"No, Vi, that's not what I mean. Why is he still here? Before it made sense, we were still finding our way back, still facing a fight with Tynan. He still unsure of his powers. But now? Why hasn't he been returned to his time? Why hasn't he faded like Tynan did when he shattered the gem that day?"

She furrowed her brow, chewing her lip.

"I don't know," she replied honestly. "Perhaps the Fates aren't done with him yet. Remember, he said I told him this was his journey, his part in our path."

Sinow was perplexed, but the day had been long and life altering, leaving him with no energy to solve yet another mystery of the Fates' intentions. Running his hands through his hair, he rose.

"Let's go back," he said pulling her up into his arms, "it's been a long day and we're both tired."

"It has been," she replied, leaning into him. He pulled her close and shifted them back to their room. They made love, slowly, the emotion of the day feeding their desire as they tried to temporarily fill the holes the loss of their Councils had left.

The next day was long. They both stayed hidden in bed as long as they could then finally ventured down to join the others, all but Paige who remained locked away. A melancholy hung over the group as they sat around, no one really knowing what to say or what to do next.

"We need a proper Irish wake," Aunt Maeve finally said, cutting the silence. They all looked up at her. "It's the proper thing to do.

"But you didn't even know them," Ren said quietly.

"No, but they were your family, and so they are our family, and we will celebrate them in the proper way."

"I think that would be nice," Sinow heard Paige say softly from across the room. He turned, as did they all, to see her walking in. Her eyes were swollen and red from crying but she wore a stoic expression as if she were ready to face the next test. Keary rose, giving her his seat next to Violissa. She sat and gave Sinow a slight smile then looked down at her hands as Violissa took one of them and squeezed it. Without saying another word, she rested her head against Violissa's as if she were the rock holding her together. Sinow glanced at Violissa and wondered if that were the case, perhaps she was the one thing that held them all together. Had she been so in Ren's lifeline or was she somehow changed in this one? He'd seen the way Ren looked at her at times as if her response or action was completely unexpected.

"Then a wake it shall be. Tomorrow morn Maeve?" Violissa asked.

"Aye, that will give us enough time to let the town know and to cook up some food. Claire go and start spreading the word."

They remained there silently sitting, letting the world pass by, no one truly knowing what to do next. Finally, Paige lifted her head and reached into the pocket of her jeans, saying, "It's time I pass this on. It no longer belongs to me."

Her hand rested on the bar in front of her and when she removed it, Sinow saw the locket lying there. The broken key to their return home.

"I can't Paige, it's not mine to take now," Violissa replied sadly.

"Not you, Violissa. Sinow."

Sinow was taken aback, not sure why she would think he needed to have it now. Violissa's face wore an expression of confusion likely matching his.

"I can't explain it, but something tells me you need to hold onto it now. It's no longer meant to be kept by me."

"Instinct?" he asked with a smile.

She gave a small laugh, "Instinct."

Violissa moved her hand over the locket, and it transformed to a small velvet black bag. "That seems more appropriate for a Dark king," she said, staring at it.

He reached over and took the bag, something about the move seeming necessary as if it were his to hold now. No power could be felt from it save a sliver of residual from Violissa's magic.

Paige rose. "I think I'd like to take a walk now."

With that she left them all to continue their contemplation of a future none could imagine. After a short time, Ren left as well, following the same path as Paige. It seemed curious to Sinow, but he let it go, his mind too numb from the other worries of their life to think on it.

He felt the weight of the bag, still in his hand, as if it also carried the weight of all they'd been through, of all they'd lost. Resting it on the bar, he opened it to allow its contents to spill out, the lifeless shards of gem free to taunt him, reminding him of what should have been. He fingered the pieces thinking that perhaps it was a blessing they were remnants of a path they would no longer tread. Their shattering had shattered the constraints of a future that held pain and agony for them both as well as a divide that neither had been able to overcome: his fear. He glanced at Violissa, her eyes keenly seeing what he was thinking, her hand reaching over to cover his.

"Not everything the Fates do can be seen in the moment. Sometimes we must wait and tread the path before looking to the past to understand them."

In that moment he saw the Elvin queen in her as he never had before, not wrapped in her nature gifts but instead as close to the Fates as one could be, seeing only as she could, understanding things that were not meant to be understood. She was blessed with a wisdom that lie beyond what any of them could have held, it was the wisdom of one who was meant to be more, the wisdom of a Fate.

"Daughter of the Fates," he mumbled, looking back down at the stone.

"What?"

Perhaps that was it all along. The trials that had been set before them were just that, a test to see if they truly deserved to be the chosen two. Two who had been created by the Fates, both children of the gods, destined to return to them, to stand by their side once the trials were passed. He chuckled then looked back at her. She had held the power of all three lines in her, enough Dark power to drive even his Council to madness, and yet, she'd survived. There was a reason she'd been able to do it, just as there was a reason the gem had been broken. The Fates were weaved through every aspect of their lives in ways he doubted he'd ever truly understand.

"We are children of the Fates, Vi. You of all people should know that. It took me some time to see it. They lead our way, and we follow, down a path we want to control, one we think is in our hands, but I don't believe has ever been ours to hold, back to the day you decided to turn away from me. All of it foreseen by them, written by them."

She studied him, as if trying to ascertain where his sudden ramblings had come from.

He continued, "I bet we discovered the same thing in Ren's lifetime, and I have a feeling the Fates were guiding our path then as well."

"You certainly got a lot out of those shards, didn't you?" she asked with a twinkle in her eyes.

"Did you happen to find any magic in them while you were finding your purpose in life?" Keary joked.

Laughing he replied, "Not a bit."

"Well, that's a bummer. I sat through all that profound junk you just laid on us only to discover there's still no way home."

"I believe that profound junk you're referring to was aimed at me Keary," Violissa said. "And I found it enlightening."

"You would Violissa. That's your kind of thing. All deep and spiritual, bonding with the trees and wind. What are you doing to my king warping him like this?"

They were all laughing now, the heaviness of the previous day lifting for just that moment, a brief escape from what they knew lay before them the next morning and every day to follow.

Paige brushed the tears away as she passed the end of the town, vowing to herself that she was done crying, that she needed to be strong. There was nothing to be done now but to move on. Her father knew the risks, they all did, and she had no doubt that her mother had been close to him when they'd died, together in life and death. She prayed that they'd both had a merciful death, but she was aware of Tynan's brutal tendencies, so she tried not to dwell on the other possibilities. The road continued before her, the turn to the fields and valleys where the lake stood lie to her right, but she couldn't fathom returning there yet, not without the support of the others. She'd have to go the next day for the wake, but they would be with her, by her side, all mourning together. Ren would be there to lean on.

She smiled thinking of him until the reality of their situation reared its head, the hopelessness overwhelming her until she pushed the thought of him away, thinking instead on the gem she'd handed to Sinow. She wasn't sure why she'd done it, but it felt like the right thing to do. Violissa's Keeper was gone, she wasn't truly her Keeper and knew it no longer belonged to her, the connection broken with her father's death. Sinow was now her Keeper, he held her heart, held the dearest parts of her and, of anyone, he seemed the best to hold it. When it had been whole, filled with the magic of the Fates, it had needed to be kept safe with Paige, something in it needing to be held away from Dark magic but now the empty shell that remained seemed as if it was meant for him. Perhaps there was a reason she had given it to him, a reason beyond her understanding. *Perhaps*, she thought.

Her thoughts were interrupted by a quick footfall approaching from behind her.

"Paige," she heard Ren's voice as she turned toward him.

"What are you doing Ren?" she asked as he jogged up to her.

"Don't tell my father you caught me running," he said with a wink.

"Why?"

"Dark kings don't run," he replied, smiling beautifully.

"What are you doing here Ren?"

For a moment he seemed uncomfortable, rubbing his neck, his eyes downcast. "I thought you might like some company."

She couldn't help but smile at how cute he was in that moment then chastised herself for thinking he was cute, someone who held the power of their world within him. Someone she would never live to see take his throne and become the ruler she knew he was capable of becoming.

"Did I misjudge?" he asked quietly.

"No, your company would be nice," she replied feeling herself drawn in by the vibrant blue his eyes shone in that moment. Lifting her hand, she brushed back the piece of hair that had dropped to his forehead. "What are we doing Ren?"

"Well, you're aimlessly wandering down a country road and I'm attempting to join you in an effort to take your mind from... well from everything."

"Then you're failing miserably," she said with a smirk.

"I am?" He appeared flustered and it made her laugh.

"Yes, because you're part of what I'm trying to free from my mind and like you, I'm failing miserably."

"So, you're able to escape the other realities of our situation but not me. Is that what I'm hearing?"

She leaned over and kissed him, against her better judgment, against the voice of reason in her head, against every bit of rational thought. It felt wonderful, her sorrow falling away, replaced with a brief moment of contentment. His hand wrapped around her waist and pulled her in closer, the moment lingering longer.

"I'd say we're both in serious trouble," she mumbled as their lips parted.

"I'd have to agree," he replied, brushing her hair back, his fingers tracing her jawline.

Her eyes searched his, looking for any answer to what they would do but finding only the anxiety that filled her soul when she thought about it.

"I'm sorry Paige. I'm sorry you have to go through any of this. I'm sorry your future has been rewritten, your life upended, your family..."

She sighed bringing her finger to his lips. "Don't. I've just managed to stop the tears, to place the pain far away in a compartment I don't want opened at this moment."

"Sorry," he said again.

"And I'm not sorry about every part of this. Most of it yes but I'm not sorry about us. It will suck, Fates it will be horrible, but I'm not sorry. I love you Ren, you know that, and I wouldn't change that for anything. The Fates have taken a lot from me, but they gave me you at least for a little while more and when this is all over...when it's all over I'll still have you here." She took his hand and placed it over her heart. "You'll be here just as my parents are. Nothing they do will ever take that away even if they physically take you from me."

"Am I to understand that sucking is a very bad thing to be?"

She laughed, "Yes, it's terribly bad."

She brought his hand down but kept hold of it. "I believe you were going to accompany me on this aimless wandering I'm going about, right?"

"Yes," he answered, bringing her hand up and kissing it as they began walking.

They walked, enjoying the silent comfort of each other until they could walk no further and so sat on a hill they found, watching the setting sun, Paige resting her head on his shoulder as he protectively held her close.

Thirty-Two

Sinow watched as the white rose petals caught the wind then delicately floated to the water. In moments, the lake looked as if it were blanketed in a layer of snow. The petals had been chosen to symbolize the Lightbearers. Paige, Violissa, and Cody stood on the shore until all had fallen, then the three moved back. Sinow, Keary, and Ren moved forward and tossed the red petals high as Violissa urged the breeze to carry them to the water. His eyes followed their descent.

It was customary in Violissa's realm to lay flower petals on the body of the mortal before it was burned. The petals were a gift to the deceased. It was thought the scent would carry to the spirit, reminding it of its mortal life, one last reminder of those who remained behind. The bodies would then be burned, the ashes collected and spread to the wind.

As immortals, one's body would disintegrate as the Council or king returned himself to the Fates. The remains, a fine sparkling dust, would be carried by the wind to join the soul collected by the Fates. It was said the dust would float upwards as far as the eye could see, collecting to join the soul and take its place among the stars. In the rare cases of those few blessed kings who were chosen to join the Fates, the dust would gather to reform the body of the new Fate, silver and glistening like the stars themselves.

The petals on the lake were symbolic, but they were the best that could be done to honor the fallen. Violissa looked over at Sinow, her eyes determined. He brought his hand out and lit the layer of petals on fire as she laid a barrier of magic below to keep the water from dousing the fire. Where their magic met, a mist of purple could be seen, the flames above roaring to life until the petals were no more than ash. He gathered the ashes with his magic as Violissa called a gentle breeze, the clouds above covering the sun at the same moment the ashes lifted to flight. They glittered a violet hue that sparkled as the breeze carried them off into the sky. No one moved, all eyes transfixed on the ashes until they were long out of sight.

Most of the day was spent celebrating the lives of those they'd lost, sharing their stories with their human families. Laughing, smiling at the memories. No tears this day for they all understood that tomorrow would bring a needed focus as they determined their next steps. Sinow still wanted to find a way back even though he sensed Violissa was right, their world was dead. He held hope that they could rebuild it, that Violissa could still restore it. Ren was that hope, the future in flesh. His hand touched the fractured remnants of the gem he now held in his pocket. Hope. It was all any of them had left, but it was enough.

Paige began to sing. It had been decided the evening would end with a farewell song. He listened to the beauty of her voice, a slight sadness passing through him that she was the last of Violissa's people, the last to carry the beauty of song that defined them. Violissa joined her, their voices blending in a sound that weaved its way around one's heart. His hand still against the gem fragments sensed a small movement, like a vibration. He looked over at Keary whose gaze remained fixed on the women. Bringing the pouch from his pocket, he dared empty its contents into his hand. As he watched, the fragments moved slightly. There was something there, unseen, a small bit of magic he could feel. He looked back up at Violissa and Paige, the gem waking as they sang. Ren joined them, his voice rich and deep with the gift of his mother's song, and the gem fragments began to glow in response. He inhaled sharply at the realization of what it meant.

"Keary," he whispered, afraid of disturbing the magic.

Keary looked over at him, his eyes growing wide upon seeing the gem fragments coming to life.

The singing stopped, Cody picking up the tune on his violin. In reaction, the gem stopped its movement, the glow dimming.

"Violissa! Keep singing!" That was it, the key they'd overlooked.

She met his eyes, concern crossing her face.

He smiled, "Sing. You're the key, all three of you. Paige is Ren's past, you are his present, and he is our hope, our future." He couldn't believe he hadn't seen it before.

"Sing."

The three of them looked at each other then Violissa sang, Paige joining her, the fragments in his hand reacting. Finally, Ren joined them, their voices filling the air, and the gem glowing once more. Sinow tossed the pieces in the air, Violissa catching them with her magic. There they floated, the pieces slowly binding with each word they sang, the light brightening. As the final fragments combined, Violissa moved it over the water. Paige and Ren stopped their song, Violissa leading the refrain, pouring her power out to encase it. On instinct, Sinow did the same. Their powers met in a purple haze that spilled out across the lake and out onto the ground around their feet. Paige and Ren added their voices in a final chorus, the light from the gem expanding to meet the bonded powers, brightening as it grew until finally in an explosion of color on the final crescendo of their song, it formed a portal.

Sinow stood frozen, unsure of what had just happened until Paige broke the silence.

"Why? Why now? Why did they wait? Why couldn't they have opened it days ago?" she cried in defeat. "Why wait until they're all gone?"

She looked at Sinow, but he had no answers. Violissa, however, somehow more attuned to the Fates than any of them, answered, "Because it wasn't the right time." She brushed a tear from Paige's cheek. "The Fates aren't always fair, but they have their reasons, and we must trust them. Now more than ever."

"Do you?" Paige asked defiantly.

Violissa remained silent.

"Do you trust them?"

"Yes. I doubted them once, Paige, and it led us down an unbound path that punished us in ways I don't fully understand. I will never stray from their path again. It cost me too much the first time."

Paige took a deep breath, then bowed her head in deference to Violissa. Sinow walked over and took Violissa's hand. "It's time to go home. Time to rebuild." He looked over at Ren. "To have hope and faith."

"You're going home now?" he heard Cody ask from behind him.

Sinow turned to see the faces of a family he'd never thought he'd have. An extended family they now had to leave behind forever.

Violissa's head was spinning. She couldn't believe the portal was open. She was angry like Paige, but she knew she had to trust the Fates. There was no other way. Now, she was faced with saying goodbye to people she'd grown to love over a lifetime in this world. The brother she'd never had, one she shouldn't have had. Had this been so hard the first time they'd gone home?

They said their goodbyes, hugged, and cried. Even Sinow seemed a bit shaken; she was certain a Dark king didn't make friends outside of his Council. She was used to growing attached to others; he was not. Finally, she came back to Cody. It broke her heart to leave him, but there was no place for him in her world; their worlds were too different. She hugged him, and he embraced her like he never wanted to let go.

"Violet, what am I supposed to do without you here?"

"Settle down, get married," she replied.

He laughed. "And you think that will ever happen?"

She cupped his face in her hands. "You're a good man, Cody, with a good heart." She choked up, her voice cracking.

"Go," he said sadly.

"You'll always be my brother, Cody."

"Even though *he* says I'm not." He motioned his head toward Sinow who laughed.

"Even though I say you're not, she'll fight me every time I say it."

She kissed his cheek. "I love you, big brother."

"Love you, little sister."

He let her go as Sinow came up beside her.

"Vi, we need to go."

He put his hand out to shake Cody's, but Cody pulled him in for a hug. Violissa couldn't help but laugh at Sinow's discomfort.

"Don't ever do that again, or I'll kill you," he said, pulling free.

"Keep her safe," Cody said.

"I will, you have my word."

"I guess I was right after all," Violissa said.

"About what?"

"Cody's not a Lightbearer. I get my I told you so."

Cody laughed and hugged her again. "I wish I were so I didn't have to let you go."

She kissed his cheek then reluctantly walked back to the others.

"Ready?" Ren asked, his voice filled with the sadness they all felt.

"We should go in the order we arrived but last goes in first," Violissa said.

"Should I bother asking why or do I already know the answer?" Sinow asked. "Never mind, I know, instinct. That means Ren goes first."

"Aye, it does," Ren responded, his eyes becoming a mix of color with the heaviness of the moment.

Sinow extended his arm, and Ren took it, meeting his before Sinow pulled him in for a tight embrace. There were no words exchanged, but Violissa could see the effect on Ren's face. When they separated, Violissa stepped up to Ren and took her hand to his cheek.

"I can't wait to meet you, to watch you grow, to love you even more than I already do. I know we loved you in your lifeline and would have been so proud of you. You are everything I could have imagined you would be, Ren, and you will make an amazing king when you ascend."

His eyes turned a deep green, revealing the emotion behind them.

He hugged her, and she took him in one last time, his smell, his aura, everything that made him Ren, made him her son.

"I love you, Ren, never doubt that."

"Never. I love you, too, Mother." It was the first time he'd purposely called her mother, an acknowledgment of the melding of their timelines.

She squeezed him tighter before finally letting go. He then moved to Paige. Saying nothing, he pulled her in and kissed her. Sinow glanced at Violissa.

"Did I know this was a thing?"

"You did, you just chose to look past it."

"Mate?"

"Sadly, yes."

"They don't make anything easy on any of us, do they?" he asked, referring to the Fates.

"No, they don't," she replied quietly.

Freed from his embrace with Paige, Ren walked toward the portal, glancing back one last time.

Violissa leaned into Sinow.

"We will be there when you emerge. I promise you that," Sinow said.

Ren nodded, then looking at Paige one more time, he took a deep breath and stepped through the portal, disappearing from their lives.

She knew she'd see him again, but it still hurt. There was an emptiness that she knew would not be filled until his birth. She knew she'd be torn, wanting the time to slow down so she could cherish every moment with Sinow yet wanting it to speed up so she could see her son again.

"That means it's our turn," Keary said, breaking through her thoughts.

"We'll see you shortly," Sinow said, knowing their timelines were the same.

"See you in a few," Paige said stoically, wiping the tears from her eyes and forcing a smile. She took Keary's hand as they walked even though Keary didn't look happy about it. "Deal with it," she said then they stepped through.

"That leaves us," Sinow said, turning to face her.

"So, it seems." She glanced back at the portal, her heart still feeling the loss of Ren.

"Vi, we don't know what awaits us on the other side, but no matter what, we have each other."

She smiled and met his eyes, deep brown the edge of night

returned her gaze. She reached up and kissed him. “Yes, we do. Let’s see what the Fates have in store for us this time around.”

He smiled then glanced back at everyone they were leaving behind. Violissa looked one last time, expecting to find sadness in their eyes. Instead, she found hope. Cody smiled at them.

“Get out of here before that thing closes, and we’re stuck with you two.”

He shook his hands, looking down at them, searching for something. “Nope, still nothing. Guess I’m an ordinary mortal.”

“You’re far from ordinary, Cody,” she said, laughing.

Sinow took her hand.

“Don’t let go,” she said as they approached the portal.

“Never again,” he answered as they stepped through.

Thirty-Three

A force hit Violissa as the portal engulfed her, her breath taken with the impact. She felt Sinow's hand around hers but couldn't see him in the darkness. Then something tugged at her center, pulling her abruptly. Her hand slipped from Sinow's, and she heard him scream her name. Just as suddenly, he was gone. She gasped for air, aware that she could breathe again, her feet now planted firmly on the ground. Opening her eyes, she blinked, the light bright after her trip through the portal.

She was standing in the middle of a room. Looking around, she recognized it as the room she'd grown up in, her room, the same room that filled her memories. But that didn't make sense, her castle had been destroyed. She tried calling out to Sinow but couldn't reach him. She could sense him but not the same way she had; it was more distant. She looked around the room, running her hand along the bed that was draped in her favorite throw, the banisters hung with the delicate green and pink flowers like she remembered. What was going on, and where was Sinow?

A knock at the door startled her.

"Violissa," Daneele said, entering the room.

She took a step back, stumbling into the bed, and brought her hand to her chest.

"You've delayed this long enough—"

He didn't have time to finish before she'd thrown herself into his arm.

"You're alive. Thank the Fates you're alive!"

She pulled back and looked at him, feeling his face and hair. "Does Paige know? Have you seen her?"

"Violissa, what are you going on about? Of course I'm alive, and who is Paige?"

He paused, seeing her startled expression. "Is this another attempt to get out of today's meeting? Well, it won't work. I've told you that you cannot turn your back on your destiny, Violissa. You will be queen soon. It's time you step into your role. You will meet the prince today no matter how much you hem and haw."

She stepped back. "The prince? I'm meeting the prince? I will be queen?"

His expression softened. "Maybe you aren't playing. Do you feel all right? Do I need to alert Cyric?"

"Cyric? The others? They're alive," she said softly, walking around the room, piecing it together. "They've taken us back. A second chance."

"Violissa?"

She looked back at him, her mind trying to contemplate the idea that she was standing there talking with him.

"I need a few minutes, Daneele. That's all, and I promise I'll be down. I'll be ready to meet the prince."

"You had better. I don't think I can keep Anwell still much longer."

With that, he turned and left the room. Violissa stood, too

stunned to move. What was happening? Had they brought Sinow back as well? She leaned on her bed in an attempt to slow her racing mind and her pounding heart. Perhaps she was dreaming? Under some spell? She thought back to her trip through the portal, but nothing seemed off about it.

Remembering that the others might be alive, she ran to the window and spotted Anwell pacing on the lawn, Brom talking away to him. She smiled, her heart filling. They were all alive again. Drawing her eyes away, she walked to her bed and sat, the weight of her new reality setting on her shoulders lightly.

"A second chance," she whispered, closing her eyes. The darkness that greeted her filled with memories. Memories that were hers in another lifetime, ones that had been hers before Tynan had disrupted their timelines. She experienced the pain, the sadness, longing, hope, dying, rebirth, and a love that never wavered. She saw her life with the man who would always hold her heart, their happiness even after the pain and even through the fear. She felt the day they settled, felt the weight of it through the millennia that followed. It remained constant, a reminder in that distance of what had been. But through it all, she saw the memories of their love, their life together. She experienced Ren's birth and all the joys of his existence in their lives. Everything filled her mind, her body, heart, and soul, the two lifelines merging as she watched the day their future world ended. Felt time disintegrate as did they, all the while safe in Sinow's arms, his hold on her tight until the very end.

She opened her eyes, feeling whole, everything she had been in her other life now part of her, both lives now intertwined and merged into one. She looked around her room, and spotting the long mirror that leaned against the far wall, she walked over to it, pulling the sheet from it, the sheet she'd always used, never caring for mirrors, for the vanity they held.

The woman looking back at her appeared the same as she had the day she'd faltered and taken the misstep off her promised path. Her hair ran in long loose golden curls skimming the bottom middle of her back, one lone wayward strand drifting defiantly along her cheek. The lilac gown that draped her curves was the same she'd chosen that morning. But the eyes that looked back at her held knowledge only the experience of time could give. They were mature, with a depth that one found in eyes that had lived a full life, a long life, a life filled with struggles that challenged and shaped the soul.

The emerald in them sparkled as she brought her hand up to the mirror. Taking a deep breath, she smiled and said, "Time to meet my husband."

Sinow grabbed for Violissa's hand, but it was gone. He screamed her name to no avail; she was too far from his reach. He closed his eyes as panic set in, and then he felt the solidness of ground below his feet. Opening his eyes, he searched frantically for her, screaming her name aloud and in enaigne. Silence greeted him. Woods thick and dense stood before him but no Violissa. He turned to see if she was behind him, and what he found surprised him. He walked closer, until the ledge of the ravine was at his toes. The ravine was lush with natural life, the river rushing through it, the roar of the water music to his ears. It was what lie beyond the ravine that caused his hesitation. Beyond where the normal eye could see standing proud was Violissa's castle. He stared at it, his mind uncertain that his eyes weren't fooling him, trying to comprehend how it could be there.

"Tynan destroyed it," he mumbled.

Something nudged his arm, and he turned, his mind still reeling. A horse, deep ebony with a mane of thick silver pawed the ground. He looked at the silver markings along its face. All horses in their world had distinct markings like tattoos, each unique.

"I know you," he said as the horse nuzzled his hand. "But

that can't be. I haven't seen you since..."

Sinow, his father's voice broke through his thoughts.

Father?

Where are you? This is the first time we've arrived before the Lightbearers, and you're not here.

Sinow's mind searched for any explanation as to how his father, who'd been dead for over a thousand years could be speaking to him. Was he in another dream, being manipulated by the Fates?

Sinow, I know you're not a fan of this union, but you'll be king soon. You need to take the Fates seriously.

King soon? he replied with a confused tone.

Son, the princess will be here any minute. Pull yourself together, put your pride aside for this one time, and get to the meeting glade.

"Princess," he said aloud, his eyes meeting those of the horse.

I'm meeting Violissa today? he asked his father.

That's enough, Sinow. Stop the foolishness and get here now, or you'll receive punishment I usually reserve for your brother.

Sinow felt his father pull away.

"I'm meeting Violissa today," he mumbled, glancing back at her castle, then at the horse who'd died well before his father had returned himself to the Fates.

"They took us back," he said softly, unsure of the words as he spoke them.

He tried reaching out to Violissa again but with no success. "Because she hasn't called me yet," he said to the horse, leaning his head against it.

As he closed his eyes, memories flooded his mind. Memories of the life that was, a lifetime with Violissa. The pain, the anguish, the loss all flooding in, drowning him, then the love, the desire, the joy of being with her. He saw their unions, the birth of Drostiren, experienced the pain of losing her to Tynan, the ecstasy of making love to her after she'd returned from his grip. The centuries, the events, the feelings of a life he had lived rushed forth along with the heaviness of fear that sat behind those memories as they became his. Two lives melded into one, the memories his to own for eternity.

He opened his eyes. This was their chance to do it all again, to make it right, to avoid the pain that came with their punishment. He ran his hand down the horse's mane then pulled his hand back to look at the union scar that remained, skimming his finger along it in disbelief. This wasn't the scar from Paige's cut, that one ragged and rushed, too short from the makeshift knife they'd hurriedly used. This was the true scar from that day in the Banished Realm when he'd watched the blood drip from Violissa's mortal wounds. The memories were his, the scars his.

Did Violissa remember? Did her hand bear the mark of their love, the mark they'd carried for thousands of years?

Sinow, they've arrived. Your father is not happy, Kanine intruded, interrupting his thoughts.

Kanine? My old friend, good to hear your aggravating voice, Sinow replied with a laugh.

My prince? Kanine asked, confused.

I'll be there momentarily, Kanine, he replied, remembering that his father was too angry at him for his lateness to inquire himself.

"I can't be on time. I'm late to this event, Kanine can't change that," he said aloud, the day's events coming back to him.

He pulled his mind away and jumped on the horse, heading back to the castle. As he approached the stables, he hopped off the horse and threw the reins to the stable boy who had run out, eyes lowered, the stable boy Sinow remembered from his younger years. He rumpled the boy's hair, the boy taking a few steps back surprised by the unusual gesture.

"Do you know what is happening today?" he asked the boy.

"Yes, sir," he answered reluctantly.

"Tell me," he commanded, needing to hear someone else affirm it.

"It's the day you meet the princess, sire."

"Ha! Yes, it is," he said, laughing, knowing he was breaking every rule of his title and not caring. He ran to the castle, up the stairs, throwing the doors open with a bolt of magic and laughing at the idea of running into the keep, knowing his father would be appalled. "Darkbearers don't run," he reminded himself.

He stopped at the entrance and took it in. Home but a home that had not been witness to the horrors it had in its past life. A home that still held the innocence of his youth.

He walked on through the halls and to his study. His father's study. And to be truthful it hadn't been his for long. After he'd returned with Violissa from the Lost Realm, they'd made their home in the meeting groves, a fresh start to a new life.

He ran his hands across his face, the confusion of memories covering his head like cobwebs. He and Violissa had been through those events yet they hadn't. It was a confusing state to be in, like waking from each life had been.

Sinow! His father's voice barreled through his aching head.

Unsure as to how he would adapt to being under his father's control again, he answered, *On my way*.

"Time to meet my wife again," he said aloud before shifting to the meeting glade.

Thirty-Four

Violissa shifted to the meeting glade moments after her Council. She heard Sinow's father ask about her just as she remembered. Too eager to wait, she pushed through her Council, realizing from his expression that she'd neglected to summon a cloak.

"I know," she said. "I'm not anything like you expected and unlike anyone you've seen before. I get that a lot."

King Drostan appeared taken aback momentarily then replied, "Princess Violissa I presume?"

"You presume correctly, your highness. Where is Sinow?"

"Eager to meet my son? I must admit he has yet to arrive."

"That's right, he's late. I'd forgotten," she mumbled.

The king looked at her curiously, but before he could respond, she felt the air stir with Sinow's shift, felt his presence, her heart racing in response.

"Sinow," she whispered. Would he remember? Had his

memory been left intact as well?

His Council moved aside as he came through, and she held her breath.

"Son," his father said sternly.

"Forgive my lateness, Father," he said, his eyes meeting Violissa's. "I was slightly preoccupied."

He walked closer to her, her breath catching as it always did.

"Do you remember?" she whispered, her eyes searching his.

He smiled. "Every moment of every day."

"All of it?"

He brought his hand up and ran his finger along her wayward curl. "Up until the moment we stepped through the portal as well as the moment time took us away as I held you in my arms."

Feeling the tears behind her eyes, she said, "They brought us back."

"Aye, they did. A second chance."

"A chance to make things right this time."

"No hesitation."

"No missteps."

She laughed, her joy too much to contain.

"Then we shouldn't make them wait any longer," he said, his smile turning to the cocky, confident one she loved so much.

"No, we shouldn't," she replied, taking a step closer to him.

He hesitated, brow furrowing, power rising.

"One thing first," he said, bringing his arm out and casting a spell that hit Tynan directly, slamming him against a tree, magic tying him to it, allowing him no movement and no voice.

Sinow's father started to question, and she heard the Councils' murmurs, all taken aback by the move.

"I'll explain in due time, Father. Now, however, I need to kiss my wife."

She giggled at the absurdity of how it must have sounded. The true meaning of the word lost on all but the two of them. He moved his hand to her face, tilted her chin up, then leaned down and kissed her, a slight delay right before his lips met hers as the significance of what they were about to do settled upon them both. Finally, his lips touched hers as it had countless times, the love she had for him rushing forth to meet his. He took her in his arms, the world around them marking the beginning step in their prophecy's path. The ground shook below her feet, and she drew back looking up at the sky, he doing the same. Colors danced across it, cascading across the land, the trees and grass momentarily changing shades. The wind stirred, picking up wishing gems and skirting them across the open space.

Sinow laughed. "I take it the Fates approve."

"I'd say we have their blessing," she said, joining his laugh.

Around her, she heard the astonished gasps of the Councils but couldn't tear her eyes from Sinow's.

"Marry me, Violissa."

"Again?" she teased.

"Third time's the charm?" he responded playfully.

She leaned into him, saying, "I believe this would be number four, but I would marry you a thousand times, Sinow."

"So, I take it that's a yes?"

She laughed. "Yes, that is definitely a yes."

He took her hand and turned it over, running his finger down her union scar, the one she hadn't realized remained. Her heart quickened. This one was different, her original scar. Her mind flashed back to the memory, the blood dripping, the fear, the panic, the heavy emotions that seemed to shroud their every memory. She brought her eyes up, meeting his again.

"This time no fear," he said as if reading her mind.

She smiled. "Only hope."

He brushed her curl back, and she caught a glimpse of his matching union scar.

"Marry me today, Vi. Marry me now."

She was about to respond when the confusion that had been contained around them broke loose.

"That's impossible," she heard Cyric under the cacophony of voices.

"What is going on here?" King Drostan asked.

"This is the prophecy?" another voice rang in.

On and on the questions came, neither Violissa nor Sinow given the opportunity to answer.

"Enough!" She recognized Keary's voice as it broke through. Everyone quieted. "They will explain in due time over quite a few rounds of ale. But now, these two need to get married as soon as possible."

Violissa looked at Sinow, then they both turned back to Keary.

"You remember?" Sinow asked cautiously.

"Every damn minute of that wild ride."

"All of it?" Violissa asked.

Keary bowed to her. "Aye, my queen. You know, I'm a little irritated that the Fates let me die before the two of you. Really, after all I did for the prophecy and that's the way they treat me."

Violissa ran over to him.

"Watch it, I believe there's a hug coming your way," Sinow joked, laughing.

She jumped into Keary's arms, and he hugged her back.

"Second chances," he said, kissing her on the head.

"Second chances." She pulled back from his arms and held his face. "You remember. If you remember, then—"

"Ren may remember," Sinow finished for her.

"And Paige," she added then grew sad momentarily as the impact of the new situation reminded her that Paige's existence was a consequence of her not following the prophecy. Without Violissa's misstep, Paige would not exist.

As if reading her mind, Sinow said, "That one we'll have to figure out."

"That's going to be a fun conversation. Can I lead that one?" Keary joked.

"Would someone please explain what in the Fates is going on here?" Sinow's father said, the frustration in his voice evident.

Sinow walked over to his father. "In due time, sir. I know this is confusing, but as Keary said, we will explain after we marry." He paused, then placed a hand on his father's arm. "It's good to see you again, Father."

"The ceremony cannot be done today, your highness," Cyric stated as Sinow's father eyed him curiously. "There are pieces that need to be practiced. It is very delicate and must be—"

"We have practiced," Sinow said.

"Trust us," Violissa finished, drawing her hands out and turning her palms up to reveal the union scars, Sinow doing the same as an audible gasp was heard all around.

Cyric grabbed her hand. "This is impossible."

He searched her eyes for an answer.

"Second chances," she said. "We know the ceremony, Cyric, and we will explain once it is performed."

Everyone started talking at once again. Violissa looked at Sinow who shrugged as if to say they would just have to deal with it. She sighed as he and Keary began the defensive while her eyes drifted beyond to where Tynan remained bound to the tree to which Sinow had pinned him. Why hadn't he broken free? Was he too weak? Her mind ran through the memories. Yes, he had yet to find the book. He was weaker than Sinow, or he was too fearful to let his father know his true power, hiding in the grass like a snake ready to strike. She dared to meet his eyes, the dark brown of them lacking the insanity they had held in their past lives. Slowly, she walked away from Sinow and toward Tynan.

"Second chances," she repeated softly.

"Vi?" she heard Sinow call her, the worry evident in his voice.

She continued walking, her eyes holding the gaze of the man who had hurt her. The memories were there. They were hers to keep forever. The pain, the terror, the humiliation of it branded on her soul for eternity. As she drew closer to him, she heard Sinow again.

"Violissa." His voice was strong and authoritative, commanding that she step away from Tynan. She looked back at him. Second chances. The thought stirred in her mind.

"Do you trust me, Sinow?"

His face dropped. "Unquestioningly."

She turned back to Tynan, facing the man who would become the monster, and with the flick of her hand, she released him from his binds.

Sinow couldn't believe Violissa had turned back to Tynan. What had been a joyous reunion had changed in moments. He watched as she undid his binding, fear ripping through him uncontrollably, a fear given life for thousands of years, kept within his heart, cast always as a shadow through the memories he now held. It hit him so deeply that it physically moved him. His father looked over at him, his eyes narrow. He could sense Sinow's fear, a weakness an ascending king should not have. Sinow drew his power forth to shield it, covering it, hiding it back in the recesses of his body. Not certain how to handle it. He turned from his father's judging eyes back to Violissa who had stepped closer to Tynan.

"Second chances," he heard her mumble. "Maybe they aren't only for us. Do you know me?" She addressed Tynan who looked confused and weak.

"What kind of question is that? Of course, I don't know you. I know of you, but this is the first time I've seen you. Father, I've been treated—"

"Silence, boy. Whatever it is you've done, you will address the princess and answer her questions."

So, his father had sensed that Tynan was part of the story.

"They've wiped your memory," she said, laughing. "They've let you free while I carry the burden. How typical." She looked toward the sky. "Even with all you've put us through, I must carry the scars."

She shook her head. It was the most Sinow had ever heard her say about her time with Tynan. They had left it in the past long ago, he forever questioning if he'd done the right thing. The memories weren't his, but they were the longer they were held in his consciousness the more they settled in like an old companion. He felt the burden of their decision as she shouldered that of her time with Tynan. Sinow ran his hand through his hair nervously, knowing deep down her intentions.

"Violissa," he said sternly, "there is no redemption for Tynan in this. There never has been." He spoke the words, remembering the first time he had made that statement.

She glanced over at him. "That is not for you to decide, Sinow, nor is it for me to decide. The Fates have spoken, and we must abide."

Not on this, he wanted to scream at her but held back.

"Your brother wants you banished until he ascends and gains the power to kill you," she said to Tynan.

"That's nonsense—"

She raised her hand to stop his talk. "I didn't say you could speak."

Tynan's eyes moved to their father who only crossed his arms. Sinow felt Tynan start to shift.

"No, you don't," he said, throwing his magic out to stop Tynan. "My queen wishes to address you for some crazy reason, so you will listen."

He felt eyes on him, knowing he had called her his queen. Habits were hard to break.

"I believe the Fates are giving all of us a second chance to get this right, no matter how much we dislike the idea. Now, I am willing to play along but only conditionally. I know what it is you seek, Tynan."

Tynan's face momentarily reflected surprise, but he masked it quickly. "You speak nothing but nonsense, woman."

"You will give up your search for the book, put aside your desire for the throne, stop the scheming. You will take your rightful place as advisor to your brother and ..." she hesitated, "... and to me. You will become who you were meant to be before the book seduced you."

Tynan looked around then met Sinow's eyes. Sinow felt his own power flare, the desire to kill Tynan again rising, the hatred for all he had done festering below.

As if sensing he was on the defensive and had been discovered, Tynan's expression changed to a more familiar one.

"And if I don't?" he snarled.

"You will succeed. You will have everything you've longed for: the throne, the realms, the power."

What's she doing, Sinow? Keary asked in enaigne.

He had no idea, but he had to trust her.

Tynan laughed but Violissa didn't give him time to talk.

"And you will die."

Tynan looked taken aback.

"Your brother will kill you, and we will take it all back."

"Sinow doesn't have the power to kill. No immortal can kill another even a king."

"He will after his ascension. I've seen it."

She brought her hand up quickly before Tynan could react and touched his temple. Memory transference. There was no doubt in Sinow's mind she was sending images of his death to Tynan's mind.

"Lightbearers can't do what I think she's doing, can they?" Keary asked.

"No," he muttered, watching Tynan's horrified face.

She drew her hand away, and Tynan stumbled back.

"Now, you have seen your fate, you have until our union to give us your decision. If you return to witness our union, we will know you have chosen to take my offer."

She turned and began to walk away then stopped.

"Oh, and Tynan," she said, her voice deepening with power as she turned to face him again. "If you deceive us, if you step one foot out of line, give me or anyone I love one wrong look … if you dare hurt anyone, dare to lay a hand on me or my son again, you won't have to fear Sinow. I will kill you myself."

Sinow smiled, pride welling in him as she started walking back to him. Tynan laughed, stopping her in her tracks.

"Lightbearers can't kill, princess. I'm well aware of your code so your words hold no power over me."

An impish grin formed on her lips, and her eyes darkened to the color of the forest behind her.

Turning back to Tynan, she said, "You are correct, my Light side would never break its code. My Elvin side, however, follows no code. It would not hesitate to kill you."

She turned, head held high and walked away, leaving Tynan with his mouth agape in surprise. Sinow wanted to laugh but checked himself as the stunned murmur of the Councils rose around them.

"I want him out of my sight," Sinow said to his father, knowing his father was the one in charge now.

"Odhran, Faolin, take him back to the keep and watch him."

The two Darkbearers moved toward Tynan who still stood, sulking. They grabbed him and shifted.

"I expect to have an explanation soon," his father said.

"Aye, you will." Sinow was about to say more when he sensed a rise in power from behind him and saw Violissa's assured face transform to a mix of horror and desperation.

"No!" she screamed and threw a blast of magic out.

Sinow swiveled to see Mackay sent flying and Cody in a crumpled ball where he'd stood.

"Shit," Keary muttered.

Violissa ran past them, oblivious to the drawn Dark power of his father and Council. Unaware that she'd just violated the treaty in their eyes and attacked one of their own. Everything had happened so fast. Sinow, knowing things were tenuous, spoke up first, stepping in front of his father.

"Father, this is not what you think."

"She attacked a Darkbearer to protect a mortal. A mortal who dares enter this glade, dares approach us? How did he get here? I thought this land was hidden from mortals?"

"It is," Cyric answered. "I've no idea how he came to be here."

"He will be punished."

Fates, Sinow thought, *how am I to fix this?*

"Father, he is a mortal, a foolish one, but he's special to Violissa."

"That is not my concern. The rules must be followed."

"He looks to be Cirillian," he heard Daneele say, but his eyes were fixed on Violissa who had raised Cody up and healed him.

She looked over at Sinow, and Cody, with the ignorance of any human, looked with her then scanned the group.

"They're all so big," he whispered to Violissa.

"He dares look at us," Sinow's father started.

"And lives," Kanine said with a tone of astonishment. "Sire, our hoods are not drawn."

"He's unique, Father. I believe the Fates have a place in mind for him in all of this," Sinow said, walking over to Cody and Violissa.

"And he's my brother," Violissa said, setting everyone off again with her announcement. "Hush, everyone. Please, we will explain in time." Her attempt to calm them only worked slightly.

"You really know how to make an entrance, Cody. What in the Fates are you doing here?" Sinow asked.

"That portal thing stayed open after you went through. Nobody knew why or what to do. Aunt Emma said it was a sign. You know how she is, Violet. She said it was waiting for me and told me to go."

"So, you just went?" Violissa asked. "Without even thinking about it, Cody?" She hit him on the chest. "What were you thinking? You could have died!"

"You went into the portal and came out here?" Sinow asked, confounded.

"Yeah, I wandered around for a while until I saw you both and then this guy yanked me out here."

Mackay glared at Cody who met his stare.

Sinow felt his father move next to him. He reached out and grabbed Cody. "Who is this mortal who can look a Dark king in the eye?"

A Lightbearer indeed, Sinow thought, looking over at Keary who tipped his head to acknowledge he was thinking the same thing.

"He's someone very special to me," Violissa said. "He is my brother in the world we just came from, and I suppose now he is in this one. Your highness, I promise all will be explained, but the story is a long one." Violissa placed her hand on his father's, and Sinow could sense his unease. "Please forgive him, he does not know our ways, but he can and will be taught."

"This other world, can all of its inhabitants face the Darkness?"

"No, Father. Only this one for reasons only the Fates know."

His father dropped Cody who stumbled back.

"I take responsibility for him, and my Council will guard him until we find a place for him."

"And you agree with this, Sinow?"

"Yes, sir. Plus, Violissa would make my life quite unbearable if I killed him like I want to right now."

"That's really no way to treat your brother-in-law, Simon," Cody quipped.

"I would shut up quickly, Cody, as your Fate is currently in my hands. And don't call me Simon," he retorted.

Sinow looked back at his father.

"This mortal presumes to talk to a Dark prince without

hesitation, to look us in the eyes without pain or death. Am I to assume this will be explained as well?"

"Not quite, your highness," Violissa answered.

"We have yet to figure it out ourselves. The Fates have their ways and given that they allowed him to follow us home, I'm certain they have a role for him yet."

Sinow could see that his father was perplexed. It was rare that a mortal went unpunished, but his father was a good king, a fair one, one from whom Sinow now realized he had learned.

"I acquiesce. He is yours but keep him out of our way and out of our matters."

"Thank you," Violissa said. "Brom, please take Cody back to Cirillia. Settle him in the keep until we figure out what to do with him."

Brom came forward and shifted with Cody before he could say anything further.

"This tale of yours I am curious to hear. We must wait?" his father asked.

"Aye, you must. We need the union before anything else can go wrong."

"Then we will wait as the union presumably is taking place today. Quite a shift from your attitude this morn I might add."

"A lot has happened since this morn, Father."

"The Council and I will return to Tenebron now. We will arrive back here at ..." He stopped, no one having discussed when the union would occur.

"At dusk," he and Violissa said simultaneously.

"When the dark—" he started.

"Meets the light," she finished for him.

"Dusk it is then. Am I to assume you'll be staying with the princess?"

"Yes, with Tynan loose ..." he trailed off, his power rising from even saying Tynan's name.

"You will keep me in your sight," Violissa said, finishing his thought again.

His father eyed him.

Fear is not something a Dark king knows, son, he said in enaigne.

"Princess," he spoke aloud, turning in her direction. Then he and his Council shifted.

Keary paused, a look of confusion on his face.

"Go, you are not my Council yet. He will punish you if you do not follow."

"Must the Fates mess with me as well? I don't know how you two keep sane with all this jumping around," Keary muttered before shifting.

"Violissa," Cyric started, "will you be returning with us to run through the ceremony?"

Violissa smiled. "Cyric, I believe I'll stay here a bit. We know the ceremony. Every word, every cut. There is no need to run through it again."

"If you've been through the ceremony, and the scars prove you have, why go through it again?" Cyric asked.

Violissa glanced at Sinow, a smile forming. "These scars are from our past, the ceremony as well. We need to do it one last time to make things right."

Cyric sighed, and Daneele put a hand on his shoulder. "I'm sure our heads will all feel a deal better once they've explained what we seem to have missed."

"I pray to the Fates they will," Cyric replied.

"We'll leave the two of you in peace," Daneele said with a slight bow. He shifted, the others following his lead, leaving them alone at last.

Sinow met Violissa's eyes, drowning in the depth of emerald.

"We're back," she said. "They've given us a second chance after all they did to us."

Her words should have brought Sinow joy, but then he thought of Tynan and felt his Darkness rise.

She must have sensed the change, her expression morphing to concern.

"Tynan?" he said, unable to hide the anger in his voice.

She pulled her lip in and chewed it.

"Did you think we wouldn't talk about it?"

"I was hoping we could put it off."

"Really, Violissa?" He ran his hand through his hair. "You should have waited. Should have discussed it with me."

"And would you think any differently if I had?"

"No. He needs to be punished."

"For what? He hasn't done anything yet."

"He's capable of it, Violissa."

"Animals are capable of biting, but do you punish them before they do so?"

"It's not the same." He was pacing now, his frustration too much to contain.

"He killed everyone we knew, destroyed our world, took you ..." He couldn't force himself to say anymore.

"He hasn't done anything. They reversed time, he has no memory of any of it. I can't let you punish him for something that hasn't happened."

"And how do you know he has no memory? He hides things very well, you know this. How do you know he's not pretending?"

"I just know," she stated.

"I'm not risking everything on your instinct this time, Violissa. Not when it comes to Tynan. I need something more concrete than that."

"He hasn't found the book, Sinow. There was no madness in his eyes."

"That's what you want me to set aside his punishment for? And how would you know he's not hiding that as well?"

Her answer made him wish he hadn't asked.

"I was forced to look into the insanity of those eyes enough to know it can't be hidden, enough to recognize it," she replied sharply. He needed no further explanation, her words a reminder of a time he'd wanted to leave behind but never quite knew how. His power rose in defense, and her expression softened.

She leaned into him and sighed. "I guess this means you'll remain by my side?"

"As long as Tynan walks the same land as you, always."

His weakness needled him, his existing self trying to comprehend the fear that ruled his older self. The memories merged but some of the feelings still unfamiliar.

"I see. Then you will oblige my instinct and trust me?"

"I don't believe you're leaving me much choice." His fingers traced the loose curl that grazed her cheek. "But if you're wrong—"

"I will kill him myself," she answered, her eyes deepening in shade.

He sighed, knowing he needed to trust her, knowing her instinct always guided her, remembering Daneele's words from their other life. It was only when she ignored her instinct that she stepped down the wrong path. Dropping his head, he threw his hands out in surrender.

"You win. I'll follow your lead on this."

She lifted his chin, her eyes a lush sage.

"I will allow him to live, but that does not mean I have to trust him, nor does it mean I want him anywhere near you." He heard the tone of his voice, felt the Darkness behind it, the fear that drove it, but he'd meant every word even if it wasn't who he'd been before they'd stepped back into their world, into a life that was now convoluted with feelings and memories that he couldn't quite grasp.

Sinow's eyes had darkened, but Violissa saw something different behind them. No, it wasn't different, she thought; she'd seen it there for thousands of years, a lifetime of it that was still settling in as her own. So, he did remember it all, inheriting a life he'd already lived, forced to accept the memories and the pain that came with it just as she was. She couldn't believe she was standing here with him, in a past they'd left behind that was now in their hands to rewrite. But she was, and he was here with her, by her side, the unsettling feeling of her future self's memories insinuating themselves in her mind just as his were. It was a strange feeling and one that was beginning to feel almost complete as if the two pieces of her were becoming one which she knew they were. She gave herself over to them and looked at him through that lens.

"You remember everything, too," she stated, studying this man whom she'd loved through two lives now.

"Yes," he answered, his voice hard. "Too much and some things I wish I didn't."

"Maybe there's a reason we have those memories," she said softly.

"Maybe but it doesn't mean I have to like them all nor does it mean I like the other parts that come with those memories. Feelings I'm not used to harboring in my mind and ..." He let go of the thought, but she knew he was going to say his heart. She sensed the difference, the fear that had driven him in their other life, fear that had been the precedent for how they had proceeded with everything they'd done.

"We don't have to retain those feelings, Sinow. This is a second chance, a chance for us to start down the path the Fates laid for us and not veer off course this time. We don't have to repeat the same mistakes, experience the same things we did before."

He searched her eyes. "Tynan is still on the path with us, Violissa."

"I know, Sinow, but he's always been on the path. Nothing will change that."

Sighing, he said, "You're right." He ran his hand through his hair then continued. "He was written into the prophecy before the alternate path was created. That doesn't mean I can't still kill him."

Her mind flashed back to a memory new to her, the prophecy changed by another Fate, the addition of Tynan, the prophecy shifting course, a branch created.

"The other Fate."

"The brother," he said. "I remember as if I had been there."

"Because we were. Sinow, we are who we were when Ren was taken from us as well as when he walked through that portal. We are the same people, two lives merged into one, and we need to own those memories, own their consequences, take the time to understand why the Fates gave them to us, why they want us to remember."

He brought his hand up, curling his finger along her loose curl.

"What lessons they want us to learn? Vi, I don't want him here, I don't want him anywhere near you, and I don't want to even look at him."

"And you call me stubborn."

"It's not stubborn, Vi. It's protective. What he did, what he's capable of doing again—"

Bringing her finger to his lips, she stopped him. "We need to play this out, Sinow. I know you don't agree with me. I know the memories are there, trust me. But we have to take this step by step and play by their rules. We're back to this specific point for a reason. It was the stepping-off point in our lives, the day I made that choice."

"The day I let you and decided I could wait, not knowing what I was signing up for," he said, a coy smile forming.

"Do you regret that wait?" she asked playfully, glad his mind was moving past Tynan.

He wrapped his hand around her waist and brought her in against him. "Not one bit."

She kissed him, losing herself in him as she had done countless times before, knowing their path was set no matter how difficult it would be to follow it this time.

Pacing his quarters, Tynan thought about all that had transpired. To say he was angry was an understatement. How had the bitch known about the book? How had she known he was searching for it? The questions abounded, and the more his mind worked at it, the more his anger grew. She had shown him an image of his death at the hands of Sinow, but that was impossible. What she had done was impossible. Only Darkbearers could transfer memories, and none he had ever studied had the power to send them to another person, they were memory stealers, stealing to confirm the guilt or intent of a mortal.

He rubbed his face and stopped pacing. Sinow hadn't questioned her knowledge of his plans as if he was aware of them as well, but that couldn't be. No one knew what he planned. The image of his death resurfaced. Had she conjured the image from her fantasy, or had it been a true memory? There was feeling there, her feelings about the incident: pity, sadness. A memory not a fantasy. But how? How could she possibly know what the future held? He thought back to Sinow's reaction again, while he hadn't questioned her knowledge, he had questioned her actions. What was it Tynan had felt? Fear. Sinow had been afraid to have her approach him. Sinow feared nothing, he had been raised to despise fear, so how had it slipped into his heart overnight?

There was more to this story, answers to all of his questions. Curious, he decided to take Violissa's proposal. He needed answers, and tonight would provide them. He would agree to her bargain and attend their blasted nuptials, nuptials he had intended to stop but somehow had been thwarted. Again, an act that left him baffled. He'd get his answers then decide whether he wanted to play along with her rules. Time would tell how he would proceed.

Thirty-Five

The union ceremony went as it should have when they first began their journey together. Their life and soul lines were cut again along their existing scars, but their wounds healed as they were meant to, immediately after the transferring of their bloodlines. When the ritual was complete, the union cloth dissolved in a sparkle of golden light, the moons watching on as the setting sun draped the land in a crimson-orange glow. The wind stirred in the trees, followed by a quiet that covered their world, a moment in which the Fates were watching and blessing them. Violissa smiled as she drew her lips from Sinow's. They'd been united again, this final time the way it had been meant. No blood, no fear, no desperation, only love. The fifth time they'd been married she realized, the third by their ritual, one by Elvin, and one by the human ceremony. Blessed on many counts in many forms but this the most special. Not because of who they were with or where they were, but because this time, they were starting a journey together from the beginning, one that held no scars, held no pain, held nothing but the potential they had ignored at the start. As long as they could move past the memories that stirred beneath the happiness, those that Violissa could see lingering behind Sinow's eyes. As long as they could get past them, then nothing would be as it had been.

After the ceremony, they told their story surrounded by mugs of ale and their family. Tynan stood apart from all of them, listening as they spoke. He had shown up, which surprised Violissa and gave her hope that perhaps her instinct was right. She felt Sinow's tension and noticed he avoided looking at or even acknowledging Tynan's presence, but there was nothing she could do about that. In fact, she, too, had a hard time looking his way and avoided it as often as possible. At one point, he began to leave, the story taking a turn to a dark period. Sinow snapped his head up and stared him down.

"You will not leave. You will stay and bear witness to everything you have done, to the pain you have caused, the destruction you wreaked. You will stay until this story has ended and own your deeds. I may not be able to physically punish you again, but this, I can do."

Tynan stayed, shifting his feet as the story progressed, their father rising then pacing far from Tynan's presence as his crimes increased. When they were through, there was silence. A silence which lingered until the king finally spoke.

"And you will leave him to live after all he has done?" he asked Violissa, his eyes a deep black, the power darkening his aura.

"Yes, the Fates have spoken, and I will not disobey them. The second chance is for all three of us."

"And you will agree to this?" Sinow's father asked him. "After what he did to her, to you both, to our people?"

Sinow's power flared, cascading across them all. Even now, prior to his ascension, his power was strong. He looked at

Violissa, the ebony of his eyes filled with pain for a brief moment, pain only she could see, before hardening.

"Yes, I will do as she wants. If her instinct says he needs to live, then I will follow her lead."

"Against your better judgment? Against your code?" his father asked.

"Violissa's instinct is to be trusted, Father. It is a part of her power. She sees things, feels things that we do not. She has a connection to the Fates that goes beyond anything I've ever heard of, and that connection guides her in ways we cannot understand. I believe it is the Elvin in her that gives her this special ability, and I no longer question it nor does she."

His father sighed. "I am king, you understand that, Violissa."

"Yes, your majesty."

"Then you know it is in my right to follow my own code and punish him for the crimes he has committed."

"Crimes he has yet to commit? Crimes he does not remember as we do?"

"Yes, even ones he has yet to commit. What is to stop me from following my duty?"

She didn't really know what could stop him. He was king, and Tynan was his son, his subject. So, she answered, "Nothing but trust."

He stared at her a moment. "You are quite vexing to my son, aren't you?"

She smiled. "So I've heard."

"It is within my right to punish him, but I shall not. You are to be king soon, Sinow, and so I will follow your judgment on this. It is your past and your future. If you feel her instinct is correct, then I will oblige."

"Thank you," she said.

"Out of my sight, Tynan. They may let you live, but if you make a wrong move before Sinow takes the throne, you will suffer the consequences."

Tynan said nothing but shifted from the glade.

Violissa, are you sure about this? Cyric asked her.

No, but it feels right.

"I had a daughter," Daneele said softly. He'd been quiet through the entire story, even as the others had asked questions.

"You will have a daughter," Violissa said, causing a riot of voices as her Council erupted.

You know how to rile them up, don't you? Sinow asked. *Don't you think we should talk about this one first?*

Paige needs to be born, Sinow. I can't ... She stopped, the sadness at the thought of Paige not in their lives hitting her.

I know. We'll figure it out, but we've got a thousand years. Let's take this one step at a time.

You do realize we're now talking in enaigne, right? she said, only now realizing it herself, the soothing feel of his voice in her mind sending a rush through her.

The union brought it back?

So, it would seem. It's nice to hear your voice again, she replied, leaning over and kissing him, forgetting everyone else was there.

"Do you think you two could stop that for two seconds?" Keary teased. "Daneele wants to know how he will have a daughter when he's bound to his code of celibacy?"

Sinow shot him a look.

"I don't want to know that, Keary. I can't even fathom it," Daneele returned.

"Good. It's not the priority at this moment," Sinow said, still staring Keary down.

"Hey, can't a guy have a little fun?" he asked, shrugging.

"I've had enough for one day," Sinow's father said. "Have either of you determined where you'll stay now that you've married?"

Neither of them had thought that far, and they both looked at each other.

"Clearly not. I'm assuming you'll want to stay together, which means boundaries will need to be opened, and the treaty amended."

"That will not be an issue on our part," Cyric told him.

They continued talking; the ascensions would take place in another moon, so the decision was made for Sinow to stay in Cirillia half the time then Violissa to stay in Tenebron until the day they took the throne. Finally, they bid farewell, Sinow following her to Cirillia, the union giving him the ability to pass through the barrier with no assistance. She wondered how many new abilities their pre-ascension union had brought as he shifted in behind her. She'd shifted to her room, not really thinking about where she'd intended to go, following her subconscious which had led her here.

"Interesting choice of places to lead me, Vi. I would have thought you'd want to check in on Cody first or show me around a bit before you seduce me in your bedroom," Sinow said, studying the room.

She lit the sconces with her magic then watched as he walked the room, running his hand along her bed.

"I remember the two times I was in this room as if they were yesterday."

"Two?" she asked, only remembering the one that had led them to war.

He turned to her, his eyes a lush brown. "I summoned the Fates here, asking them to send me after you." He looked down at his hands as if remembering the moment. "Offered everything in exchange for the chance to find you."

She moved closer to him. "I think it's time we make some better memories here," she whispered, looking up at him.

"I'm not going to argue with that," he replied, pulling her in and kissing her. "You do know this will be our first time in this life," he continued, his lips moving down to her neck, butterflies flitting in her stomach as if it were truly their first time.

"Are you seducing me in an attempt at my virginity once again? And on my wedding night?" she responded playfully.

"That I am," he said, his hand unfastening her dress with his magic, then sliding it down her back.

Her pulse quickened, her breathing tightening in anticipation of his touch, his hands moving the material from her body. Chills followed his fingers as they made their way upwards, tracing her curves, his eyes never leaving hers. His fingers finally weaving through her hair, he pulled her in and kissed her passionately. Her body responded, desire rushing through her. She wanted him desperately as if she'd never had him before, as if it were indeed their first time. Her hands grabbed at his shirt, her fingers fumbling at the buttons on his pants, missing the ease of zippers the human world provided. When she'd finally succeeded, he drew her in tight against him, his skin hot against hers, the pounding of his heart intense against her chest as he moved her to the bed. Feeling the need in him rise, she raised her leg, his hand running along it as he entered her. The pleasure ran in waves as they made love until it finally crested, crashing with his in one final moment of heated ecstasy.

He dropped his head to her neck, his body relaxing atop hers, the weight of him a welcome feeling of strength which she clung to, her own body responding once again, warmth spreading through her. He kissed her neck then licked the sweat from it, drawing his tongue along her skin until he found her lips. His own body reacting to her re-emerging desire. They made love again, the mix of memories and lives merging to give them a mixed feeling of familiarity and newness. The weight of all they now knew had happened, the discovery that they were alive, that after all they'd lost, they were with each other to experience it all anew, intensifying their need and emotion.

The night passed and finally both lay in her bed exhausted. Violissa swept her hand down Sinow's chest, feeling each muscle and the strength that lay beneath them. She'd made the same movement more times than she could count, yet there was something new about it.

He kissed her head. "What's on your mind? Don't tell me you're up for another round already."

She peeked up at him, pushing her fallen hair from her face. "Are you?"

"Do you need to ask?" he replied, laughing. "I can't resist you Vi, no matter how many times I've had you."

Heat rose in her cheeks as a rush of blood flowed through her body, sending a warmth through her in answer to his response. She kissed his chest, her fingers grazing his skin.

"I am, but that wasn't what I was thinking about."

"Hmmm, so that leaves me with a dilemma. Be a good husband and ask what's on your mind or a selfish one and take advantage of you again," he said, his eyes darkening.

"I think the Dark king in you just made the decision," she responded playfully.

"Dark prince and yes, he's a selfish bastard," he said, kissing her, his fingers brushing her breast. All thoughts fled, and she gave herself to him again, wondering how after thousands of years with him she still felt no control over her need for him. The memories affirmed her suspicion that the need never wavered, that it always took hold, always took priority.

This final lovemaking did them both in. Their eyes too weary for more, they drifted off in each other's arms.

Sinow never had the chance to ask Violissa what she'd been thinking about. When they'd woken, they'd made love again then finally found their way down to the dining room to scavenge for food. Mid-day had passed, but someone had left food out for them, something that would not have happened in his home. Violissa sat down next to him as he ate, enjoying the taste of their food, clean and savory, unprocessed. He smiled as she took a bite of fruit, the juice escaping to dribble down her chin. It was a small thing but one that reminded him of her childlike nature, the innocence that filled her every move.

"That was quite lady-like, wasn't it?" she joked, smiling back at him.

He reached his finger out, catching the drop then wiping the rest up to her lip where she licked it off. Desire flared in her eyes, and he traced the curve of her lip, fighting the rising urge to kiss her again, to take her again. There were two sides of him vying to do so, the one who had died that day, holding her in his arms, hating the idea of never touching her again, cursing death and all it held but accepting his fate, their fate. The other, the man who'd been reborn to live another lifetime with her, wanting her with a passion that came with knowing they were just beginning their journey, that they had been blessed with a second chance, that he would savor every moment he had with her knowing what it meant to lose her.

He dropped his hand, but as if she'd read his every thought, she leaned over and kissed him hungrily. He was ready to fling everything from the table and take her on it when Cody's voice interrupted his intention.

"There you are!" he said, running into the room. "Don't you guys ever stop? Seriously, you act like a couple of teenagers."

Violissa dropped her head against Sinow's chest.

"Is killing him out of the question, Vi?" he asked, feeling the Darkness rise at the interruption.

Cody, paying no attention, plopped in a chair across from them.

"Yes," she said, sighing, lifting her head and composing herself.

Can I get a rain check? she asked seductively.

Definitely.

"Your friend, the really serious guy, Cyric, has me working, too hard I might add. Nobody said this was part of the deal."

At that moment, Sinow wanted to do nothing more than take Cody and pound his face in with every word he spoke, but he forced himself to pull his attention from Violissa and listen.

"What deal, Cody? You stepped through that portal knowing

very well you could be killed. You're lucky the Darkbearers didn't kill you."

"I followed you, Violet. I wasn't about to let you leave me. We're a team, remember?"

"First of all, you need to address her by her true name," Sinow said. "Secondly, you are not a team. You're a mortal, Cody, one who took a huge risk. Now that you're stuck here, there's no going back." Sinow crossed his arms as his desire was quickly replaced by irritation.

Cody looked hurt. "I won't leave my sister, Simon." Sinow held back the urge to punch him and let him continue. "She's my sister, I've been protecting her since she was a baby, and I will continue to do so even if it means jumping into some Alice in Wonderland type wormhole."

Violissa put her hand on Sinow's leg and squeezed, he assumed in an attempt to let her handle the conversation. He looked over at her; the lush sage of her eyes had cooled to emerald.

"There's no sense in fighting about what's in the past. We can't change what's happened and now we move forward."

He had a distinct feeling her words held a deeper meaning that was directed at him as well. Had he thought her innocent just a few minutes prior? He made a mental note to re-evaluate that observation.

"So, what has Cyric been making you do?" she asked.

Cody groaned. "He's making me learn. All kinds of boring stuff from your world, and it's all from these boring old books. You guys really should consider upgrading to technology. All that power you have, and you still use books? And don't even get me started on the bathroom situation. Bathtubs? Seriously, where are the showers?"

Running his hands through his hair, Sinow laughed. "I don't think bathrooms are our main priority right now, Cody."

"A shower would be a nice upgrade," Violissa said. *Imagine what we could do in one.*

He cocked his brow, his mind momentarily envisioning what he would do to her in one. Then he remembered they had added a shower in their past life, his memory confirming all he had imagined. Shaking his head to free himself from the images, he returned, *I do believe your Elvin side is as bad as my Dark side, Vi.*

"Hello, I'm still here," Cody said.

"Unfortunately," he muttered.

"So, Cyric is teaching you our history," Violissa said. "That's not a bad thing, Cody."

"He's training you," Sinow said. "Training always starts with the history, and ours is an extensive one that you need to understand, especially to understand where we stand today and why our union is so important to our world."

"You sound just like him. It's boring."

"It's necessary," Violissa said, bringing her hand out to cover Cody's. "Look, Sinow believes you're a future Lightbearer. If that's true, Cyric is taking you down the path where every new Lightbearer begins. To understand your future powers, you need to understand the past that shapes them."

"Are you starting to believe now, Violissa?" Sinow asked her.

"No, I still don't see it, but there's no harm in training him. If anything, he can be an advisor."

"That sounds dull. I think I prefer the power thing."

Sinow rose, stretching, bored with the conversation and eager to have Violissa to himself again.

Unfortunately, he never got the chance. He found himself drawn into the world of Cirillia, following Violissa through her day, learning that her style of ruling was not anything like his, something he already knew but never from this perspective. When they had ruled together, it had started as a joint rule, both adjusting to each other's differences as they ruled. Now, she was ruler of Cirillia, still the princess, but the Councils let her run free. He was still prince, his father the one in charge, he still on the sideline. It was an odd feeling and one he knew would be hard to adjust to when they returned to Tenebron. Thankfully, it would only encompass a few weeks, and then he would take the throne again.

The days went by quickly, filled with trips to her villages, he always keeping his distance as he watched her interact, taking him back to memories of their former life. He felt the guilt that accompanied those memories, the fear that filled them, and he didn't like it. Cyric pulled her from him several times to prepare for her ascension, no matter how many times she resisted, arguing that she'd been through it and knew what to expect. During that time, Sinow wandered her castle, studying her life through a lens he'd never had, seeing the world of the Lightbearers from a setting in which he was unfamiliar. This was their world, not a shared one, not a united one: theirs completely. He wondered if this was how Violissa had felt in their last life when they'd taken back Tenebron and settled in his castle. It left a feeling of being out of sorts, and it was a state to which he wasn't accustomed.

On the morning of their departure for Tenebron, Violissa led him away, saying she wanted to do one last thing before they left. Something she needed to do. She led him down a corridor that stirred memories of their past, until he finally remembered this was the route to the hidden entrance to the Lost Realm. He grabbed her hand and stopped as they came upon the dead end that hid the secret corridors.

"Vi, what are you doing?"

She chewed her lip, furrowing her brow. "I'm going to see my parents."

"And you think that's a wise idea at this stage?" He wasn't certain it was, unsure if this would tempt the Fates to think twice about their new beginning.

"I do. I can't explain it, Sinow."

He sighed. "Is there anything you can ever explain, Vi? Does instinct rule your every move?"

Shrugging, she replied, "Pretty much. Don't you know that

by now?"

She leaned up and kissed him then turned and moved through the hidden entrance before he could stop her. Groaning, he followed, knowing there was no stopping her once she had an idea in her head. He knew too well how difficult that would be. When they finally reached the doorway, he couldn't help but be overcome with awe, just as he had the first time. This was something ancient, created by power that was greater than theirs, power that had ruled their lives every step they had taken. This was where it had all begun, where she had been hidden, waiting for his birth, waiting for him.

He looked over at her. "You know, I never realized this, but you are really old. You know how many millennia older you are than me?"

She threw him an irritated look and opened her mouth to come back at him but was stopped short when Daneele shifted behind her.

"What in the Fates are you two doing here? And how did you get here?"

Sinow tried not to laugh; Daneele was not one to ever show his anger, and when he did, it never settled right on him. It had been a fact Keary had exploited throughout their former life.

"We're going to see my parents. We told you we've been here before. You know that's why I'm aware of my heritage."

"Yes, I'd forgotten. But, Violissa, you can't come down here whenever you feel like it. This is sacred ground, and it's reserved for your Keeper."

She crossed her arms, and Sinow could feel her Elvin temper rising.

"I wouldn't push her, Daneele. She's got it in her head, and you're not going to persuade her to do anything besides what she's intending."

"Just because you gained access once—"

"Twice," Sinow corrected.

Violissa spun her head around. "Twice? I don't remember

that."

"You wouldn't. I went in a second time."

"You went into the Hidden Realm through this entrance?" Daneele asked, surprise on his face.

"I was trying to find Violissa. Trying to find you when Tynan had you." Just speaking the words brought the memory of the pain and desperation back. "I knew you were locked in there with him and thought they could let me in. I raised the entranceway from the rubble of your castle, and the Fates granted me access."

She stared at him, her eyes a mix of awe and sadness. "You raised it from the ruins?"

He shrugged. "I didn't really think about it. I was in a unique frame of mind."

"And you entered unaccompanied?" Daneele asked.

He nodded in affirmation.

"Fine, if the Fates granted you entrance without me, if you've both been granted access, then I'll let the Fates decide your path again," Daneele said with a sigh, rubbing his beard. "They let you in by yourself?" he mumbled, Sinow watching as he tried to figure it out.

"Don't try. The Fates are entirely too hard to interpret, Daneele," he said, putting his hand on the man's shoulder.

He looked from Sinow to Violissa then back again before shifting to leave them be. Violissa was still staring at him. He took his finger and closed her mouth, inwardly proud at having impressed her, then placed his hand on the door just as they had centuries before. Never casting her eyes from him, she placed her hand on the door, across from his. Within seconds, he felt the familiar prick as the door began its opening ritual. Violissa didn't react this time, her eyes still locked on his as the entranceway opened to reveal the haven of the guardians, her parents. He lowered his hand, then taking hers, they walked in together for the first time as one.

Upon her first step through, the gardens burst to life. Colors like Sinow had seen in her shared memory as well as in his new ones, brightened, the fountain repairing with each step, emerald water dripping slowly from it at first then increasing its flow to fill the room with its sound. Everything awoke as if awaiting their return, awaiting proof of their union.

"Why didn't this happen the first time?" she asked in a hushed tone.

"Because the prophecy had become unbound," he heard a woman's voice say. Aradisa stood next to the fountain, no longer a shade but in physical form as he remembered her in their past life. Her straight golden, almost white hair shone in the sunlight that streamed through the broken ceiling of the garden. King Viliren, Violissa's father, stood by her side.

"You're whole again."

"No, child. We remain as we were when we left you," her father said.

"You remember," Sinow stated, realizing that their memories had been left intact just as their form had been.

"Yes. Our memories remain as well. The Fates blessed us, keeping us as we were, keeping our memories whole just as they have blessed you with yours."

"Blessed?" Sinow asked. "Are you certain it's not a curse, another punishment for straying?"

Aradisa smiled, moving closer to them, and he saw the silver glimmer that accompanied her movements.

"Dark child, your memories are there for a reason, for many reasons that even I do not know. The Fates chose to leave them so that you can learn from them perhaps."

He looked at Violissa who returned his look, a moment of guilt flashing across her face before she covered it.

"Shhhh, my child," Aradisa said, running her hand down Violissa's hair. "You must follow your heart and your instinct, let them guide you. Second chances do not come often, and you have been given one. Don't let your past define how you move forward from here." Her last comment was directed at Sinow.

"Why are you both still mortal?" Violissa asked, in an effort, he suspected, to change the subject.

"They're not," he answered for them.

Her father smiled. "Often my daughter sees things we cannot, but you find ways to see what is often right in front of her. Her awareness and yours complement each other, they always have."

"Sinow?"

"They're with the Fates, Vi." He kneeled and moved his hand to sweep the silver dust that barely lay upon the ground.

"But—"

"We are no longer part of this story, my daughter. You freed us, you brought us back, gave us a chance to live the life we did not have, a chance to finish our lives together. You gave us our second chance."

"The prophecy is nearly complete, you've seen its outcome, you know your path. There is no longer a need for us in this story. We have played our part and been rewarded for it. Our part in the prophecy as well as yours has come to an end. There is no more to it than the final step."

"Ren," he said.

"Aye, he is the end, the purpose to it all. Your love was created so that you could start our world down the path to his rule. His birth is the reason for it all, you discovered that in both timelines."

"The blended powers," Violissa said. "All of it for the merging of the three lines."

"And a final everlasting peace to our world. Ren is what you've both been fighting for," the king said.

"I started us down this path, the day I met your father—"

"That was the day I fell in love with you."

"And the day that I gave you my heart," Aradisa said softly. "We never knew that you would be the result, Violissa. We had no idea what we were putting in motion. I simply followed the flickering silver light that led me to his path that day, through the now sacred forest and to the border of the three realms. Now I see that it was a sign of all that was to come, that by simply following my intuition, trusting in the Fates, in the silver glow that led me to him, I was unleashing the power of prophecy."

Sinow wasn't sure what to say, he'd had no idea that the Fates had brought Violissa's parents together nor had she.

"Why tell us all this now when you never mentioned it before?" she asked.

"Because you need to know. The Fates work in ways we do not understand, and we should not question. You learned that lesson, and now, both of you need to trust in it."

"Pawns," she mumbled.

Her father laughed. "Some might say that."

"We were all pawns in their game."

"Vi?"

She turned her eyes to him. "Something I learned in a dark time. I thought it was just the three of us, locked in this game that needed to be played out. But it was more than that, the players greater. My parents, your father, the Councils, us, Tynan, all playing a part to bring us to the climax of the story. All part of the branch that we saw in the Dream Realm. The one created by the other Fate, the brother. I remember watching with you. That's why we have our memories, to remind us that they still control us."

Her eyes grew sad. "But we fulfilled the prophecy, we've married."

"The prophecy is not complete until they determine it is complete, my child," her mother said.

Her face dropped, and Sinow saw the fear, the same fear

he'd carried for far too long. He lifted her chin. "We will not waver from the path, we will fulfill our destiny even if it means waiting until Ren ascends."

She nodded in agreement then turned back to her parents. "But you're no longer part of this. You won't be here when I bring the Hidden Realm back. Everything in our future has changed, all the steps we took to get to where we were the day the Fates took us. Ren is still the end outcome but..." she paused, getting a wild look about her. "He has his own path, his own part of the prophecy. Our end in the story is not the end of the prophecy, is it?"

"You ask too many questions, daughter, just as your husband does. Know this. Your prophecy is yours alone. It began with your mother and me, and it ends with the two of you. Ren is the outcome, he is the result of what the Fates desired, but your story is more than just Ren. You know this to be true."

"The Fates. The three of them, Vi. Orlaina—"

"Shhh, you do not invoke the name of the Mother Fate," Aradisa said in a hushed tone.

"Mother Fate. It wasn't about us, it was about them. I remember now."

"That's why the prophecy's end is in their hands. You must await their sign, their blessing, and then you will know when you have made it to your destination," Aradisa replied.

"Now, you must both go. Our time here has passed, they allowed us one last visit, one last time to say goodbye," her father said.

"That's why I needed to come. You called me."

Her mother smiled and placed her hands on Violissa's cheeks. "Your father and I were blessed to be given time with you now and in your past life. We could not be prouder, you both have been challenged with events that no other could have survived, but you did, and your love grew through it all. I have watched you from afar, we both have, watching you flourish as a queen and a mother. Now, you will do it all again but the way you should have been allowed that first life. I will be there with you the entire way, and if you need me, call for me. I will find a way to be by your side."

She hugged Violissa tightly then kissed her head before moving to Sinow. "Dark Child, take care of her as you always have." *Remember, she is stronger than you think, let her go this life and you will live freer than you ever have.*

She kissed his cheek quickly then faded, a silvery dust glittering in the sunlight.

"Your mother has always been the better one with words," her father said. Violissa hugged him, and Sinow watched as he stroked her hair. "I only ever wished for your happiness," he said, letting go of her. "Don't take this second life for granted. Remember the Fates have blessed you with it. Live each day with that knowledge."

He grasped Sinow's arm. "You are a good king, Sinow, and a good man. There is no other I would wish for her and no other I would wish to rule by her side."

He, too, faded, leaving the same silver trail. The room felt empty as if their presence had always filled it. He took Violissa in his arms as she shed her tears, the same she had shed when her mother had first died, and her father had returned himself to the Fates. He didn't know what was harder, losing them once or losing them a second time. He held her until her tears had faded, and she peeked her head up to see him. Her eyes were a deep green, but as they met his they lightened.

Taking his fingers and wiping her stray tear, he asked, "Will you be all right?"

"Yes, I suppose I am, but I didn't expect that. I thought they'd be here again, that we'd have more time."

"Second chances, but they'd already had theirs."

She moved from his arms and walked slowly through the gardens. As she did, he noticed the broken ceiling repair itself, the walls reform, the sun grow brighter, beams of sunlight filling the space. Images appeared, moments in time, a time before theirs, a time that defined their existence. He saw Aradisa and Viliren youthful and happy, saw her gardening as Violissa always did, watched her laugh with her brother, the garden fading to reveal them both young and running through the forests, Aradisa's power evident even then as the plants blossomed in her path. The garden became a room filled with men he knew to be Lightbearers but none he recognized save Cyric, music streamed through it, laughter, people a mix of Elvin and Cirillian, a celebration, a union between Viliren and Aradisa, their lives together just beginning as they danced together, the love they felt for each other evident in their eyes. The scene shifted to the garden once again, Aradisa with Viliren, her hand on her stomach as he rested his atop hers.

"Do you feel her?" she asked. "Feel the power?"

"Aye, it's strong even now. Aradisa, there has never been a child born with such power."

"There has never been a female ruler born Viliren," she whispered. "You know what this means."

"It means we must protect her from Theonelle. The Dark king will kill her and you, Aradisa."

She placed her finger on his lips. "It means she is the one. The Light child of the prophecy."

The scene shifted once again, the room dark, the noise of war filling the space. Sinow felt the fear that permeated the room even before he saw Aradisa and Viliren. She was holding something against her stomach, speaking softly to it. When she lifted it, he could see the infant within the sphere, tiny and asleep, waiting for her mate to be born. Aradisa placed her in the fountain water and within moments, the water had taken her, the brilliant green of its power flooding the room. When it cleared, the image was gone. Violissa stood next to the fountain, her eyes meeting his. She looked around. "Their story," she said. "It's a story I don't think we ever heard fully."

"And one we may never completely know."

"But one they have shared pieces of with us. They loved each other, Sinow, as you and I do. Their love started us down this path, and now, we must finish it. We must see it to its end, whatever that may be."

He held his hand out to her, and she took it, moving into his arms. "We will get to the end," he said assuredly.

"Yes, we will," she replied, kissing him. "Let's go back. It's time we headed to Tenebron. You've an ascension to prepare for."

Thirty-Six

Tenebron was just as Violissa remembered: dark, ominous, and dreary. Stepping into Sinow's castle did not, however, carry the same weight as it did the first time she had arrived. There was another sense to it as she walked through the corridors: home. Not hers but Sinow's. This was his world as it should have been when they'd first lived, unsullied by Tynan's corrupt magic. The pain and anguish that had layered the air did not exist without it. Instead, it felt like Sinow: warm, protective, strong. It did not, however, feel comfortable to her Light side, and she had to keep her powers quelled as Sinow had needed to in Cirillia. Upon her first step into the keep, her power had flared, lighting up the entire bottom floor. Sinow's father and several of the Council had shifted to investigate.

It was strange seeing Sinow with his father. They were more alike than she would have guessed. It wasn't simply their appearance but their mannerisms, the slight softness that she would catch in his eyes, the care he had for his people. He wasn't the scary monster she'd been led to believe, but then again, neither was Sinow. Both had been judged by their predecessor's actions. She supposed it was as unfair as judging Sinow against Tynan, the difference between Dark power when it did not tip one over the edge of sanity.

As the first few days passed, Violissa noticed Sinow's tension at a higher level than it had been in her home. He kept close to her, always on edge, waiting for Tynan to strike. It saddened her to know the fear that had encompassed their prior life had clawed its way into this one. His father took notice as well; she could see the look of concern that crossed his face when he sensed it.

On the third day, his father insisted he spend time with Sinow alone, asking Violissa to give them the time to which she did not object. Sinow, however, voiced his discontent with the idea but was overruled by his father. As she left the room, she glanced back at Sinow, his knuckles tight with tension, muscles strained. She knew this went against his own instinct, but he was not in a position to disobey his father, as strange as that seemed. She glanced at the king who gave her a quick wink. Walking down the hall, she laughed to herself. He did know, and he was forcing Sinow out of his comfort, forcing him away from her, forcing him to leave her alone with Tynan in the same building in an attempt to break him of his fear. *Would it work?* she wondered as she tried to find her way to the library.

She weaved herself down the dark hallways, trying to remember where the library had been from their first life. She had told Sinow she'd be fine without a tour, she knew the keep, at least she thought she did. Like her castle, there were many winding corridors that led to many more corridors. Turning down another, she noticed the sconces were fewer, the lighting less. She shivered, the natural reaction to the thick Dark presence that seemed to congregate in certain areas of the castle, this one in particular. Throwing a light sphere out, she realized she was in the wrong corridor and began to turn when she noticed something, portraits hung further down the wing, similar to the wing in her own castle where portraits of her forefathers were placed. She didn't remember this wing from when they'd taken back the castle in their previous life. Perhaps Tynan had destroyed it, or he'd simply destroyed the portraits that held his history. Curious, she walked further, the sphere moving forward with her every step. She evaluated the men in the pictures, all with the same glare, the same pitch-black eyes, the same fear invoking presence. All strikingly similar in appearance to Sinow and, she recalled, Tynan at his full power. As she reached the end of the hall, the walls closing in the further she walked, she realized that most held the same proud, powerful look that Sinow and his father shared. Only a few held the crazed, maniacal eyes that Tynan had once held, the corruption of their Dark power visible in them. She stood before the second to last portrait, the man within glaring out at her with eyes that twisted the soul. Sinow's grandfather, there was no doubt, the similarities between this man and Tynan were terrifying. Both bore the same insanity, the same disregard for their code screaming from their presence and their hardened eyes. A chill crossed her spine at the memory of looking into those eyes. Tentatively, she reached up on her tiptoes and touched her fingers to the face before her, remembering the small glint of man she had sometimes seen beneath Tynan's madness. Had his grandfather held it as well? This man before her looked as if he never had, as if the madness was all he craved.

"My grandfather was a different breed." She heard behind her, so lost in thought that she hadn't felt a presence. She swirled around, nearly stumbling, Tynan's eyes meeting hers. He reached out to catch her, but she backed away, slamming into the portrait, her breaths coming out in short pants, the fear too great to hide. He remained quiet, studying her, his eyes never leaving hers, eyes that were yet untouched by corruption, ones that reminded her greatly of Sinow's. She quickly recovered, composing herself as best she could, considering the moment of vulnerability she'd shown.

"I've heard if you stand too close to his portrait, you might just lose your mind, his presence lingering even in death." His eyes drifted to the portrait behind her. "Was I like him?"

She wasn't certain how to react to his question. Was he goading her? Forcing her to bring up memories he knew would bother her? Wanting to witness her reaction? Or was she misjudging him, her thoughts influenced by her preconceptions? She turned to look at the portrait, knowing he was behind her, knowing she was making herself even more vulnerable.

Stop it, Violissa. He's not the same man. The book has not corrupted him.

"Yes," she answered honestly, looking in the eyes again. "Very much."

"Hmmm. I've always been told that's a bad thing, that the madness that runs in our veins is something we strive to overcome. I'm not certain it can be though."

She turned quickly, unsure as to what he had meant with the comment.

"Dark power is madness itself. All of our line has the potential to tilt over that edge because the power drives it, it craves it as I suppose some of us do as well."

"Do you crave it?" she asked, unsure why she had asked the question.

"No, I can't say that I do," he replied absently, his eyes still directed toward his grandfather's menacing stare. "Why are you down here, Violissa? And why is my brother not with you? Father forcing him from your side?"

His eyes dropped back to hers as she noted the coldness in the last statement.

"I can function quite well on my own," she replied, straightening her posture.

"I see that," he said with a smirk. "That would explain why you've wandered down toward the lower levels where the dungeons lie."

She couldn't help the reaction she had at the thought of the dungeons, remembering them in the aftermath of Tynan's destruction. She'd never returned after that day and never once ventured into the dungeons of any of their castles. That remained Sinow's territory, and she chose never to see what lie below.

"I was trying to find the library."

He raised his eyebrow. "The library?"

"I wanted to do some reading, and I find the quiet space of a library peaceful when I can't be outside."

"Hmmm, I can see how you became lost then. My brother is not one to tarry near any of the libraries in our home. You are headed toward the lower library, but I doubt that's the one you had in mind. Come, I'll lead you to the better one, the one I prefer when my mood is not dark."

She thought of asking if there was a time his mood was ever anything but dark but refrained as he walked off. Did he really intend to have her follow him? And why was he not going back the way she came? She stood there, pondering her next move when he stopped and turned back to her.

"Coming?"

Gulping, she followed, listening for her instinct to scream for her to run but hearing nothing. *Where are you?* she asked it but again no sensation, no internal scream. She caught up with him, and they walked in silence, her heartrate increasing as they passed the stairwell to the dungeons. Eventually, she could see only a dead end in front of them and her concern grew.

"Where are you taking me?" she finally asked.

"To the library."

"This isn't the way to the library. Now tell me why you're leading me down this dead end," she said, stopping and crossing her arms.

Slowly he turned, a smirk on his face, his eyes slightly darker even in the dimly lit hallway.

Fool, she told herself. *Why didn't you turn back?*

"There are multiple libraries here, Violissa. I assumed you wanted the main wing library, did you not?"

"Well, yes, but this isn't the way I remember."

He eyed her. "It's not the way most enter it, but," he started, thumping his fist on the wall, causing her to jump, a response she instantly regretted. "A bit jumpy, are we? As I was saying, this is the way I enter." He stepped aside, and she noticed a corridor had appeared where the wall had been.

Cautiously, she walked past him and into the tunnel. "It's a secret passage," she said, throwing a light sphere out to light her path. "But why didn't I know about it? Why didn't Sinow?"

He laughed. "There's quite a bit my brother doesn't know, princess."

"But it wasn't here when I lived her."

"I would venture I likely destroyed it. My grandfather had it sealed off. It's said the slaves would hide from him here." He paused and ran his fingertips along marks in the wall. "I've been told he caught one in here, sealing off both ends, locking her in with no escape."

Violissa took a step back upon realizing the marks were scratches. The slave had tried clawing her way out. She swallowed back the sadness she felt for the woman.

"All that was left when I discovered it was her bones." He kneeled down and sifted a white powder through his fingers. "Which I playfully ground down as a child."

Standing, he reached across her and bumped the wall to the right of her. It moved open, revealing the library. She backed up, his body too close to hers, but the wall hit her. There was nowhere to go.

He chuckled then walked past her, his body brushing hers. Revulsion rose, but she pushed it back down, remembering he wasn't the same man, none of the things he had done had been done in this life. She followed him through, taking a deep breath in the open room.

"I do suggest you take the main route next time. I don't believe my brother would like knowing you were wandering about the wing where I found you. It's a bit too close to my wing."

He closed the secret door as he spoke but didn't leave.

"Why are you being nice to me?" she asked.

He turned back to her and studied her, his eyes intense. "I find you curious. You had every reason to let my father banish me, to have me killed again as you say I was in your first life. Yet, you didn't. That behavior is unlike any with which I'm familiar, and it interests me."

"So, I'm something to study?"

"Perhaps." He stepped closer to her. "I've had many mortals in my time, Violissa. I can have any one I take regardless of whether they live or die. With the power you say I had, I could have had them all. Why the fascination with you?"

If he expected an answer, she gave none.

"The curiosity not only involves you but me as well. You stir something in me...not anything you need be worried about yet. But it's something I don't understand. Perhaps I never did understand it, perhaps," he paused as if wanting to say something further but hesitated. "Keep out of that wing, the dungeons are too close and you too fragile."

He shifted, and she finally exhaled the breath she'd been holding, collapsing in the nearest seat, her legs no longer able to hold her or to hide the shaking she'd kept at bay.

Violissa didn't mention her encounter with Tynan to Sinow that evening. She hated not telling him but knew it would only upset him. As she entered the library the next day, the last thing she expected was to see Tynan there.

"My father keeping Sinow occupied again? Weaning him from you?" he said with a chuckle that seemed oddly placed.

"Why are you here? I thought you preferred the other libraries."

When she'd entered, he'd had three books in his hands but

now only two were there. "What are you up to, Tynan?"

She walked up to him and looked at the books. "Elvin history?" she asked then grabbed the hand to his side, the one hiding the third book. This one, worn and tattered, looked to be well read. She ripped it from his hand and felt the stir of his Dark power.

"Elvin. Why are you studying the Elvin?" She flipped the pages of the book, scratched writing lie in margins and all throughout it. She remembered Sinow mentioning it one time. One of the few times they had discussed the book.

Backing away, she said, "You're still looking for it. I told you I would kill you, Tynan. I told you to give it up."

He snatched the book from her hand, his eyes black with anger. "You couldn't kill me if you tried. Your ascension is too close, the shake in your hands is evident just as Sinow's has been the last moon, your power too unpredictable, too erratic. You don't stand a chance against me, and you know it."

She felt her own power shift, the Elvin surfacing. "Tell me you're not looking for the book, Tynan."

"I'm not looking for it, Violissa," he replied, his power calming, eyes lightening. "Interesting how your eyes shift. How they darken so that they could almost be black. Just a few shades more, and they would be."

He shifted, leaving her to wonder what had just happened. Was he telling her the truth? Or was she being naïve as Sinow thought she was? She glanced down at her hands and noticed the slight quiver. He was right, the pre-ascension effects were increasing, and her powers as well as Sinow's were unreliable. Taking a deep breath, she decided to let the incident go. Although it had been intense, she had felt no threat. She walked toward the seat she'd claimed as her own, noticing a piece of parchment mostly hidden under the table closest to her. Leaning down, she picked it up and unfolded it, noticing the yellowed age of it, the delicate thinness from wear and time. It was a letter to Tynan. As she scanned it, she saw it was from his mother. Knowing she shouldn't read it, that it was something private, she refolded it. It wasn't hers to read, and he had dropped it in his haste, perhaps letting it slip from the book she had grabbed. What she didn't know was how to get it back to him.

Biting her lip, she was tempted to go after him but thought twice about it. The last thing she wanted was to be anywhere near his quarters. Instead, she tucked it away then tucked herself into a chair and read until Sinow found her.

"You know, I forgot how cute you are when you're reading," he said playfully, kneeling down next to her and peering over the edge of the book. "I think Kanine forced me to read that during training. Is our book selection that bad?"

She laughed, closing the book. "No, I never had a chance to learn all the quirks of your realm, the things that make it distinct from mine other than the power. Most of those books were destroyed by Tynan or lost in the fire that destroyed his wing."

Sinow's face dropped slightly. She'd heard from Paige that he had destroyed it, but they had never spoken of it. For a moment, she wanted to force him to talk, wanted to scream that they needed to get past this, that everything that they had pushed aside in their last life needed to come out, but she didn't. Instead, she reached her hand up and caressed his cheek, the understanding passing through their eyes that this wasn't the time nor the place. Would it ever be the time? She sat up on her knees and kissed him, the book dropping to the floor as she let go of the crushing weight of that time in their past life for just a moment. His hand weaved through her hair, and as he pulled her in, lifting her from the chair, the need she felt from him was mixed with something more, a heaviness that he couldn't escape but longed to. They were both trapped under the constraints of a past life neither could free themselves from, and in that kiss, they revealed the pain of it, the exhaustion, the desperation to break free. Yet, as the kiss ended, and they pulled apart, he dropped his head, resting it against hers. She felt the tear slip from her eye, knowing nothing would change, watching as it landed quietly on the stone floor and seeped into a crack hidden away as the past would do once again.

He lifted her chin, and as she felt the Darkness in him rise to bury his emotion, she stoically swallowed back her longing and met his eyes. His finger caressed her cheek, passing over the remaining dampness from the tear, his eyes flickering lightly with the feel of it on his skin. Then as she had for thousands of years, as she had that day, she acquiesced, this time not needing his strength but instead needing the man below, knowing he wasn't ready, and she would need to wait. Why? She couldn't answer only knowing it had to be this way. It was he who would need to take the step and free them from the chains of their past.

Giving him a small smile, she reached back up and kissed him. This time, the emotion had settled, there was a sadness to the kiss as if he realized what he had asked of her, what she was again giving up, but the heaviness that had layered the first kiss was gone, vanquished to the depths of his mind once again by the king within.

"I believe you promised me a tour of Tenebron," she said softly, her fingers tracing his bottom lip.

"But you've seen all of Tenebron," he replied, his voice reflecting the relief that she'd moved past the moment.

"Aye, but that was in another life. I've never seen it whole from the start, only after we rebuilt it. You promised to show me the land."

"So, I did." His eyes softened to a rich brown as they searched hers, looking for any indication of regret.

She sighed and leaned into him, resting her head on his chest. "I think now would be the perfect time for that tour."

He kissed her head and rested his chin against it. "Then that's what we'll do."

Closing her eyes, she fought the urge to turn back, instead

setting it aside until the time was right, knowing in this life it would come, praying it came soon before both of them broke from the weight of the emotions their merged memories had forced upon them.

Thirty-Seven

The letter weighed heavily on Violissa. She needed to get it back to Tynan; the urge to read it was high, and the fear Sinow would find it was even greater. It had been a few days since she'd seen him. No, it had been two days since Sinow had left her side, his father not pulling him away until this day. She should have told Sinow about her run in with Tynan, but each time she started, she pulled back, knowing exactly how he would react, the emotions of their experience the few days prior still fresh in her mind. Plus, she didn't know why, but something told her she needed to keep this to herself, that whatever was happening with Tynan was something that belonged between the two of them at this time. Maybe she was losing her mind, the Dark energy of the castle warping her senses. Was she insane? Tempting fate by playing with fire. Still her intuition told her this was right, that this version of Tynan was capable of change.

As she entered the library after two days away, she again prayed she was right. Tynan wasn't there when she arrived, so she found a book and snuggled into her chair. Sinow's father had once again found an excuse to steal him away, giving her the chance to sneak off on her own again. It didn't surprise her that Tynan appeared a few minutes later as if he sensed her there.

"You have something of mine," he stated flatly, a frightening gleam to his eyes. She thought momentarily of fleeing but stopped herself.

This is not the same man you knew, she told herself. *But he's capable of becoming that man,* the fearful side of her said.

"I do," she said, pulling the letter from where she'd tucked it in her skirts and handing it to him. She stood, uncomfortable with him towering over her. He remained where he stood which left her too close to him and unsure what to do to change their proximity.

"Did you read it?" he asked, the accusation heavy in his tone.

"No," she replied, forcing herself to take normal breaths. Her mind flashed back to the memories she now held, his face in hers, his body on hers, his hands.

He studied her, and she knew he had felt her pulse increase, her fear rise. "I scare you still."

It was a statement, not a question. A simple fact that could not be denied, no matter how she wanted to believe her instinct of his second chance. The fear remained, the memories, their history too damaging to deny.

"Yes," she answered honestly.

"That will never change, will it?"

"I don't know, but I don't know that I have reason for it to change yet."

His eyes dropped to the letter. "No, no, you don't. Nor do I have reason to say you shouldn't fear me."

She said nothing but followed his eyes to the letter. He did not move back from her, still closer than she liked.

"This is a letter from my mother, written while she was carrying me. Did you know they locked her away?"

She could feel his eyes looking at her again, feeling vulnerable below his stare, so she brought them back up to meet his.

"Yes, she attacked Sinow."

"So, I've been told. But she tells a different tale. She should have been queen. It is I who should have been born first. His mother stole our father from her, stole her right to bear the next king, stole the throne from me."

His eyes darkened, and she felt the air thicken with his power.

"Sinow has everything that should have been mine. She tells me so in this letter. All of it spelled out."

A letter. A letter written by a woman maddened from the Dark power of the very child she carried was the impetus of it all, the trigger to the events that had shaped their lives and turned them into a nightmare.

"You had everything, Tynan, and yet ... yet in the end, you still had nothing. You remained unhappy and alone."

She felt the Darkness dissipate a bit.

"If I follow your path, I still have nothing. If I follow mine, I have power."

"Power does nothing to feed your needs, Tynan, trust me."

"Why should I trust you, Violissa?"

"Because I've looked into the madness that power gives you, Tynan. I've seen what it does to you, seen how it changes you. But mostly because I've witnessed you fight against it. Whatever that power did to you, it took every piece of the man you are today and destroyed him."

"I don't want to live as second to Sinow."

"Then you will lose everything, Tynan."

He laughed. "That's what you don't understand, Violissa. I have nothing to lose now. There is nothing in this life for which I would fight."

On instinct, she reached her hand out and placed it on his,

saying, “You can fight for me.”

She didn’t know why she’d said it or where it had come from, but it felt right.

He glanced down at her hand then looked back up at her, his eyes searching hers.

“You had moments, Tynan. You don’t have to be that same man. You have a place here.”

“With you and Sinow? Do you seriously think he likes that idea? You are naïve, aren’t you? I would kill me in a heartbeat if I were him.”

“But you’re not, and he has me to balance out that impulse.”

He pulled his hand back, stepping away from her. “You don’t know my brother then.”

“I know him better than he knows himself,” she replied.

He said nothing, shifting from the room. She let out the breath that had been frozen in her lungs the entire time and rubbed her arms, unsure of what had just occurred and what it had all meant. Was it a sign that he was changing or was he still going after the book? She wanted to have faith, to trust her instinct, but then in times like this she wondered if she’d actually gone mad. Talking to the man who had done so much to hurt her. She sighed, looking at the book in her chair, knowing she would not be picking it back up today, her moment of calm lost.

Guard duty again. That’s what this was. “Keep Violissa company while I’m away,” Sinow had told him, but Keary knew exactly what this was. Guard duty. Sinow dragged off grounds to the ascension caverns by the king on the premise of some excuse his father had created. Keary had wanted to tell the king that it was no use, the fear couldn’t be broken, but he risked punishment if he dared voice an opposing opinion. So, here he sat, pretending that guard duty was an honor. He met Violissa’s eyes and saw that she understood all too well why he and Ailin were trailing her around this eve. They were sitting together, playing a game of marfoirn, a game similar to marbles in the human world.

Violissa sat back, saying, "When does it end, Keary?"

"I don't know, but you've invited the devil into his house, Violissa. Did you really think he'd react any different?"

"Does this mean the game is over?" Ailin asked.

"You didn't think though, did you? You never do."

"That hurts, Keary."

He stood and stretched. "You run on instinct and that strange sixth sense you have. It confounds all of us, especially Sinow. You know how he is. For Fates' sake, Violissa, you lived an eternity with him, and you didn't think to discuss keeping Tynan alive with him?"

"There wasn't time," she answered defensively. "He would have banished him there and then."

"And that would have been a bad thing?" Ailin muttered.

"I believe so."

"You believe so, but we don't, none of us do. I don't trust him, I wouldn't expect Sinow to trust him. So here we are, back to the same awkward spot. You imprisoned me on guard duty and Sinow drowning in fear."

She looked down at her hands. "I didn't know that would happen. The memories weren't settled like they are now, they weren't completely mine yet."

"But they are now, and Sinow can't seem to escape them."

She stood and gave him a look he knew all too well, that Elvin side of her slipping out. "Violissa," he warned.

"I'm going for a walk, and you two are not going to follow me."

She turned and walked from the room.

"The hell we're not!" he yelled after her, the human word slipping out.

"Hell? What does that mean?" Ailin asked.

"Never mind. Let's go follow, trust me, if anything happens to her, we'll both regret it greatly."

They stayed back as Violissa wandered through the keep, running her hands along the walls, lost in thought. After a time, she wandered down an older wing they rarely used, one that had been destroyed by Tynan during his reign, Sinow deciding not to rebuild it. She stopped, opening the doors to what had been their meeting room ages before Keary had been Council. Slowly, she walked in, surveying the now empty room.

He put a hand out to stop Ailin from entering, and they both remained outside the doors. He wondered if she even remembered they were there. He hated having to follow her around, part of him on edge like Sinow with Tynan around, the other tired of seeing her shackled. In their past life, Sinow had clipped her wings when she'd returned even though all of them could tell she'd returned stronger, more self-assured than she had been. He had caged her and, in doing so, had caged himself. And to everyone's frustration, she had allowed it.

He watched as she reached the windows to the room, one of the reasons he'd been told the room had been abandoned, one of the prior kings thinking it too light for his taste. He heard her voice, sad and soft, the words of a song forming. It weaved through the room, enchanting everything it touched. The dust in the air seemed to freeze and sparkle, the moonlight seemed to stream brighter as if reaching to her.

"What in the Fates'?" Ailin said.

"Shhhh, give her the moment."

He couldn't drag his eyes from her though; she didn't sing often, but when she did, it was like a magic of its own that called to everyone.

The words of the song reached him, and he recognized them along with the melody. It was one she and Paige had sung several times. He didn't remember the name but knew the words spoke of being bound speechless, caged to stay silent against an inner spirit that wanted to finally be free and break the bounds that held it.

As if forgetting he and Ailin were there, she lost herself to the song, waving her hand to bring the music to life, filling the room with it. She danced among the dust particles, turning her force to the windows which blew free from their panes, shattering with the power of her voice and her emotion. The outside world reached in, climbing and crawling to be closer to her, the moonlight shimmering along her skin and hair, her eyes vibrant within it.

From the corner of his eye, he saw movement.

"Tynan," Ailin whispered, seeing the same thing and moving as if to attack.

Keary threw his hand out, waiting to see what would happen. Was she right, was he different this time? Would Keary regret not acting or would his eyes be opened to whatever it was that Violissa saw?

He waited, but Tynan did nothing, merely stood to the side watching her, his expression revealing the same wonder that Keary felt every time he heard the magic of her voice. As her song finished, everything in the room seemed to freeze around her, groping for her last note, not wanting the magic to end. She stopped to catch her breath, waking from whatever trance she had pulled herself into, her eyes filled with sadness, the defiance of the song now gone.

Tynan stepped into the room, and she swirled to his direction, clearly startled by his appearance. Keary tensed, but Tynan moved no further.

"Did I ever hear you sing?" he asked, his voice carrying a bit of awe to it.

"No, I don't believe so," she replied. "Why?"

He looked curiously at her before saying, "I can't imagine ever wanting to harm something that beautiful."

As if realizing the honesty of what he'd just stated, Tynan shifted, leaving Violissa standing alone in the room. Keary watched as she dropped her hands to her knees, her arms shaking with nerves, a sob escaping.

He pulled Ailin and urged him back; what they'd witnessed had not been for their eyes. She needed her privacy this time, and Tynan was not a threat to her right now. Walking down the hall, Ailin said, "He didn't hurt her. He had the chance, and he did nothing."

Keary rubbed his hands over his face. "Maybe Violissa was right. Maybe there's something changing in him."

"Or maybe she's changing him."

Keary looked at him.

"You know you really are strangely deep thinking sometimes. Isn't that Kanine's job to say things like that?"

They laughed then continued down the hall, both still too overtaken with the sight they had just witnessed to speak anymore and both vowing the need to neglect mentioning the incident to Sinow when he returned. There was no way they could explain the event and no way they could defend not stopping Tynan from approaching Violissa. It was better to leave it alone, safer to let it lie.

Tynan paced his quarters, unnerved by his experience with Violissa. What was happening to him? He felt weak in her presence, something with which he was unfamiliar. Yet, he couldn't help being drawn to her, sensing her, as if a connection were there that had not been severed as his memories had. Had he a connection with her in his previous life? Had he been drawn to her as he was now?

He stopped pacing. But he wasn't drawn to her physically. Oh, but she was alluring, and that smell that permeated the air around her. He certainly understood why he would have desired her in another life, but he didn't in this one. Had he truly desired her in his past life, or had he mistaken the connection for something more? Why was there a connection at all?

Too many questions and none with answers. All he knew was that something drew him to her, and tonight he felt it deeper than he had before. Her voice had weaved its way into his consciousness like a snake coiling around its prey. It was sensual, seductive, commanding, and most of all powerful. There was magic to her voice, and in the rhapsody of hearing it, he had been lost. He wanted to do nothing more than to protect her; that was the feeling that kept washing through him, the one he had felt after their first encounter but not recognized.

Ever since she had spoken to him that day in the meeting grove, he couldn't get her out of his mind, couldn't stop himself from finding out more about her, from bumping into her whenever Sinow wasn't near. Fates, what was happening to him?

Fates. Fates, that was it. What had they said in their story about the Fates? There were three central to the story. Two brothers. That's what this was, why hadn't he seen that? Violissa had, Sinow had, but they had been immersed in the story, he now on the fringe. The part he had played in their original story was different in this one, but it was still his part. The Fates still wanted him here; they still had a role for him. Was Violissa right? Was this his second chance? Had he missed his true potential in his last life, assuming it was power driven, lost in that power, lost to the vengeance he felt was deserved?

He stopped and stared out the window. He didn't like being out of control, preferring to be the one behind the reins, driving everyone else's behaviors. He'd been doing it for centuries now, making the others see what he wanted them to see, the illusion of a weaker man, blending into the background, hiding his true self, his true power. He stood taller, to his natural height, rolling his neck and loosening his constraint on his power, letting it course through him. He was his brother's equal, hiding in the shadows until the right time came. Now should have been that time, and in another life, it had been. Could he be this person Violissa thought he was meant to be?

He didn't know what it was like to be seen for who he was, looked upon with respect. Could he be that man without the power of the throne? Without the power the book offered? Or was she fooling herself and tempting him with something that could never be? Time would tell. He would continue to give her the chance, to follow her lead. She remained curious to him, something that needed to be studied. The feelings she aroused in him needed to be understood. He would wait and watch as time was on his side, and he would use it to his advantage.

Thirty-Eight

The next few days dragged for Violissa. She felt cooped up in the Dark keep, the overbearing Darkness weighing heavy on her, as if drawing the Light from her. She and Sinow took walks, went riding, spent time at the ravine overlooking the river below, but it wasn't home, and he knew it, understanding, just as he had in their prior life that she needed to be somewhere her power could be free, where her spirit could be free.

Each day, Sinow's father would take him away, insisting he wanted to spend his final days with his son. Violissa still wasn't certain if he did it simply to give her some space or if there was a true longing to spend more time with Sinow, knowing he would be returning to the Fates soon. She spent her time as she always did, wandering the castle, happy that Sinow hadn't insisted on having Keary guard her like he had the one night. She supposed Keary kept talking him out of it and silently thanked him every time she was left to explore on her own.

She'd recently begun talking with the servants, getting to know them, getting them used to someone who wouldn't murder them for looking up without permission.

She was used to it, familiar with the rules of the Dark world, but this was a different experience. She had seen it from the other side, one where everyone adapted to the rules just as she had. This time, the rules had been in place since the start of time, and she was the one adapting to it on her own. Sinow warned her that getting them comfortable with her might risk their lives if they accidently grew too content, daring to meet a Darkbearer's eyes, or worse their king's. Servants in the castle were the only mortals to ever witness the Darkbearers without their hoods drawn, the only ones given complete permission, but the rules of respect were still to be applied. None spoke nor raised their eyes until addressed first. And these rules were never broken.

The remainder of Violissa's time was spent in the library, and as it happened over those next few days, Tynan could conveniently be found there. The interactions were brief, but he would do something each time that surprised her. Sometimes, he would bring a book from the other library, and other times, he would suggest a book or a good view from the castle grounds to take in or places to avoid. She wasn't sure what to make of it, but something had changed after that night he'd seen her sing, his demeanor different, respectful, almost protective. She continued to avoid mention of it to Sinow, feeling that this was meant for her, a healing of sorts, if that was possible. She still felt uncomfortable in his presence, but then he never lingered. Secretly, she wondered if that was the reason he made their encounters brief—out of some purpose to respect her feelings. It seemed an odd thought, but everything about the situation was odd. She could still see the look of wonder he'd had that night, his eyes wide like those of a child. There was something about the way he'd spoken to her that made her think perhaps she had been right in letting him live—perhaps there was a chance he was changing.

As time drew closer to their ascension, Violissa noticed Sinow spending less time with his father. If the time he had pulled Sinow away had been meant to break him of his fear she wasn't certain it had worked. He remained by her side most days now unless something required his attention, and it was rare that he let her wander the castle grounds without accompaniment. It irked her, but she kept her mouth shut, knowing it wasn't the time to deal with the issue. They were too close to ascension, and there were other priorities that needed attention. She would, however, put an end to it once they had both taken the throne. She'd stayed silent through one lifetime, but she was a different person this time around and would not remain silent in this life.

Two days prior to their ascension she was breaking fast with Sinow when his father shifted into the room.

"Father," Sinow said, addressing him.

"We've a problem in the town of Danfin. I would like you to accompany me."

"You're going yourself?" Sinow asked, surprised.

"It's serious. Odhran and Ristear have already been to the town. Something's sickening the villagers, and they don't know the cause. Several have died already. I was hoping your bride might join us and allow me the opportunity to see healing magic before I return to the Fates." He gave her a smile that would frighten most, but she saw the genuineness in it and returned with her own smile.

"I'd be honored to," she said, standing. "Did they tell you anything about how long the sickness has been present?"

"Only a few days according to the message we received."

Sinow drew a cloak with his magic and pulled the hood up, his father doing the same. Violissa conjured her own white cloak and pulled her curls in as she drew up the hood.

"Well, you won't stand out in a crowd of Darkbearers, will you?" his father teased.

"Black isn't really my color," she replied.

His father shifted, and Sinow grabbed her elbow. "Violissa, this is serious. It will be nothing like when you and I ruled. If my father is going, and there is any trouble, he will not hesitate to kill or have a Darkbearer do his bidding. You cannot question his authority. Understood?"

"You act as if I'm going to do something to cause trouble. Do you think I would do such a thing?"

"I know it," he said, kissing her. "Follow my shift and stay quiet unless my father addresses you. I'll be doing the same."

He shifted, and she followed, arriving in the small village, dirt paths worn through to the different buildings. A few stray dogs bolted upon their arrival, and anyone out and about had already dropped to their knees in the familiar deference she had come to know through her time with Sinow. Even after thousands of years, she had never grown accustomed to it.

Two Darkbearers came forward with a man whose head remained bowed, eyes staring at the ground.

"Tell them," one commanded.

"There is sickness," the man replied, his voice shaking. "We've lost several of our people. Others keep falling ill, and we've nothing to stop it, we've nothing to tell us where it comes from."

Violissa wanted to ask questions, to investigate, but she remembered what Sinow had said.

Sinow, I need to ask him questions, she said in enaigne, hoping he would pass the message to his father.

A moment later, the king turned toward her, asking, "What do you need to know?"

"Do I have permission to address this man myself?" she asked cautiously.

"Yes" was the only answer she received.

"Is there any connection between those who have died or those who have fallen sick?"

"No, my lady. They are from different families and some

from different ends of the village."

That didn't seem right. Typically, illness would travel through a family, marking it as a virus or disease.

"May I see the ill?"

"Begging my pardon, but do you think that wise? To expose yourself?" the man asked, eyes still pinned to the ground.

"I'll be fine, please take me to them."

She followed him to a building toward the end of the village, Sinow and the others following. As she approached one of the victims, she felt it, a distinct difference to the aura, not one of natural illness but something foul. She kneeled down next to a body that had been draped with a cloth, touching the woman's cool hand. She hadn't been dead for long. Honing her power, she dived deep into the body with her mind, feeling the frozen blood, stuck in limbo, no heart to pump it further. With her power, she pulled at it, breaking it into strands, moving aside the natural parts of it until she found the cause. Finding it, she pushed back on her feet and dropped the hand quickly.

"Poison," she mumbled.

"What?" the king asked.

Her mind was racing, and she wandered past them all, sending her senses out at the same time as she tried to determine why so many of them had been poisoned. Then she felt it. Lifting her head, she noticed the auras with her Light power. They were all sick. The entire village. The thought overwhelmed her. What could poison an entire village? She'd had cases where one or two had been poisoned, the wrong herb picked and eaten, meat that had turned too quickly. But never an entire village of this size. She stumbled out of the building and through the town, trying to find the source, sending her Light power out but finding nothing. She stopped, Sinow calling to her, *Violissa, my father is not a patient man, and I'm having trouble convincing him that you haven't lost your mind.*

I haven't. But I need another minute, she replied distantly.

Out of desperation, she threw her nature powers out, trying to sense anything out of place. The field was filled with what was left of the harvest, but that wasn't right. The season was too early. She moved closer to the field and noticed the crop had deteriorated; it was dry and brittle. Kneeling, she sifted the dirt through her hands.

"Where's the water source for this field?" she said loudly.

"Over here, my lady," the man said from a distance. He turned and pointed beyond the last house, walking toward her once given permission by the Darkbearers.

"Is it a shared water source?" she asked.

He looked at her questioningly.

"Do you source it for drinking water as well as irrigation?"

"Aye, we do."

She rushed past him and ran past the houses, past the people kneeling, knowing the others were watching, were judging, knowing Sinow was trying to excuse her strange behavior, but she didn't care. The closer she came to it, the more she felt the pain of the ground around it, the more her head hurt, her bones ached. She stopped in front of the stream that flowed from north of the town and continued south as it wound through the field then disappeared back underground. Removing the shoes she had worn out of respect, she lifted her skirts and stepped into the water, the cool feel of it comforting until the sting of the poison hit her. She closed her eyes, listening to the flow of the water, the flow of the poison, following it with her senses up through the town and past the hills where it stopped a few miles away. Then she stooped down, running her hand through the water, feeling the familiarity of what should be there mixed with the corrupt feel of what shouldn't. She let her nature power pry further into the corruption until she found the culprit.

Finally, she walked back out of the stream, her dress and feet drying as her magic flowed over them. She left her shoes behind, knowing she needed her feet free for what was to come. She aimed her sight at Sinow and his father, meaning to tell them what she'd discovered once she reached them. She was sidetracked when she heard murmuring to her left.

"It's her, daughter, it's her. She's here. The princess. A Lightbearer here, just as your mother always said there would be."

"Father, calm down," she heard, detecting the strain in the woman's voice as she held him down.

Violissa also detected the slight disillusion in his brain, the sign of his nearing death. Before she could react, he broke free from his daughter and ran toward her. She felt the Dark magic even before it hit as the Darkbearers reacted. Sinow knew better, but they were under his father's rule, and this was unacceptable. The man screamed in pain as the power hit him, bending him over so that he crumpled into a ball.

"Granda!" a small girl screamed as her father held her down.

Violissa's hand flew to her mouth at the sight, and she began to run toward the man.

Violissa! Sinow commanded. She halted in her tracks, knowing things were on edge, that her next move could cost both her and this man dearly.

As Sinow had stood and watched Violissa kneel in the water, he'd been mesmerized by her. Her golden curls flowed around her, some resting gently in the stream as she had stooped down to let her fingers run through the water.

What is she doing? his father had asked, irritation evident in his voice.

Being Violissa, he'd replied.

She'd discovered something, he knew enough to see that. The way she had run to the stream told him that. It was something in the water source. Her head had lifted and stared north then she'd risen from the water, her clothes and skin drying as she stepped out. She'd looked directly to where he and his father stood, intent on explaining when they were all caught off guard. Her hood down, someone had noticed her, realizing who she was. There was no hiding it, she was light in the darkness of their world, her golden hair, her emerald eyes too unique to go unnoticed.

In an instant, everything changed. Sinow heard the man's words then felt the Dark magic in the air as it hit him, punishing him for a crime that would mean death in their land. His eyes, however, never left Violissa's face, watching as it filled with horror then determination. He knew what she would do and knew what it would mean if she attempted to do it.

Violissa! he'd commanded, knowing she wanted to run to the man and heal him.

She'd stopped, but he knew that look in her eyes, they had darkened slightly, whether it was in response to what she saw as an injustice or to being commanded, he couldn't say. Now, as she defiantly stared back at him, he attempted to remind her that the rules here were no longer as they were when they had reigned in their last life.

Violissa, don't. Remember where you are. No one approaches a Darkbearer.

She didn't need to respond; her face said it all. She stood taller, her Light power subtle but enough to surround her in an aura that told of her power. Her eyes held his as if waiting for him to change the situation, to do what she needed him to do.

"Dammit," he muttered. He turned to his father who spoke before he had the chance.

"Do not, son. This is our realm. She knows the rules."

"Aye, but those rules apply to us, sire. They do not apply to her. She is not a Darkbearer. Her people, our people are able to approach her. She welcomes them, she talks with them, touches them as they are allowed to do so to her."

"Our people approach an immortal?"

"They approach their queen. Violissa needs the people as

much as the people need her," he said, smiling at the memory of those words first being told to him. "It is who she is, and she will be their queen in a matter of days."

"You allow this?"

"I would be in grave trouble if I did not. You have yet to see her Elvin side in full force, Father."

"Do the same exceptions pertain to you and your Council?"

"No, the law remains. I do not interact with them. I watch from afar, and they know the consequence of approaching any of us, particularly me."

He heard his father sigh. "A different world indeed."

"Stand back," he commanded to Ristear. "No one approaches a Darkbearer, but it would seem the Light have different laws regarding their presence." Then he looked to Violissa. "You may heal him as he approached you and not one of us. But know this, if anyone dares beak law with a Darkbearer, there will be swift punishment."

"Thank you," Sinow heard her say then she ran over to the old man. A small child broke free from her mother and ran to them. Ristear started to react again, but Sinow's father raised his hand to stop him.

"Sire?" Ristear asked, walking back to them.

"Sinow is right. She will be queen in a few days' time. We must adapt as he has. The realm is his now."

By now, the mortals had realized they were not only in the presence of the future Light queen but also of the king and prince. Murmurs could be heard, and several of them backed away further in fear.

Violissa bowed slightly in respect then quickly kneeled next to the man, moving the small girl aside so she could heal him. Sinow felt her Light power increase then felt his father's power rise in response. He watched as the man stirred, the pain Ristear had left in him diminishing. Slowly, he sat up, his granddaughter helping him.

"You are the Light queen," he said weakly in a tone of awe.

"I will be soon. Now you should know better than to risk the wrath of a Darkbearer, kind sir, regardless of whom you see. You could have been killed." She looked at the child. "And you as well. Listen to your mother next time, or I won't be here to save you."

She knows our laws well and enforces them? his father said.

Aye, we have a mutual understanding. I respect her powers as she respects mine. The same goes for our laws.

He listened as she continued to speak with the man.

"My Leeza wanted nothing more than to see this day. She was a true believer in the prophecy, carried down through the generations of her family."

"Leeza? Was she your wife?"

"Aye, that she was. She couldn't hold on though. We lost her three moons ago. The last thing she told me was to keep living so that I could see the day the realms were united."

Violissa's smile brightened, the purity of it reflected in the man's face, his eyes wide with astonishment.

"You will have done just that in a few days' time. Now, I must go and fix this sickness, or there will be more of you who do not make it to that day."

She rose, but he grabbed her wrist, urging her to kneel beside him again. Sinow felt his father's power flare at the action. Violissa, not fazed by it, dropped back to his level.

"My Leeza would sing a song to me. She learned it from her mother who learned it from hers. The song was taught to her line by a Cirillian slave her family once owned."

Violissa's back straightened at the word slave, and Sinow could feel her indignity at the thought, but slavery had been outlawed by his father well before he had been born. Those slaves left in the realm returned to the Lightbearers as part of the treaty.

"Your wife sang? I didn't realize Tenebrons sang."

The man drew closer to her, and Sinow heard him whisper, "The Darkbearers frown upon it, but song can be found when you look for it."

"I bet she sounded quite lovely."

"Ha! It was awful, the Fates likely cringed. But it came from the heart. She always wanted to hear you sing. Said you had the voice of the Fates."

"It's an exaggeration," Violissa said, starting to rise again. She bent down and kissed the girl on the head. "Take care of your grandfather and remember to follow the laws."

As she walked away, the old man said, "Would you sing a song? Her spirit is still here, out among the fields. I feel her stir sometimes, and I know it would settle her."

Violissa stopped, raising her head to look at Sinow then turning back to the man. *What is she doing?* he wondered. She couldn't be contemplating granting his wish.

"What did she sing?" she asked. Sinow couldn't believe she was considering it.

The man named a song with which Sinow was unfamiliar.

"I know that song, it's a beautiful song. One my people still sing today. I suppose—"

"That's enough, Violissa," he said, stepping away from his father and walking angrily toward her, his hood falling with the impact of his steps. He ignored the rush of fear he felt around them, savoring it as it fed his power. He knew his father wouldn't be happy with the open display, but he cared naught, knowing he needed to stop her. He'd heard enough. She met him halfway, a puzzled expression on her face.

"You cannot sing here, not yet," he commanded, keeping his voice low.

She stared at him, her eyes growing a deeper green, her face reflecting her annoyance at having been commanded by him. *You will need to give me a good reason, or I will simply defy your tone, Sinow.*

He wanted to laugh but suppressed it and instead moved closer to her, saying softly. "You can't sing to my people. Your voice is sacred, Violissa. You told me long ago that it is forbidden for you to sing outside of your realm. I remember distinctly sitting in the meeting ground and wondering at the absurdity of it. You cannot sing here, not yet, not until the realms are united, and my people are yours as well."

She smiled, her eyes filling with love. "I sang in the Banished Realm, Sinow. I sang after we freed our realms. I've always done so."

"Yes, but that was our last life," he whispered. "That was a thousand years after our world was in chaos. The norms of both our realms no longer applied. The situation was different. Now, you would be breaking a vow asked of you by your people."

"It's a foolish vow, isn't it?" she said playfully.

"I don't see why she can't sing now, even if her people say they can be the only ones to hear her voice. Although singing at this moment seems quite out of place," his father said quietly upon approaching them. "I am quite intrigued to hear it now though."

"But, Father—"

"Our people will be hers upon your ascensions. You've already united, so in essence they're already her people. And from what I've seen here, she will be exactly what our people need."

"And it will help me heal the people and the land, Sinow. You know that."

"You don't need song to use your nature power."

"No, but I've yet to ascend, and my powers are not as strong now. The song will enhance what I do have."

"Really?" his father said. "How fascinating."

Sinow ran his hand through his hair, pulling his hood back up after realizing he'd neglected to do so. "Fine. I take it you found what's making them sick?"

"The problem is in the water," she said. "It's been poisoned. The water is the source of nourishment for the crops and the people."

"Poisoned?" his father said, his Dark power rising again.

"Yes. I believe the source is further up where the river splits off to the stream. I can't tell exactly where."

"Do you know what's poisoning it?" Sinow asked.

"Nibas."

"Nibas?" his father asked. "But that grows nowhere near this part of the realm. It's only found past the mountain range to the northwest corner of the realm."

Nibas was an herb that was innocent in its natural form but if ground to a powder was lethal. Its strength was so feared that it had been uprooted and burned in most of the realm except the desolate northwestern corner. One plant's essence was enough to kill twenty men.

"This was deliberate," he said.

Odhran and Ristear came closer, leading the village head, called in enaigne by his father.

"What lies north of the water?" Sinow's father asked the man.

"Nothing for a few miles," he replied, his head dropped, eyes to the ground.

"What about where the river forks to the stream?" Violissa asked.

"That would be Liam's place."

"Liam? He lives that far outside the village?" Sinow asked.

"Aye, his family has lived there for centuries. Owns a farm, never comes here..." he paused, thinking. "Well, never did, but a few weeks ago he came, asking to expand his crops into the village crops. We told him he had no right to our land and sent him home."

"And you haven't seen him since?" his father asked.

"No."

His father was quiet then looked at Odhran and Ristear. "You both know what to do."

They shifted, on the hunt for the culprit and ready to dole out a punishment fitting the crime.

"Thank you. You've been very helpful, but you may go now."

The man bowed further and backed away from them. "Violissa, can you fix this? Can you heal them?"

"Yes."

"And singing a song for that man will help you?"

"Yes. I can heal them all and restore the water source to its original purity."

"Then do it. My people need to be healed."

With a quick glance to Sinow, she returned to the man and his granddaughter.

I do believe you're in for quite a treat, Father.

I'd best be, singing is not good for our image, Sinow. Nor is your reaction to Violissa. Dropping your hood in front of mortals? Best not to forget who you are and let your emotions rule for you. You are not like her, Sinow. You are Dark blood, you rule with the Darkness.

He knew that more than anyone, the memories reminding him that the Darkness hadn't been enough to tame those emotions in their past life.

Violissa leaned down to the girl and said, "Do you know the words to the song?"

"Yes," she said softly.

"I want you to start it, and when you do, don't be surprised by your voice," she whispered. He'd forgotten that her voice brought out the beauty in her people's voices, enhancing them. He didn't remember his people singing and wondered if the same would apply to them. He found out within moments as the girl began to sing. Her voice wasn't beautiful, his people not singers like the Cirillians, but it was nice, and from her startled expression, it must have been a great improvement.

As she sang the first verse, Violissa joined her, the girl's voice gaining another element of what was almost beauty. The sound of Violissa's voice stirred his people, eyes peered up, risking the wrath of Sinow and his father just to see her. He watched as she did the same thing he'd seen her do countless times, each time as awe inspiring as the first, her voice weaving the magic that ingrained her place in their people's heart. She reached her hand out and drew it over the child's hair, flowers following gently through it. Then she rose, turning to the grandfather, whose eyes had teared. Breaking for a moment, she leaned over and kissed his cheek then continued her song, walking away from them and toward the stream. With each step she took, the ground awoke, flowers springing in her wake, grass brightening, stretching to touch her. The wind blew gently, her cape stirring until it slipped from her body. She drew her arms out, her face looking upward, peaceful, hauntingly beautiful. As if in answer, clouds cleared, the sun streaming down to touch her hair with golden light that sparkled upon it. The nearer she came to the water the more it churned until finally it rose from its bed to greet her, an arch that stretched and leaned waiting for her.

"Amazing," his father said.

"Yes, she is."

The water flowed from its arch and wrapped around her, her fingers running through it as it found its way back to its home, a strange fog left in its wake.

"What in the Fates?" Ristear muttered, having returned from his work.

"That's the poison?" Odhran asked.

The fog encased her, and for a moment, they could only hear her. Then it funneled, rising upward and changing, cleansed, renewed as it transformed into tiny petals that the wind picked up to travel throughout the village. Her voice strengthened, her eyes brightening as he felt her call her Light power. A wave of healing magic weaved through the village, passing through each of the mortals, lifting the poison from them and healing those it had already affected. As the blue of her Light magic faded, she dropped her body, crouching on the ground, and digging her fingers deep into the ground. The familiar green of her nature magic rolled across the land, healing it, the crops rising, rich and healthy. Standing, she looked to the sky, her eyes closed, and finished her last note, its power weaving through Sinow's heart as he knew it was doing to everyone. The song stopped, and her eyes opened, their color a brilliant emerald that spilled out around her.

"Showing off again?" he heard Keary behind him.

He turned to see several of the Council around them.

"Heard the commotion and couldn't help but bring a few to see. It's not every day we get to see a Light queen at work."

His father composed himself as Violissa approached them, her smile as bright as her eyes.

"Impressive," he said. "Is it cleansed?"

"Aye," she returned, her voice still musical.

He turned to Odhran and Ristear. "Punishment has been served?"

He noticed Violissa flinch at the blood that still shone on their capes.

"Yes, my liege. The mortal and his two sons confessed. All three will no longer be of any problem."

Sinow knew what that meant, and from Violissa's look, she did as well. Dark power was there to protect and punish; she knew all three were dead, likely having suffered greatly. He was surprised they hadn't saved one to take to the dungeons but perhaps they had been distracted by Violissa's magic.

"Good. The village may take their land and their belongings. It is time to return home."

He shifted, with all following but Ristear who spoke to the village head.

"Not a man of many words, is he?" Violissa asked Sinow.

"Just discovering that?"

She laughed then looked back toward the mortals.

"Go, my father won't mind."

"You'll stay here with me?" she asked, a slight sadness in her eyes.

He wanted to, the fear screaming for him to stay. "No, I will return with the others. You know how to get back. Do not tarry long though."

Tynan was not a threat out here. The only time he ever visited a town was to find a bedmate.

She smiled. "I won't. I'd really like to kiss you right now, but that would be pushing it, wouldn't it?"

"Ha, yes, it would."

He watched as she made her way back to the old man and his granddaughter. Ristear shifted, and Sinow followed, knowing Violissa would be here for hours, getting to know the people and letting them see for the first time the blessing the prophecy had truly given them.

Upon her return, Violissa shifted to where she sensed Sinow. Relief filled his eyes the moment he saw her, but he covered it quickly, pulling her in tight against him and kissing her.

"Miss me?" she said seductively.

"Too much," he responded, kissing her again.

"Ahem," she heard from behind him.

"Did you forget to warn me that someone was with you?" she asked.

"I forgot someone was with me," he answered.

"Thanks. That makes me feel really important," Keary responded.

She laughed then pulled out of Sinow's arms. "Sorry, Keary," she said, still laughing.

"I'm not," Sinow joked. "That could have continued to be a nice moment for me."

It was only then that she saw they were outside on the front steps of the castle. "You two were outside? Without me persuading you?"

"You know, just because we're Darkbearers doesn't mean we live constantly in the dark innards of our keep like vampires,

Violissa," Keary answered.

"This is true. We actually do get outdoors at times."

"And what were you doing in said outdoors this time?"

"Reminiscing a bit," Sinow answered, surprising her.

"We lived a long life before it was started again," Keary said. "There are some memories that deserve being relived."

"Living in the past can be detrimental to one's future," she heard Sinow's father say as he walked down the steps toward them. "You should keep that in mind, son, and Keary, you should never forget to remind him of that fact."

"Noted, Father, thank you."

"I'd like a few minutes alone with your future queen."

"But she just returned," Sinow replied.

"And she will join you shortly. I will only take a few moments. I'd like to have a word with her. As you have her company for the rest of eternity, I believe you can spare her for a short time."

Violissa squeezed Sinow's arm. "I'll join you shortly." *In our room,* she continued silently.

That I can agree with, he replied, kissing her quickly. He shifted, Keary following after a quick bow to the king.

"My son does not like to leave your side, my dear," his father said, sitting down on the stone steps and patting the seat next to him, signaling for her to sit. She took his signal and sat, her skirts settling around her.

"No, he does not." She sighed. "I thought perhaps it would change, but it hasn't."

"Fear is weakness—"

"And a Dark king has no weakness," she finished for him.

"Ah, you have been trained well."

"You don't stay happily married to a Dark king for nearly six thousand years without knowing that." She looked down at her hands. "It is not the Dark king who holds the fear but the man within."

"The man and the king are one. There should be no

difference."

"But Sinow is different, you know this. He has me, and that keeps the man in him separate."

"Aye, he has always been different. I saw that from the beginning." He stopped talking for a moment, staring out at the grounds. "He will be a good king, and he has you to help guide him, to keep him balanced. I see that now. You know, when they first came to me, telling me that Kathala was carrying the chosen child, I didn't believe them. I doubted, but when I told her, she said, 'Drostan he is special, listen to them.' I trusted her, and when I first felt his power, still small in her womb, I knew she had been correct."

"What was she like, Sinow's mother?" she asked, curious.

"She was beautiful. Not to your level of beauty, but she stood out amongst any other woman, and she had a smile that could wind its way into your heart."

Violissa smiled at the thought.

"I loved her, everything about her. Even when she discovered she was pregnant, she didn't grow fearful. She was exuberant, wondrous about the experience. There was goodness in her that I believe she passed on to Sinow, a kindness that spread from her as it does you. She would have liked you."

"I'm sure I would have liked her. She sounds like a wonderful woman."

"Aye, she was up to the last moment. Even in the pain of bearing Sinow she remained that way. When most women would have cursed him for taking their life, she willingly gave it up with nothing but love for him."

"But you had a second chance for love?" she dared ask, curious about the difference between Sinow's mother and Tynan's.

"That I did, lucky enough to have it twice. Although I did find Tabitha before I discovered Kathala, I had wondered briefly if she was the one to carry my son, but never did I have that feeling my father had told me of, the pull that distinctly named her my mate. It wasn't until she introduced me to her sister that I realized it wasn't Tabitha but Kathala who would bear him."

"Wait, they were sisters?" she asked, the world collapsing around her with the shock.

"Aye, that they were. Tabitha worked here at the castle, so she was here most days. Her family lived in the closest village, and she went home at times. It was during one of those times that I ... well, let's just say I felt the urge to see her."

Violissa blushed, knowing why he'd gone to the village.

"I sent one of my Council in to retrieve her, and she foolishly brought her sister along to meet me. As if I were some mortal man courting her. I should have punished her there and then, but upon seeing Kathala, I felt the pull. I knew she was my mate in that instant."

"They were sisters," she said again. It all made sense why Tynan's mother would be so angry about being passed over by the king. Why she would hold a grudge. It also explained why Sinow and Tynan were so alike. Not only did they share king's blood, but they shared the same blood from their mothers' sides. They were in essence, true brothers, not half-brothers. "And Tabitha hated you for taking Kathala over her."

"No. Where did you hear that?" he said, surprising her again.

"I just assumed she wouldn't like being passed over."

"It is true she wasn't happy, but she loved her sister and put her sister's happiness ahead of hers. In some morbid way, I suppose she knew her sister's life would end at the birth of our son and that I would return to her. As it happened, I did. I gave her time to mourn Kathala as I gave myself time, and when I knew that I missed Tabitha, I called for her. I had no idea she would bear Tynan." His tone changed at the mention of Tynan as if he resented his birth, resented the fact that he had stolen his second chance at love. "He took her away too soon."

"Does he know? Do either of them know their mothers were sisters?"

"No, I chose to keep it from them. In the end, both were

dead, what did it matter?"

They didn't know the connection, but would it have mattered to them? She doubted it, but in the grand scheme of things, it did. Still curious, she said, "Sinow told me she went mad."

"She did. She had the same demeanor as Kathala; she was sweet, caring, had the same welcoming smile. Something changed when she became pregnant, Tynan's blood corrupted her, drove her mad."

"She was kind?"

"They both were. When I married Tabitha, she took right to Sinow. She was his aunt after all. The first time a Dark prince ever had family other than his father. It was only after she carried Tynan that her mind went."

"That's when you had to remove her from Sinow."

"Aye, she tried to hurt him, and he protected himself. He was young, his powers too strong for him at that age, stronger than any prince before him in fact. He didn't know how to control them at the time, and he nearly killed her. I couldn't punish him for protecting himself, and I couldn't punish the woman carrying my child for trying to hurt him. So, we did the only thing we knew, we had her locked away until Tynan's birth. If I'd known then what I know now, I would have killed her then."

"You would have killed her and Tynan?"

"Tynan was an abomination. At first, I thought it was a blessing, two sons, the first Dark king ever to produce two heirs. But then he was weak, his powers minimal compared to Sinow's. He spent his time locked away in the library, preferring to study rather than practice using his magic, what little he had. I despised him from the moment he was born, so small and puny, a drain on the Council and on Sinow."

"But they were friends I thought."

"I suppose they were when they were younger. Sinow always stuck up for him. If I went to punish him, Sinow would defy me and take the punishment for him. I punished them both to teach him not to disobey me. He followed Sinow around like a lost puppy, no confidence, no pride like a Dark prince should have. Finally, I separated them. I didn't want my heir to be influenced by his weaker half."

"You separated them," she mumbled. "You made the first step on the path just as my parents did. All of you players in the game All of you pawns just as we were."

He looked at her, studying her. "You speak of the Fates as if they planned all of this. As if you know from experience..." he drifted off. "But you do, don't you?"

"We know more than you could ever imagine. Each of us had our own part to play, even Tynan."

"That's why you let him live. Why you gave him the second chance. You still feel there's a part for him even after all he's done."

She thought about what he'd said. She'd acted on instinct, something that told her he shared their second chance, something that said his part wasn't complete.

"Yes."

"I've lived a long life, a good life, but I have my regrets about certain things I've chosen to do in that time. Regrets can sometimes haunt not only you but those around you. Sinow is already haunted by regret. He lives with a fear that is fueled by that regret. Don't let this decision become something that comes to haunt you as well."

He stood and stretched, then leaned down and kissed her head. "You will be a good queen, Violissa. I'm disappointed I won't live to see what the two of you will become. The potential is unimaginable." She stood, and he took her hand. "You bring out the good in my son, the part of him that will make him the kind of king he's meant to be. Don't let his fear bury him, don't let it burden you through another lifetime."

In the wake of his shift, she thought of what he had said. Regret, Sinow's fear was fueled by regret. It was a concept she'd never thought about. He regretted leaving her that day, leaving an opening for Tynan. He regretted not being able to save her, to protect her. That regret had indeed led to his fear upon her return. She thought about all she'd gone through in that time. It wasn't burdened by regret but instead by a self-awareness, that if she could survive that experience, if she could come out of it stronger, more self-assured than when she'd entered, then she could survive anything. Sinow had simply never taken the time to see that, to respect the power of it.

Sighing, she looked back at the keep, feeling his eyes upon her, knowing he would be out at her side within moments. They'd only had their memories back for less than a moon and already, his demons had settled in. He had left her in the village earlier, however, a decision that had surprised her. But then, she was amongst the people, someplace Tynan would never care to be. Tynan was in the castle where Sinow could keep an eye on him. What freedom she may have thought he'd given her was still far from what it needed to be for them to live this second life as they were meant to.

Thirty-Nine

The day had been a long one. Sinow's father had forced him to spar, keeping him from Violissa for longer than Sinow liked. He knew what his father was up to, purposely keeping him busy, forcing his separation from her, forcing the fear to abate. It hadn't worked; the fear had remained. He had washed up upon returning and felt for Violissa, sensing her somewhere in the east wing. Likely in the library. He'd asked her to stay within the confines of the castle while he was away, and she had respected his request even though he knew how hard it was for her to stay cooped up. Stretching his muscles, he decided to walk to her rather than shift. He needed to loosen up, relax from being under the influence of his Dark power for so many hours. Walking closer to the library, he was surprised to hear Violissa talking to someone and alarmed to hear Tynan's voice respond to her. It sounded like a civil conversation, which did nothing to allay his fear and everything to inflame his ire.

Refraining from barging into the library only due to Violissa's calm demeanor, he peered around the door, unseen by either of them.

They were talking, Violissa holding a book in her hand.

"Thank you, Tynan. That was nice of you to think of me. I'm sure I'll find it engaging."

"I'm not sure why it was in our library. It was clearly written by a Lightbearer or someone who had up close interaction with the Elvin."

"Tynan," she said, looking up from the book, "why are you still studying the Elvin? You're not still—"

"No, I told you, Violissa. I've given up the search."

"And how can I truly trust you on that, Tynan?"

He looked down at his hands as if contemplating something, and then moved them atop each other. Sinow could feel the magic coming from his brother. When Tynan's hands separated, a weathered book appeared. Sinow recognized it, his future self having once held that book in his hands. It had been his grandfather's, the clue to finding the entrance to the Lost Realm. His heart rushed, but he kept himself hidden, curious to see what would happen.

"Here. This book holds the key to finding the Lost Realm and the book. It was my grandfather's, at least it has his writing in it, his notes on finding it. Take it," he said, handing the book to Violissa.

"Why?"

"Second chances, right? Perhaps you were correct, Violissa. Maybe there is a different path for all of us."

"Maybe," she said quietly.

"Can I ask you something?"

"Sure," she answered.

"If you could ask the Fates to remove your memories like they did mine, if you could take them all away and start it over, thinking none of it had ever happened, would you?"

She was quiet for a few moments and then, to Sinow's

surprise, she looked directly in Tynan's eyes, no fear, no reaction, and said, "No, I wouldn't change a thing."

As if anticipating another answer, Tynan asked, "But why? If the things I did were so terrible, why would you want to keep those memories?"

To keep an eye on you, Sinow expected her to say, but then realized those were his thoughts, not hers.

"We were different people back then, young and naïve. The things Sinow and I went through are the things that made us who we are today. They shaped us. If you hadn't cast me to the human realm, we wouldn't have fought for each other through a thousand years of lives, we wouldn't have come to realize how deeply we love each other, just how strong our love really is. We came out of that experience changed people. Having to rebuild the realms, to recreate our world toughened us yet broadened both of our views. It gave us insight into each other we never would have had." She paused momentarily.

"And if you hadn't taken me, hadn't done the horrible things you did, I would not be who I am today. That trauma shaped me in ways you could never imagine, in ways even Sinow doesn't recognize. I am who I am because of that experience. I found my people, my Elvin family, discovered a world I thought no longer existed, I found my parents, I found myself. You see, life gives us lessons whether we see them that way or not. The Fates may have played with us, they may have laid this path to torture us, but they really," her voice quivered as she took a breath, her eyes growing wide as the thought hit her, "they really completed us."

Tynan didn't respond, taking a moment to let her words sink in as Sinow was doing. She wouldn't change anything? Even the torture, the pain she endured? His mind couldn't grasp it because he would have given anything to take that moment back, to not let her go by herself that day. He would have turned time back in a heartbeat.

"You have an odd way of looking at things, Violissa."

"So I've been told."

"I should go, I've lingered too long. Enjoy the books."

"Tynan," she said, stopping him, "are you still curious?"

He laughed softly. "No, intrigued perhaps but no longer curious. More like settled."

With that, he shifted, leaving her alone in the library. Sinow shifted as well, not wanting her to know he'd been there, that he'd heard the conversation. He left the castle, shifting to his spot overlooking the ravine, pacing the moment he landed. The conversation had been civil, as if the two had spoken to each other more than just this one time. How could that be though? Why wouldn't she have told him? Why would she purposely leave a detail like that out?

The more he thought about it, the angrier he became. He knew he couldn't go back, he wasn't ready to broach the subject yet, so he stayed away until he was forced to return when she called for him to find out why he wasn't sitting down for dinner with her. Replying that he'd be there shortly, he ignored her questioning, *Is everything all right?*

He shifted back to the castle and joined Violissa and his father, both already seated. Avoiding her questioning look, he tried to focus on his father's talking, and she, clearly reading his mood, led his father into a discussion about something trivial. Eventually though, she'd had enough of his silence and called him out.

"What is it, Sinow? Something's bothering you," she said, worry in her voice.

"Now is not the time," he answered curtly, the response only encouraging her to push for an answer.

"Have I done something? You don't hide it well when you're irritated, Sinow."

"She's right, son. I've noticed it since you arrived. What's on your mind?"

Now, both of them were hounding him. He slammed his fork down, the move causing the table to shake and Violissa to jump.

"I asked you to leave it, Violissa," he said as her eyes darkened with his tone. "But you both pushed. I saw you today with Tynan."

She couldn't hide the shock on her face, the guilt that flashed.

"Why? After all you went through? Why would you be alone with him? Why would you even talk to him? And why would you hide it from me?"

His father stayed silent, knowing this wasn't his argument, that he was merely a witness.

"Because I knew you would react this way."

"Of course, I would react this way. How else am I supposed to act? You're spending time with the man who stole you, who hurt you! Am I supposed to be happy about that?" he yelled.

"You're overreacting, Sinow. It was innocent, and he's not the same person as he was then."

"Not the same person? Are you insane? He's deceiving you. He lies, he tricks, he connives. You are playing into his hands again."

She lowered her silverware and glared at him, but he continued. "You are not to go near him again."

"What?"

He looked down at his food and stabbed a piece of meat with his fork.

"You will not bind me like you did before."

He jerked his head up.

"I can talk to him any time I like, and you will not stop me."

"Don't push me, Violissa. I won't allow you to get hurt again, I won't allow him to take you. You act like you have no idea what he's capable of. Are you that naïve?"

She stood abruptly, throwing her chair back, her eyes turning a rich sage. "I have more idea than you ever cared to discover. I am the only one who has a right to decide whether I talk to Tynan, whether I allow him in my presence. You have no right, you have no right to even think you do. I am the one he kidnapped, I am the one he beat, the one he abused, the one he raped," her voice cracked, and his heart dropped. "Don't you ever assume to know more about what he can do than I. And don't you ever put your fear before my rights again."

She turned and stormed out of the dining room, her skirts emphasizing the anger in her steps. He sat, too stunned to move. What had just happened? What had he done?

"It would seem your wife has finally spoken," his father said quietly.

Sinow looked at him, unsure what to say.

"You've put your needs in this matter ahead of hers for too long, Sinow. Everyone has their breaking point, and she just had hers. It's time to listen to her, it's time."

"I don't—"

"Go after her, Sinow. She loves you, I promise you she'll forgive you as long as you learn to forgive yourself. Your past is your past, nothing can change that, but given all she went through, she came out of it in far better shape than you."

He left the dining room, feeling for her, sensing her presence. Walking instead of shifting, his mind ran through their argument. They'd never truly had one. The last time he could remember was in the Banished Realm. Another moment in time marred by his fear and by what he saw now as his underestimation of her. Had he always underestimated her, always putting his fear first? Raking his hands through his hair, he thought about what she'd said. She was right; while he'd gone through his own struggles in her absence, she had gone through the physical ones. She had endured the true pain, the abuse. His thoughts slipped back to the words she'd spoken to Tynan. How her experiences had made her the person she was today, how they had defined her. Had he ever taken the time to see her perspective or had he only thought of himself, only thinking of his own pain through it all? This was their second chance as she called it. Maybe it was time for him to start treating it as such.

He found her sitting on the roof outside their room.

"The balcony not enough for you?" he asked, sitting next to her.

She remained silent, staring out at the moons.

"Vi, I'm sorry."

She turned and looked at him, her eyes a crystal green. "Will we ever move past this, Sinow? In nearly six thousand years, we couldn't. Will we this time around?"

He sighed, bringing his hand out to tuck her curl back. "I asked too much that day, Vi." He looked out at the night sky. "I should have stopped myself. I should have put your needs before mine, but it had been so hard imagining what you'd gone through that having you speak the words, having to confront the reality of it was too much for me." His eyes dropped to his hands. "I did this to us. I made the choice for both of us."

Her hand moved to his, and her head rested on his shoulder. "What is it you always say when I blame myself for our crooked path? We both made that choice. You asked, but I accepted. We both acquiesced, lost in what we needed in that moment, and afterwards, by then, it was too late to turn back."

He kissed her head. "You said the Fates have given us all a second chance. I think it's time to use it wisely. Let's go back to that moment, Vi."

She brought her head up and looked at him curiously.

"Tell me what you should have told me that day."

Her eyes grew damp, and she brought her hand up, running her fingers along his cheek, a small smile on her lips. "Are you sure you're ready?"

"I should have been ready centuries ago."

And so, he listened as she spoke. Listening to her story for the first time. He heard the horrors, the validation of all he had imagined was happening to her, of all the things Tynan had done, but then he discovered something he hadn't expected. The story of her strength. The strength she'd had in even the direst of situations to persevere, to find her way home.

To stand up to Tynan, to stand up for her people even when the odds were against her. He heard stories of the people who helped her, never bothering to ask in the past for fear of hearing her pain. In that space, he saw her as he never had before but should have: strong, independent, determined, capable. She didn't need his protection, didn't need his fear. The only thing she had needed from him was his love and the knowledge that it was always there for her. With each word, his love for her grew as did his pride, pride he had always felt but never acknowledged.

When she spoke her last word, the story finished as it should have been all those centuries before, she sat, quietly waiting for his response. He could sense her nervousness, likely wondering if his fear would increase, if his anger would rise. He looked into her emerald eyes sparkling in the light of the moons and did what he should have that day. He took her in his arms and kissed her, letting go of the fear, of the anger, letting go of it all just as she had done when she'd soaked her feelings into the nightmare tree in the human world. Feeling the change, her lips curved to a smile, and she kissed him back, relaxing into him. Finally, she dropped her head and leaned it against his chest.

Kissing her hair, he said, "I'm sorry I never took the time to listen, to understand."

"Shhh," she replied. "We both needed something that day, Sinow. You took my silence, and I took your strength. We did what we had to— survive in the moment."

He lifted her face. "That moment lasted too long, and I promise you I will not cage you in this life."

She smiled. "You didn't cage me, Sinow."

"I bound your wings so that you lost your free spirit, that part of you that I failed to realize gives you the strength I never saw."

Kissing him again, she said, "I love you, Sinow. I always have, and I always will."

"I love you, Vi, and that will never change."

"It's the one thing that's unbreakable," she said. "The one constant that we have and the thing that drove me to survive."

"No, Vi. You drove yourself, you found the strength in yourself, your true power. I had nothing to do with it."

"You don't see it, do you? Your love is what gives me my strength. Without it, I don't know that I could have gone on to face another day. There were times when it was the only thing that kept me sane, the only thing that kept me alive."

He hadn't seen it that way, but now that she'd said it, he realized it had been the same for him. His love for her was the driving force behind everything he had done in the past and everything he would continue to do. It had driven him to chase her through lifetimes in the human realm and kept him from sliding into the insanity of his Dark power when Tynan had taken her.

He kissed her again, this time passion filling the kiss, his need for her rising as hers rose to meet it. Breathless, she drew back from him, resting her hand upon his chest.

"Are you planning to make love to me out here, or should we move inside so we don't fall off the roof?" Violissa asked. "We may be unbreakable, but that fall would still hurt."

Laughing, Sinow stood and helped her up. "Inside is the better option." Then he pulled her in against him and shifted them to their room where they made love, finally free of the chains of their past that had tethered them and the fear that had encapsulated it.

The next morning upon waking, Violissa looked up at Sinow, taking in his beauty as she often did, thanking the Fates for him. She kissed his cheek and rose, not wanting to wake him. The events of the previous night ran through her head. It had felt good to finally talk it through, a weight now lifted from her shoulders, one she hadn't realized was there, like a veil lifting from the world. She felt free for the first time in ages. Looking out from the bedroom balcony, she sent her vision far beyond where the normal eye could see and set her sight northward. Something dawned on her. Today was the ascension. They'd been through the preparation again, dealt with their expected pre-ascension jitters, talked through most of the details, but as she looked out upon the realm, far into the Sacred Groves, she felt a pull, something calling her.

Lost in thought, she jumped when Sinow came up behind her, wrapping his arm around her waist and bringing his hand up to brush her hair back from her neck, his lips grazing it.

"Jumpy this morning?" he asked playfully.

"A little too far lost in my mind," she replied. "Sinow?"

"Yes."

"What if we aren't meant to follow the same pattern with our ascension as we did in the past?"

He stopped kissing her neck and sighed. "Do I want to know what you mean?"

She laughed. "Maybe not. I'm not sure I mean anything, just wondering if it should all be done the same way."

"But it won't be the same. We've made changes. You'll be ascending without your people this time and with all of my Council attending to witness, and your Council will all witness mine."

"That's not what I mean," she said, turning to face him. "What if we're missing something?"

"With your instinct, I find it doubtful anything would be missed."

She looked back out, something nudging her but nothing she could pinpoint. "Maybe you're right, maybe it's nothing."

"Violissa, your intuition is usually right," he said, worry in his voice.

"It was nothing," she said, trying to sound confident.

Normally, if she had a feeling about something, she had some clarity, but there was nothing this time, just a feeling. "Whatever it is, if it is something, then I'll figure it out in time."

He eyed her suspiciously. "Are you trying to convince me or yourself?"

Smiling, she leaned in and kissed him. "Let's get ready. We've a big day ahead."

They had agreed to separate until mid-day when her ascension would take place, she returning to Cirillia and he remaining in Tenebron. Surprisingly, he seemed relaxed about letting her go, no worry evident when she kissed him goodbye. Had their talk really helped or was it simply that there was no way for Tynan to get through the boundary to Cirillia? She wanted to believe it was the first option, but she wasn't certain she could truly say so.

Returning to Cirillia had made her fully aware of the connection they now shared. She felt lost without him. In truth, she hadn't been without him by her side for millennia, and the miles that lie between them seemed endless. Thankful that it was only for a few hours, she turned her attention to matters with her Council. Cody had been driving Cyric mad, unwilling to sit still long enough to get a proper education. Violissa tried not to laugh, but with Cody's ADHD, it was impossible to get him to sit still long enough to hold a conversation, let alone learn the dull history of their world. When she asked where he currently was, Daneele awkwardly told her he'd been chasing a few of the servants around, and they'd lost track of him.

She finally found him making out with one of the servant girls and duly slapped him across the back of his head upon the discovery.

"What are you doing?" she said, dragging him away by his

ear as she had when they were young and in the human world.

"Ouch, ouch! Let me go Violet," he whined.

She let go and faced him, arms crossed. "You cannot chase the servants around, Cody! This is not what goes on in my realm or in my castle!"

"But—"

"No buts! You cannot chase every girl you see like you did at home. This world or at least, this realm, is not the same. Not to mention, Sinow thinks you're a future Lightbearer, and my Lightbearers do not do this!"

"Daneele did," he argued and received a kick in the shin for it.

"That's not the same, and that's not what happened. Now, today is my special day, and you will take yourself back to your room and get ready. Be prepared to leave by mid-day, or I'll pull more than your ear."

She shifted, too annoyed to look at him anymore. Instead, she returned to her own room to ready herself. This time she was alone, no seamstress to make her gown, no one to put her hair up in some fashion that she would never wear nor to color her cheeks. She sat on her bed, taking the time alone to think about all that had happened and all that had changed.

"Nothing has changed," she said. "Nothing, that is, but us."

Then it dawned on her. They were the only part of this story, this timeline that had changed, and with their change came change they would now ignite. A change to their own paths, a change to the paths of their people, to everyone they knew. This life was new, even if no one but they really saw it. Their union had been the first step, and today's ascension would be the next. Rising, she walked over to her window. No balcony lined her room as it did Sinow's, but her view was similar; out beyond the villages and meadows lie the Sacred Groves. Again, she felt drawn to them, but once again, she had no idea why. What was it that she was missing? She turned and paced her room. Had she been wrong? Should her ascension include the groves? As she thought it, Daneele's voice broke through.

It is time.

It was time. She glanced back out, the feeling growing again, but once more, she set it aside and told Daneele she was on her way.

When she arrived in the meadow where they'd held her ascension prior, she called Sinow who arrived dragging Keary and Kanine with him. The others arrived with two of her Council after they were passed through the boundary, Sinow able to bring two through with his shift, his ability to pass through the boundary by himself still present. Everyone was there to witness, even Cody. *Almost everyon*e, she thought. How she wished Paige were here. For a moment, she let the thought in, and sadness washed through her. But Paige would not be born for another thousand years, and they weren't even sure how she would be born this time around, another change impacted by the new direction in their path.

Vi, Sinow called to her softly. *Everything ok?*

She looked up and smiled. *Yes, just thinking how nice it would be if Paige were here.*

His eyes softened. *I know you miss her. We'll figure it out.*

We always do, right? she replied.

"I hate to interrupt your internal discussion, but we need to get started, Violissa," Cyric said.

Things moved quickly from there, the ritual the same as she remembered, but this time, more personal, more intimate than it had been her first time. Sinow, along with his father and the Darkbearers stood to the side, observers to what would be the final Light ascension as she and her Council would bear witness to the final Dark ascension. Ren's ascension would be new, different, and begin a ritual that would then be passed on through every ascending king to follow.

As the Council returned the powers her father had passed to them upon assuming his role as guardian, Violissa prepared herself to accept her Fate-given powers. The final words were spoken, and she closed her eyes, waiting to feel the increase in Light power course through her. After a few moments, she opened her eyes and looked up at the sky. Nothing had changed, no clouds, no streaming light, no sense that they were even in the tail end of a ritual. She looked over at Daneele who was kneeling with the others.

What's going on? she called to him.

Violissa, pay attention and wait for it, he replied curtly.

It should already be here, Daneele. Nothing's happening. "Something's wrong," she whispered aloud.

She met Sinow's eyes, and he mouthed, "What's wrong?"

Turning her eyes to the sky, she tried feeling for Fate's magic, feeling for anything that told her things were just delayed even though she knew that wasn't true. The ritual was specific, done at just the right time, the words said in just the right order. There would never be a delay. She chewed her bottom lip as it dawned on her.

"I'm not ascending."

The spoken words fell heavy in the silence. She could tell Sinow wanted to talk but was hesitant to interrupt the ritual.

"This is the final punishment," she said. "I won't ascend this lifetime."

"Violissa," Daneele said in a hushed tone.

"No, Daneele. It should have happened already, it happened right after you gave up the king's power."

"Maybe there's a delay? Did we get the timing wrong?" Sinow finally said.

She shook her head. "You know we didn't. You remember it just as I do." She dropped her eyes to her hands. "They're not blessing me with my Fate-given powers this time."

"Vi, you can't know that," he responded.

But she did know it. Her instinct confirmed that she would not ascend here today. "It's not happening, I can feel it. The Fates have spoken, and they've made their final judgment."

"You can't simply not ascend, Violissa," Cyric said. "It's unprecedented. Every king ascends."

"I'm not a king, Cyric," she said absently. "And everything about my life has been unprecedented."

Her eyes wandered to the north, toward the Sacred Groves. "There's something I missed. Something I can't quite figure."

She felt Sinow's hand on hers, and drawing her attention back to him said, "Now, we wait to see if they serve you the same judgment. When does it end, Sinow?"

He brushed her loose curl back. "I don't know, but this can't be how it ends, Vi. There has to be more."

"Are you certain, Violissa?" Daneele asked.

"You know as well as I what should have happened, Daneele. You are my Keeper after all. There will be no ascension for me today. We shall see what happens with Sinow."

The day wore on, too slow for Sinow's comfort. Violissa couldn't sit still, pacing, wandering, muttering; she sounded half mad, and it worried him. The entire day worried him. Why had she not ascended? No one could find a reason or any history of it ever happening. Her Council had spent hours looking, first searching their records, then with the help of his Council, combing the records of his ancestors. The effort left them empty-handed and perplexed.

His ascension would be after sunset, only another half hour. The sun was already lowering. Running his hand through his hair, he walked across the grounds of his keep to where she stood staring off toward the north east, muttering about the forests.

"Vi, it's time you rest. It's nearly time for my ascension, and we need to prepare."

She turned her eyes to him; they were a kaleidoscope of colors, something he hadn't seen since her ascension. They were wild with a look that teetered on the edge of insanity, and her hands shook.

"Vi?"

"Why hasn't it happened, Sinow? Why are they punishing me like this? I can feel it." She raised her shaking hands. "There's something I can't see. It's right here." She reached out grasping for something.

Grabbing her hands, he said, "Stop this. You are making yourself sick, and you even appear a bit mad. There is nothing we can do about it now until the Fates speak to us."

She yanked her hands back, her eyes widening then narrowing. "The Fates. They always speak to us in ways we don't see."

"That's it. I'm getting Cyric to look at you. This is craziness."

"Is it?" Her eyes drifted toward the ground. "Is it madness? Is my final punishment to live like this?" The hues in her eyes froze, one eye blue, one eye green. "What have I done to deserve any more than they've laid upon my shoulders? What have I done?" She yelled at the sky, backing away from him. "What are you trying to tell me? What did I not do this time?" Her voice grew in anger, clouds forming above them. "What did I not do?" she muttered, turning her back to him and stepping away.

Why were her eyes pre-ascension as if preparing for her gifts? What was he missing? And then he saw it. A beilcan flitted in the air, just above her hand. Beilcan didn't exist in this realm, they were creatures from Cirillia who nested in the groves.

"The Sacred Groves," she mumbled.

Her head tipped in the direction of the groves, and he heard her voice, soft yet full of emotion, the song stirring his Dark power, drawing on his ire, her voice growing as she bellowed her feelings to the creature. In the power of her voice, it faded, a golden sparkle left in its place.

Something's happening, he called to his Council. *Get the Lightbearers.*

"Does she sing about everything?" he heard Tynan behind him. Violissa ran off after what looked like a trail of gold, her song filling the air.

"What are you doing here?" he asked curtly, his attention on Violissa, momentarily forgetting his animosity toward him.

"I heard her."

He looked at Tynan, surprised but with no time to react, turned back to see Violissa shift.

"What in the Fates?" he muttered, running then hearing her voice farther from him. He shifted, feeling Tynan and the others all shift in next to him, the Lightbearers following shortly after. He should have confronted Tynan for even daring to be in his presence, but his mind was on Violissa.

Her song cascaded through the air, the golden sparkle leading her on, the words filled with her anger at the Fates, at her destiny, her punishments. She had shifted to the tip of the ravine where it converged with the boundary and Cirillia's border. The golden light shimmered across the ravine, and she paused then leapt.

"Violissa!" he yelled, running to watch her land, her song crescendoing, the river below splitting as she hit the water, forming a wall around her, then pushing into one massive wave in front of her, her words pushing it further north.

He shifted to her level, the river bed now bursting with life, grass and wild flowers blooming with her every step.

"What's going on?" he heard his father ask.

"I think the Fates are calling her," he answered, moving closer.

With her last note belted out louder and with a force he'd only heard one time when she'd burst the boundary to the Lost Realm open, she ended her song.

"What do we do?" Daneele asked him.

"We wait," Sinow replied. "This is Violissa's moment. We follow her lead."

He walked forward, as close as he felt he needed to be. The golden light shimmered around her and he heard her voice again, low and vulnerable, her strength gone, her anger dissipated. This tone was respectful, full of wonder as the golden light spread out before her, the water standing at attention as if awaiting her command. She took a step, and the water separated, her fingers reaching up to drape through it. It dawned on him that they were no longer in the ravine, that they were now ground level, trees on either side of them. As she had moved further up the ravine, she had changed the very foundation of the world they knew, she had created a river through the Sacred Groves where before there had been none, and she had raised the bed of the ravine and bound their realms.

But how had they even gotten this far north in the few steps she had taken?

A voice, sweet and demure but laced with power, joined hers. It emanated from the golden sparkle that had grown to encompass the space before her.

"Fates," he mumbled, moving closer but putting his hand out to stop the others, knowing this wasn't meant for them. Knowing it was something bigger than them.

Violissa's voice grew in force, her excitement palpable, the other voice growing with hers until they matched a note that shook the world around them. The golden light shimmered and shifted to a glimmering silver that slowly faded until forms could be seen taking shape within it. Violissa stopped singing, but the Fate did not, and as her form became clear, she brought her hand out to Violissa who raised her voice to join hers, bringing her hand out to take the Fate's.

The world exploded all around upon their contact, a flood of power bursting from them. They continued to sing while the other Fates appeared behind the female. What was her name?

He tried to dredge it from his memory, his eyes moving to the male Fates he had seen in the vision they'd been shown. Orlaina. The Mother Fate.

Violissa dropped her hand, stepping back as hues of magic encased her. He felt the rush of Dark magic as it poured into him, his eyes meeting the Fate who'd come to him that day. They were ascending. Power engulfed him, taking over all of his senses, power greater than he'd had even in their past life. He didn't fight it, instead letting it find its place, harboring in his every cell, feeling the familiarity of it, the ecstasy of the ascension. As he felt the darkening of his eyes, he looked back at Violissa; she shimmered in a blur of colors, the forest around them responding to her ascension, the colors brightening to the ones he knew marked this land as Elvin touched. They were colors that matched no other.

The ascension ended, his power settled within, a part of him once more. The Fates, all clearly visible now, stood silently. These were the true Fates, the originals who had built this world, created the races, orchestrated their destinies. Orlaina met his eyes and beckoned him closer. As he joined Violissa, he could feel the power that emanated from them, but he could also feel Violissa's; it was stronger than it had been, different.

"You have my spirit, my child," Orlaina said to Violissa. "We were waiting for you to call us and now you have."

Violissa, never the one to pause, too familiar with her creator to find fear in questioning her, asked, "Waiting for us to call? Why would that be on our shoulders? Why would you not simply come to us?"

The Dark Fate, the one Sinow remembered was brother to Orlaina's lover, his ancestor, laughed. "You push too much, child, and Orlaina allows it. If it were up to us—"

"But it is no longer," Orlaina interrupted. "You have all had your say in their path for far too long, and they have suffered because of it."

"Orlaina," he warned, but his brother stepped forward.

"We are here to bless your ascensions. You have faced the challenges, followed a path unbound, and we have watched."

"Your new life awaits," Orlaina said. "You have reached the end of your part of the prophecy, and you have done well."

"Done well?" Violissa asked. "You tortured us, and you say we've done well?"

Orlaina's eyes grew dark. "Do not push too hard, child. I favor you, but that favor could be tested."

"Sorry," she said, dropping her eyes.

"She may not push, but I will," Sinow said. "How do we know this is the end? We thought we were there in our last lifetime, but you couldn't leave us be."

The Dark Fate stepped forward, but Orlaina answered, her eyes lightening. "The prophecy was not complete."

Then he saw it. "Ren. He was the last piece. The prophecy couldn't be complete until the new way was established, a true merging of all the races through one king. And Ren refused his ascension."

Orlaina smiled. "His part needs to be played just as yours did. Without him, the prophecy is incomplete." She stepped up to Sinow. "You have both been tested greatly, and now, you are rewarded. Sometimes, you need to face the fire, own the fear to come through a stronger, better king and man."

She touched his face, and he could feel the nature magic that coursed through her, power on a level he couldn't fathom. Then she dropped her hand and moved to Violissa.

"You, my child, are stronger than you realize. There is potential you have yet to discover. Others see it, your mate sees it, but you turn a blind eye to it, seeing the best in everyone else but yourself. You still do not see what he sees." She looked over at Sinow. "But you see it, don't you?"

He thought about it, all the times he'd seen Violissa use her magic. His was concentrated in Darkness, but hers was multilayered, like Ren's. Very much like Ren's, especially now. His mind went back to the moment she had taken his power to restore the Councils. He'd witnessed it then and not fully comprehended what it was he'd seen. He laughed, "Aye, I do, I always have but never fully understood what it meant."

"I don't understand," Violissa said.

Orlaina took her hand, drawing her forward. "Look at where you are, my daughter. Look where you have called us."

She looked around, moving her hand, the shimmer of the boundary upon which she stood sparkling around her. She walked on, dropping Orlaina's hand and brought hers up to touch the boundary that lay before her, a light frost spread from her finger upward toward the sky and down along the ground, running the distance of the boundary walls, both the one dividing their realms and the one hiding the realm of her Elvin ancestors. She lowered her head, and Sinow could sense the wave of emotion that drifted through her. He heard her voice, delicate and vulnerable, the song she sang in a language similar to her Elvin heritage, but the dialect was different, unique. His eyes drifted to Orlaina who met his, a smile lifting on her lips. It was the language of the Fates, one not spoken in this world. His eyes, drawn back to Violissa, watched as the boundary magic warped and changed with her voice, the ground below them trembling as if in anticipation to what it knew was coming, the trees shaking nervously behind the water, water he now saw had been standing at attention the entire time. As she sang, it drifted up in droplets until the entire river hung in gleaming emerald pearls all around them. He heard the gasps behind him but kept his eyes on Violissa. She raised her head, her hand dropping, her voice rising, full of pride and reverence. In that moment, she was the queen he had always known her to be but never truly seen her as. Her hair sparkled, her eyes shone a vibrant hue that lit the boundaries. With the crescendo of her final note, she lifted her left hand, palm upwards, a flare of arcane blue magic flowing from it. Then she lifted the right hand, a splash of sage meeting the arcane, the two covering the sky above them in a dance. She turned and faced them, the hues of her power blanketing her then. Throwing her head back up, she finished her note as a blast of Dark magic, gray and mist-like joined the other two powers, weaving amongst them in a dance that ended with a flash of violet that filled the sky, the boundaries shimmering then turning to dust. Dropping her head back down, her eyes opened to reveal the violet eyes he had once seen on his son.

He smiled as the Councils reacted, trying to keep their shock quiet but unable to contain it. Orlaina moved to her, followed by the Light Fate who Sinow remembered seeing when they had created the prophecy. He was joined by the Dark Fate who had spoken to Sinow, Orlaina's lover.

"Now, you know who you are?" Orlaina asked.

"I am the conduit," she said softly, her eyes fading to green and meeting Sinow's. "I am the first to bear the powers of our world. The conduit between the races."

"Born of Light and nature but blessed through union with Dark. Our union necessary o that you could bear the future. Ren," he said, moving closer to her.

"You knew?" she asked.

For a moment, everything fell away and he was alone with her, lost in her eyes. "I've always suspected even in our first life. You carried Ren with no repercussions, your hair turning ebony the day he was born. I saw the signs, but the moment I truly knew was the moment you took the power I gave you. There's no Darkbearer that could tolerate that much power, and you asked for more, taking it, controlling it as if you owned it. I knew that day that you were more special than we'd ever thought."

"The prophecy is now complete," the Light Fate said.

Violissa turned to them. "Truly?"

"Yes," Orlaina answered, brushing Violissa's hair back as a mother would. "You are free to live your lives unburdened by the words of your birth."

Sinow felt a weight lifted from him. It was over. He took

Violissa's hand.

"Know this, however," she continued. "You will now be adrift in life. We will be onlookers only, no more able to shape the events that happen. Your life is your own, but you will be alone, adrift in the unpredictable events of life."

"I think we can manage," he replied.

The Dark Fate smiled. "I've no doubt you both can. Orlaina, it is time."

To Sinow's surprise, he bowed to them and was joined by all the other Fates who faded in a silver shimmer, Orlaina remaining.

"It has been a long journey, one I started when your mother was just a child. It is hard to say goodbye to you, my daughter." She tilted Violissa's head and kissed it. "You've one last thing to do, and I believe you know what that is."

"Yes, I do," she replied, touching her hand to her heart.

Orlaina smiled, turned to Sinow, and took his hands. "You are a good man, Sinow. You've both been left with scars, be sure to shed them as she has, and you will live the life you were destined to live. You will finally be free."

She faded with her last word, the powdery feel of silver residue on his hands, the only evidence she had ever been there.

No one moved, nor did they say anything. Who could? They had been visited by the true Fates, something no one had ever witnessed. They had learned their final ending in the prophecy's path, they had discovered the end was finally here. Violissa left his side and began walking forward.

Vi?

Shhh, I have one last thing to do.

He looked back at the Councils who were now beginning to stand, having taken to the ground before out of deference to the Fates. His father and Tynan stood to the side; he'd forgotten they were there. A flash of Darkness rose in him upon seeing Tynan there then he thought of the three Fates, Orlaina and the two brothers. He would tolerate Tynan's presence in their life, but he would not invite him in nor would he call him brother. His father looked at him questioningly, bringing him back.

"What is she doing?" he mouthed.

I don't know, but why are you still here if I've ascended? He looked back toward Violissa who was still walking. *Maybe the Fates still want you to see something.*

He followed her, the others doing the same. He heard a splash behind them and turned to see the river water pouring to the ground, running down the ravine which no longer existed, instead, a river bed in its place. When Violissa had broken the boundaries and lifted the Lost Realm back to their world it had lifted as well, the realms no longer divided, an entirely new landscape created.

Follow me.

Violissa shifted, and he followed, landing outside the ruins of her parent's castle. The others shifted in next to them.

"Home," she said, waving her hand in the air, the ruins of the castle shifting and morphing until a perfect rendition of the original castle stood in their place.

"This is the Lost Realm?" his father asked.

"Yes, this is my home. The land of my birth, the land where the prophecy was brought to fruition."

He ran his hands over his face. "This has been a lot to take in. We saw the Fates. You spoke with the Fates."

His hands were shaking slightly so Sinow took one. "And you will soon join them. Trust me, Father, you'll like your new life."

His father squeezed his hand. "I had my doubts. When Cyric first told me all of this would be the outcome, I never believed him. He, all the Lightbearers, Kanine, all of them kept telling me to trust, to let you follow the path and now ... now you walk in the presence of the Fates. And you," he said, turning toward Violissa, "You are something extraordinary." Turning back to Sinow, he said, "I thought the union would bring you equal power? She holds three forms of magic, Sinow."

"We are equal," Violissa said. "Sinow's power is equal to mine. Mine is simply divided among the three, the Dark power the lesser of the other powers. It skirts the surface while my other two powers play in the sun. It is our son who will hold them all equally and whose power will eclipse ours."

"You said you had something else to do, Violissa?" Daneele asked.

"Yes, we will need to walk though."

She turned again and walked along the castle toward the back and to the path he'd taken so often in their former life. The path that led to the Elvin enclave. She draped her hand along the tree trunks as she walked, humming a low tune that seemed to stir the sleeping world, colors rising within the plants and trees, life coming back to a world encased in a spell to shield it from the tides of time. When they reached the cusp of the valley, the moons had risen to their peak, full and bright, lighting the valley below in a spectral essence.

"The Elvin are alive?" he heard Tynan ask, Sinow's irritation growing again at his presence until he shook it off, not caring to let it spoil the moment.

"They will be," she answered, then opened her mouth and began to sing, the language of the Elvin weaving through the air, stirring her sleeping kin. Eventually, movement appeared, one by one, the Elvin rising from the different places along the valley, some in the grass, some in buildings, some along the river, the river that now glowed an emerald that matched the water that had collapsed behind them as they'd walked to the castle.

Sinow looked to his left and saw the river had followed them, silently spreading along. It pooled at the edge of the hillside awaiting Violissa's command. With the rise of her voice, she raised her hand, and it poured over the ridge, thickening and spreading out until it became a massive waterfall that landed next to her uncle's castle and flowed across the ground to meet the existing river below. Where before the flow of the water had been underground, disappearing at the end of the ravine to then travel unseen into the Elvin enclave, now, it streamed across the three realms, connecting them all as he and Violissa now did and as Ren would continue to do.

She turned and focused her attention back on the castle, her eyes darkening to the color of Sinow's. The ground trembled, and thunder ripped through the silence. Her commanding voice called to something and only after she stepped forward did Sinow see the book, battered and dusty floating in the air.

He heard Tynan emit a sound of surprise, and a moment of worry surfaced. He forced himself to stay calm and called to Cyric in enaigne, knowing the ascension had sealed the connection between them all as it had in their past life: *I need the Lightbearers to raise a shield around all of us. Now.*

Cyric didn't question, and in moments, Sinow felt the touch of Light power. His father looked at

him, but he put his finger up to his lip and shook his head. He wanted no words, no chance that the book would sense another source of Dark power and falter in its connection to Violissa.

The book flitted in the air, its pages rustling as Violissa controlled it. She drew on her nature power, and he could feel its stir in the air as it flipped open, the pages fluttering through, words lifting from them. Out of the corner of his eye, he watched Tynan's reaction, ready to strike if needed, but all he saw was an expression of astonishment.

The words floated in the air all around Violissa, the book's pages now blank. Then with a blast of nature magic, she sang a commanding note, and the words turned to ash, falling to the ground, the pages of the book torn from its spine and shredded to miniscule pieces then finally dissolving to a light silver dust that was carried away by a sudden gust of air. The spine smoked, deep black tendrils of it filling the air then dissipating before them as Violissa ended her song.

"You destroyed it?" Tynan asked. Sinow's power flared, but then he felt the calming spell from Violissa.

"I am its Keeper, and it was no longer needed," she replied. She glanced back at Sinow. "It had served its purpose, and it was ready to rest for the remains of eternity."

"Its purpose?" Tynan asked.

"You," she returned. "It serves no purpose in this lifeline."

Tynan stared at her in disbelief, all of them did, all of them understanding the meaning of her words. The book had only served one purpose, to corrupt Tynan and bring about the events that had led them to this point, yet another piece in the Fates' plan.

"Niece, I assume?" A voice broke all of them from their thoughts. Violissa's uncle stood on the path, his smile full of pride.

She turned and smiled at him. "Hello, Uncle. I do believe we have some catching up to do."

As Violissa's uncle led the others into the valley, Violissa remained by Sinow's side.

"We made it," she said.

"Yes, we finally did. Took you long enough to get here," he said jokingly.

She laughed. "Now, what should we do with the rest of eternity?"

"I have a few ideas, but first, I think I'll start with a kiss." He pulled her in and took the first kiss of their new life together, tasting the sweetness of the magic on her, reveling in the power and the knowledge that this time they were shaping their own path, adrift in the unexpected surprises that life would now hand them and happily looking forward to it.

Epilogue

Silence greeted Ren when he stepped from the portal. It was a strange stillness that settled heavily on his ears. He looked around, his instinct telling him he'd arrived outside the castle. The land was right, the woods the same he'd spent most of his life escaping to; however, no castle stood where it should have. He took a step closer to where he remembered it, his feet stirring a fine silver dust that glittered on the shafts of grass. The smell of lilac grazed his senses, a stir of familiarity in this now unfamiliar terrain.

His parents had been here, it all had been here. He leaned down and touched the silver dust, rubbing it between his fingers, an intense feeling of sadness overwhelming him. They were gone, this timeline interrupted, now erased just as his parents had been. But they weren't really gone, they were being recreated, their path rewritten, bound perhaps once again to the prophecy that ruled their lives. With Tynan gone, they would live free, unburdened from the pain he would have caused them.

Standing, he took one more look around the quiet landscape then closed his eyes.

"I'm ready," he said as he accepted that his place in this time was ending. He felt the tingle as the Fates took him; his future now lie with the parents he'd left on the other side of the portal, and it was a future he knew he would welcome, for no matter the time nor the place, they would always be his parents, and he would always love them. As the breeze slowly took him away, his last thoughts settled on Paige, her warm blue eyes beaming from a face he knew he would forever long to see once more.

Silver dust fell gently to the ground mingling with the remnants of silver that had awaited his return, the gentle breeze then lifting the combination, filling the space where Ren had once stood then floating away, coaxed by the breeze into the sky beyond.

Look for the final installment in the Unbound Prophecy series in spring 2022

Adrift

J. L. Jackola discovered her passion for writing in grade school when she wrote a short story that earned her a spot in a local writing workshop. She has been creating fantasy worlds ever since. When she's not weaving tales, she can be found logging miles in her running shoes, watching movies with her family, or curled up with a book. She resides in Delaware with her husband and three children.

To learn more, visit her website at www.jljackola.com.

CPSIA information can be obtained
at www.ICGtesting.com
Printed in the USA
BVHW071202051021
618194BV00002B/74

9 781954 175112